OXFORD WORLD'S CLASSICS

OROONOKO

AND OTHER WRITINGS

APHRA BEHN'S biographical details, especially those concerned with her birth and early life, remain contested and obscure. No firm date or place of birth have been established. It now seems certain that Behn went to Surinam while still a young woman, around 1663, returning to London probably in 1664. Her marriage also remains obscure; she began using the name Behn in 1666, but no mention of her husband or his presumed death occur in her writings. In the middle of 1666 she acted as a spy in the Netherlands, returning to England in debt. Her career as a dramatist began with the staging of *The Forced Marriage* in 1670. She was soon established as a prolific playwright, with eleven of her plays performed in the following decade. When opportunities for staging her plays diminished, she published a collection of her poetry in 1684, as well as her first prose narrative: *Love Letters Between a Nobleman and His Sister*, based on a current scandal. She then produced a wide range of fiction, poetry, and translations until her death on 16 April 1689.

PAUL SALZMAN is a Senior Lecturer in the English Department at La Trobe University, Melbourne, Australia. He is the author of *English Prose Fiction 1558–1700: A Critical History* (Oxford, 1985), has edited two selections of Renaissance fiction for Oxford World's Classics, and has also published widely in the area of Australian literature, including *The New Diversity* (written with Ken Gelder, Melbourne, 1989) and *'Helplessly Tangled in Female Arms and Legs': Elizabeth Jolley's Fictions* (University of Queensland Press, 1993).

OXFORD WORLD'S CLASSICS

*For almost 100 years Oxford World's Classics have brought
readers closer to the world's great literature. Now with over 700
titles—from the 4,000-year-old myths of Mesopotamia to the
twentieth century's greatest novels—the series makes available
lesser-known as well as celebrated writing.*

*The pocket-sized hardbacks of the early years contained
introductions by Virginia Woolf, T. S. Eliot, Graham Greene,
and other literary figures which enriched the experience of reading.
Today the series is recognized for its fine scholarship and
reliability in texts that span world literature, drama and poetry,
religion, philosophy and politics. Each edition includes perceptive
commentary and essential background information to meet the
changing needs of readers.*

OXFORD WORLD'S CLASSICS

APHRA BEHN

Oroonoko
and Other Writings

Edited with an Introduction and Notes by
PAUL SALZMAN

Oxford   New York
OXFORD UNIVERSITY PRESS

Oxford University Press, Great Clarendon Street, Oxford OX2 6DP

Oxford New York

Athens Auckland Bangkok Bogota Bombay Buenos Aires
Calcutta Cape Town Dar es Salaam Delhi Florence Hong Kong Istanbul
Karachi Kuala Lumpur Madras Madrid Melbourne Mexico City
Nairobi Paris Singapore Taipei Tokyo Toronto Warsaw

and associated companies in
Berlin Ibadan

Oxford is a trade mark of Oxford University Press

Editorial material © Paul Salzman 1994

First published as a World's Classics paperback 1994
Reissued as an Oxford World's Classics paperback 1998

British Library Cataloguing in Publication Data

Data available

Library of Congress Cataloging in Publication Data

Behn, Aphra, 1640–1689.
Oroonoko, and other writings / Aphra Behn; edited with an
introduction by Paul Salzman.
p. cm.—(Oxford World's classics).
1. Slaves—Surinam—Fiction. I. Salzman, Paul. II. Title.
823'.4—dc20 PR3317.A6 1994 93–8875
ISBN 0-19-283460-6

1 3 5 7 9 10 8 6 4 2

Printed in Great Britain by
Caledonian International Book Manufacturing Ltd.
Glasgow

ACKNOWLEDGEMENTS

The work for this edition was done during study leave granted by La Trobe University, but made possible by the co-operation of my department, and especially of the then chairperson, Dr Lucy Frost. I am particularly grateful to her, and to my colleagues, for undertaking the additional work that my stay in Cambridge necessitated. Thanks to a small grant from the La Trobe University School of Humanities, I was able to employ Michael Connor, who offered useful assistance at the early stages of this project. In Cambridge, I would like to thank the Master and Fellows of Pembroke College, and especially Dr Howard Erskine-Hill, for their hospitality. Professor Janet Todd cheerfully answered my queries, and provided the invaluable resource of her fine edition of Behn's poetry; I only regret that her edition of the prose was not available to me when I prepared this book. As usual, Susan Bye ungrudgingly offered her services as a research assistant, repaid only by occasional reciprocity on my part in relation to her own research.

CONTENTS

viii CONTENTS

INTRODUCTION

Aphra Behn has always been an enigma. For her own contemporaries, she was a threatening figure who undermined certain assumptions about the masculine realms of letters, drama, politics, intrigue. She offered disingenuous reassurance that hers was only a 'female pen',[1] though she also attested to a 'masculine part' that may have alarmed her detractors.[2] Behn was known as Astrea from the time of her flirtatious relationship with the Republican William Scot in Surinam, during her attempts, as a spy for Charles II, to turn Scot around and run him as an agent for the crown, and throughout her literary career, even to the burial record at Westminster Abbey, where she is registered as 'Astrea Behn'.[3] Astrea is a romance name (taken from the French pastoral romance *l'Astrée*, by d'Urfé), but Behn, as a writer and as a woman who entered the world of writers, challenged many of the superficial associations of such a name. Modern interest in Behn, following the edition of her works published in 1915 by Montague Summers, has been fuelled by the characterization of her in Virginia Woolf's *A Room of One's Own* (1929) as a figure of symbolic importance for women writers; indeed all women, Woolf suggested, should pay Behn homage: 'All women together ought to let flowers fall upon the tomb of Aphra Behn, which is, most scandalously but rather appropriately, in Westminster Abbey, for it was she who earned them the right to speak'.[4] But this was a homage to an iconic figure, rather than to an actual writer.[5] Accordingly,

---

[1] In *Oroonoko*, below, 40.

[2] 'All I ask is the privilege for my masculine part the poet in me', Preface to *The Lucky Chance* (1686).

[3] Noted by Maureen Duffy, *The Passionate Shepherdess* (London, 1977), 288. Most of Behn's works were simply signed 'Mrs A. Behn'. She was referred to as 'Afra' in the early biographical account, *Memoirs of the Life of Mrs Behn* (1696), and 'Aphra' is the name used by all critics and biographers since the 1915 edition of her work edited by Montague Summers.

[4] Virginia Woolf, *A Room of One's Own* (London, 1929), 98.

[5] 'She made, by working very hard, enough to live on. The importance of that fact outweighs anything that she actually wrote, even the splendid "A Thousand Martyrs I Have Made", or "Love in Fantastic Triumph Sat", for here begins the freedom of the mind.' Ibid. 95.

when biographers went in search of 'Aphra Behn' it is fitting that they found a series of puzzles, and despite much effort, controversy still surrounds Behn's family background, her date and place of birth, her upbringing—even her acquisition of the name 'Behn' remains clouded.

Until very recently, such biographical speculation has taken precedence over any detailed critical discussion of Behn's writing, with the exception of *Oroonoko*, and even critical discussion of *Oroonoko* has tended to concentrate on its relationship to Behn's biography. Behn's current reputation rests mainly on the revival of interest in her plays, particularly *The Rover*, which was successfully staged (in an adapted version) by the Royal Shakespeare Company in 1986. This selection of her fiction and poetry should provide ample evidence of the range of her work beyond the drama.

Up until this time, only one work of fiction, *Oroonoko*, has really been subjected to close critical scrutiny, and the changing approaches taken to *Oroonoko* offer an interesting paradigm for Behn's general critical fortunes during this century. It tells the story of the noble African, Oroonoko, who loves Imoinda, as does his grandfather the king. Both lovers are sold into slavery and meet again in Surinam. There Oroonoko inspires a slaves' revolt, is betrayed and cruelly beaten. He kills Imoinda, a willing victim, and is executed for the murder. The story is remarkable both for Behn's critical analysis of the slave trade and depiction of native morality and Christian hypocrisy, and for its philosophical content. First published in 1688, it was Behn's most popular work from a very early stage in its history, a popularity enhanced by its dramatic adaptation by Thomas Southerne in 1696, an adaptation which was performed throughout the eighteenth century. The work was also much acclaimed in France in the eighteenth century, following the first French translation in 1745 (there were seven altogether).[6] In this context, *Oroonoko* was read as an anti-slavery novel, particularly in the period when anti-slavery sentiment began to intensify.

[6] See Edward Seeber, '*Oroonoko* in France in the 18th Century', *PMLA* 51 (1936).

Then the popularity of *Oroonoko* waned until a revival of interest in the early part of the twentieth century. This new attention, however, was focused on a very different aspect of Behn's work: its 'validity' as an autobiographical account. In 1913, Ernest Bernbaum published two essays castigating Behn for passing off a fictional account as truth.[7] Bernbaum's account of Behn's authorial crimes takes a particularly affronted tone: 'Mrs Behn in *Oroonoko* deliberately and circumstantially lied'.[8] This had the effect of turning criticism for the next seventy years or so into a contest over the truth of Behn's account of her stay in Surinam.[9] In general, as more and more information has been uncovered, the autobiographical aspect of *Oroonoko* (only an aspect) has been confirmed. But that is not so important; rather, the paradoxical situation was created whereby Behn's 'defenders' had to prove she was a truth-teller, not a liar, and this very defence involved the destruction of her claim to be taken seriously as a *creative* writer.[10] Just at the

[7] 'Mrs Behn's *Oroonoko*', *George Lyman Kittredge Anniversary Papers* (Boston, 1913); 'Mrs Behn's Biography a Fiction', *PMLA* 28 (1913).

[8] 'Mrs Behn's Biography', *PMLA* 28, 434.

[9] The most important contributions to this debate are: Harrison Platt, 'Astrea and Celadon: An Untouched Portrait of Aphra Behn', *PMLA* 49 (1934); Wylie Sypher, 'A Note on the Realism of Mrs Behn's *Oroonoko*', *MLQ* 3 (1942); J. A. Ramsaran, '*Oroonoko*: A Study of the Factual Elements', *Notes and Queries*, 205 (1960); W. J. Cameron, *New Light on Aphra Behn* (Auckland, 1961); Ruthe Sheffey, 'Some Evidence for a New Source of Aphra Behn's *Oroonoko*', *Studies in Philology*, 59 (1962); B. Duhuicq, 'Further Evidence on Aphra Behn's Stay in Surinam', *Notes and Queries*, 224 (1979); Katherine M. Rogers, 'Fact and Fiction in Aphra Behn's *Oroonoko*', *Studies in the Novel*, 20 (1988); all biographical accounts add to the evidence for Behn's stay in Surinam, see Duffy, *Passionate Shepherdess*; Angeline Goreau, *Reconstructing Aphra* (Oxford, 1980); Sara Heller Mendelson, *The Mental World of Stuart Women* (Brighton, 1987); and Jane Jones, 'New Light on the Background and Early Life of Aphra Behn', *Notes and Queries*, 235 (1990).

[10] The best account of this double bind is Robert L. Chibka, ' "Oh! Do Not Fear a Woman's Invention": Truth, Falsehood, and Fiction in Aphra Behn's *Oroonoko*', *Texas Studies in Literature and Language*, 30 (1988), which also offers a very sophisticated analysis of Behn's narrative strategies and their effect on the reader. See also Martine Brownley, 'The Narrator in *Oroonoko*', *Essays in Literature*, 4 (1977). The effect on attitudes towards Behn is also discussed in Dale Spender, *Mothers of the Novel* (London, 1986). The whole truth–lie double bind is seen as an important element in the history of the novel as a form in

time when criticism might have been expected to have been concentrating attention on Behn's literary achievements, by far the most effort was being diverted towards biographical debate. This is not to say that the biography behind *Oroonoko* is unimportant, but it has dominated at the expense of other aspects of the work until very recently.[11]

A change in this critical preoccupation can be traced since the appearance of studies which placed Behn more firmly in a female creative tradition.[12] Since 1987, *Oroonoko* has become the focus of a much more sophisticated account of Behn's narrative skill, and, most importantly, it has been seen from the perspective of a feminist criticism alert to new implications of race and gender issues raised by the treatment of slavery in relation to Oroonoko and Imoinda, and to the figure of the (white female) narrator.[13] This is best seen in a particularly suggestive article by Margaret Ferguson, who brilliantly connects the account of slavery, the figure of the female slave in *Oroonoko*,

the sophisticated account by Lennard Davis, *Factual Fictions: The Origins of the English Novel* (New York, 1983), which includes a brief account of how *Oroonoko* fits into this context. See also the account in Michael McKeon, *The Origins of the English Novel 1600–1740* (Baltimore, 1987), which stresses the manipulation of the reader. Also relevant is the discussion of truth and lies in early travel narratives in Percy G. Adams, *Travel Literature and the Evolution of the Novel* (Lexington, 1983), ch. 3.

[11] The early exception to this trend is George Guffey's reading of *Oroonoko* as a narrative concerned with the fortunes of James II in his year of crisis, 1688, in George Guffey 'Aphra Behn's *Oroonoko*: Occasion and Accomplishment', in Guffey and Wright, *Two English Novelists* (Los Angeles, 1975). Maureen Duffy also reads *Oroonoko* as a political narrative which glances at the Stuarts: see *Passionate Shepherdess*, ch. 26.

[12] For example, see Janet Todd, *The Sign of Angellica: Women, Writing and Fiction 1660–1800* (London, 1989); Jane Spencer, *The Rise of the Woman Novelist* (Oxford, 1986); Elaine Hobby, *Virtue of Necessity: English Women's Writing 1649–88* (London, 1988); and Ros Ballaster, *Seductive Forms: Women's Amatory Fiction from 1684–1740* (Oxford, 1992).

[13] See Duhuicq, 'Further Evidence'; Laura Brown, 'The Romance of Empire and the Trade in Slaves', in Brown and Nussbaum (eds.), *The New Eighteenth Century* (New York, 1987); Ros Ballaster, 'New Hystericism: Aphra Behn's *Oroonoko*: The Body, the Text and the Feminist Critic', in Isobel Armstrong (ed.), *New Feminist Discourses* (London, 1992); for a psychoanalytical account, see Beverley Houston, 'Usurpation and Dismemberment: Oedipal Tyranny in *Oroonoko*', *Literature and Psychology*, 32 (1986).

and Behn's position as a female author: 'her textual staging of an implicit competition between the white English female author and the black African female slave-wife-mother-to-be. The competition is for Oroonoko's body and its power to engender something in the future, something that will outlive it.'[14] Ferguson stresses the fact that the narrative of *Oroonoko* cannot be romanticized into a purely emancipatory text, not merely in relation to colonialism, but also in relation to Behn as a woman writer:

Playing a version of Othello to both her slaves, and thus dramatizing a complex mode of authorial 'ownership' of characters cast in the role of enthralled audience, Behn represents herself creating a paradoxical facsimile of freedom, for herself, her immediate audience, and by implication, her largely female English readers as well, in which servitude is rendered tolerable by being eroticized, fantasized, diverted from activities, either sexual or military, that might work to dislodge the English from their precarious lordship of this new world land.[15]

It seems significant that the narrative of *Oroonoko* is virtually framed by two teasingly contradictory statements by Behn (or her narrator) concerning her power as an author. In contrast to the early statement that hers is 'only a female pen', Behn finishes *Oroonoko* with a 'hope' that implies a large claim for her status: 'Thus died this great man; worthy of a better fate, and a more sublime wit than mine to write his praise; yet I hope the reputation of my pen is considerable enough to make his glorious name to survive to all ages, with that of the brave, the beautiful and the constant Imoinda' (p. 73). Like so many of Behn's works represented here, *Oroonoko* is partly concerned with Behn's struggle to represent herself as a female writer, to assume a certain power that would go with such a representation.

This whole question of power and representation is evident in the other works of fiction presented in this volume, however much they may also testify to the diversity of fictional genres

---

[14] Margaret Ferguson, 'Juggling the Categories of Race, Class and Gender: Aphra Behn's *Oroonoko*', *Women's Studies*, 19 (1991), 170.

[15] Ibid. 171; although the claim of a largely female readership is open to dispute, at least when *Oroonoko* was first published.

within which Behn worked. *The Fair Jilt*, published in 1688, the same year as *Oroonoko*, is a very different narrative in what might be called Behn's style of high melodrama, albeit based upon a true account of a man claiming to be Prince Tarquin, a descendant of the last Roman kings. Behn does not concentrate on the evidently notorious figure of Tarquin, but rather on his fiery consort Miranda, who is a fascinating study of amoral desire. Throughout the account of Miranda, Behn stresses her total resourcefulness and sense of self-determination (perhaps a salutary counter to the passive female figure of Imoinda in *Oroonoko*). Miranda is not really presented as a moral example for the reader; in fact, we are asked to admire her ability to dissemble, to assume an identity in the imaginative manner of a writer. A good example is her treatment of the unfortunate Father Francisco, who spurns her overtures, whereupon Miranda is easily able to convince her superiors that he has raped her: 'a shower of tears burst from her fair dissembling eyes, and sobs so naturally acted and so well managed as left no doubt upon the good men but all she had spoken was truth' (p. 95). This figure who manipulates truth so easily stands in an interesting relationship to her narrator, who protests vehemently that she too is a truth-teller: 'For however it may be imagined that poetry (my talent) has so greatly the ascendant over me, that all I write must pass for fiction, I now desire to have it understood that this is reality, and matter of fact' (p. 74).

The story which follows *The Fair Jilt* could be seen as a comic treatment of this same theme of deception and truth. *The Court of the King of Bantam* demonstrates the range of Behn's fiction. It is narrated in the knowing and sophisticated tones of a Restoration raconteur, full of cynical asides and wry humour. The story of a man who would be king (because of his name, in an example, this time, of farcical self-representation) is very like a Restoration comedy, and indeed, the theatre itself is prominent in the course of the narrative. The elaborate intrigue plot is worthy of Behn's dramatic talents, and the narrative voice never falters.

The History of the Nun, published in 1689, the year of Behn's death, explores a character somewhat similar to Miranda.

However, Isabella is seen much more as a victim of an unfortunate, premature constraint, described by a very sympathetic narrator: 'The young beauty therefore who dedicates herself to Heaven and weds herself forever to the service of God ought first very well to consider the self-denial she is going to put upon her youth.... The resolution we promise and believe we shall maintain, is not in our power, and nothing is so deceitful as human hearts' (p. 140). *The History of the Nun* is a narrative of desire as an irresistible force, and unlike *The Fair Jilt*, Isabella's tragic decision to murder her two husbands (however melodramatic such a plot development may sound) is treated with considerable sympathy.

The Adventure of the Black Lady has been included here as an example of one of Behn's short stories which offers a realistic glimpse of a female dilemma. Much depends, as is the case with *The Court of the King of Bantam*, upon the witty narrative tone. However, Bellamora's independence is offered as a more serious case history than Wou'dbe King's laughable obsession, and Behn also offers an interesting glance at the social constraints placed upon women who generally cannot rely on the fortunate denouement with which Behn supplies her protagonist.

The last example of Behn's fiction, *The Unfortunate Bride*, offers a startling tonal shift from apparent comedy to tragedy and then back to a version of comic wish fulfilment, as the 'blind lady' Celesia gains her love Frankwit (not to mention her sight), but only at the cost of the death of his first love, her cousin Belvira. There is a savage fairy-tale quality about this narrative of the innocent Celesia's acquisition of happiness. *The Unfortunate Bride*, like all the fiction, turns upon a question of identity and representation, as the jaunty account of Celesia's true 'sight' when blind turns out to be all too true. Behn is particularly interested in the contradictions inherent in narrative claims to truth, just as her critics have engaged so fiercely in a hunt for biographical 'truths' about Behn herself.

Indeed, it is possible to see this paradox at work in Behn's writing, as well as in her own placement of herself as a professional woman writer in a Restoration world of hostility and, to a large degree, social and literary misogyny. Behn's fiction, as represented in this selection, is constantly turning on the question of how her characters represent themselves, and how their own representations are seized from them, or, from a social perspective, imposed on them. This is especially the case with her female characters, from tough women who scheme and intrigue (and murder) their way through the restrictions placed upon them, such as Miranda in *The Fair Jilt* and Isabella in *The Nun*, to women captured by their circumstances, such as Bellamora in *The Adventure of the Black Lady* and Belvira in *The Unfortunate Bride*. Behn often presents a split between female resourcefulness and female entrapment, an aspect of her fiction aptly described by Elaine Hobby:

Aphra Behn's stories map out a world of female possibilities and limits: a bleak world, since the options open to her heroines are shown to be few indeed. It is rescued from despair only by the sparkling courage and daring of her women protagonists, who with great determination negotiate their way through a universe where men have all the power.[16]

This aspect of Behn's fiction has been complicated by recent criticism which has drawn attention to the nature of her use of a largely female narrative voice, a voice which offers a controlling perspective more reflective of Behn's personal achievements and independence than of the restricted situations of so many of her female protagonists. Janet Todd, for example, observes that 'The narrator is all-important in this fiction, emerging as a definite character, and in a way all the tales become part of a larger fictionalized autobiography of the author.'[17]

Behn's poetry similarly offers shifting perspectives, as she writes in all the Restoration modes, from the public style of her political poems, such as 'A Pindaric on the Death of Our Late Sovereign', to the racy voice of a typical conversational poem such as 'A Letter to a Brother of the Pen in Tribulation'. There is a kind of 'staging' taking place in the multiple voices

---

[16] Hobby, *Virtue of Necessity*, 96.
[17] Todd, *The Sign of Angellica*, 77; see also the extended discussion of narrative voice in Jacqueline Pearson 'Gender and Narrative in the Fiction of Aphra Behn', *RES* 42 (1991, two parts); and on Behn's self-presentation, Ballaster, *Seductive Forms*, 71.

of Behn's poetry, which may be compared to the acute account
of her drama put forward in an important essay by Elin
Diamond, who suggests that:

In Behn's texts, the painful bisexuality of authorship, the conflict
between (as she puts it) her 'defenceless' woman's body and her
'masculine part' is staged in her insistence, in play after play, on
the equation between female body and fetish, fetish and
commodity—the body in the 'scene'. Like the actress, the woman
dramatist is sexualized, circulated, denied a subject position in the
theatre hierarchy.[18]

There is a greater self-consciousness and self-control than this,
it seems to me, in Behn's 'staging' of her poetry, where she is
equally compelled to enter a world dominated by male writers
working in specifically misogynistic forms. This is most evident
in the satirical poetry of the Restoration, and in the bawdy
lyrics of writers like Rochester and Sedley.[19] Angeline Goreau,
among others, notes 'the physical repulsion that feminine
sexuality inspired in the male poets of Aphra Behn's genera-
tion'.[20] At times, it is true, Behn's poetry simply seems to
reflect a watered-down version of this perspective, with the
benign view of the seducer in 'Song. "Cease, cease Amynta to
complain"' and the homage to Rochester in 'On the Death of
the Late Earl of Rochester'.[21] But she also writes counter
poems, such as 'To Alexis in Answer to his Poem Against
Fruition', a sharp portrait of the rake's unstable insatiability,
which wittily overturns the misogynistic attitudes of the male
poet. Even sharper is the critique inherent in her version of

[18] Elin Diamond, 'Gestus and Signature in Aphra Behn's *The Rover*', *ELH* 56
(1989), 535.
[19] For an excellent discussion of the satire, see Felicity Nussbaum, *The
Brink of All We Hate: English Satire on Women 1660–1750* (Lexington, 1984), chs. 2–4.
[20] Angeline Goreau, 'Last Night's Rambles· Restoration Literature and the
War Between the Sexes', in Alan Bold (ed.), *The Sexual Dimension in Literature*
(London, 1982), 66; see also Jacqueline Pearson, *The Prostituted Muse: Images of
Women and Women Dramatists 1642–1737* (London, 1988).
[21] It was, one should remember, Rochester who wrote '*Whore is scarce a more
reproachful name| Than poetess ...*', a taunt echoed by Robert Gould specifically
to attack Behn; quoted in Pearson, *Prostituted Muse*, 9.

the impotence poem which a number of male writers produced, where, for Behn, the astonished woman's disappointment is more important than the man's anger. Such an unsettling of Restoration lyric conventions could be seen to culminate in Behn's analysis of female passion in 'On Desire', and most notably in her unfixing of sexual categories in 'To The Fair Clarinda, Who Made Love To Me, Imagined More Than Woman', which offers a potential lesbian solution to the Restoration male sexual marauder.

One of Behn's most perceptive accounts of the relationship between sexual and economic exchange is the finely wrought lyric 'To Lysander, On Some Verses He Writ, And Asking More For His Heart Than 'Twas Worth', which sees clearly the process which forces women to play out the role of their own femininity as they become objects of exchange in a patriarchal society.[22] From the beginning of the poem, Behn offers the possibility of a female discernment of the terms by which the market operates:

> Take back that heart, you with such caution give,
>   Take the fond valued trifle back:
> I hate love-merchants that a trade would drive;
>   And meanly cunning bargains make.

In Behn's world, in her society in general, and in the perhaps even more patriarchal literary world, this perception seldom results in any opting out (for that is scarcely possible), but the macho ethos can be deflated and the game can be joined from a position of knowledge rather than ignorance:

> Let us then love upon the honest square,
>   Since interest neither have designed,
> For the sly gamester, who ne'er plays me fair,
>   Must trick for trick expect to find.

However, Behn's most famous lyric, 'Love Armed', first published in her tragedy *Abdelazar* (1677), makes it clear that the

---

[22] For a suggestive discussion of this situation, see Luce Irigaray, *This Sex Which is Not One*, trans. Catherine Porter (Cornell University Press: Ithaca, NY, 1985).

general state of affairs invariably results in a female victim and a male conqueror:

> From me he took his sighs and tears,
> From thee his pride and cruelty;
> From me his languishments and fears,
> And every killing dart from thee;
> Thus thou and I the god have armed,
> And set him up a deity;
> But my poor heart alone is harmed,
> Whilst thine the victor is, and free.

Behn as a writer circumvents this situation by the very range of her output, not simply in the fiction and poetry represented here, of course, but notably in her large dramatic output, where Jacqueline Pearson has noted the importance of masquerade and the unsettling—at least—of some gender conventions: 'Cross-wooings, disguise, misunderstandings and masquerades are her stock in trade'.[23] Behn is aware of the gap between the position society writes her into (woman) and the position she wants to write herself into (with a masculine pen), as well as the way such a gap may be dramatized through her sense of femininity within her own position as writer, narrator, and poet. Behn's characters, especially her female characters, are always acting out roles and disguises which respond to their sense of entrapment, just as Behn's poetry is so often concerned with the gap between a conventional lyric stance and the unsettling of lyric conventions by way of a (self-)knowing voice. I would associate this process of masquerade, in Behn's case, with the idea of the spy. Of course, Behn, like all professional writers, had to be versatile, but it is tempting to see the spy still present in the many voices, narrators, and disguises evident throughout her output. The tone of Behn's fiction ranges from the knowing voice of a raconteur, who narrates the sophisticated satire of *The Court of the King of Bantam*, to the sympathetic and engaged narrator of *Oroonoko*, concerned to provide evidence of her own authenticity, as well as that of her narrative. Like her poetry, Behn's fiction seems

---

[23] Pearson, *Prostituted Muse*, 145.

to change its nature according to the occasion and the intended readership—such versatility being, of course, the true mark of a skilled professional writer, but in Behn's case, this versatility always has something of a masquerade quality.

However, it would be wrong to characterize Behn simply as a ventriloquist; she creates a space for herself and for her writing by unsettling fixed positions, but she also offers a certain commitment, particularly at a political level, to a set of coherent ideas. As a translator, for instance, Behn always moved away from literal renderings, inserting a personal note, for example, in her translation of part of Cowley's *Of Plants* (see p. 249), which moved the text away from the original towards a work that Behn might claim as more her own.[24] Behn's poetry was not on call for any cause. She wrote, as she notes in 'A Letter to Mr Creech at Oxford', Tory propaganda, but when urged by Burnet to turn towards the winning cause of William of Orange, she refused to write to order, and eloquently defended a certain ideological integrity in her moving 'A Pindaric Poem to the Reverend Doctor Burnet'.

This political side to Behn's writing has been neglected in much of the criticism thus far, which has (understandably) concentrated on issues of gender. But it is important to examine how Behn took her place as a significant commentator (from the Tory side) on a whole range of current political issues.[25] This is most obvious in her grand, public poems. The example I have included here, 'A Pindaric on the Death of Our Late Sovereign: With an Ancient Prophecy on His Present Majesty', is one of a number of poems which are typical of the hagio-

[24] Behn offered a sophisticated account of her views on translation in the preface to her translation of Fontenelle's *A Discovery of New Worlds* (1688).

[25] The critic who has been most interested in this side of Behn is Germaine Greer, who stresses the political nature of Behn's poetry throughout her edition *The Uncollected Verse of Aphra Behn* (Stump Cross, 1989). Mendelson also sets Behn in a political context in her biographical study: see *Stuart Women*. For an important account of the way that a Tory ideology was available for 17th-c. women writers who wanted to break some of the boundaries of their patriarchal society, see Catherine Gallagher, 'Embracing the Absolute: The Politics of the Female Subject in 17th Century England', *Genders*, 1 (1988).

graphical public poetry of the period.[26] It is difficult for modern readers to see past what seem like exaggerated praise and artificial poetic conventions to the context which meant that such poetry was an intervention in public affairs. This is especially true of Behn, who clearly did not simply write such poetry for financial gain alone. Poems such as 'The Cabal at Nickey Nackeys' (from her satirical play *The Roundheads* of 1681, a telling piece of anti-Whig propaganda) show Behn stating her political views in more robust, comic form.

Ros Ballaster's recent study of Behn's 'amatory fiction' offers the interesting argument that in Behn's work 'the battle for control over sexual representation acts as an analogy for women's search for political "representation" or agency'.[27] Ballaster notes how Behn's treatment of sexuality and gender issues may be linked to a wider context—'Behn's success lay in her dual articulation of Tory myth and feminocentric individualism'[28]—though without offering much in the way of concrete illustration. This suggestion may be extended by noting how Behn is constantly turning to the question of authority and rule in her fiction, as well as in her poetry. Behn treats this subject with high seriousness in a tragedy such as *Oroonoko*, which is certainly an acute examination of the morality of authoritarian rule, whether or not it may be seen as an analogy for the situation of James II in 1688. Even more interesting is the fascination with what we might call a masquerade of authority. Not only do we have the example of Prince Tarquin in *The Fair Jilt*, who passes himself off as a descendant of the last kings of Rome, but we also have the farcical protagonist-dupe of *The Court of the King of Bantam*, a desperate pretender who takes his role as Twelfth Night King entirely

---

[26] Behn's major poem in this mode is the long Pindaric which celebrated the coronation of James II. She also wrote a poem of sympathy to Charles's widow Catherine; poems to James's queen on her expectation of an heir, as well as a poem to James commemorating the birth of the expected (and ill-fated) heir; an important riposte to a satirical attack by John Baber on the birth; and a poem to congratulate Mary on her arrival in England (which is as close as she got to writing to order as Burnet suggested she should).

[27] Ballaster, *Seductive Forms*, 40.

[28] Ibid. 79.

seriously.[29] This concern of Behn's refers back to the Civil War and its aftermath, and, more immediately, to the exclusion crisis and the revolution of 1688. Behn's audience would have been alert to the implications of such allusions as the story of Prince Henrick, usurped by his brother. Indeed, *The Fair Jilt* examines the nature of power and authority even more interestingly through Miranda, who offers an exemplary picture of political ruthlessness, especially in comparison to the rather spineless Tarquin. Once again, this political dimension meshes with the idea of masquerade, and even with the intersection of gender and economic exchange, notably in the cynical opening sentence of *The Court of the King of Bantam*: 'This money, certainly, is a most dev'lish thing!', and the following story of economic and sexual manipulation. The same theme runs through *The Adventure of the Black Lady* and *The Unfortunate Bride*. This political dimension to Behn's work needs to be borne in mind as, without taking it into account, we are left with a much narrower view of her as a writer. Even Behn's more conventional pastoral poetry frequently sees the shifting balance of power between the lovers in political terms, and often there is a slight sting in the tail of even the most apparently benign lyric, as it deflates the (male) lover's pretensions to conquest:

> Content thee with this victory,
> Think me as fair and young as she:
> I'll make thee garlands all the day,
> And in the groves we'll sit and sing;
> I'll crown thee with the pride o'th' spring,
> When thou art lord of May.

('The Invitation')

Behn offers the modern reader an intriguing mixture of views we would now classify as conservative (her Tory propaganda offered in support of the Stuarts), and 'counter-views' evident in her ability to shift suddenly into the more cynical, radical

---

[29] Mendelson has suggested that Wou'dbe King represents a satire directed at Mulgrave, who was exiled from court for his aspirations to the hand of James's daughter, Anne: see *Stuart Women*, 213. I think that it is more likely to be a general satire. For further information, see the explanatory note on p. 274.

mode of the Restoration sceptic, as she does, for example, in her poem which commemorated Creech's translation of Lucretius. The following sceptical account of faith was actually only printed when the poem appeared in her own collection, *Poems Upon Several Occasions* (1684), while the sentiment was eliminated from the poem as it appeared amongst the commemorative verses at the beginning of Creech's translation:

> Beyond poor feeble faith's dull oracles.
> Faith, the despairing soul's content,
> Faith, the last shift of routed argument.

However, this stance in the Restoration normally went hand in hand with the misogynistic attitudes of the Restoration rake, as noted above, so that Behn is particularly interesting in her efforts to dramatize the shortcomings of the mode associated with the predatory seducer, while at the same time making use of the disruptive potential of some of the more challenging philosophical premises associated with figures like Rochester.

The selection of Behn's fiction and poetry in this volume is designed to offer some sense of just how many masks Behn could put on, of how many voices she spoke in, how many narrative forms she had at her disposal. Some evidence of her success in her own self-representation is registered in tributes to her such as 'A Pindaric to Mrs Behn on her Poem on the Coronation, Written by a Lady', which begins: 'Hail, thou sole Empress of the land of wit'.[30] Yet even here, there is perhaps a trace of irony in her being described as the sole empress in a land of male writers. However, Behn was able to look back at a small but none the less important tradition of women writers when she made her most eloquent plea to attain lasting recognition, within her translation of Abraham Cowley's *Of Plants*:

> Let me with Sappho and Orinda be
> O ever sacred nymph adorned by thee;
> And give my verses immortality.[31]

---

[30] Aphra Behn, *Lycidus* (1688), 89.
[31] Orinda is the poet Katherine Philips (1632–64).

Her immortality now seems assured, but there is still a great deal of work to be done on her *œuvre* before its significance is fully established. This volume, like a number of recent editions devoted to expanding readers' access to her writing, should help to facilitate such work. Behn herself, appropriately, remains an elusive actor in the masquerades of her work, staging her own reception in her many addresses to her reader.

A NOTE ON THE TEXTS

Original sources have been used for all the texts provided here—first editions in the case of all the prose, and for the poetry, either first printings or later printings supervised by Behn, such as *Poems Upon Several Occasions* (1684). I have undertaken a limited collation, occasionally indicating interesting variants, and have noted all emendations. A full collation of Behn's work is provided in the scholarly edition by Janet Todd. I have modernized spelling throughout, and, in the case of the prose, I have also modernized punctuation and introduced paragraphs where necessary. While the punctuation of the published poetry is clearly that of the printer rather than Behn herself (as a comparison of the holograph of 'On The Death of E. Waller, Esquire' and the published version makes clear), I have tried to retain it where possible, as it provides some sense of how Restoration poetry was read. Full textual information on sources is provided in the notes for each item.

SELECT BIBLIOGRAPHY

Bibliography

There is an excellent bibliography of Behn's work, which includes an annotated bibliography of criticism up to 1985: Mary Ann O'Donnell, *Aphra Behn: An Annotated Bibliography of Primary and Secondary Sources* (New York, 1986).

Editions

The pioneering edition by Montague Summers, published in 1915, though used extensively by scholars, has proved fairly unreliable. It is now being replaced by an authoritative scholarly edition published by Pickering/Chatto under the editorship of Janet Todd: *The Works of Aphra Behn*, Volume 1, *Poetry* (London, 1992); Volume 2, *Prose* (London, 1993); further volumes to follow. An earlier volume, edited by Germaine Greer, intended to supplement Summers by publishing all the poems he left out of his edition, remains a valuable adjunct to Todd for fifteen poems because of its extensive notes: *The Uncollected Verse of Aphra Behn* (Stump Cross, 1989). For an important account of the manuscript in the Bodleian Library which contains poems transcribed in Behn's hand, some of which may be by her, see Mary Ann O'Donnell, 'A Verse Miscellany of Aphra Behn: Bodleian Library MS Firth c.16', *English Manuscript Studies*, 2 (1990). A selection of Behn's fiction has been edited by Maureen Duffy as *Oroonoko and Other Stories* (London, 1986); Duffy has also edited Behn's important long fiction *Love Letters Between a Nobleman and His Sister* (London, 1988). A good general selection of Behn's work in one volume is edited by Janet Todd, *Oroonoko, The Rover and Other Works* (Harmondsworth, 1992).

Biography

Three major biographies of Behn are available: Maureen Duffy, *The Passionate Shepherdess* (London, 1977), which remains an excellent general introduction; Angeline Goreau, *Reconstructing Aphra* (New York, 1980), particularly good on social background; and Sara Heller Mendelson, *The Mental World of Stuart Women* (Brighton, 1987), ch. 3, which is the most reliable, though less detailed. These should be supplemented with Jane Jones, 'New Light on the Background and

Early Life of Aphra Behn', *Notes and Queries*, 235 (1990), who offers new claims about Behn's much disputed background. A full account of Behn's time in Surinam and her spying activities, complete with reprinted documents, is contained in W. J. Cameron, *New Light on Aphra Behn* (Auckland, 1961). Further information about Behn's stay in Surinam is provided in B. Duhuicq, 'Further Evidence on Aphra Behn's Stay in Surinam', *Notes and Queries*, 224 (1979), and the strongest claim for Behn's Catholicism (still a matter of some dispute) is made in Gerald Duchovnay, 'Aphra Behn's Religion', *Notes and Queries*, 221 (1976). A good discussion of the earliest biographical accounts of Behn is Robert A. Day, 'Aphra Behn's First Biography', *Studies in Bibliography*, 22 (1969).

Criticism

The best brief critical–biographical introduction to Behn is Mary Ann O'Donnell, 'Aphra Behn: Tory Wit and Unconventional Woman', in Katharina Wilson and Frank Warnke (eds.), *Women Writers of the 17th Century* (Athens, Ga., 1989), 341–74. George Woodcock, *The Incomparable Aphra* (London, 1948), is now rather outdated, though still useful. There is a helpful general study in the Twayne series: Frederick Link, *Aphra Behn* (New York, 1968).

Behn is placed in the context of other women writers in Elaine Hobby, *Virtue of Necessity: English Women's Writing 1649–88* (London, 1988). For studies which include discussions of Behn's fiction, see Jane Spencer, *The Rise of the Woman Novelist* (Oxford, 1986); Janet Todd, *The Sign of Angellica: Women, Writing and Fiction 1660–1800* (London, 1989); Paul Salzman, *English Prose Fiction 1558–1700: A Critical History* (Oxford, 1985); Charles C. Mish, 'English Short Fiction in the 17th Century', *Studies in Short Fiction*, 6 (1969); Paula Backschieder, 'Women's Influence', *Studies in the Novel*, 11 (1979); Rose A. Zimbardo, 'Aphra Behn in Search of the Novel', *Studies in Eighteenth Century Culture*, 19 (1989). The fiction is analysed in greatest detail in Ros Ballaster, *Seductive Forms: Women's Amatory Fiction from 1684 to 1740* (Oxford, 1992). See also Jacqueline Pearson, 'Gender and Narrative in the Fiction of Aphra Behn', *RES* 42 (1991, two parts); Gary Kelly, ' "Intrigue" and "Gallantry": The 17th Century French Nouvelle and the "Novels" of Aphra Behn', *Revue de littérature comparée*, 55 (1981); Robert A. Day, 'Aphra Behn and the Works of the Intellect', in Schofield and Macheski (eds.), *Fetter'd or Free* (Athens, Oh., 1986).

There is, as yet, no detailed study of Behn's poetry, though see the introduction to Todd's edition, discussion in Hobby, and an excellent article on the metamorphoses of a single poem: Bernard Duyfhuizen, '"That Which I Dare Not Name": Aphra Behn's "The Willing Mistress"', *ELH* 58 (1991).

Two impressive articles which concentrate on plays offer suggestive accounts of Behn's practices as a writer from complementary feminist perspectives: Elin Diamond, 'Gestus and Signature in Aphra Behn's *The Rover*', *ELH* 56 (1989) and Catherine Gallagher, '"Who Was That Masked Woman": The Prostitute and the Playwright in the Comedies of Aphra Behn', *Women's Studies*, 15 (1988).

On *Oroonoko*, see especially George Guffey, 'Aphra Behn's *Oroonoko*: Occasion and Accomplishment', in Guffey and Wright, *Two English Novelists* (Los Angeles, 1975); Martine Brownley, 'The Narrator in *Oroonoko*', *Essays in Literature*, 4 (1977); William C. Spengemann, 'The Earliest American Novel: Aphra Behn's *Oroonoko*', *Nineteenth Century Fiction*, 38 (1984); Elaine Campbell, 'Aphra Behn's Surinam Interlude', *Kunapipi*, 7 (1985); Laura Brown, 'The Romance of Empire: *Oroonoko* and the Trade in Slaves', in Nussbaum and Brown (eds.), *The New Eighteenth Century* (New York, 1987); Katherine M. Rogers, 'Fact and Fiction in Aphra Behn's *Oroonoko*', *Studies in the Novel*, 20 (1988); Robert L. Chibka, '"Oh! Do Not Fear a Woman's Invention": Truth, Falsehood and Fiction in Aphra Behn's *Oroonoko*', *Texas Studies in Literature and Language*, 30 (1988); Margaret Ferguson, 'Juggling the Categories of Race, Class and Gender: Aphra Behn's *Oroonoko*', *Women's Studies*, 19 (1991); Ros Ballaster, 'New Hystericism: Aphra Behn's *Oroonoko*: The Body, The Text and the Feminist Critic', in Isobel Armstrong (ed.), *New Feminist Discourses* (London, 1992).

CHRONOLOGY OF
APHRA BEHN'S LIFE AND WORKS

1640   Most probable year of Behn's birth, possibly to Bartholomew and Elizabeth Johnson in Kent, though this is far from conclusively proven.

1663–4 Probably in Surinam during this time, then returned to London, and perhaps then married 'Mr Behn', but no records of the marriage have been uncovered.

1666–7 Spy in the Netherlands.

1670   First performance of a play by Behn: *The Forced Marriage*, by The Duke's Company.

1671   Performance of *The Amorous Prince*.

1672   Behn commonly accepted as editor of the poetic miscellany *Covent Garden Drollery*.

1673   Performance of *The Dutch Lover*.

1676   Performance of Behn's tragedy *Abdelazar*.

1677   Performance of *The Rover*; also of *The Debauchee* and *The Counterfeit Bridegroom* (both attributed to Behn).

1678   Performance of *Sir Patient Fancy*.

1679   Performances of *The Feigned Courtezan* and *The Young King*.

1680   Performance of *The Revenge*.

1681   Perforances of *The Rover Part Two*, *The False Count* and *The Roundheads*.

1682   Performances of *Like Father, Like Son*; *The City Heiress*.

1684   Publication of Behn's *Poems Upon Several Occasions*, and the first part of the *roman-à-clef Love Letters Between a Nobleman and His Sister*.

1685   Poems on the death of Charles II and the accession of James II.

1686   Performance of *The Lucky Chance*.

1687   Performance of *The Emperor of the Moon*.

1688   Publication of *Oroonoko*, *The Fair Jilt*, translation of Tallemant's *Lycidus* together with *Miscellany* collection of original poems, poems on the birth of the Prince of Wales; *To Poet Bavius*.

1689   Publication of *The History of the Nun*, *The Lucky Mistake*, translation of Cowley's *Of Plants* Bk. 6. April 16, Behn dies and is buried in Westminster Abbey. *The Widow Ranter* performed posthumously.

1696   Publication of *The Younger Brother*, collection of Behn's fiction, including previously unpublished works: *The Adventure of the Black Lady*, *The Unfortunate Happy Lady*, *The Court of the King of Bantam*, *The Wandering Beauty*, *The Unfortunate Bride*, *The Unhappy Mistake*.

PART ONE

Prose

OROONOKO,

OR,

THE ROYAL SLAVE.

A TRUE HISTORY.

To The Right Honourable The Lord Maitland.[*]

My Lord, since the world is grown so nice and critical upon
dedications, and will needs be judging the book by the wit of
the patron, we ought with a great deal of circumspection, to
choose a person against whom there can be no exception, and
whose wit and worth truly merits all that one is capable of
saying upon that occasion.

The most part of dedications are charged with flattery, and
if the world knows a man has some vices, they will not allow
one to speak of his virtues. This, my Lord, is for want of
thinking rightly; if men would consider with reason, they
would have another sort of opinion and esteem of dedications
and would believe almost every great man has enough to make
him worthy of all that can be said of him there. My Lord, a
picture drawer, when he intends to make a good picture,
essays the face many ways, and in many lights, before he
begins, that he may choose from the several turns of it which
is most agreeable and gives it the best grace; and if there be a
scar, an ungrateful mole, or any little defect, they leave it out;
and yet make the picture extremely like. But he who has the
good fortune to draw a face that is exactly charming in all its
parts and features, what colours or agreements can be added to
make it finer? All that he can give is but its due; and glories in
a piece whose original alone gives it its perfection. An ill hand
may diminish, but a good hand cannot augment its beauty. A
poet is a painter in his way; he draws to the life, but in another
kind; we draw the nobler part, the soul and mind; the pictures
of the pen shall outlast those of the pencil, and even worlds
themselves. 'Tis a short chronicle of those lives that possibly
would be forgotten by other historians, or lie neglected there,

however deserving an immortal fame; for men of eminent parts are as exemplary as even monarchs themselves: and virtue is a noble lesson to be learned, and 'tis by comparison we can judge and choose. 'Tis by such illustrious precedents as your Lordship the world can be bettered and refined; when a great part of the lazy nobility shall with shame behold the admirable accomplishments of a man so great and so young.

Your Lordship has read innumerable volumes of men and books, not vainly for the gust* of novelty, but knowledge, excellent knowledge: like the industrious bee, from every flower you return laden with the precious dew, which you are sure to turn to the public good. You hoard no one perfection, but lay it all out in the glorious service of your religion and country; to both which you are a useful and necessary honour: they both want such supporters, and 'tis only men of so elevated parts and fine knowledge, such noble principles of loyalty and religion this nation sighs for.* Where shall we find a man so young, like Saint Augustine, in the midst of all his youth and gaiety, teaching the world divine precepts, true notions of faith, and excellent morality, and, at the same time, be also a perfect pattern of all that accomplish a great man? You have, my Lord, all that refined wit that charms, and the affability that obliges; a generosity that gives a lustre to your nobility; that hospitality and greatness of mind that engages the world and that admirable conduct that so well instructs it. Our nation ought to regret and bemoan their misfortunes, for not being able to claim the honour of the birth of a man who is so fit to serve His Majesty and his kingdoms in all great and public affairs, and to the glory of your nation be it spoken, it produces more considerable men, for all fine sense, wit, wisdom, breeding, and generosity (for the generality of the nobility) than all other nations can boast; and the fruitfulness of your virtues sufficiently make amends for the barrenness of your soil: which, however, cannot be incommode* to your Lordship, since your quality and the veneration that the commonalty naturally pay their lords creates a flowing plenty there—that makes you happy. And to complete your happiness, my Lord, Heaven has blessed you with a lady, to whom it has given all the graces, beauties, and virtues of her sex; all the youth, sweetness of nature, of a most illustrious family, and who is a most rare example to all wives of quality for her eminent piety, easiness, and condescension: and as absolutely merits respect from all the world, as she does that passion and resignation she receives from your Lordship: and which is, on her part, with so much tenderness returned. Methinks your tranquil lives are an image of the new made and beautiful pair in paradise: and 'tis the prayers and wishes of all, who have the honour to know you, that it may eternally so continue with additions of all the blessings this world can give you.

My Lord, the obligations I have to some of the great men of your nation, particularly to your Lordship, gives me an ambition of making my acknowledgements, by all the opportunities I can; and such humble fruits as my industry produces I lay at your Lordship's feet. This is a true story* of a man gallant enough to merit your protection; and, had he always been so fortunate, he had not made so inglorious an end: the royal slave I had the honour to know in my travels to the other world; and though I had none above me in that country, yet I wanted power to preserve this great man. If there be anything that seems Romantic, I beseech your Lordship to consider these countries do, in all things, so far differ from ours, that they produce unconceivable wonders; at least they appear so to us because new and strange. What I have mentioned I have taken care should be truth, let the critical reader judge as he pleases. 'Twill be no commendation to the book to assure your Lordship I writ it in a few hours, though it may serve to excuse some of its faults of connection, for I never rested my pen a moment for thought: 'tis purely the merit of my slave that must render it worthy of the honour it begs; and the author of that of subscribing herself,

My Lord,
your Lordship's most obliged
and obedient servant
A. Behn.

THE HISTORY OF THE ROYAL SLAVE

I do not pretend, in giving you the history of this royal slave, to entertain my reader with the adventures of a feigned hero, whose life and fortunes fancy may manage at the poet's pleasure; nor in relating the truth, design to adorn it with any accidents, but such as arrived in earnest to him: and it shall come simply into the world, recommended by its own proper merits and natural intrigues, there being enough of reality to support it, and to render it diverting, without the addition of invention.

I was myself an eye-witness to a great part of what you will find here set down, and what I could not be witness of I received from the mouth of the chief actor in this history, the hero himself, who gave us the whole transactions of his youth, and though I shall omit, for brevity's sake, a thousand little accidents of his life, which, however pleasant to us, where history was scarce, and adventures very rare, yet might prove tedious and heavy to my reader in a world where he finds diversions for every minute new and strange. But we who were perfectly charmed with the character of this great man were curious to gather every circumstance of his life.

The scene of the last part of his adventures lies in a colony in America called Surinam* in the West Indies. But before I give you the story of this gallant slave, 'tis fit I tell you the manner of bringing them to these new colonies; for those they make use of there are not natives of the place, for those we live with in perfect amity, without daring to command 'em, but on the contrary, caress 'em with all the brotherly and friendly affection in the world; trading with 'em for their fish, venison, buffaloes' skins and little rarities, as marmosets, a sort of monkey as big as a rat or weasel, but of a marvellous and delicate shape, and has face and hands like an human creature, and cousheries,* a little beast in the form and fashion of a lion, as big as a kitten, but so exactly made in all parts like that noble beast that it is it in miniature. Then for little parakeetoes, great parrots, macaws, and a thousand other birds and beasts of wonderful and surprising forms, shapes, and colours, for skins of prodigious snakes, of which there are some threescore yards in length, as is the skin of one that may be seen at His Majesty's antiquary's, where are also some rare flies, of amazing forms and colours, presented to 'em by myself, some as big as my fist, some less, and all of various excellencies, such as art cannot imitate. Then we trade for feathers, which they order into all shapes, make themselves little short habits of 'em, and glorious wreaths for their heads, necks, arms, and legs, whose tinctures are unconceivable. I had a set of these presented to me, and I gave 'em to the King's theatre, and it was the dress of the Indian Queen,* infinitely admired by persons of quality, and were unimitable. Besides these, a thousand little knacks and rarities in nature, and some of art, as their baskets, weapons, aprons, etc. We dealt with 'em with beads of all colours, knives, axes, pins, and needles, which they used only as tools to drill holes with in their ears, noses, and lips, where they hang a great many little things, as long beads, bits of tin, brass, or silver, beat thin, and any shiny trinket. The beads they weave into aprons about a quarter of an ell* long, and of the same breadth, working them very prettily in flowers of several colours of beads, which apron they wear just before 'em, as Adam and Eve did the fig leaves; the men wearing a long strip of linen, which they deal with us for. They thread these beads also on long cotton threads, and make girdles to tie their aprons to, which come twenty times or more about the waist and then cross, like a shoulder belt, both ways and round their necks, arms and legs. This adornment, with their long black hair and the face painted in little specks or flowers here and there, makes 'em a wonderful figure to behold. Some of the beauties, which indeed are finely shaped, as almost all are, and who have pretty features, are very charming and novel, for they have all that is called beauty, except the colour, which is a reddish yellow or, after a new oiling, which they often use to themselves, they are of the colour of a new brick, but smooth, soft, and sleek.

They are extreme modest and bashful, very shy, and nice of being touched. And though they are all thus naked, if one lives forever among 'em, there is not to be seen an indecent action, or glance, and being continually used to see one another unadorned, so like our first parents before the Fall,* it seems as if they had no wishes, there being nothing to heighten curiosity, but all you can see, you see at once, and every moment see; and where there is no novelty, there can be no curiosity. Not but I have seen a handsome young Indian dying for love of a very beautiful young Indian maid; but all his courtship was to fold his arms, pursue her with his eyes, and sighs were all his language, while she, as if no such lover were present, or rather, as if she desired none such, carefully guarded her eyes from beholding him, and never approached him, but she looked down with all the blushing modesty I have seen in the most severe and cautious of our world. And these people represented to me an absolute idea of the first state of innocence, before Man knew how to sin, and 'tis most evident and plain that simple Nature is the most harmless, inoffensive, and virtuous mistress. 'Tis she alone, if she were permitted, that better instructs the world than all the inventions of Man. Religion would here but destroy that tranquillity they possess by ignorance, and laws would but teach 'em to know offence, of which now they have no notion. They once made mourning and fasting for the death of the English governor, who had given his hand to come on such a day to 'em, and neither came, nor sent; believing, when once a man's word was passed, nothing but death could or should prevent his keeping it, and when they saw he was not dead, they asked him what name they had for a man who promised a thing he did not do. The governor told them such a man was a liar,* which was a word of infamy to a gentleman. Then one of 'em replied, 'Governor, you are a liar and guilty of that infamy.' They have a native justice which knows no fraud, and they understand no vice, or cunning, but when they are taught by the white men. They have plurality of wives, which, when they grow old, they serve those that succeed 'em, who are young, but with a servitude easy and respected, and unless they take slaves in war, they have no other attendants.

Those on that continent where I was had no king, but the oldest war captain was obeyed with great resignation. A war captain is a man who has led them on to battle with conduct and success, of whom I shall have occasion to speak more hereafter, and of some other of their customs and manners as they fall in my way.

With these people, as I said, we live in perfect tranquillity and good understanding, as it behoves us to do, they knowing all the places where to seek the best food of the country and the means of getting it; and for very small and unvaluable trifles, supply us with what 'tis impossible for us to get, for they do not only in the wood and over the savannahs in hunting supply the parts of hounds by swiftly scouring through those almost impassable places, and by the mere activity of their feet, run down the nimblest deer, and other eatable beasts, but in the water one would think they were gods of the rivers, or fellow citizens of the deep, so rare an art they have in swimming, diving, and almost living in water, by which they command the less swift inhabitants of the floods. And then for shooting, what they cannot take or reach with their hands, they do with arrows, and have so admirable an aim, that they will split almost an hair, and at any distance that an arrow can reach they will shoot down oranges and other fruit, and only touch the stalk with the darts' points that they may not hurt the fruit. So that they being on all occasions very useful to us, we find it absolutely necessary to caress 'em as friends and not to treat 'em as slaves; nor dare we do other, their numbers so far surpassing ours in that continent. Those then whom we make use of to work in our plantations of sugar are negroes,* black slaves altogether, which are transported thither in this manner.

Those who want slaves make a bargain with a master, or captain of a ship and contract to pay him so much a piece, a matter of twenty pound a head for as many as he agrees for and to pay for 'em when they shall be delivered on such a plantation. So that when there arrives a ship laden with slaves, they who have so contracted go aboard and receive their number by lot; and perhaps in one lot that may be for ten, there may happen to be three or four men, the rest, women and children. Or, be there more or less of either sex, you are obliged to be contented with your lot.

Coramantien,* a country of blacks so called, was one of those places in which they found the most advantageous trading for these slaves, and thither most of our great traders in that merchandise trafficked, for that nation is very warlike and brave and, having a continual campaign, being always in hostility with one neighbouring prince or other, they had the fortune to take a great many captives, for all they took in battle were sold as slaves; at least, those common men who could not ransom themselves. Of these slaves so taken, the general only has all the profit and of these generals, our captains and masters of ships buy all their freights.

The king of Coromantien was himself a man of a hundred and odd years old, and had no son, though he had many beautiful black wives; for most certainly there are beauties that can charm of that colour. In his younger years he had had many gallant men to his sons, thirteen of which died in battle, conquering when they fell, and he had only left him for his successor one grandchild, son to one of these dead victors, who, as soon as he could bear a bow in his hand, and a quiver at his back, was sent into the field to be trained up by one of the oldest generals to war, where from his natural inclination to arms, and the occasions given him with the good conduct of the old general, he became, at the age of seventeen, one of the most expert captains and bravest soldiers that ever saw the field of Mars. So that he was adored as the wonder of all that world, and the darling of the soldiers. Besides, he was adorned with a native beauty so transcending all those of his gloomy race, that he struck an awe and reverence even in those that knew not his quality, as he did in me, who beheld him with surprise and wonder when afterwards he arrived in our world.

He had scarce arrived at his seventeenth year when fighting by his side the general was killed with an arrow in his eye, which the Prince Oroonoko (for so was this gallant Moor called) very narrowly avoided; nor had he, if the general, who saw the arrow shot, and perceiving it aimed at the prince, had not bowed his head between, on purpose to receive it in his own body rather than it should touch that of the prince, and so saved him. 'Twas then, afflicted as Oroonoko was, that he was proclaimed general in the old man's place, and then it was, at the finishing of that war, which had continued for two years, that the prince came to court, where he had hardly been a month together, from the time of his fifth year to that of seventeen; and 'twas amazing to imagine where it was he learned so much humanity; or, to give his accomplishments a juster name, where 'twas he got that real greatness of soul, those refined notions of true honour, that absolute generosity, and that softness that was capable of the highest passions of love and gallantry, whose objects were almost continually fighting men, or those mangled, or dead, who heard no sounds but those of war and groans. Some part of it we may attribute to the care of a French man of wit and learning, who finding it turn to very good account to be a sort of royal tutor to this young black, and perceiving him very ready, apt, and quick of apprehension, took a great pleasure to teach him morals, language, and science, and was for it extremely beloved and valued by him. Another reason was he loved when he came from war to see all the English gentlemen that traded thither, and did not only learn their language, but that of the Spaniards also, with whom he traded afterwards for slaves.

I have often seen and conversed with this great man, and been a witness to many of his mighty actions, and do assure my reader, the most illustrious courts could not have produced a braver man, both for greatness of courage and mind, a judgement more solid, a wit more quick, and a conversation more sweet and diverting. He knew almost as much as if he had read much; he had heard of and admired the Romans, he had heard of the late Civil Wars in England and the deplorable death of our great monarch, and would discourse of it with all the sense, and abhorrence of the injustice imaginable. He had an extreme good and graceful mien, and all the civility of a well-bred great man. He had nothing of barbarity in his nature, but in all points addressed himself as if his education had been in some European court.

This great and just character of Oroonoko gave me an extreme curiosity to see him, especially when I knew he spoke French and English and that I could talk with him. But though I had heard so much of him, I was as greatly surprised when I saw him as if I had heard nothing of him; so beyond all report I found him. He came into the room and addressed himself to me and some other women with the best grace in the world. He was pretty tall, but of a shape the most exact that can be fancied. The most famous statuary could not form the figure of

a man more admirably turned from head to foot. His face was
not of that brown, rusty black which most of that nation are,
but a perfect ebony, or polished jet. His eyes were the most
aweful that could be seen and very piercing, the white of 'em
being like snow, as were his teeth. His nose was rising and
Roman, instead of African and flat. His mouth, the finest
shaped that could be seen, far from those great turned lips,
which are so natural to the rest of the Negroes. The whole
proportion and air of his face was so noble and exactly formed
that, bating* his colour, there could be nothing in nature more
beautiful, agreeable, and handsome. There was no one grace
wanting that bears the standard of true beauty. His hair came
down to his shoulders, by the aids of art, which was by pulling
it out with a quill and keeping it combed, of which he took
particular care. Nor did the perfections of his mind come short
of those of his person, for his discourse was admirable upon
almost any subject, and whoever had heard him speak would
have been convinced of their errors, that all fine wit is confined
to the white men, especially to those of Christendom, and
would have confessed that Oroonoko was as capable even of
reigning well and of governing as wisely, had as great a soul, as
politic maxims, and was as sensible of power, as any prince
civilized in the most refined schools of humanity and learning,
or the most illustrious courts.

This prince, such as I have described him, whose soul and
body were so admirably adorned, was (while yet he was in the
court of his grandfather), as I said, as capable of love as 'twas
possible for a brave and gallant man to be; and in saying that, I
have named the highest degree of love, for sure, great souls are
most capable of that passion. I have already said, the old general
was killed by the shot of an arrow, by the side of this prince in
battle, and that Oroonoko was made general. This old dead
hero had one only daughter left of his race: a beauty that to
describe her truly one need say only she was female to the
noble male, the beautiful black Venus to our young Mars, as
charming in her person as he and of delicate virtues. I have seen
an hundred white men sighing after her and making a thousand
vows at her feet, all vain and unsuccessful. And she was indeed
too great for any but a prince of her own nation to adore.

Oroonoko, coming from the wars, which were now ended, after he had made his court to his grandfather, he thought in honour he ought to make a visit to Imoinda, the daughter of his foster father, the dead general, and to make some excuses to her, because his preservation was the occasion of her father's death, and to present her with those slaves that had been taken in this last battle, as the trophies of her father's victories. When he came, attended by all the young soldiers of any merit, he was infinitely surprised at the beauty of this fair queen of night, whose face and person was so exceeding all he had ever beheld, that lovely modesty with which she received him, that softness in her look and sighs upon the melancholy occasion of this honour that was done by so great a man as Oroonoko, and a prince of whom she had heard such admirable things, the awefulness wherewith she received him, and the sweetness of her words and behaviour while he stayed, gained a perfect conquest over his fierce heart and made him feel the victor could be subdued. So that having made his first compliments, and presented her an hundred and fifty slaves in fetters, he told her with his eyes that he was not insensible of her charms; while Imoinda, who wished for nothing more than so glorious a conquest, was pleased to believe she understood that silent language of new-born love, and from that moment put on all her additions to beauty.

The prince returned to court with quite another humour than before; and though he did not speak much of the fair Imoinda, he had the pleasure to hear all his followers speak of nothing but the charms of that maid, insomuch that, even in the presence of the old king, they were extolling her and heightening, if possible, the beauties they had found in her. So that nothing else was talked of, no other sound was heard in every corner where there were whisperers, but 'Imoinda! Imoinda!'.

'Twill be imagined Oroonoko stayed not long before he made his second visit, nor, considering his quality, not much longer before he told her he adored her. I have often heard him say that he admired by what strange inspiration he came to talk things so soft, and so passionate, who never knew love, nor was used to the conversation of women, but (to use his own words) he said, most happily, some new, until then unknown power instructed his heart and tongue in the language of love and at the same time in favour of him inspired Imoinda with a sense of his passion. She was touched with what he said and returned it all in such answers as went to his very heart, with a pleasure unknown before. Nor did he use those obligations ill that love had done him, but turned all his happy moments to the best advantage; and as he knew no vice, his flame aimed at nothing but honour, if such a distinction may be made in love, and especially in that country, where men take to themselves as many as they can maintain and where the only crime and sin with woman is to turn her off, to abandon her to want, shame, and misery. Such ill morals are only practised in Christian countries where they prefer the bare name of religion and, without virtue or morality, think that's sufficient. But Oroonoko was none of those professors; but as he had right notions of honour, so he made her such propositions as were not only and barely such but, contrary to the custom of his country, he made her vows she should be the only woman he would possess while he lived; that no age or wrinkles should incline him to change, for her soul would be always fine and always young, and he should have an eternal idea in his mind of the charms she now bore and should look into his heart for that idea when he could find it no longer in her face.

After a thousand assurances of his lasting flame and her eternal empire over him, she condescended to receive him for her husband; or rather, received him as the greatest honour the gods could do her. There is a certain ceremony in these cases to be observed, which I forgot to ask him how performed; but 'twas concluded on both sides that, in obedience to him, the grandfather was to be first made acquainted with the design, for they pay a most absolute resignation to the monarch, especially when he is a parent also.

On the other side, the old king, who had many wives and many concubines, wanted not court flatterers to insinuate in his heart a thousand tender thoughts for this young beauty, and who represented her to his fancy as the most charming he had ever possessed in all the long race of his numerous years.

At this character his old heart, like an extinguished brand most apt to take fire, felt new sparks of love, and began to kindle, and now, grown to his second childhood, longed with impatience to behold this gay thing with whom, alas!, he could but innocently play. But how he should be confirmed she was this wonder, before he used his power to call her to court (where maidens never came unless for the king's private use) he was next to consider, and while he was so doing, he had intelligence brought him that Imoinda was most certainly mistress to the Prince Oroonoko. This gave him some chagrin; however, it gave him also an opportunity, one day, when the prince was a-hunting, to wait on a man of quality as his slave and attendant who should go and make a present to Imoinda, as from the prince; he should then, unknown, see this fair maid and have an opportunity to hear what message she would return the prince for his present, and from thence gather the state of her heart and degree of her inclination. This was put in execution, and the old monarch saw and burnt; he found her all he had heard, and would not delay his happiness, but found he should have some obstacle to overcome her heart, for she expressed her sense of the present the prince had sent her in terms so sweet, so soft and pretty, with an air of love and joy that could not be dissembled, insomuch that 'twas past doubt whether she loved Oroonoko entirely. This gave the old king some affliction, but he salved it with this: that the obedience the people pay their king was not at all inferior to what they paid their gods, and what love would not oblige Imoinda to do, duty would compel her to.

He was therefore no sooner got to his apartment but he sent the royal veil to Imoinda; that is, the ceremony of invitation: he sends the lady he has a mind to honour with his bed a veil, with which she is covered and secured for the king's use and 'tis death to disobey; besides, held a most impious disobedience. 'Tis not to be imagined the surprise and grief that seized this lovely maid at this news and sight. However, as delays in these cases are dangerous, and pleading worse than treason, trembling and almost fainting, she was obliged to suffer herself to be covered and led away.

They brought her thus to court, and the king, who had

caused a very rich bath to be prepared, was led into it where he sat under a canopy in state to receive this longed-for virgin, whom he having commanded should be brought to him, they (after disrobing her) led her to the bath and, making fast the doors, left her to descend. The king, without more courtship, bade her throw off her mantle and come to his arms. But Imoinda, all in tears, threw herself on the marble on the brink of the bath and besought him to hear her. She told him, as she was a maid, how proud of the divine glory she should have been of having it in her power to oblige her king, but as by the laws he could not, and from his royal goodness would not, take from any man his wedded wife, so she believed she should be the occasion of making him commit a great sin, if she did not reveal her state and condition, and tell him she was another's, and could not be so happy to be his.

The king, enraged at this delay, hastily demanded the name of the bold man, that had married a woman of her degree without his consent. Imoinda, seeing his eyes fierce and his hands tremble, whether with age or anger I know not, but she fancied the last, almost repented she had said so much, for now she feared the storm would fall on the prince; she therefore said a thousand things to appease the raging of his flame, and to prepare him to hear who it was with calmness, but before she spoke he imagined who she meant, but would not seem to do so, but commanded her to lay aside her mantle and suffer herself to receive his caresses; or, by his gods, he swore that happy man whom she was going to name should die, though it were even Oroonoko himself.

'Therefore', said he, 'deny this marriage, and swear thyself a maid.'

'That', replied Imoinda, 'by all our powers I do, for I am not yet known to my husband.'

''Tis enough,' said the king, ''tis enough to satisfy both my conscience and my heart.' And rising from his seat, he went and led her into the bath, it being in vain for her to resist.

In this time the prince, who was returned from hunting, went to visit his Imoinda, but found her gone, and not only so, but heard she had received the royal veil. This raised him to a storm and, in his madness, they had much ado to save him from laying violent hands on himself. Force first prevailed, and then reason. They urged all to him that might oppose his rage, but nothing weighed so greatly with him as the king's old age uncapable of injuring him with Imoinda. He would give way to that hope because it pleased him most and flattered best his heart. Yet this served not altogether to make him cease his different passions, which sometimes raged within him, and sometimes softened into showers. 'Twas not enough to appease him, to tell him his grandfather was old, and could not that way injure him, while he retained that aweful duty which the young men are used there to pay to their grave relations. He could not be convinced he had no cause to sigh and mourn for the loss of a mistress he could not with all his strength and courage retrieve. And he would often cry: 'O my friends! were she in walled cities, or confined from me in fortifications of the greatest strength, did enchantments or monsters detain her from me, I would venture through any hazard to free her. But here, in the arms of a feeble old man, my youth, my violent love, my trade in arms, and all my vast desire of glory avail me nothing. Imoinda is as irrecoverably lost to me as if she were snatched by the cold arms of death. O she is never to be retrieved! If I would wait tedious years till fate should bow the old king to his grave, even that would not leave me Imoinda free, but still that custom that makes it so vile a crime for a son to marry his father's wives or mistresses would hinder my happiness, unless I would either ignobly set an ill precedent to my successors, or abandon my country and fly with her to some unknown world who never heard our story.'

But it was objected to him that his case was not the same, for Imoinda being his lawful wife by solemn contract, 'twas he was the injured man and might, if he so pleased, take Imoinda back, the breach of the law being on his grandfather's side; and that if he could circumvent him and redeem her from the Otan, which is the palace of the king's women, a sort of seraglio, it was both just and lawful for him so to do.

This reasoning had some force upon him, and he should have been entirely comforted but for the thought that she was possessed by his grandfather; however, he loved so well, that he was resolved to believe what most favoured his hope, and to endeavour to learn from Imoinda's own mouth what only she could satisfy him in: whether she was robbed of that blessing which was only due to his faith and love. But as it was very hard to get a sight of the women, for no men ever entered into the Otan, but when the king went to entertain himself with some one of his wives or mistresses, and 'twas death at any other time for any other to go in, so he knew not how to contrive to get a sight of her.

While Oroonoko felt all the agonies of love, and suffered under a torment the most painful in the world, the old king was not exempted from his share of affliction. He was troubled for having been forced by an irresistible passion to rob his son of a treasure he knew could not but be extremely dear to him, since she was the most beautiful that ever had been seen, and had besides all the sweetness and innocence of youth and modesty with a charm of wit surpassing all. He found that, however she was forced to expose her lovely person to his withered arms, she could only sigh and weep there and think of Oroonoko, and oftentimes could not forbear speaking of him, though her life were by custom forfeited by owning her passion. But she spoke not of a lover only, but of a prince dear to him to whom she spoke, and of the praises of a man who, till now, filled the old man's soul with joy at every recital of his bravery, or even his name. And 'twas this dotage on our young hero that gave Imoinda a thousand privileges to speak of him without offending; and this condescension in the old king that made her take the satisfaction of speaking of him so very often.

Besides, he many times enquired how the prince bore himself, and those of whom he asked, being entirely slaves to the merits and virtues of the prince, still answered what they thought conduced best to his service; which was, to make the old king fancy that the prince had no more interest in Imoinda, and had resigned her willingly to the pleasure of the king; that he diverted himself with his mathematicians, his fortifications, his officers, and his hunting.

This pleased the old lover, who failed not to report these things again to Imoinda, that she might, by the example of her young lover, withdraw her heart and rest better contented in his arms. But however she was forced to receive this unwelcome news, in all appearance with unconcern and content, her heart was bursting within, and she was only happy when she could get alone to vent her griefs and moans with sighs and tears.

What reports of the prince's conduct were made to the king, he thought good to justify as far as possibly he could by his actions; and when he appeared in the presence of the king, he showed a face not at all betraying his heart: so that in a little time the old man, being entirely convinced that he was no longer a lover of Imoinda, he carried him with him, in his train, to the Otan, often to banquet with his mistress. But as soon as he entered, one day, into the apartment of Imoinda with the king, at the first glance from her eyes, notwithstanding all his determined resolution, he was ready to sink in the place where he stood, and had certainly done so, but for the support of Aboan, a young man who was next to him, which, with his change of countenance, had betrayed him, had the king chanced to look that way. And I have observed, 'tis a very great error in those who laugh when one says a Negro can change colour, for I have seen 'em as frequently blush and look pale, and that as visibly as ever I saw in the most beautiful white. And 'tis certain that both these changes were evident this day in both these lovers. And Imoinda, who saw with some joy the change in the prince's face, and found it in her own, strove to divert the king from beholding either by a forced caress, with which she met him; which was a new wound in the heart of the poor dying prince. But as soon as the king was busied in looking on some fine thing of Imoinda's making, she had time to tell the prince with her angry but love-darting eyes that she resented his coldness, and bemoaned her own miserable captivity. Nor were his eyes silent, but answered hers again, as much as eyes could do, instructed by the most tender, and most passionate heart that ever loved; and they spoke so well and so effectually, as Imoinda no longer doubted but she was the only delight and the darling of that soul she found pleading in 'em its right of love, which none was more willing to resign than she. And 'twas this powerful language alone that in an instant conveyed all the thoughts of their souls to each other, that they both found there wanted but opportunity to make them both entirely happy.

But when he saw another door opened by Onahal, a former old wife of the king's, who now had charge of Imoinda, and saw the prospect of a bed of state made ready with sweets and flowers for the dalliance of the king, who immediately led the trembling victim from his sight into that prepared repose, what rage, what wild frenzies seized his heart, which forcing to keep within bounds, and to suffer without noise, it became the more insupportable, and rent his soul with ten thousand pains. He was forced to retire to vent his groans, where he fell down on a carpet and lay struggling a long time, and only breathing now and then, 'O Imoinda!'. When Onahal had finished her necessary affair within, shutting the door, she came forth to wait till the king called, and hearing someone sighing in the other room, she passed on, and found the prince in that deplorable condition, which she thought needed her aid. She gave him cordials, but all in vain, till finding the nature of his disease by his sighs and naming Imoinda, she told him he had not so much cause as he imagined to afflict himself, for if he knew the king so well as she did, he would not lose a moment in jealousy, and that she was confident that Imoinda bore at this minute part in his affliction. Aboan was of the same opinion, and both together persuaded him to reassume his courage, and all sitting down on the carpet, the prince said so many obliging things to Onahal, that he half persuaded her to be of his party. And she promised him she would thus far comply with his just desires that she would let Imoinda know how faithful he was, what he suffered, and what he said.

This discourse lasted till the king called, which gave Oroonoko a certain satisfaction, and with the hope Onahal had made him conceive, he assumed a look as gay as 'twas possible a man in his circumstances could do, and presently after, he was called in with the rest who waited without. The king commanded music to be brought, and several of his young wives and mistresses came altogether by his command to dance before him, where Imoinda performed her part with an air and grace so passing all the rest as her beauty was above

'em, and received the present ordained as a prize. The prince
was every moment more charmed with the new beauties and
graces he beheld in this fair one, and while he gazed and she
danced, Onahal was retired to a window with Aboan.

This Onahal, as I said, was one of the cast-mistresses of the
old king, and 'twas these (now past their beauty) that were
made guardians or governants to the new and the young ones
and whose business it was to teach them all those wanton arts
of love with which they prevailed and charmed heretofore in
their turn, and who now treated the triumphing happy ones
with all the severity, as to liberty and freedom, that was
possible, in revenge of those honours they robbed them of,
envying them those satisfactions, those gallantries, and presents
that were once made to themselves while youth and beauty
lasted, and which they now saw pass regardless by, and paid
only to the bloomings. And certainly nothing is more afflicting
to a decayed beauty than to behold in itself declining charms
that were once adored and to find those caresses paid to new
beauties, to which once she laid a claim; to hear 'em whisper
as she passes by, 'That once was a delicate woman.' These
abandoned ladies therefore endeavour to revenge all the des-
pites and decays of time on these flourishing happy ones. And
'twas this severity that gave Oroonoko a thousand fears he
should never prevail with Onahal to see Imoinda. But, as I
said, she was now retired to a window with Aboan.

This young man was not only one of the best quality, but a
man extremely well made and beautiful; and coming often to
attend the king to the Otan, he had subdued the heart of the
antiquated Onahal, which had not forgot how pleasant it was
to be in love. And though she had some decays in her face, she
had none in her sense and wit; she was there agreeable still,
even to Aboan's youth, so that he took pleasure in entertaining
her with discourses of love. He knew also that to make his
court to these she-favourites was the way to be great, these
being the persons that do all affairs and business at court. He
had also observed that she had given him glances more tender
and inviting than she had done to others of his quality and
now, when he saw that her favour could so absolutely oblige
the prince, he failed not to sigh in her ear, and to look with

eyes all soft upon her, and give her hope that she had made some impressions on his heart. He found her pleased at this and making a thousand advances to him, but the ceremony ending and the king departing broke up the company for that day and his conversation.

Aboan failed not that night to tell the prince of his success and how advantageous the service of Onahal might be to his amour with Imoinda. The prince was overjoyed with this good news, and besought him if it were possible to caress her so as to engage her entirely; which he could not fail to do if he complied with her desires. 'For then,' said the prince, 'her life lying at your mercy, she must grant you the request you make in my behalf.' Aboan understood him and assured him he would make love so effectually that he would defy the most expert mistress of the art to find out whether he dissembled it, or had it really. And 'twas with impatience they waited the next opportunity of going to the Otan.

The wars came on, the time of taking the field approached, and 'twas impossible for the prince to delay his going at the head of his army, to encounter the enemy, so that every day seemed a tedious year till he saw his Imoinda; for he believed he could not live if he were forced away without being so happy. 'Twas with impatience, therefore, that he expected the next visit the king would make, and, according to his wish, it was not long. The parley of the eyes of these two lovers had not passed so secretly, but an old jealous lover could spy it; or rather, he wanted not flatterers who told him they observed it. So that the prince was hastened to the camp and this was the last visit he found he should make to the Otan. He therefore urged Aboan to make the best of this last effort, and to explain himself so to Onahal that she, deferring her enjoyment of her young lover no longer, might make way for the prince to speak to Imoinda.

The whole affair being agreed on between the prince and Aboan, they attended the king, as the custom was, to the Otan; where, while the whole company was taken up in beholding the dancing, and antic postures the women royal made to divert the king, Onahal singled out Aboan, whom she found most pliable to her wish. When she had him where she believed she could not be heard, she sighed to him, and softly cried: 'Ah, Aboan! When will you be sensible of my passion? I confess it with my mouth, because I would not give my eyes the lie and you have but too much already perceived they have confessed my flame; nor would I have you believe that because I am the abandoned mistress of a king, I esteem myself altogether divested of charms. No, Aboan, I have still a rest of beauty enough engaging, and have learned to please too well not to be desirable. I can have lovers still, but will have none but Aboan.'

'Madam,' replied the half-feigning youth, 'you have already, by my eyes, found you can still conquer; and I believe 'tis in pity of me you condescend to this kind confession. But, Madam, words are used to be so small a part of our country courtship, that 'tis rare one can get so happy an opportunity as to tell one's heart; and those few minutes we have are forced to be snatched for more certain fruits of love than speaking and sighing and such I languish for.'

He spoke this with such a tone that she hoped it true, and could not forbear believing it; and being wholly transported with joy, for having subdued the finest of all the king's subjects to her desires, she took from her ears two large pearls and commanded him to wear 'em in his. He would have refused 'em, crying, 'Madam, these are not the proofs of your love that I expect; 'tis opportunity, 'tis a lone hour only that can make me happy.' But forcing the pearls into his hand, she whispered softly to him, 'O do not fear a woman's invention when love sets her a-thinking.' And pressing his hand she cried, 'This night you shall be happy. Come to the gate of the orange groves behind the Otan and I will be ready about midnight to receive you.'

'Twas thus agreed, and she left him, that no notice might be taken of their speaking together. The ladies were still dancing and the king, laid on a carpet, with a great deal of pleasure was beholding them, especially Imoinda, who that day appeared more lovely than ever, being enlivened with the good tidings Onahal had brought her of the constant passion the prince had for her. The prince was laid on another carpet at the other end of the room, with his eyes fixed on the object of his soul; and as she turned, or moved, so did they, and she alone gave his eyes and soul their motions; nor did Imoinda employ her eyes to any other use than in beholding with infinite pleasure the joy she produced in those of the prince. But while she was more regarding him than the steps she took, she chanced to fall, and so near him as that, leaping with extreme force from the carpet, he caught her in his arms as she fell, and 'twas visible to the whole presence the joy wherewith he received her. He clasped her close to his bosom and quite forgot that reverence that was due to the mistress of a king, and that punishment that is the reward of a boldness of this nature; and had not the presence of mind of Imoinda (fonder of his safety than her own) befriended him, in making her spring from his arms and fall into her dance again, he had, at that instant, met his death; for the old king, jealous to the last degree, rose up in rage, broke all the diversion and led Imoinda to her apartment, and sent out word to the prince to go immediately to the camp and that if he were found another night in court he should suffer the death ordained for disobedient offenders.

You may imagine how welcome this news was to Oroonoko, whose unseasonable transport and caress of Imoinda was blamed by all men that loved him; and now he perceived his fault, yet cried that for such another moment he would be content to die.

All the Otan was in disorder about this accident, and Onahal was particularly concerned because on the prince's stay depended her happiness, for she could no longer expect that of Aboan. So that, ere they departed, they contrived it so that the prince and he should come both that night to the grove of the Otan, which was all of oranges and citrons, and that there they should wait her orders.

They parted thus, with grief enough, till night, leaving the king in possession of the lovely maid. But nothing could appease the jealousy of the old lover. He would not be imposed on, but would have it that Imoinda made a false step on purpose to fall into Oroonoko's bosom, and that all things looked like a design on both sides, and 'twas in vain she protested her innocence: he was old and obstinate and left her more than half assured that his fear was true.

The king, going to his apartment, sent to know where the prince was, and if he intended to obey his command. The messenger returned, and told him he found the prince pensive and altogether unpreparing for the campaign; that he lay negligently on the ground and answered very little. This confirmed the jealousy of the king, and he commanded that they should very narrowly and privately watch his motions, and that he should not stir from his apartment, but one spy or other should be employed to watch him. So that the hour approaching wherein he was to go to the citron grove, and taking only Aboan along with him, he leaves his apartment and was watched to the very gate of the Otan, where he was seen to enter, and where they left him to carry back the tidings to the king.

Oroonoko and Aboan were no sooner entered, but Onahal led the prince to the apartment of Imoinda; who, not knowing anything of her happiness, was laid in bed. But Onahal only left him in her chamber to make the best of his opportunity, and took her dear Aboan to her own, where he showed the height of complaisance for his prince when, to give him an opportunity, he suffered himself to be caressed in bed by Onahal.

The prince softly wakened Imoinda, who was not a little surprised with joy to find him there, and yet she trembled with a thousand fears. I believe he omitted saying nothing to this young maid that might persuade her to suffer him to seize his own, and take the rights of love; and I believe she was not long resisting those arms, where she so longed to be; and having opportunity, night, and silence, youth, love, and desire, he soon prevailed and ravished in a moment what his old grand-father had been endeavouring for so many months.

'Tis not to be imagined the satisfaction of these two young lovers, nor the vows she made him, that she remained a spotless maid till that night, and that what she did with his grandfather had robbed him of no part of her virgin honour, the gods, in mercy and justice, having reserved that for her plighted Lord, to whom of right it belonged. And 'tis impossible to express the transports he suffered, while he listened to a discourse so charming from her loved lips and clasped that

body in his arms for whom he had so long languished; and
nothing now afflicted him but his sudden departure from her,
for he told her the necessity, and his commands; but should
depart satisfied in this, that since the old king had hitherto not
been able to deprive him of those enjoyments which only
belonged to him, he believed for the future he would be less
able to injure him; so that, abating the scandal of the veil,
which was no otherwise so, than that she was wife to another,
he believed her safe, even in the arms of the king, and
innocent—yet would he have ventured at the conquest of the
world, and have given it all, to have had her avoided that
honour of receiving the royal veil. 'Twas thus, between a
thousand caresses, that both bemoaned the hard fate of youth
and beauty, so liable to that cruel promotion. 'Twas a glory
that could well have been spared here, though desired and
aimed at by all the young females of that kingdom.

But while they were thus fondly employed, forgetting how
time ran on, and that the dawn must conduct him far away
from his only happiness, they heard a great noise in the Otan,
and unusual voices of men, at which the prince, starting from
the arms of the frighted Imoinda, ran to a little battleaxe he
used to wear by his side, and having not so much leisure as to
put on his habit, he opposed himself against some who were
already opening the door, which they did with so much
violence that Oroonoko was not able to defend it, but was
forced to cry out with a commanding voice, 'Whoever ye are
that have the boldness to attempt to approach this apartment
thus rudely, know, that I, the Prince Oroonoko, will revenge it
with the certain death of him that first enters. Therefore stand
back and know this place is sacred to love and me this night;
tomorrow 'tis the king's.'

This he spoke with a voice so resolved and assured that
they soon retired from the door, but cried, ''Tis by the king's
command we are come, and being satisfied by thy voice, O
Prince, as much as if we had entered, we can report to the king
the truth of all his fears, and leave thee to provide for thy own
safety, as thou art advised by thy friends.'

At these words they departed, and left the prince to take a
short and sad leave of his Imoinda, who trusting in the

strength of her charms, believed she should appease the fury of a jealous king by saying she was surprised, and that it was by force of arms he got into her apartment. All her concern now was for his life, and therefore she hastened him to the camp, and with much ado prevailed on him to go. Nor was it she alone that prevailed: Aboan and Onahal both pleaded and both assured him of a lie that should be well enough contrived to secure Imoinda. So that at last, with a heart sad as death, dying eyes, and sighing soul, Oroonoko departed and took his way to the camp.

It was not long after the king in person came to the Otan, where beholding Imoinda with rage in his eyes, he upbraided her wickedness and perfidy, and threatening her royal lover— she fell on her face at his feet, bedewing the floor with her tears, and imploring his pardon for a fault which she had not with her will committed, as Onahal, who was also prostrate with her, could testify: that, unknown to her, he had broke into her apartment and ravished her. She spoke this much against her conscience, but to save her own life, 'twas absolutely necessary she should feign this falsity. She knew it could not injure the prince, he being fled to an army that would stand by him against any injuries that should assault him. However, this last thought of Imoinda's being ravished changed the measures of his revenge; and whereas before he designed to be himself her executioner, he now resolved she should not die. But as it is the greatest crime in nature amongst 'em to touch a woman, after having been possessed by a son, a father, or a brother, so now he looked on Imoinda as a polluted thing, wholly unfit for his embrace; nor would he resign her to his grandson, because she had received the royal veil. He therefore removes her from the Otan with Onahal, whom he put into safe hands, with order they should be both sold off as slaves to another country, either Christian or heathen, 'twas no matter where.

This cruel sentence, worse than death, they implored might be reversed; but their prayers were vain, and it was put in execution accordingly, and that with so much secrecy, that none, either without or within the Otan, knew anything of their absence or their destiny. The old king, nevertheless, executed this with a great deal of reluctancy, but he believed

he had made a very great conquest over himself, when he had
once resolved, and had performed what he resolved. He believed now that his love had been unjust, and that he could not
expect the gods, or captain of the clouds (as they call the
unknown power), should suffer a better consequence from so
ill a cause. He now begins to hold Oroonoko excused, and to
say he had reason for what he did; and now everybody could
assure the king how passionately Imoinda was beloved by the
prince, even those confessed it now who said the contrary
before his flame was abated. So that the king being old, and
not able to defend himself in war, and having no sons of all his
race remaining alive, but only this to maintain him on his
throne, and looking on this as a man disobliged, first by the
rape of his mistress, or rather, wife, and now by depriving of
him wholly of her, he feared might make him desperate, and
do some cruel thing either to himself or his old grandfather,
the offender. He began to repent him extremely of the contempt he had, in his rage, put on Imoinda. Besides, he considered he ought in honour to have killed her for this offence—if
it had been one. He ought to have had so much value and
consideration for a maid of her quality, as to have nobly put
her to death, and not to have sold her like a common slave, the
greatest revenge and the most disgraceful of any, and to which
they a thousand times prefer death and implore it, as Imoinda
did, but could not obtain that honour. Seeing therefore it was
certain that Oroonoko would highly resent this affront, he
thought good to make some excuse for his rashness to him,
and to that end he sent a messenger to the camp, with orders
to treat with him about the matter, to gain his pardon, and to
endeavour to mitigate his grief; but that by no means he
should tell him she was sold, but secretly put to death, for he
knew he should never obtain his pardon for the other.

When the messenger came, he found the prince upon the
point of engaging with the enemy, but as soon as he heard of
the arrival of the messenger, he commanded him to his tent,
where he embraced him, and received him with joy, which was
soon abated by the downcast looks of the messenger, who was
instantly demanded the cause by Oroonoko, who, impatient of
delay, asked a thousand questions in a breath, and all concern-

ing Imoinda. But there needed little return, for he could
almost answer himself of all he demanded from his sighs and
eyes. At last, the messenger casting himself at the prince's feet
and kissing them with all the submission of a man that had
something to implore which he dreaded to utter, he besought
him to hear with calmness what he had to deliver to him, and
to call up all his noble and heroic courage to encounter with
his words, and defend himself against the ungrateful things he
must relate. Oroonoko replied with a deep sigh and a languishing voice,' —I am armed against their worst efforts—for I know
they will tell me Imoinda is no more—and after that, you may
spare the rest.' Then commanding him to rise, he laid himself
on a carpet under a rich pavilion, and remained a good while
silent, and was hardly heard to sigh. When he was come a little
to himself, the messenger asked him leave to deliver that part
of his embassy, which the prince had not yet divined, and the
prince cried, 'I permit thee——' Then he told him the affliction the old king was in for the rashness he had committed in
his cruelty to Imoinda, and how he deigned to ask pardon for
his offence, and to implore the prince would not suffer that
loss to touch his heart too sensibly, which now all the gods
could not restore him, but might recompense him in glory,
which he begged he would pursue; and that death, that
common revenger of all injuries, would soon even the account
between him and a feeble old man.

Oroonoko bade him return his duty to his lord and master,
and to assure him, there was no account of revenge to be
adjusted between them; if there were, 'twas he was the aggressor, and that death would be just and, maugre* his age, would
see him righted; and he was contented to leave his share of
glory to youths more fortunate and worthy of that favour from
the gods. That henceforth he would never lift a weapon or
draw a bow, but abandon the small remains of his life to sighs
and tears, and the continual thoughts of what his lord and
grandfather had thought good to send out of the world, with
all that youth, that innocence, and beauty.

After having spoken this, whatever his greatest officers and
men of the best rank could do, they could not raise him from
the carpet or persuade him to action and resolutions of life,

but commanding all to retire, he shut himself into his pavilion all that day, while the enemy was ready to engage, and wondering at the delay, the whole body of the chief of the army then addressed themselves to him, and to whom they had much ado to get admittance. They fell on their faces at the foot of his carpet, where they lay, and besought him with earnest prayers and tears to lead 'em forth to battle, and not let the enemy take advantages of them, and implored him to have regard to his glory, and to the world, that depended on his courage and conduct. But he made no other reply to all their supplications but this: that he had now no more business for glory; and for the world, it was a trifle not worth his care.

'Go', continued he, sighing, 'and divide it amongst you, and reap with joy what you so vainly prize, and leave me to my more welcome destiny.'

They then demanded what they should do, and whom he would constitute in his room, that the confusion of ambitious youth and power might not ruin their order, and make them a prey to the enemy. He replied, he would not give himself the trouble—but wished 'em to choose the bravest man amongst 'em, let his quality or birth be what it would. 'For, O my friends,' said he, 'it is not titles make men brave, or good, or birth that bestows courage and generosity, or makes the owner happy. Believe this, when you behold Oroonoko, the most wretched and abandoned by fortune of all the creation of the gods.' So turning himself about, he would make no more reply to all they could urge or implore.

The army, beholding their officers return unsuccessful, with sad faces and ominous looks that presaged no good luck, suffered a thousand fears to take possession of their hearts, and the enemy to come even upon 'em before they would provide for their safety by any defence; and though they were assured by some, who had a mind to animate 'em, that they should be immediately headed by the prince, and that in the mean time Aboan had orders to command as general, yet they were so dismayed for want of that great example of bravery, that they could make but a very feeble resistance, and at last, downright fled before the enemy, who pursued 'em to the very tents, killing 'em. Nor could all Aboan's courage, which that day gained him immortal glory, shame 'em into a manly defence of themselves. The guards that were left behind about the prince's tent, seeing the soldiers flee before the enemy, and scatter themselves all over the plain in great disorder, made such outcries as roused the prince from his amorous slumber, in which he had remained buried for two days without permitting any sustenance to approach him. But, in spite of all his resolutions, he had not the constancy of grief to that degree as to make him insensible of the danger of his army, and in that instant he leaped from his couch and cried, 'Come, if we must die, let us meet death the noblest way; and 'twill be more like Oroonoko to encounter him at an army's head, opposing the torrent of a conquering foe, than lazily on a couch to wait his lingering pleasure and die every moment by a thousand wreck-ing thought[s]; or be tamely taken by an enemy and led a whining, love-sick slave, to adorn the triumphs of Jamoan, that young victor, who already is entered beyond the limits I had prescribed him.'

While he was speaking he suffered his people to dress him for the field; and sallying out of his pavilion, with more life and vigour in his countenance than ever he showed, he ap-peared like some divine power descended to save his country from destruction and his people had purposely put him on* all things that might make him shine with most splendour, to strike a reverent awe into the beholders. He flew into the thickest of those that were pursuing his men, and being animated with despair, he fought as if he came on purpose to die, and did such things as will not be believed that human strength could perform, and such as soon inspired all the rest with new courage and new order. And now it was that they began to fight indeed, and so, as if they would not be outdone, even by their adored hero, who turning the tide of the victory, changing absolutely the fate of the day, gained an entire conquest, and Oroonoko, having the good fortune to single out Jamoan, he took him prisoner with his own hand, having wounded him almost to death.

This Jamoan afterwards became very dear to him, being a man very gallant, and of excellent graces, and fine parts; so that he never put him amongst the rank of captives, as they used to do, without distinction, for the common sale or market, but kept him in his own court, where he retained nothing of the prisoner but the name, and returned no more into his own country, so great an affection he took for Oroonoko, and by a thousand tales and adventures of love and gallantry, flattered his disease of melancholy and languishment, which I have often heard him say, had certainly killed him but for the conversation of this prince and Aboan, and* the French governor he had from his childhood, of whom I have spoken before, and who was a man of admirable wit, great ingenuity, and learning, all which he had infused into his young pupil. This Frenchman was banished out of his own country for some heretical notions he held, and though he was a man of very little religion, he had admirable morals, and a brave soul.

After the total defeat of Jamoan's army, which all fled, or were left dead upon the place, they spent some time in the camp, Oroonoko choosing rather to remain a while there in his tents, than enter into a place, or live in a court where he had so lately suffered so great a loss. The officers therefore who saw and knew his cause of discontent, invented all sorts of diversions and sports to entertain their prince. So that what with those amusements abroad, and others at home—that is, within their tents—with the persuasions, arguments, and care of his friends and servants that he more peculiarly prized, he wore off in time a great part of that chagrin and torture of despair which the first efforts* of Imoinda's death had given him, insomuch as having received a thousand kind embassies from the king, and invitations to return to court, he obeyed, though with no little reluctancy, and when he did so, there was a visible change in him, and for a long time he was much more melancholy than before. But time lessens all extremes and reduces 'em to mediums and unconcern; but no motives or beauties, though all endeavoured it, could engage him in any sort of amour, though he had all the invitations to it, both from his own youth and others' ambitions and designs.

Oroonoko was no sooner returned from this last conquest, and received at court with all the joy and magnificence that could be expressed to a young victor who was not only returned triumphant, but beloved like a deity, when there arrived in the port an English ship. This person had often before been in these countries, and was very well known to Oroonoko, with whom he had trafficked for slaves, and had used to do the same with his predecessors. This commander was a man of a finer sort of address and conversation, better bred and more engaging than most of that sort of men are, so that he seemed rather never to have been bred out of a court, than almost all his life at sea. This captain therefore was always better received at court than most of the traders to those countries were, and especially by Oroonoko, who was more civilized, according to the European mode, than any other had been, and took more delight in the white nations and, above all, men of parts and wit. To this captain he sold abundance of his slaves, and for the favour and esteem he had for him, made him many presents, and obliged him to stay at court as long as possibly he could, which the captain seemed to take as a very great honour done him, entertaining the prince every day with globes and maps and mathematical discourses and instruments, eating, drinking, hunting, and living with him with so much familiarity that it was not to be doubted but he had gained very greatly upon the heart of this gallant young man. And the captain, in return of all these mighty favours, besought the prince to honour his vessel with his presence some day or other to dinner before he should set sail, which he condescended to accept and appointed his day. The captain, on his part, failed not to have all things in a readiness in the most magnificent order he could possibly. And the day being come, the captain in his boat, richly adorned with carpets and velvet cushions, rowed to the shore to receive the prince, with another long boat, where was placed all his music and trumpets, with which Oroonoko was extremely delighted, who met him on the shore, attended by his French governor, Jamoan, Aboan, and about an hundred of the noblest youths of the court. And after they had first carried the prince on board, the boats fetched the rest off, where they found a very splendid treat, with all sorts of fine wines, and were as well entertained as 'twas possible in such a place to be.

The prince, having drunk hard of punch, and several sorts of wine, as did all the rest (for great care was taken they should want nothing of that part of the entertainment), was very merry and in great admiration of the ship, for he had never been in one before, so that he was curious of beholding every place where he decently might descend. The rest, no less curious, who were not quite overcome with drinking, rambled at their pleasure fore and aft, as their fancies guided 'em. So that the captain, who had well laid his design before, gave the word and seized on all his guests, they clapping great irons suddenly on the prince, when he was leaped down in the hold to view that part of the vessel, and locking him fast down, secured him. The same treachery was used to all the rest, and all in one instant, in several places of the ship, were lashed fast in irons and betrayed to slavery. That great design over, they set all hands to work to hoist sail, and with as treacherous and fair a wind, they made from the shore with this innocent and glorious prize, who thought of nothing less than such an entertainment.

Some have commended this act as brave in the captain, but I will spare my sense of it, and leave it to my reader to judge as he pleases. It may be easily guessed in what manner the prince resented this indignity, who may be best resembled to a lion taken in a toil; so he raged, so he struggled for liberty, but all in vain, and they had so wisely managed his fetters that he could not use a hand in his defence to quit himself of a life that would by no means endure slavery, nor could he move from the place where he was tied to any solid part of the ship, against which he might have beat his head, and have finished his disgrace that way. So that being deprived of all other means, he resolved to perish for want of food, and pleased at last with that thought, and toiled and tired by rage and indignation, he laid himself down and sullenly resolved upon dying, and refused all things that were brought him. This did not a little vex the captain, and the more so because he found almost all of 'em of the same humour, so that the loss of so many brave slaves, so tall and goodly to behold, would have been very considerable. He therefore ordered one to go from him (for he would not be seen himself) to Oroonoko, and to assure him he was afflicted for having rashly done so unhospitable a deed, and which could not be now remedied, since they

were far from shore. But since he resented it in so high a
nature, he assured him he would revoke his resolution, and set
both him and his friends ashore in the next land they should
touch at, and of this the messenger gave him his oath, provided
he would resolve to live. And Oroonoko, whose honour was
such as he never had violated a word in his life himself, much
less a solemn asseveration, believed in an instant what this
man said, but replied, he expected for a confirmation of this to
have his shameful fetters dismissed. This demand was carried
to the captain, who returned him answer that the offence had
been so great which he had put upon the prince, that he durst
not trust him with liberty while he remained in the ship, for
fear lest by a valour natural to him, and a revenge that would
animate that valour, he might commit some outrage fatal to
himself and the King his master, to whom his vessel did
belong. To this Oroonoko replied, he would engage his honour
to behave himself in all friendly order and manner, and obey
the command of the captain as he was lord of the King's vessel,
and general of those men under his command.

This was delivered to the still-doubting captain, who could
not resolve to trust a heathen, he said, upon his parole, a man
that had no sense or notion of the god that he worshipped.
Oroonoko then replied, he was very sorry to hear that the
captain pretended to the knowledge and worship of any gods
who had taught him no better principles than not to credit as
he would be credited; but they told him the difference of their
faith occasioned that distrust, for the captain had protested to
him upon the word of a Christian, and sworn in the name of a
great god, which if he should violate, he would expect eternal
torment in the world to come. 'Is that all the obligation he has
to be just to his oath?', replied Oroonoko. 'Let him know I
swear by my honour, which to violate would not only render
me contemptible and despised by all brave and honest men,
and so give myself perpetual pain, but it would be eternally
offending and diseasing all mankind, harming, betraying, cir-
cumventing, and outraging all men; but punishments hereafter
are suffered by oneself, and the world takes no cognisances
whether this god have revenged 'em or not, 'tis done so
secretly, and deferred so long, while the man of no honour

suffers every moment the scorn and contempt of the honester world, and dies every day ignominiously in his fame, which is more valuable than life. I speak not this to move belief, but to show you how you mistake, when you imagine that he who will violate his honour will keep his word with his gods.'

So turning from him with a disdainful smile, he refused to answer him when he urged him to know what answer he should carry back to his captain, so that he departed without saying any more. The captain pondering and consulting what to do, it was concluded that nothing but Oroonoko's liberty would encourage any of the rest to eat, except the Frenchman, whom the captain could not pretend to keep prisoner, but only told him he was secured because he might act something in favour of the prince, but that he should be freed as soon as they came to land. So that they concluded it wholly necessary to free the prince from his irons, that he might show himself to the rest, that they might have an eye upon him, and that they could not fear a single man.

This being resolved, to make the obligation the greater, the captain himself went to Oroonoko, where, after many compliments and assurances of what he had already promised, he, receiving from the prince his parole and his hand for his good behaviour, dismissed his irons and brought him to his own cabin, where, after having treated and reposed him a while, for he had neither eat nor slept in four days before, he besought him to visit those obstinate people in chains, who refused all manner of sustenance, and entreated him to oblige 'em to eat, and assure 'em of their liberty the first opportunity.

Oroonoko, who was too generous not to give credit to his words, showed himself to his people, who were transported with excess of joy at the sight of their darling prince, falling at his feet, and kissing and embracing 'em, believing as some divine oracle all he assured 'em. But he besought 'em to bear their chains with that bravery that became those whom he had seen act so nobly in arms, and that they could not give him greater proofs of their love and friendship, since 'twas all the security the captain (his friend) could have, against the revenge, he said, they might possibly justly take for the injuries sustained by him. And they all, with one accord, assured him, they could not suffer enough when it was for his repose and safety.

After this they no longer refused to eat, but took what was brought 'em, and were pleased with their captivity, since by it they hoped to redeem the prince, who, all the rest of the voyage, was treated with all the respect due to his birth, though nothing could divert his melancholy, and he would often sigh for Imoinda, and think this a punishment due to his misfortune in having left that noble maid behind him that fatal night in the Otan, when he fled to the camp.

Possessed with a thousand thoughts of past joys with this fair young person, and a thousand griefs for her eternal loss, he endured a tedious voyage, and at last arrived at the mouth of the river of Surinam, a colony belonging to the King of England, and where they were to deliver some part of their slaves. There the merchants and gentlemen of the country going on board to demand those lots of slaves they had already agreed on, and, amongst those, the overseers of those planta- tions where I then chanced to be,* the captain, who had given the word, ordered his men to bring up those noble slaves in fetters whom I have spoken of, and having put 'em, some in one, and some in other lots with women and children (which they call piccaninnies), they sold 'em off as slaves to several merchants and gentlemen, not putting any two in one lot, because they would separate 'em far from each other, not daring to trust 'em together, lest rage and courage should put 'em upon contriving some great action to the ruin of the colony.

Oroonoko was first seized on, and sold to our overseer, who had the first lot, with seventeen more of all sorts and sizes, but not one of quality with him. When he saw this, he found what they meant; for, as I said, he understood English pretty well, and being wholly unarmed and defenceless, so as it was in vain to make any resistance, he only beheld the captain with a look all fierce and disdainful, upbrading him with eyes that forced blushes on his guilty cheeks. He only cried, in passing over the side of the ship, 'Farewell, Sir. 'Tis worth my suffering to gain so true a knowledge both of you and of your gods by whom you swear.' And desiring those that held him to forbear their pains, and telling 'em he would make no resistance, he cried, 'Come, my fellow slaves, let us descend and see if we can meet with more honour and honesty in the next world we shall touch upon.' So he nimbly leaped into the boat and, showing no more concern, suffered himself to be rowed up the river with his seventeen companions.

The gentleman that bought him was a young Cornish gentleman whose name was Trefry,* a man of great wit and fine learning and was carried into those parts by the lord governor to manage all his affairs. He, reflecting on the last words of Oroonoko to the captain, and beholding the richness of his vest, no sooner came into the boat but he fixed his eyes on him, and finding something so extraordinary in his face, his shape, and mien,* a greatness of look and haughtiness in his air, and finding he spoke English, had a great mind to be inquiring into his quality and fortune; which, though Oroonoko endeavoured to hide by only confessing he was above the rank of common slaves, Trefry soon found he was yet something greater than he confessed, and from that moment began to conceive so vast an esteem for him, that he ever after loved him as his dearest brother, and showed him all the civilities due to so great a man.

Trefry was a very good mathematician and a linguist, could speak French and Spanish, and in the three days they remained in the boat (for so long were they going from the ship to the plantation) he entertained Oroonoko so agreeably with his art and discourse, that he was no less pleased with Trefry than he was with the prince; and he thought himself at least fortunate in this: that since he was a slave, as long as he would suffer himself to remain so, he had a man of so excellent wit and parts for a master. So that before they had finished their voyage up the river, he made no scruple of declaring to Trefry all his fortunes and most part of what I have here related, and put himself wholly into the hands of his new friend, whom he found resenting all the injuries were done him, and was charmed with all the greatness of his actions, which were recited with that modesty and delicate sense, as wholly vanquished him and subdued him to his interest. And he promised him on his word and honour he would find the means to reconduct him to his own country again, assuring him he had a perfect abhorrence of so dishonourable an action, and that he would sooner have died, than have been the author of such a perfidy. He found the prince was very much concerned to know what became of his friends, and how they took their slavery, and Trefry promised to take care about the enquiring after their condition, and that he should have an account of 'em.

Though, as Oroonoko afterwards said, he had little reason to credit the words of a Backearary,* yet he knew not why, but he saw a kind of sincerity and aweful truth in the face of Trefry; he saw an honesty in his eyes, and he found him wise and witty enough to understand honour, for it was one of his maxims: a man of wit could not be a knave or villain.

In their passage up the river, they put in at several houses for refreshment, and ever when they landed, numbers of people would flock to behold this man, not but their eyes were daily entertained with the sight of slaves, but the fame of Oroonoko was gone before him, and all people were in admiration of his beauty. Besides, he had a rich habit on, in which he was taken, so different from the rest, and which the captain could not strip him of, because he was forced to surprise his person in the minute he sold him. When he found his habit made him liable, as he thought, to be gazed at the more, he begged Trefry to give him something more befitting a slave, which he did, and took off his robes. Nevertheless, he shone through all, and his osenbrigs (a sort of brown Holland suit he had on) could not conceal the graces of his looks and mien; and he had no less admirers than when he had his dazzling habit on; the royal youth appeared in spite of the slave, and people could not help treating him after a different manner, without designing it. As soon as they approached him, they venerated and esteemed him; his eyes insensibly commanded respect, and his behaviour insinuated it into every soul, so that there was nothing talked of but this young and gallant slave, even by those who yet knew not that he was a prince.

I ought to tell you, that the Christians never buy any slaves but they give 'em some name of their own, their native ones being likely very barbarous and hard to pronounce; so that Mr Trefry gave Oroonoko that of Caesar, which name will live in that country as long as that (scarce more) glorious one of the great Roman, for 'tis most evident he wanted no part of the personal courage of that Caesar, and acted things as memorable, had they been done in some part of the world replenished with people and historians that might have given him his due. But his misfortune was to fall in an obscure world, that afforded only a female pen* to celebrate his fame; though I doubt not but it had lived from others' endeavours, if the Dutch, who, immediately after his time, took that country, had not killed, banished and dispersed all those that were capable of giving the world this great man's life much better than I have done. And Mr Trefry, who designed it, died before he began it, and bemoaned himself for not having undertook it in time.

For the future, therefore, I must call Oroonoko Caesar, since by that name only he was known in our Western world, and by that name he was received on shore at Parham House, where he was destined a slave. But if the King himself (God bless him) had come ashore, there could not have been greater expectations by all the whole plantation, and those neighbouring ones, than was on ours at that time, and he was received more like a governor than a slave. Notwithstanding, as the custom was, they assigned him his portion of land, his house, and his business up in the plantation. But as it was more for form than any design to put him to his task, he endured no more of the slave but the name, and remained some days in the house, receiving all visits that were made him without stirring towards that part of the plantation where the Negroes were.

At last, he would needs go view his land, his house and the business assigned him. But he no sooner came to the houses of the slaves, which are like a little town by itself, the Negroes all having left work, but they all came forth to behold him, and found he was that prince who had at several times sold most of 'em to these parts; and, from a veneration they pay to great men, especially if they know 'em, and from the surprise and awe they had at the sight of him, they all cast themselves at his feet, crying out in their language: 'Live, O King, long live, O King!', and kissing his feet, paid him even divine homage. Several English gentlemen were with him, and what Mr Trefry had told 'em was here confirmed, of which he himself before had no other witness than Caesar himself. But he was infinitely glad to find his grandeur confirmed by the adoration of all the slaves.

Caesar, troubled with their overjoy, and overceremony, besought 'em to rise, and to receive him as their fellow-slave, assuring them he was no better. At which they set up with one accord a most terrible and hideous mourning and condoling, which he and the English had much ado to appease; but at last they prevailed with 'em, and they prepared all their barbarous music, and everyone killed and dressed something of his own stock (for every family has their land apart on which, at their leisure times, they breed all eatable things) and clubbing it together, made a most magnificent supper, inviting their grandee captain, their prince, to honour it with his presence, which he did, and several English with him, where they all waited on him, some playing, others dancing before him all the time according to the manners of their several nations, and with unwearied industry endeavouring to please and delight him.

While they sat at meat, Mr Trefry told Caesar that most of these young slaves were undone in love with a fine she-slave, whom they had had about six months on their land; the prince, who never heard the name of love without a sigh, nor any mention of it without the curiosity of examining further into that tale, which of all discourses was most agreeable to him, asked how they came to be so unhappy as to be all undone for one fair slave. Trefry, who was naturally amorous, and loved to talk of love as well as anybody, proceeded to tell him they had the most charming Black that ever was beheld on their plantation, about fifteen or sixteen years old, as he guessed, that, for his part, he had done nothing but sigh for her ever since she came, and that all the white beauties he had seen never charmed him so absolutely as this fine creature had done, and that no man of any nation ever beheld her that did not fall in love with her, and that she had all the slaves perpetually at her feet, and the whole country resounded with the fame of Clemene, 'For so,' said he, 'we have christened her. But she denies us all with such a noble disdain, that 'tis a miracle to see that she, who can give such eternal desires, should herself be all ice and all unconcerned. She is adorned with the most graceful modesty that ever beautified youth; the softest sigher—that, if she were capable of love, one would swear she languished for some absent, happy man, and so retired, as if she feared a rape even from the god of day, or that the breezes would steal kisses from her delicate mouth. Her task of work some sighing lover every day makes it his petition to perform for her, which she accepts, blushing, and with reluctancy, for fear he will ask her a look for a recompense, which he dares not presume to hope, so great an awe she strikes into the hearts of her admirers.'

'I do not wonder', replied the prince, 'that Clemene should refuse slaves, being as you say so beautiful, but wonder how she escapes those who can entertain her as you can do; or why, being your slave, you do not oblige her to yield.'

'I confess', said Trefry, 'when I have, against her will, entertained her with love so long as to be transported with my passion, even above decency, I have been ready to make use of those advantages of strength and force nature has given me. But O, she disarms me with that modesty and weeping so tender and so moving that I retire and thank my stars she overcame me.'

The company laughed at his servility to a slave, and Caesar only applauded the nobleness of his passion and nature, since that slave might be noble, or, what was better, have true notions of honour and virtue in her. Thus passed they this night, after having received from the slaves all imaginable respect and obedience. The next day Trefry asked Caesar to walk, when the heat was allayed, and designedly carried him by the cottage of the fair slave, and told him, she whom he spoke of last night lived there retired. 'But', says he, 'I would not wish you to approach, for I am sure you will be in love as soon as you behold her.' Caesar assured him he was proof against all the charms of that sex, and that if he imagined his heart could be so perfidious to love again after Imoinda, he believed he should tear it from his bosom. They had no sooner spoke, but a little shock dog,* that Clemene had presented her, which she took great delight in, ran out, and she, not knowing anybody was there, ran to get it in again, and bolted out on those who were just speaking of her, when seeing them, she

would have run in again, but Trefry caught her by the hand
and cried, 'Clemene, however you fly a lover, you ought to
pay some respect to this stranger', pointing to Caesar. But she,
as if she had resolved never to raise her eyes to the face of a
man again, bent 'em the more to the earth when he spoke and
gave the prince the leisure to look the more at her. There
needed no long gazing or consideration to examine who this
fair creature was; he soon saw Imoinda all over her: in a
minute he saw her face, her shape, her air, her modesty, and
all that called forth his soul with joy at his eyes, and left his
body destitute of almost life; it stood without motion and, for a
minute, knew not that it had a being, and I believe he had
never come to himself, so oppressed he was with overjoy, if he
had not met with this allay: that he perceived Imoinda fall
dead in the hands of Trefry. This awakened him, and he ran to
her aid, and caught her in his arms, where, by degrees, she
came to herself, and 'tis needless to tell with what transports,
what ecstasies of joy they both awhile beheld each other
without speaking, then snatched each other to their arms, then
gaze again, as if they still doubted whether they possessed the
blessing they grasped; but when they recovered their speech,
'tis not to be imagined what tender things they expressed to
each other, wondering what strange fate had brought 'em again
together. They soon informed each other of their fortunes, and
equally bewailed their fate, but, at the same time, they mutually
protested that even fetters and slavery were soft and easy, and
would be supported with joy and pleasure while they could be
so happy to possess each other, and to be able to make good
their vows. Caesar swore he disdained the empire of the world
while he could behold his Imoinda, and she despised grandeur
and pomp, those vanities of her sex, when she could gaze on
Oroonoko. He adored the very cottage where she resided, and
said that little inch of the world would give him more happiness
than all the universe could do; and she vowed it was a palace,
while adorned with the presence of Oroonoko.

Trefry was infinitely pleased with this novel,* and found
this Clemene was the fair mistress of whom Caesar had before
spoke, and was not a little satisfied that Heaven was so kind to
the prince as to sweeten his misfortunes by so lucky an

accident; and leaving the lovers to themselves, was impatient to come down to Parham House (which was on the same plantation) to give me an account of what had happened. I was as impatient to make these lovers a visit, having already made a friendship with Caesar, and from his own mouth learned what I have related, which was confirmed by his Frenchman, who was set on shore to seek his fortunes, and of whom they could not make a slave, because a Christian, and he came daily to Parham Hill to see and pay his respects to his pupil prince. So that concerning and interesting myself in all that related to Caesar, whom I had assured of liberty as soon as the governor arrived, I hasted presently to the place where the lovers were, and was infinitely glad to find this beautiful young slave (who had already gained all our esteems for her modesty and her extraordinary prettiness) to be the same I had heard Caesar speak so much of. One may imagine then, we paid her a treble respect, and though, from her being carved in fine flowers and birds all over her body, we took her to be of quality before, yet when we knew Clemene was Imoinda we could not enough admire her.

I had forgot to tell you that those who are nobly born of that country are so delicately cut and razed all over the fore part of the trunk of their bodies, that it looks as if it were japanned, the works being raised like highpoint round the edges of the flowers. Some are only carved with a little flower or bird at the sides of the temples, as was Caesar, and those who are so carved over the body resemble our ancient Picts, that are figured in the chronicles, but these carvings are more delicate.

From that happy day, Caesar took Clemene for his wife, to the general joy of all people; and there was as much magnificence as the country would afford at the celebration of this wedding. And in a very short time after, she conceived with child, which made Caesar even adore her, knowing he was the last of his great race. This new accident made him more impatient of liberty, and he was every day treating with Trefry for his and Clemene's liberty; and offered either gold, or a vast quantity of slaves, which should be paid before they let him go, provided he could have any security that he should go when his ransom was paid. They fed him from day to day with promises, and delayed him till the lord governor should come, so that he began to suspect them of falsehood, and that they would delay him till the time of his wife's delivery, and make a slave of that too, for all the breed is theirs to whom the parents belong. This thought made him very uneasy, and his sullenness gave them some jealousies of him, so that I was obliged by some persons who feared a mutiny (which is very fatal sometimes in those colonies, that abound so with slaves that they exceed the whites in vast numbers) to discourse with Caesar, and to give him all the satisfaction I possibly could; they knew he and Clemene were scarce an hour in a day from my lodgings, that they eat with me, and that I obliged 'em in all things I was capable of. I entertained him with the lives of the Romans and great men, which charmed him to my company; and her, with teaching her all the pretty works that I was mistress of, and telling her stories of nuns,* and endeavouring to bring her to the knowledge of the true God. But of all the discourses Caesar liked that the worst, and would never be reconciled to our notions of the Trinity, of which he ever made a jest; it was a riddle, he said, would turn his brain to conceive, and one could not make him understand what faith was. However, these conversations failed not altogether so well to divert him, that he liked the company of us women much above the men, for he could not drink, and he is but an ill companion in that country that cannot. So that obliging him to love us very well, we had all the liberty of speech with him, especially myself, whom he called his great mistress; and indeed my word would go a great way with him. For these reasons, I had opportunity to take notice to him that he was not well pleased of late as he used to be, was more retired and thoughtful, and told him, I took it ill he should suspect we would break our words with him, and not permit both him and Clemene to return to his own kingdom, which was not so long a way; but when he was once on his voyage, he would quickly arrive there. He made me some answers that showed a doubt in him, which made me ask him what advantage it would be to doubt. It would but give us a fear of him, and possibly compel us to treat him so, as I should be very loath to behold; that is,

it might occasion his confinement. Perhaps this was not so
luckily spoke of me, for I perceived he resented that word
which I strove to soften again in vain. However, he assured me
that whatsoever resolutions he should take, he would act
nothing upon the white people; and as for myself, and those
upon that plantation where he was, he would sooner forfeit his
eternal liberty, and life itself, than lift his hand against his
greatest enemy on that place. He besought me to suffer no
fears upon his account, for he could do nothing that honour
should not dictate; but he accused himself for having suffered
slavery so long. Yet he charged that weakness on love alone,
who was capable of making him neglect even glory itself, and
for which now he reproaches himself every moment of the
day. Much more to this effect he spoke, with an air impatient
enough to make me know he would not be long in bondage;
and though he suffered only the name of a slave, and had
nothing of the toil and labour of one, yet that was sufficient to
render him uneasy, and he had been too long idle, who used to
be always in action, and in arms. He had a spirit all rough and
fierce, and that could not be tamed to lazy rest; and though all
endeavours were used to exercise himself in such actions and
sports as this world afforded, as running, wrestling, pitching
the bar, hunting and fishing, chasing and killing tigers of a
monstrous size, which this continent affords in abundance, and
wonderful snakes such as Alexander is reported to have encountered at the river of Amazons, and which Caesar took great
delight to overcome, yet these were not actions great enough
for his large soul, which was still panting after more renowned
action.

Before I parted that day with him I got, with much ado, a
promise from him to rest yet a little longer with patience, and
wait the coming of the lord governor, who was every day
expected on our shore. He assured me he would, and this
promise he desired me to know was given perfectly in complaisance to me, in whom he had an entire confidence. After
this, I neither thought it convenient to trust him much out of
our view, nor did the country, who feared him; but with one
accord it was advised to treat him fairly and oblige him to
remain within such a compass, and that he should be permitted

as seldom as could be to go up to the plantations of the Negroes, or, if he did, to be accompanied by some that should be rather in appearance attendants than spies. This care was for some time taken, and Caesar looked upon it as a mark of extraordinary respect, and was glad his discontent had obliged 'em to be more observant to him. He received new assurance from the overseer, which was confirmed to him by the opinion of all the gentlemen of the country, who made their court to him. During this time that we had his company more frequently than hitherto we had had, it may not be unpleasant to relate to you the diversions we entertained him with, or rather he us.

My stay was to be short in that country, because my father* died at sea and never arrived to possess the honour was designed him (which was lieutenant general of six and thirty islands, besides the continent of Surinam), nor the advantages he hoped to reap by them, so that though we were obliged to continue on our voyage, we did not intend to stay upon the place. Though, in a word, I must say thus much of it, that certainly had his late Majesty* of sacred memory but seen and known what a vast and charming world he had been master of in that continent, he would never have parted so easily with it to the Dutch.* 'Tis a continent whose vast extent was never yet known, and may contain more noble earth than all the universe besides, for they say it reaches from East to West one way as far as China, and another to Peru. It affords all things both for beauty and use; 'tis there eternal spring, always the very months of April, May and June; the shades are perpetual, the trees bearing at once all degrees of leaves and fruit, from blooming buds to ripe autumn; groves of oranges, lemons, citrons, figs, nutmegs, and noble aromatics, continually bearing their fragrancies. The trees appearing all like nosegays adorned with flowers of different kind; some are all white, some purple, some scarlet, some blue, some yellow; bearing at the same time ripe fruit and blooming young, or producing every day new. The very wood of all these trees have an intrinsic value above common timber; for they are, when cut, of different colours, glorious to behold, and bear a price considerable to inlay withal. Besides this, they yield rich balm and gums, so that we make our candles of such an aromatic substance as does not only give a sufficient light, but, as they burn, they cast their perfumes all about. Cedar is the common firing, and all the houses are built with it. The very meat we eat, when set on the table, if it be native, I mean of the country, perfumes the whole room, especially a little beast called an armadilly,* a thing which I can liken to nothing so well as a rhinoceros; 'tis all in white armour so jointed that it moves as well in it as if it had nothing on. This beast is about the bigness of a pig of six weeks old. But it were endless to give an account of all the diverse wonderful and strange things that country affords, and which we took a very great delight to go in search of, though those adventures are often times fatal and at least dangerous. But while we had Caesar in our company on these designs we feared no harm, nor suffered any.

As soon as I came into the country, the best house in it was presented me, called St John's Hill.* It stood on a vast rock of white marble, at the foot of which the river ran a vast depth down, and not to be descended on that side; the little waves, still dashing and washing the foot of this rock, made the softest murmurs and purlings in the world, and the opposite bank was adorned with such vast quantities of different flowers eternally blowing, and every day and hour new, fenced behind 'em with lofty trees of a thousand rare forms and colours, that the prospect was the most raving* that sands can create. On the edge of this white rock, towards the river, was a walk or grove of orange and lemon trees, about half the length of the Marl* here, whose flowery and fruity bare branches meet at the top, and hindered the sun, whose rays are very fierce there, from entering a beam into the grove; and the cool air that came from the river made it not only fit to entertain people in at all the hottest hours of the day, but refreshed the sweet blossoms and made it always sweet and charming; and sure the whole globe of the world cannot show so delightful a place as this grove was. Not all the gardens of boasted Italy can produce a shade to outvie this, which nature had joined with art to render so exceeding fine, and 'tis a marvel to see how such vast trees, as big as English oaks, could take footing on so solid a rock, and in so little earth as covered that rock, but all things by nature there are rare, delightful and wonderful. But to our sports.

Sometimes we would go surprising and in search of young tigers in their dens, watching when the old ones went forth to forage for prey; and oftentimes we have been in great danger and have fled apace for our lives, when surprised by the dams. But once above all other times we went on this design, and Caesar was with us, who had no sooner stolen a young tiger from her nest but, going off, we encountered the dam bearing a buttock of a cow, which he* had torn off with his mighty paw, and going with it towards his den; we had only four women, Caesar, and an English gentleman, brother to Harry Martin, the great Oliverian;* we found there was no escaping this enraged and ravenous beast. However, we women fled as fast as we could from it, but our heels had not saved our lives if Caesar had not laid down his cub, when he found the tiger quit her prey to make the more speed towards him, and taking Mr Martin's sword, desired him to stand aside, or follow the ladies. He obeyed him, and Caesar met this monstrous beast of might, size, and vast limbs, who came with open jaws upon him, and fixing his aweful stern eyes full upon those of the beast, and putting himself into a very steady and good aiming posture of defence, ran his sword quite through his breast down to his very heart, home to the hilt of the sword; the dying beast stretched forth her paw and going to grasp his thigh, surprised with death in that very moment, did him no other harm than fixing her long nails in his flesh very deep, feebly wounded him but could not grasp the flesh to tear off any. When he had done this, he holloed to us to return, which after some assurance of his victory we did, and found him lugging out the sword from the bosom of the tiger, who was laid in her blood on the ground. He took up the cub and, with an unconcern that had nothing of the joy or gladness of a victory, he came and laid the whelp at my feet. We all extremely wondered at his daring and at the bigness of the beast, which was about the height of an heifer, but of mighty, great, and strong limbs.

Another time, being in the woods, he killed a tiger which had long infested that part, and borne away abundance of sheep and oxen and other things that were for the support of those to whom they belonged. Abundance of people assailed

this beast, some affirming they had shot her with several
bullets quite through the body at several times, and some
swearing they shot her through the very heart, and they
believed she was a devil rather than a mortal thing. Caesar had
often said he had a mind to encounter this monster, and spoke
with several gentlemen who had attempted her; one crying, 'I
shot her with so many poisoned arrows', another with his gun
in this part of her, and another in that; so that he, remarking
all these places where she was shot, fancied still he should
overcome her, by giving her another sort of a wound than any
had yet done, and one day said (at the table), 'What trophies
and garlands, ladies, will you make me if I bring you home the
heart of this ravenous beast that eats up all your lambs and
pigs?' We all promised he should be rewarded at all our hands.
So taking a bow, which he choosed out of a great many, he
went up in the wood with two gentlemen, where he imagined
this devourer to be. They had not passed very far in it but
they heard her voice growling and grumbling as if she were
pleased with something she was doing. When they came in
view, they found her muzzling in the belly of a new-ravished
sheep, which she had torn open, and seeing herself approached,
she took fast hold of her prey with her forepaws, and set a very
fierce raging look on Caesar, without offering to approach him
for fear, at the same time, of losing what she had in possession.
So that Caesar remained a good while only taking aim and
getting an opportunity to shoot her when he designed. 'Twas
some time before he could accomplish it, and to wound her
and not kill her would but have enraged her more and
endangered him. He had a quiver of arrows at his side, so that
if one failed he could be supplied; at last, retiring a little, he
gave her opportunity to eat, for he found she was ravenous,
and fell to as soon as she saw him retire, being more eager of
her prey than of doing new mischiefs. When he, going softly to
one side of her, and hiding his person behind certain herbage
that grew high and thick, he took so good aim that, as he
intended, he shot her just into the eye, and the arrow was sent
with so good a will, and so sure a hand, that it stuck in her
brain, and made her caper, and become mad for a moment or
two, but being seconded by another arrow, he fell dead upon

the prey. Caesar cut him open with a knife to see where those wounds were that had been reported to him, and why he did not die of 'em. But I shall now relate a thing that possibly will find no credit among men, because 'tis a notion commonly received with us, that nothing can receive a wound in the heart and live; but when the heart of this courageous animal was taken out, there were seven bullets of lead in it, and the wounds seamed up with great scars, and she lived with the bullets a great while, for it was long since they were shot. This heart the conqueror brought up to us, and 'twas a very great curiosity, which all the country came to see, and which gave Caesar occasion of many fine discourses of accidents in war and strange escapes.

At other times he would go a-fishing and discoursing on that diversion, he found we had in that country a very strange fish, called a numb-eel* (an eel of which I have eaten), that while it is alive, it has a quality so cold that those who are angling, though with a line of never so great a length with a rod at the end of it, it shall, in the same minute the bait is touched by this eel, seize him or her that holds the rod with benumbedness, that shall deprive 'em of sense for a while; and some have fallen into the water, and others dropped as dead on the banks of the rivers where they stood, as soon as this fish touches the bait. Caesar used to laugh at this, and believed it impossible a man could lose his force at the touch of a fish, and could not understand that philosophy, that a cold quality should be of that nature. However, he had a great curiosity to try whether it would have the same effect on him it had on others, and often tried, but in vain. At last the sought-for fish came to the bait as he stood angling on the bank, and instead of throwing away the rod, or giving it a sudden twitch out of the water, whereby he might have caught both the eel and have dismissed the rod, before it could have too much power over him, for experiment's sake he grasped it but the harder, and fainting fell into the river, and being still possessed of the rod, the tide carried him senseless as he was a great way till an Indian boat took him up and perceived, when they touched him, a numbness seize them, and by that knew the rod was in his hand, which, with a paddle (that is, a short oar) they struck away and snatched it into the boat, eel and all. If Caesar were almost dead with the effect of this fish, he was more so with that of the water, where he had remained the space of going a league, and they found they had much ado to bring him back to life. But, at last, they did, and brought him home, where he was in a few hours well recovered and refreshed, and not a little ashamed to find he should be overcome by an eel, and that all the people who heard his defiance would laugh at him. But we cheered him up, and he, being convinced, we had the eel at supper, which was a quarter of an ell about, and most delicate meat, and was of the more value since it cost so dear as almost the life of so gallant a man.

About this time we were in many mortal fears about some disputes the English had with the Indians,* so that we could scarce trust ourselves without great numbers to go to any Indian towns or place where they abode, for fear they should fall upon us, as they did immediately after my coming away, and that it was in the possession of the Dutch, who used 'em not so civilly as the English, so that they cut in pieces all they could take, getting into houses and hanging up the mother and all her children about her; and cut a footman I left behind me all in joints, and nailed him to trees.

This feud began while I was there, so that I lost half the satisfaction I proposed in not seeing and visiting the Indian towns. But one day, bemoaning of our misfortunes upon this account, Caesar told us we need not fear, for if we had a mind to go, he would undertake to be our guard. Some would, but most would not venture; about eighteen of us resolved and took barge, and, after eight days, arrived near an Indian town, but approaching it, the hearts of some of our company failed, and they would not venture on shore, so we polled who would and who would not. For my part, I said if Caesar would, I would go. He resolved, so did my brother and my woman, a maid of good courage. Now none of us speaking the language of the people, and imagining we should have a half-diversion in gazing only, and not knowing what they said, we took a fisherman that lived at the mouth of the river who had been a long inhabitant there, and obliged him to go with us. But because he was known to the Indians as trading among 'em, and being by long living there become a perfect Indian in colour, we, who resolved to surprise 'em by making 'em see something they never had seen (that is, white people), resolved only myself, my brother and woman should go; so Caesar, the fisherman and the rest, hiding behind some thick reeds and flowers that grew on the banks, let us pass on towards the town, which was on the bank of the river all along. A little distant from the houses, or huts, we saw some dancing, others busied in fetching and carrying of water from the river; they had no sooner spied us, but they set up a loud cry that frighted us at first. We thought it had been for those that should kill us, but it seems it was of wonder and amazement. They were all naked, and we were dressed so as is most commode for the hot countries, very glittering and rich, so that we appeared extremely fine. My own hair was cut short, and I had a taffety cap, with black feathers on my head. My brother was in a stuff suit, with silver loops and buttons, and abundance of green ribbon. This was all infinitely surprising to them, and because we saw them stand still till we approached 'em, we took heart and advanced, came up to 'em, and offered 'em our hands, which they took and looked on us round about, calling still for more company, who came swarming out, all wondering and crying out: 'Tepeeme', taking their hair up in their hands and spreading it wide to those they called out to, as if they would say (as indeed it signified) 'numberless wonders', or not to be recounted, no more than to number the hair of their heads. By degrees they grew more bold, and from gazing upon us round, they touched us, laying their hands upon all the features of our faces, feeling our breasts and arms, taking up one petticoat, then wondering to see another; admiring our shoes and stockings, but more our garters, which we gave 'em, and they tied about their legs, being laced with silver lace at the ends, for they much esteem any shining things. In fine, we suffered 'em to survey us as they pleased, and we thought they would never have done admiring us. When Caesar and the rest saw we were received with such wonder, they came up to us, and finding the Indian trader whom they knew (for 'tis by these fishermen, called Indian traders, we hold a commerce with 'em, for they love not to go far from home, and we never go to them), when they saw him, therefore, they set up a new joy, and cried, in their language, 'Oh, here's our Tiguamy, and we shall now know whether those things can speak'. So, advancing to him, some of 'em gave him their hands and cried, 'Amora, Tiguamy'—which is as much as, 'How do you' or 'Welcome friend'; and all, with one din, began to gabble to him and asked if we had sense and wit, if we could talk of affairs of life and war, as they could do, if we could hunt, swim, and do a thousand things they use. He answered 'em we could. Then they invited us into their houses, and dressed venison and buffalo for us, and, going out, gathered a leaf of a tree called a sarumbo leaf, of six yards long, and spread it on the ground for a tablecloth, and cutting another in pieces instead of plates, setting us on little low Indian stools, which they cut out of one entire piece of wood and paint in a sort of japan work, they serve everyone their mess on these pieces of leaves, and it was very good, but too high seasoned with pepper. When we had eat, my brother and I took out our flutes, and played to 'em, which gave 'em new wonder, and I soon perceived, by an admiration that is natural to these people, and by the extreme ignorance and simplicity of 'em, it were not difficult to establish any unknown or extravagant religion among them, and to impose any notions or fictions upon 'em. For seeing a kinsman of mine set some paper afire with a burning glass, a trick they had never before seen, they were like to have adored him for a god, and begged he would give them the characters or figures of his name, that they might oppose it against winds and storms, which he did, and they held it up in those seasons, and fancied it had a charm to conquer them, and kept it like a holy relic. They are very superstitious, and called him the Great Peeie; that is, prophet. They showed us their Indian Peeie, a youth of about sixteen years old, as handsome as nature could make a man. They consecrate a beautiful youth from his infancy, and all arts are used to complete him in the finest manner, both in beauty and shape. He is bred to all the little arts and cunning they are capable of, to all the legerdemain, tricks, and sleight of hand, whereby he imposes upon the rabble, and is both a doctor in physic and divinity, and by these tricks makes the sick believe he sometimes eases their

pains by drawing from the afflicted part little serpents, or odd
flies, or worms, or any strange thing, and though they have
besides undoubted good remedies for almost all their diseases,
they cure the patient more by fancy than by medicines, and
make themselves feared, loved, and reverenced. This young
Peeie had a very young wife, who seeing my brother kiss her,
came running and kissed me; after this, they kissed one another,
and made it a very great jest, it being so novel, and new
admiration and laughing went round the multitude, that they
never will forget that ceremony never before used or known.
Caesar had a mind to see and talk with their war captains, and
we were conducted to one of their houses, where we beheld
several of the great captains, who had been at council. But so
frightful a vision it was to see 'em no fancy can create, no such
dreams can represent so dreadful a spectacle. For my part, I
took 'em for hobgoblins, or fiends, rather than men; but
however their shapes appeared, their souls were very humane
and noble, but some wanted their noses, some their lips, some
both noses and lips, some their ears, and others cut through
each cheek with long slashes through which their teeth appeared. They had other several formidable wounds and scars,
or rather dismemberings; they had Comitias,* or little aprons
before 'em, and girdles of cotton, with their knives naked stuck
in it, a bow at their backs and a quiver of arrows on their
thighs, and most had feathers on their heads of diverse colours.
They cried, 'Amora Tiguamy' to us at our entrance, and were
pleased we said as much to 'em; they seated us and gave us
drink of the best sort, and wondered, as much as the others
had done before, to see us. Caesar was marvelling as much at
their faces, wondering how they should all be so wounded in
war; he was impatient to know how they all came by those
frightful marks of rage or malice, rather than wounds got in
noble battle. They told us, by our interpreter, that when any
war was waging, two men chosen out by some old captain,
whose fighting was past, and who could only teach the theory
of war, these two men were to stand in competition for the
generalship, or great war captain, and being brought before the
old judges, now past labour, they are asked what they dare do
to show they are worthy to lead an army. When he who is first

asked, making no reply, cuts off his nose and throws it contempt-
ibly on the ground, and the other does something to himself
that he thinks surpasses him, and perhaps deprives himself of
lips and an eye. So they slash on till one gives out, and many
have died in this debate. And 'tis by a passive valour they
show and prove their activity: a sort of courage too brutal to
be applauded by our black hero, nevertheless he expressed his
esteem of 'em.

In this voyage Caesar begot so good an understanding
between the Indians and the English, that there were no more
fears or heart-burnings during our stay, but we had a perfect,
open, and free trade with 'em. Many things remarkable and
worthy reciting we met with in this short voyage, because
Caesar made it his business to search out and provide for our
entertainment, especially to please his dearly adored Imoinda,
who was a sharer in all our adventures, we being resolved to
make her chains as easy as we could, and to compliment the
prince in that manner that most obliged him.

As we were coming up again, we met with some Indians of
strange aspects; that is, of a larger size, and other sort of
features than those of our country. Our Indian slaves that
rowed us asked 'em some questions, but they could not understand us, but showed us a long cotton string with several knots
on it, and told us they had been coming from the mountains so
many moons as there were knots. They were habited in skins
of a strange beast and brought along with 'em bags of gold dust
which, as well as they could give us to understand, came
streaming in little small channels down the high mountains
when the rains fell, and offered to be the convoy to any body
or persons that would go to the mountains. We carried these
men up to Parham, where they were kept till the lord governor
came, and because all the country was mad to be going on this
golden adventure, the governor, by his letters, commanded
(for they sent some of the gold to him) that a guard should be
set at the mouth of the river of Amazons (a river so called,
almost as broad as the river of Thames), and prohibited all
people from going up that river, it conducting to those moun-
cains of gold. But we going off for England before the project
was further prosecuted, and the governor being drowned in a

hurricane, either the design died, or the Dutch have the advantage of it, and 'tis to be bemoaned what His Majesty lost by losing that part of America.

Though this digression is a little from my story, however, since it contains some proofs of the curiosity and daring of this great man, I was content to omit nothing of his character.

It was thus for some time we diverted him, but now Imoinda began to show she was with child, and did nothing but sigh and weep for the captivity of her lord, herself and the infant yet unborn, and believed, if it were so hard to gain the liberty of two, 'twould be more difficult to get that for three. Her griefs were so many darts in the great heart of Caesar, and taking his opportunity one Sunday, when all the whites were overtaken in drink, as there were abundance of several trades and slaves for four years that inhabited among the Negro houses, and Sunday was their day of debauch (otherwise they were a sort of spies upon Caesar), he went pretending out of goodness to 'em to feast amongst 'em, and sent all his music and ordered a great treat for the whole gang, about three hundred Negroes, and about a hundred and fifty were able to bear arms, such as they had, which were sufficient to do execution with spirits accordingly, for the English had none but rusty swords, that no strength could draw from a scabbard, except the people of particular quality, who took care to oil 'em and keep 'em in good order. The guns also, unless here and there one, or those newly carried from England, would do no good or harm, for 'tis the nature of that country to rust and eat up iron, or any metals but gold and silver. And they are very unexpert at the bow, which the Negroes and Indians are perfect masters of.

Caesar, having singled out these men from the women and children, made an harangue to 'em of the miseries and ignominies of slavery, counting up all their toils and sufferings under such loads, burdens, and drudgeries as were fitter for beasts than men, senseless brutes than human souls. He told 'em it was not for days, months or years, but for eternity; there was no end to be of their misfortunes. They suffered not like men who might find a glory and fortitude in oppression, but like dogs that loved the whip and bell and fawned the more they were beaten; that they had lost the divine quality of men, and were become insensible asses, fit only to bear; nay worse, an ass, or dog, or horse, having done his duty, could lie down in retreat, and rise to work again, and while he did his duty, endured no stripes, but men, villainous, senseless men such as they, toiled on all the tedious week till black Friday, and then whether they worked or not, whether they were faulty or meriting, they promiscuously, the innocent with the guilty, suffered the infamous whip, the sordid stripes from their fellow slaves till their blood trickled from all parts of their body, blood whose every drop ought to be revenged with a life of some of those tyrants that impose it.

'And why,' said he, 'my dear friends and fellow sufferers, should we be slaves to an unknown people? Have they vanquished us nobly in fight? Have they won us in honourable battle? And are we by the chance of war become their slaves? This would not anger a noble heart, this would not animate a soldier's soul; no, but we are bought and sold like apes or monkeys, to be the sport of women, fools, and cowards, and the support of rogues, runagates, that have abandoned their own countries for rapine, murders, thefts, and villainies. Do you not hear every day how they upbraid each other with infamy of life, below the wildest salvages,* and shall we render obedience to such a degenerate race, who have no one humane* virtue left to distinguish 'em from the vilest creatures? Will you, I say, suffer the lash from such hands?'

They all replied, with one accord, 'No, no, no! Caesar has spoke like a great captain, like a great king.'

After this he would have proceeded, but was interrupted by a tall Negro of some more quality than the rest. His name was Tuscan, who, bowing at the feet of Caesar, cried: 'My Lord, we have listened with joy and attention to what you have said, and, were we only men, would follow so great a leader through the world. But O, consider, we are husbands and parents too, and have things more dear to us than life: our wives and children, unfit for travel in these unpassable woods, mountains and bogs; we have not only difficult lands to overcome, but rivers to wade and monsters to encounter, ravenous beasts of prey—' To this, Caesar replied that honour was the first principle in nature that was to be obeyed; that as no man would pretend to that without all the acts of virtue, compassion, charity, love, justice, and reason, he found it not inconsistent with that to take an equal care of their wives and children, as they would of themselves, and that he did not design, when he led them to freedom and glorious liberty, that they should leave that better part of themselves to perish by the hand of the tyrant's whip. But if there were a woman among them so degenerate from love and virtue to choose slavery before the pursuit of her husband, and with the hazard of her life, to share with him in his fortunes, that such an one ought to be abandoned and left as a prey to the common enemy.

To which they all agreed—and bowed. After this, he spoke of the impassable woods and rivers, and convinced 'em, the more danger, the more glory. He told them that he had heard of one Hannibal, a great captain, had cut his way through mountains of solid rocks, and should a few shrubs oppose them, which they could fire before 'em? No, 'twas a trifling excuse to men resolved to die, or overcome. As for bogs, they are with a little labour filled and hardened, and the rivers could be no obstacle, since they swam by nature, at least by custom, from their first hour of their birth; that when the children were weary they must carry them by turns, and the woods and their own industry would afford them food. To this they all assented with joy.

Tuscan then demanded what he would do. He said, they would travel towards the sea, plant a new colony, and defend it by their valour, and when they could find a ship, either driven by stress of weather or guided by providence that way, they would seize it and make it a prize, till it had transported them to their own countries; at least, they should be made free in his kingdom, and be esteemed as his fellow sufferers, and men that had the courage and the bravery to attempt, at least, for liberty, and if they died in the attempt, it would be more brave than to live in perpetual slavery.

They bowed and kissed his feet at this resolution, and with one accord vowed to follow him to death. And that night was appointed to begin their march. They made it known to their wives and directed them to tie their hamaca* about their shoulder, and under their arm like a scarf, and to lead their children that could go, and carry those that could not. The wives, who pay an entire obedience to their husbands, obeyed, and stayed for 'em where they were appointed. The men stayed but to furnish themselves with what defensive arms they could get, and all met at the rendezvous, where Caesar made a new encouraging speech to 'em, and led 'em out.

But, as they could not march far that night, on Monday early, when the overseers went to call 'em all together to go to work, they were extremely surprised to find not one upon the place, but all fled with what baggage they had. You may imagine this news was not only suddenly spread all over the plantation, but soon reached the neighbouring ones, and we had by noon about six hundred men, they call the militia of the country, that came to assist us in the pursuit of the fugitives. But never did one see so comical an army march forth to war. The men, of any fashion, would not concern themselves, though it were almost the common cause, for such revoltings are very ill examples, and have very fatal consequences oftentimes in many colonies. But they had a respect for Caesar, and all hands were against the Parhamites, as they called those of Parham Plantation, because they did not, in the first place, love the lord governor, and secondly, they would have it that Caesar was ill-used and baffled with; and 'tis not impossible but some of the best in the country was of his council in this flight, and depriving us of all the slaves, so that they of the better sort would not meddle in the matter. The deputy governor, of whom I have had no great occasion to speak, and who was the most fawning, fair-tongued fellow in the world, and one that pretended the most friendship to Caesar, was now the only violent man against him, and though he had nothing, and so need fear nothing, yet talked and looked bigger than any man. He was a fellow whose character is not fit to be mentioned with the worst of the slaves. This fellow would lead his army forth to meet Caesar, or rather, to pursue him; most of their arms were of those sort of cruel whips they call cat-with-nine-tails; some had rusty, useless guns for show, others old basket-hilts whose blades had never seen the light in this age, and others had long staffs and clubs. Mr Trefry went along, rather to be a mediator than a conqueror in such a battle, for he foresaw, and knew, if by fighting they put the Negroes into despair, they were a sort of sullen fellows, that would drown or kill themselves before they would yield, and he advised that fair means was best. But Byam* was one that abounded in his own wit, and would take his own measures. It was not hard to find these fugitives, for as they fled they were forced to fire and cut the woods before 'em, so that night or day they pursued 'em by the light they made, and by the path they had cleared. But as soon as Caesar found he was pursued, he put himself in a posture of defence, placing all the women and children in the rear, and himself, with Tuscan by his side, or next to him, all promising to die or conquer. Encouraged thus, they never stood to parley, but fell on pellmell upon the English and killed some, and wounded a good many, they having recourse to their whips as the best of the weapons. And as they observed no order, they perplexed the enemy so sorely, with lashing 'em in the eyes, and the women and children seeing their husbands so treated, being of fearful, cowardly dispositions, and hearing the English cry out, 'Yield and live; yield and be pardoned!', they all run in amongst their husbands and fathers, and hung about 'em, crying out, 'Yield, yield, and leave Caesar to their revenge', that by degrees the slaves abandoned Caesar and left him only Tuscan and his heroic Imoinda, who grown big as she was, did nevertheless press near her lord, having a bow and a quiver full of poisoned arrows, which she managed with such dexterity that she wounded several, and shot the governor into the shoulder, of which wound he had like to have died, but that an Indian woman, his mistress, sucked the wound, and cleansed it from the venom. But however, he stirred not from the place till he had parleyed with Caesar, who he found was resolved to die fighting, and would not be taken; no more would Tuscan or Imoinda. But he, more thirsting after revenge of another sort than that of depriving him of life, now made use of all his art of talking and dissembling, and besought Caesar to yield himself upon terms which he himself should propose, and should be sacredly assented to and kept by him. He told

him, it was not that he any longer feared him, or could believe
the force of two men, and a young heroine, could overcome all
them, with all the slaves now on their side also, but it was the
vast esteem he had for his person, the desire he had to serve so
gallant a man, and to hinder himself from the reproach hereafter of having been the occasion of the death of a prince whose
valour and magnanimity deserved the empire of the world. He
protested to him, he looked upon this action as gallant and
brave, however tending to the prejudice of his lord and master
who would, by it, have lost so considerable a number of slaves;
that this flight of his should be looked on as a heat of youth
and rashness of a too-forward courage, and an unconsidered
impatience of liberty, and no more, and that he laboured in
vain to accomplish that which they would effectually perform
as soon as any ship arrived that would touch on his coast.

'So that if you will be pleased', continued he, 'to surrender
yourself, all imaginable respect shall be paid you, and yourself,
your wife, and child, if it be here born, shall depart free out of
our land.' But Caesar would hear of no composition, though
Byam urged, if he pursued and went on in his design, he
would inevitably perish, either by great snakes, wild beasts, or
hunger, and he ought to have regard to his wife, whose
condition required ease and not the fatigues of tedious travel,
where she could not be secured from being devoured. But
Caesar told him, there was no faith in the white men or the
gods they adored, who instructed 'em in principles so false that
honest men could not live amongst 'em; though no people
professed so much, none performed so little; that he knew
what he had to do when he dealt with men of honour, but with
them a man ought to be eternally on his guard, and never to
eat and drink with Christians without his weapon of defence in
his hand, and for his own security never to credit one word
they spoke. As for the rashness and inconsiderateness of his
action, he would confess the governor is in the right, and that
he was ashamed of what he had done, in endeavouring to
make those free who were by nature slaves, poor, wretched
rogues, fit to be used as Christians' tools, dogs treacherous and
cowardly fit for such masters, and they wanted only but to be
whipped into the knowledge of the Christian gods to be the

vilest of all creeping things, to learn to worship such deities as had not power to make 'em just, brave, or honest. In fine, after a thousand things of this nature, not fit here to be recited, he told Byam he had rather die than live upon the same earth with such dogs.

But Trefry and Byam pleaded and protested together so much, that Trefry, believing the governor to mean what he said, and speaking very cordially himself, generously put himself into Caesar's hands, and took him aside, and persuaded him, even with tears, to live by surrendering himself, and to name his conditions. Caesar was overcome by his wit and reasons, and in consideration of Imoinda, and demanding what he desired, and that it should be ratified by their hands in writing, because he had perceived that was the common way of contract between man and man amongst the whites. All this was performed, and Tuscan's pardon was put in, and they surrender to the governor, who walked peaceably down into the plantation with 'em, after giving order to bury their dead. Caesar was very much toiled with the bustle of the day, for he had fought like a Fury, and what mischief was done, he and Tuscan performed alone, and gave their enemies a fatal proof that they durst do anything, and feared no mortal force.

But they were no sooner arrived at the place where all the slaves receive their punishments of whipping, but they laid hands on Caesar and Tuscan, faint with heat and toil, and, surprising them, bound them to two several stakes, and whipped them in a most deplorable and inhumane manner, rending the very flesh from their bones, especially Caesar, who was not perceived to make any moan, or to alter his face, only to roll his eyes on the faithless governor, and those he believed guilty, with fierceness and indignation; and to complete his rage, he saw every one of those slaves who, but a few days before, adored him as something more than mortal, now had a whip to give him some lashes, while he strove not to break his fetters, though if he had, it were impossible. But he pronounced a woe and revenge from his eyes that darted fire, that 'twas at once both aweful and terrible to behold.

When they thought they were sufficiently revenged on him, they untied him, almost fainting with loss of blood from a thousand wounds all over his body, from which they had rent his clothes, and led him bleeding and naked as he was, and loaded him all over with irons, and then rubbed his wounds, to complete their cruelty, with Indian pepper, which had like to have made him raving mad, and in this condition made him so fast to the ground that he could not stir, if his pains and wounds would have given him leave. They spared Imoinda, and did not let her see this barbarity committed towards her lord, but carried her down to Parham, and shut her up, which was not in kindness to her, but for fear she should die with the sight, or miscarry, and then they should lose a young slave, and perhaps the mother.

You must know, that when the news was brought on Monday morning that Caesar had betaken himself to the woods and carried with him all the Negroes, we were possessed with extreme fear which no persuasions could dissipate that he would secure himself till night, and then, that he would come down and cut all our throats. This apprehension made all the females of us fly down the river to be secured, and while we were away they acted this cruelty. For I suppose I had authority and interest enough there, had I suspected any such thing, to have prevented it, but we had not gone many leagues but the news overtook us that Caesar was taken, and whipped like a common slave. We met on the river with Colonel Martin,* a man of great gallantry, wit and goodness, and whom I have celebrated in a character of my new comedy by his own name in memory of so brave a man. He was wise and eloquent, and, from the fineness of his parts, bore a great sway over the hearts of all the colony. He was a friend to Caesar, and resented this false dealing with him very much. We carried him back to Parham thinking to have made an accommodation. When we came, the first news we heard was that the governor was dead of a wound Imoinda had given him, but it was not so well; but it seems he would have the pleasure of beholding the revenge he took on Caesar, and before the cruel ceremony was finished, he dropped down, and then they perceived the wound he had on his shoulder was by a venomed arrow which, as I said, his Indian mistress healed by sucking the wound.

We were no sooner arrived, but we went up to the plantation

to see Caesar, whom we found in a very miserable and un-expressible condition, and I have a thousand times admired how he lived in so much tormenting pain. We said all things to him that trouble, pity and good nature could suggest, protesting our innocency of the fact, and our abhorrence of such cruelties, making a thousand professions of services to him, and begging as many pardons for the offenders, till we said so much that he believed we had no hand in his ill treatment, but told us he could never pardon Byam; as for Trefry, he confessed he saw his grief and sorrow for his suffering, which he could not hinder, but was like to have been beaten down by the very slaves for speaking in his defence. But for Byam, who was their leader, their head, and should, by his justice and honour, have been an example to 'em—for him, he wished to live to take a dire revenge of him and said, 'It had been well for him if he had sacrificed me instead of giving me the contemptible whip'. He refused to talk much, but begging us to give him our hands, he took 'em and protested never to lift up his to do us any harm. He had a great respect for Colonel Martin, and always took his counsel like that of a parent, and assured him he would obey him in anything, but his revenge on Byam.

'Therefore,' said he, 'for his own safety, let him speedily dispatch me, for if I could dispatch myself, I would not till that justice were done to my injured person and the contempt of a soldier. No, I would not kill myself, even after a whipping, but will be content to live with that infamy, and be pointed at by every grinning slave, till I have completed my revenge, and then you shall see that Oroonoko scorns to live with the indignity that was put on Caesar.'

All we could do could get no more words from him, and we took care to have him put immediately into a healing bath to rid him of his pepper, and ordered a chirurgeon* to anoint him with healing balm, which he suffered, and in some time he began to be able to walk and eat. We failed not to visit him every day, and to that end had him brought to an apartment at Parham.

The governor was no sooner recovered and had heard of the menaces of Caesar but he called his council who (not to disgrace them, or burlesque the government there) consisted of such notorious villains as Newgate never transported, and possibly originally were such, who understood neither the laws of God or man, and had no sort of principles to make 'em worthy the name of men, but at the very council table would contradict and fight with one another; and swear so bloodily that 'twas terrible to hear and see 'em. (Some of 'em were afterwards hanged when the Dutch took possession of the place; others sent off in chains.) But calling these special rulers of the nation together, and requiring their counsel in this weighty affair, they all concluded that (damn 'em) it might be their own cases, and that Caesar ought to be made an example to all the Negroes to fright 'em from daring to threaten their betters, their lords and masters, and, at this rate, no man was safe from his own slaves and concluded *nemine contradicente**   that Caesar should be hanged.

Trefry then thought it time to use his authority, and told Byam his command did not extend to his lord's plantation, and that Parham was as much exempt from the law as Whitehall, and that they ought no more to touch the servants of the lord (who there represented the King's person) than they could those about the King himself, and that Parham was a sanctuary, and though his lord were absent in person, his power was still in being there, which he had entrusted with him, as far as the dominions of his particular plantations reached, and all that belonged to it—the rest of the country, as Byam was lieutenant to his lord, he might exercise his tyranny upon. Trefry had others as powerful, or more, that interested themselves in Caesar's life, and absolutely said he should be defended. So turning the governor and his wise council out of doors (for they sat at Parham House), they set a guard upon our landing place and would admit none but those we called friends to us and Caesar.

The governor, having remained wounded at Parham till his recovery was completed, Caesar did not know but he was still there, and indeed, for the most part, his time was spent there, for he was one that loved to live at other people's expense, and if he were a day absent, he was ten present there, and used to play and walk and hunt and fish with Caesar, so that Caesar did not at all doubt, if he once recovered strength, but he should find an opportunity of being revenged on him, though, after such a revenge, he could not hope to live, for if he escaped the fury of the English mobile,* who perhaps would have been glad of the occasion to have killed him, he was resolved not to survive his whipping; yet he had some tender hours a repenting softness, which he called his fits of coward, wherein he struggled with love for the victory of his heart, which took part with his charming Imoinda there. But, for the most part, his time was passed in melancholy thought and black designs; he considered, if he should do this deed and die, either in the attempt or after it, he left his lovely Imoinda a prey or, at best, a slave to the enraged multitude. His great heart could not endure that thought. 'Perhaps', said he, 'she may be first ravished by every brute, exposed first to their nasty lusts, and then a shameful death.' No, he could not live a moment under that apprehension, too insupportable to be borne. These were his thoughts, and his silent arguments with his heart, as he told us afterwards, so that now resolving not only to kill Byam, but all those he thought had enraged him, pleasing his great heart with the fancied slaughter he should make over the whole face of the plantation, he first resolved on a deed that (however horrid it at first appeared to us all) when we had heard his reasons, we thought it brave and just. Being able to walk and, as he believed, fit for the execution of his great design, he begged Trefry to trust him into the air, believing a walk would do him good, which was granted him and, taking Imoinda with him as he used to do in his more happy and calmer days, he led her up into a wood, where, after (with a thousand sighs and long gazing silently on her face, while tears gushed in spite of him from his eyes) he told her his design, first of killing her, and then his enemies, and next himself, and the impossibility of escaping and therefore he told her the necessity of dying. He found the heroic wife faster pleading for death than he was to propose it, when she found his fixed resolution, and on her knees besought him not to leave her a prey to his enemies. He, grieved to death, yet pleased at her noble resolution, took her up and embracing her with all the passion and languishment of a dying lover, drew his knife to kill this treasure of his soul, this pleasure of his eyes; while tears trickled down his cheeks, hers were smiling with joy she should die by so noble a hand, and be sent in her own country (for that's their notion of the next world) by him she so tenderly loved and so truly adored in this, for wives have a respect for their husbands equal to what any other people pay a deity, and when a man finds any occasion to quit his wife, if he love her, she dies by his hand, if not, he sells her or suffers some other to kill her. It being thus, you may believe the deed was soon resolved on, and 'tis not to be doubted, but the parting, the eternal leave-taking of two such lovers, so greatly born, so sensible, so beautiful, so young, and so fond, must be very moving, as the relation of it was to me afterwards.

All that love could say in such cases being ended, and all the intermitting irresolutions being adjusted, the lovely, young and adored victim lays herself down before the sacrificer, while he, with a hand resolved, and a heart breaking within, gave the fatal stroke; first cutting her throat, and then severing her yet smiling face from that delicate body, pregnant as it was with the fruits of tenderest love. As soon as he had done, he laid the body decently on leaves and flowers, of which he made a bed and concealed it under the same coverlid of nature; only her face he left yet bare to look on, but when he found she was dead and passed all retrieve, never more to bless him with her eyes and soft language, his grief swelled up to rage, he tore, he raved, he roared like some monster of the wood, calling on the loved name of Imoinda; a thousand times he turned the fatal knife that did the deed toward his own heart, with a resolution to go immediately after her, but dire revenge, which now was a thousand times more fierce in his soul than before, prevents him, and he would cry out, 'No, since I have sacrificed Imoinda to my revenge, shall I lose that glory which I have purchased so dear as at the price of the fairest, dearest, softest creature that ever nature made? No, no!'. Then, at her name, grief would get the ascendant of rage, and he would lie down by her side, and water her face with showers of tears, which never were wont to fall from those eyes, and however bent he was on his intended slaughter, he had not power to stir from the sight of this dear object, now more beloved and more adored than ever.

He remained in this deploring condition for two days, and never rose from the ground where he had made his sad sacrifice; at last, rousing from her side, and accusing himself with living too long now Imoinda was dead, and that the deaths of those barbarous enemies were deferred too long, he resolved now to finish the great work. But, offering to rise, he found his strength so decayed that he reeled to and fro like boughs assailed by contrary winds, so that he was forced to lie down again, and try to summon all his courage to his aid. He found his brains turn round and his eyes were dizzy, and objects appeared not the same to him they were wont to do; his breath was short, and all his limbs surprised with a faintness he had never felt before. He had not eat in two days, which was one occasion of this feebleness, but excess of grief was the greatest; yet still he hoped he should recover vigour to act his design, and lay expecting it yet six days longer, still mourning over the dead idol of his heart, and striving every day to rise, but could not.

In all this time you may believe we were in no little affliction for Caesar and his wife; some were of opinion he was escaped never to return, others thought some accident had happened to him. But however, we failed not to send out an hundred people several ways to search for him; a party of about forty went that way he took, among whom was Tuscan, who was perfectly reconciled to Byam. They had not gone very far into the wood, but they smelt an unusual smell, as of a dead body, for stinks must be very noisome that can be distinguished among such a quantity of natural sweets as every inch of that land produces. So that they concluded they should find him dead, or somebody that was so; they passed on towards it, as loathsome as it was, and made such a rustling among the leaves that lie thick on the ground by continual falling, that Caesar heard he was approached, and though he had, during the space of these eight days endeavoured to rise, but found he wanted strength, yet looking up and seeing his pursuers, he rose and reeled to a neighbouring tree, against which he fixed his back, and being within a dozen yards of those that advanced and saw him, he called out to them, and bid them approach no nearer if they would be safe, so that they stood still and hardly believing their eyes, that would persuade them that it was Caesar that spoke to 'em, so much was he altered. They asked him what he had done with his wife, for they smelt a stink that almost struck them dead. He, pointing to the dead body, sighing, cried: 'Behold her there'. They put off the flowers that covered her with their sticks and found she was killed, and cried out, 'Oh monster that hast murdered thy wife.' Then asking him why he did so cruel a deed, he replied he had no leisure to answer impertinent questions. 'You may go back', continued he, 'and tell the faithless governor he may thank fortune that I am breathing my last, and that my arm is too feeble to obey my heart in what it had designed him.' But his tongue faltering and trembling, he could scarce end what he was saying.

The English, taking advantage by his weakness, cried, 'Let us take him alive by all means.' He heard 'em, and as if he had revived from a fainting, or a dream, he cried out, 'No Gentlemen, you are deceived, you will find no more Caesars to be whipped, no more find a faith in me. Feeble as you think me, I have strength yet left to secure me from a second indignity.' They swore all anew, and he only shook his head and beheld them with scorn. Then they cried out, 'Who will venture on this single man? Will nobody?'

They stood all silent while Caesar replied, 'Fatal will be the attempt to the first adventurer, let him assure himself', and at that word held up his knife in a menacing posture. 'Look ye, ye faithless crew,' said he, ''Tis not life I seek, nor am I afraid of dying,' and at that word cut a piece of flesh from his own throat and threw it at 'em, 'yet still I would live if I could till I had perfected my revenge. But oh it cannot be, I feel life gliding from my eyes and heart, and if I make not haste, I shall yet fall a victim to the shameful whip.' At that he ripped up his own belly, and took his bowels and pulled 'em out with what strength he could, while some, on their knees imploring, besought him to hold his hand. But when they saw him tottering, they cried out, 'Will none venture on him?' A bold English cried, 'Yes, if he were the devil' (taking courage when he saw him almost dead) and swearing a horrid oath for his farewell to the world, he rushed on Caesar [who]* with his armed hand met him so fairly as stuck him to the heart and he fell dead at his feet.

Tuscan, seeing that, cried out, 'I love thee, O Caesar, and therefore will not let thee die if possible' and, running to him, took him in his arms, but, at the same time, warding a blow that Caesar made at his bosom, he received it quite through his arm, and Caesar, having not the strength to pluck the knife forth, though he attempted it, Tuscan neither pulled it out himself, nor suffered it to be pulled out, but came down with it sticking in his arm, and the reason he gave for it was, because the air should not get into the wound. They put their hands across and carried Caesar between six of 'em, fainted as he was, and they thought dead, or just dying, and they brought him to Parham, and laid him on a couch, and had the chirurgeon immediately to him, who dressed his wounds and sewed up his belly and used means to bring him to life, which they effected. We ran all to see him, and, if before we thought him so beautiful a sight, he was now so altered that his face was like a death's head blacked over, nothing but teeth and eye-holes. For some days we suffered nobody to speak to him, but caused cordials to be poured down his throat, which sustained his life, and in six or seven days he recovered his senses, for you must know that wounds are almost to a miracle cured in the Indies, unless wounds in the legs, which rarely ever cure.

When he was well enough to speak, we talked to him and asked him some questions about his wife, and the reasons why he killed her, and he then told us what I have related of that resolution, and of his parting, and he besought us we would let him die and was extremely afflicted to think it was possible he might live. He assured us, if we did not dispatch him, he would prove very fatal to a great many. We said all we could to make him live, and gave him new assurances, but he begged we would not think so poorly of him, or of his love to Imoinda, to imagine we could flatter him to life again. But the chirurgeon assured him he could not live, and therefore he need not fear. We were all (but Caesar) afflicted at this news, and the sight was gashly;* his discourse was sad and the earthly smell about him so strong that I was persuaded to leave the place for some time (being myself but sickly, and very apt to fall into fits of dangerous illness upon any extraordinary melancholy), the servants and Trefry and the chirurgeons promised all to take what possible care they could of the life of Caesar, and I, taking boat, went with other company to Colonel Martin's, about three days' journey down the river. But I was no sooner gone, but the governor, taking Trefry about some pretended earnest business a day's journey up the river, having communicated his design to one Banister,* a wild Irishman, and one of the council, a fellow of absolute barbarity, and fit to execute any villainy, but was rich. He came up to Parham and forcibly took Caesar and had him carried to the same post where he was whipped, and causing him to be tied to it, and a great fire made before him, he told him he should die like a dog, as he was. Caesar replied, this was the first piece of bravery that ever Banister did, and he never spoke sense till he pronounced that word, and if he would keep it, he would declare in the other world that he was the only man, of all the whites, that ever he heard speak truth.

And turning to the men that bound him, he said, 'My friends, am I to die, or to be whipped?', and they cried, 'Whipped! No, you shall not escape so well.' And then he replied, smiling, 'A blessing on thee', and assured them, they need not tie him, for he would stand fixed like a rock, and endure death so as should encourage them to die. 'But if you whip me,' said he, 'be sure you tie me fast.'

He had learnt to take tobacco, and when he was assured he should die, he desired they would give him a pipe in his mouth ready lighted, which they did, and the executioner came, and first cut off his members, and threw them into the fire; after that, with an ill-favoured knife, they cut his ears, and his nose, and burned them. He still smoked on, as if nothing had touched him. Then they hacked off one of his arms, and still he bore up, and held his pipe; but at the cutting off the other arm, his head sunk and his pipe dropped, and he gave up the ghost without a groan or a reproach. My mother and sister were by him all the while, but not suffered to save him, so rude and wild were the rabble, and so inhumane were the justices, who stood by to see the execution, who after paid dearly enough for their insolence. They cut Caesar in quarters and sent them to several of the chief plantations. One quarter was sent to Colonel Martin, who refused it, and swore he had rather see the quarters of Banister and the governor himself, than those of Caesar, on his plantations, and that he could govern his Negroes without terrifying and grieving them with frightful spectacles of a mangled king.

Thus died this great man; worthy of a better fate, and a more sublime wit than mine to write his praise; yet I hope the reputation of my pen is considerable enough to make his glorious name to survive to all ages, with that of the brave, the beautiful, and the constant Imoinda.

THE FAIR JILT;

OR;

THE HISTORY OF PRINCE TARQUIN AND MIRANDA

To Henry Pain, Esq.,*

Sir, dedications are like love, and no man of wit or eminence escapes them; early or late, the affliction of the poet's compliment falls upon him, and men are obliged to receive 'em as they do their wives: for better, for worse—at least with a feigned servility.

It was not want of respect, but fear that has hitherto made us keep clear of your judgement, too piercing to be favourable to what is not nicely valuable. We durst not awaken your criticism, and by begging your protection in the front of a book, give you an occasion to find nothing to deserve it. Nor can this little history lay a better claim to that honour than those that have not pretended to it; which has but this merit to recommend it, that it is truth: truth, which you so much admire. But 'tis a truth that entertains you with so many accidents diverting and moving that they will need both a patron and an asserter in this incredulous world. For however it may be imagined that poetry (my talent) has so greatly the ascendant over me, that all I write must pass for fiction, I now desire to have it understood that this is reality, and matter of fact,* and acted in this our later age, and that, in the person of Tarquin,* I bring a prince to kiss your hands who owned himself, and was received, as the last of the race of the Roman kings, whom I have often seen, and you have heard of, and whose story is so well known to yourself, and many hundreds more, part of which I had from the mouth of this unhappy great man, and was an eye-witness to the rest.

'Tis true, Sir, I present you with a prince unfortunate, but still the more noble object for your goodness and pity, who never valued a brave man the less for being unhappy. And whither should the afflicted flee for refuge, but to the generous? Amongst all the race, he cannot find a better man, or more certain friend, nor amongst all his ancestors match your greater soul, and magnificence of mind. He will behold in one English subject a spirit as illustrious, a heart as fearless, a wit and eloquence as excellent as Rome itself could produce. Its senate scarce boasted of a better statesman, nor Augustus of a more faithful subject; as your imprisonment and sufferings,* through all the course of our late national distractions have sufficiently manifested. But nothing could press or deject your great heart; you were the same man still, unmoved in all terms, easy and innocent, no persecution being able to abate your constant good humour or wonted gallantry. If, Sir, you find here a prince of less fortitude and virtue than yourself, charge his miscarriages on love, a weakness of that nature you will easily excuse (being so great a friend to the fair), though possibly, he gave a proof of it too fatal to his honour. Had I been to have formed his character, perhaps I had made him something more worthy of the honour of your protection. But I was obliged to pursue the matter of fact, and give a just relation of that part of his life which, possibly, was the only reproachful part of it. If he be so happy as to entertain a man of wit and business, I shall not fear his welcome to the rest of the world, and 'tis only with your passport he can hope to be so.

The particular obligations I have to your bounty and goodness, O noble friend and patron of the Muses, I do not so much as pretend to acknowledge in this little present; those being above the poet's pay, which is a sort of coin not current in this age, though perhaps may be esteemed as medals in the cabinets of men of wit. If this be so happy to be of that number, I desire no more lasting a fame, than that it may bear this inscription: that I am, Sir, your most obliged and most humble servant,

A. Behn.

THE FAIR HYPOCRITE; OR, THE AMOURS OF PRINCE TARQUIN AND MIRANDA

As love is the most noble and divine passion of the soul, so is it that to which we may justly attribute all the real satisfactions of life; and without it, man is unfinished, and unhappy.

There are a thousand things to be said of the advantages

this generous passion brings to those whose hearts are capable
of receiving its soft impressions, for 'tis not everyone that can
be sensible of its tender touches. How many examples, from
history and observation, could I give of its wondrous power;
nay, even to a degree of transmigration? How many idiots has
it made wise? How many fools eloquent? How many home-
bred squires accomplished? How many cowards brave? And
there is no sort or species of mankind on whom it cannot work
some change and miracle, if it be a noble, well-grounded
passion, except on the fop in fashion; the hardened, incorrigible
fop, so often wounded but never reclaimed. For still, by a dire
mistake, conducted by vast opinionatreism,* and a greater
portion of self-love, than the rest of the race of man, he
believes that affectation in his mien and dress, that mathematical movement, that formality in every action, that face managed
with care, and softened into ridicule, the languishing turn, the
toss, and the back-shake of the perrywig,* is the direct way to
the heart of the fine person he adores, and instead of curing
love in his soul, serves only to advance his folly, and the more
he is enamoured, the more industriously he assumes (every
hour) the coxcomb. These are Love's playthings, a sort of
animals with whom he sports, and whom he never wounds but
when he is in good humour and always shoots laughing. 'Tis
the diversion of the little god to see what a fluttering and
bustle one of these sparks, new-wounded, makes; to what
fantastic fooleries he has recourse. The glass is every moment
called to counsel, the valet consulted and plagued for new
invention of dress, the footman and scrutore* perpetually
employed; billet-doux* and madrigals take up all his mornings,
till playtime in dressing, till night in gazing; still, like a
sunflower turned towards the beams of the fair eyes of his
Celia, adjusting himself in the most amorous posture he can
assume, his hat under his arm, while the other hand is put
carelessly into his bosom, as if laid upon his panting heart; his
head a little bent to one side, supported with a world of
cravat-string,* which he takes mighty care not to put into
disorder, as one may guess by a never-failing and horrid
stiffness in his neck, and if he have an occasion to look aside,
his whole body turns at the same time, for fear the motion of

the head alone should incommode the cravat or perrywig. And sometimes the glove is well-managed, and the white hand displayed. Thus, with a thousand other little motions and formalities, all in the common place or road of foppery, he takes infinite pains to show himself to the pit and boxes,* a most accomplished ass. This is he, of all humankind, on whom love can do no miracles, and who can nowhere, and upon no occasion, quit one grain of his refined foppery, unless in a duel or a battle, if ever his stars should be so severe and ill-mannered to reduce him to the necessity of either. Fear then would ruffle that fine form he had so long preserved in nicest order, with grief considering that an unlucky, chance wound in his face, if such a dire misfortune should befall him, would spoil the sale of it forever.

Perhaps it will be urged that, since no metamorphosis can be made in a fop by love, you must consider him one of those that only talks of love, and thinks himself that happy thing, a lover, and wanting fine sense enough for the real passion, believes what he feels to be it. There are in the quiver of the god a great many different darts; some that wound for a day, and others for a year. They are all fine, painted, glittering darts, and show as well as those made of the noblest metal, but the wounds they make reach the desire only, and are cured by possessing, while the short-lived passion betrays the cheats. But 'tis that refined and illustrious passion of the soul, whose aim is virtue, and whose end is honour, that has the power of changing nature, and is capable of performing all those heroic things of which history is full. How far distant passions may be from one another, I shall be able to make appear in these following rules. I'll prove to you the strong effects of love in some unguarded and ungoverned hearts, where it rages beyond the inspirations of a god all soft and gentle, and reigns more like a fury from Hell. I do not pretend here to entertain you with a feigned story, or anything pieced together with romantic accidents, but every circumstance, to a tittle, is truth. To a great part of the main, I myself was an eye-witness, and what I did not see, I was confirmed of by actors in the intrigue, holy men of the order of St Francis. But for the sake of some of her relations, I shall give my fair jilt a feigned name, that of

Miranda; but my hero must retain his own, it being too illustrious to be concealed.

You are to understand, that in all the Catholic countries where holy orders are established, there are abundance of differing kinds of religious, both of men and women. Amongst the women there are those we call nuns, that make solemn vows of perpetual chastity. There are others who make but a simple vow, as, for five or ten years, or more or less, and that time expired, they may contract anew for longer time, or marry, or dispose of themselves as they shall see good. And these are ordinarily called galloping nuns.* Of these there are several orders; as, Chanonesses, Beguines, Quests, Swart-Sisters, and Jesuitesses,* with several others I have forgot. Of those of the Beguines was our fair votress.

These orders are taken up by the best persons of the town, young maids of fortune, who live together, not enclosed, but in palaces that will hold about fifteen hundred or two thousand of these fille-devotes,* where they have a regulated government, under a sort of abbess, or prioress, or rather, a governant. They are obliged to a method of devotion, and are under a sort of obedience. They wear an habit much like our widows of quality in England, only without a bando;* and their veil is of a thicker crepe than what we have here, through which one cannot see the face, for when they go abroad, they cover themselves all over with it, but they put 'em up in the churches and lay 'em by in the houses. Every one of these have a confessor, who is to 'em a sort of steward, for, you must know, they that go into these places have the management of their own fortunes, and what their parents design 'em. Without the advice of this confessor, they act nothing, nor admit of a lover that he shall not approve of; at least, this method ought to be taken, and is by almost all of 'em, though Miranda thought her wit above it, as her spirit was.

But as these women are, as I said, of the best quality, and live with the reputation of being retired from the world a little more than ordinary, and because there is a sort of difficulty to approach 'em, they are the people the most courted and liable to the greatest temptations, for as difficult as it seems to be, they receive visits from all the men of the best quality,

especially strangers. All the men of wit and conversation meet
at the apartments of these fair fille-devotes, where all manner
of gallantries are performed, while all the study of these maids
is to accomplish themselves for these noble conversations.
They receive presents, balls, serenades, and billets. All the
news, wit, verses, songs, novels, music, gaming, and all fine
diversion, is in their apartments, they themselves being of the
best quality and fortune. So that to manage these gallantries,
there is no sort of female arts they are not practised in, no
intrigues they are ignorant of, and no management of which
they are not capable.

Of this happy number was the fair Miranda, whose parents
being dead, and a vast estate divided between herself and a
young sister (who lived with an unmarried, old uncle, whose
estate afterwards was all divided between 'em) put herself into
this unenclosed religious house, but her beauty, which had all
the charms that ever nature gave, became the envy of the
whole sisterhood. She was tall and admirably shaped; she had a
bright hair, and hazel eyes, all full of love and sweetness. No
art could make a face so fair as hers by nature, which every
feature adorned with a grace that imagination cannot reach.
Every look, every motion, charmed, and her black dress showed
the lustre of her face and neck. She had an air, though gay as
so much youth could inspire, yet so modest, so nobly reserved,
without formality or stiffness, that one who looked on her
would have imagined her soul the twin angel of her body, and
both together made her appear something divine. To this she
had a great deal of wit, read much, and retained all that served
her purpose. She sung delicately, and danced well, and played
on the lute to a miracle. She spoke several languages naturally,
for being co-heiress to so great a fortune, she was bred with
nicest care in all the finest manners of education, and was now
arrived to her eighteenth year.

'Twere needless to tell you how great a noise the fame of
this young beauty, with so considerable a fortune, made in the
world; I may say the world, rather than confine her fame to
the scanty limits of a town: it reached to many others, and
there was not a man of any quality that came to Antwerp, or
passed through the city, but made it his business to see the

lovely Miranda, who was universally adored. Her youth and beauty, her shape and majesty of mien and air of greatness, charmed all her beholders, and thousands of people were dying by her eyes, while she was vain enough to glory in her conquest, and make it her business to wound. She loved nothing so much as to behold sighing slaves at her feet of the greatest quality, and treated 'em all with an affability that gave 'em hope. Continual music as soon as it was dark, and songs of dying lovers, were sung under her windows, and she might well have made herself a great fortune (if she had not been so already) by the rich presents that were hourly made her, and everybody daily expected when she would make someone happy by suffering herself to be conquered by love and honour, by the assiduities and vows of some one of her adorers. But Miranda accepted their presents, heard their vows with pleasure, and willingly admitted all their soft addresses; but would not yield her heart, or give away that lovely person to the possession of one who could please itself with so many. She was naturally amorous, but extremely inconstant. She loved one for his wit, another for his face, a third for his mien, but above all, she admired quality; quality alone had the power to attack* her entirely, yet not to one man; but that virtue was still admired by her in all: wherever she found that, she loved, or at least acted the lover with such art that (deceiving well) she failed not to complete her conquest, and yet she never durst trust her fickle humour with marriage. She knew the strength of her own heart, and that it could not suffer itself to be confined to one man, and wisely avoided those inquietudes and that uneasiness of life she was sure to find in that married life which would, against her nature, oblige her to the embraces of one, whose humour was to love all the young and the gay. But love, who had hitherto but played with her heart and given it nought but pleasing, wanton wounds, such as afforded only soft joys and not pains, resolved, either out of revenge to those numbers she had abandoned, and who had sighed so long in vain, or to try what power he had upon so fickle a heart, sent an arrow dipped in the most tormenting flames that rage in hearts most sensible. He struck it home and deep, with all the malice of an angry god.

There was a church belonging to the cordeliers,* whither Miranda often repaired to her devotion, and being there one day, accompanied with a young sister of the order, after the mass was ended, as 'tis the custom, some one of the fathers goes about the church with a box for contribution, or charity money. It happened that day that a young father, newly initiated, carried the box about, which, in his turn, he brought to Miranda. She had no sooner cast her eyes on this young friar, but her face was overspread with blushes of surprise; she beheld him steadfastly, and saw in his face all the charms of youth, wit, and beauty. He wanted no one grace that could form him for love, he appeared all that is adorable to the fair sex, nor could the misshapen habit hide from her the lovely shape it endeavoured to cover, nor those delicate hands that approached her too near with the box. Besides the beauty of his face and shape, he had an air altogether great; in spite of his professed poverty, it betrayed the man of quality, and that thought weighed greatly with Miranda. But love, who did not design she should now feel any sort of those easy flames with which she had heretofore burnt, made her soon lay all those considerations aside which used to invite her to love, and now loved she knew not why.

She gazed upon him, while he bowed before her, and waited for her charity, till she perceived the lovely friar to blush and cast his eyes to the ground. This awakened her shame, and she put her hand into her pocket and was a good while in searching for her purse, as if she thought of nothing less than what she was about; at last she drew it out, and gave him a pistole,* but that with so much deliberation and leisure as easily betrayed the satisfaction she took in looking on him, while the good man, having received her bounty, after a very low obeisance, proceeded to the rest, and Miranda casting after him a look all languishing, as long as he remained in the church, departed with a sigh as soon as she saw him go out, and returned to her apartment without speaking one word all the way to the young fille-devotes who attended her, so absolutely was her soul employed with this young holy man. Cornelia (so was this maid called who was with her) perceiving she was so silent, who used to be all wit and good humour, and observing her little disorder at the sight of the young father, though she was far from imagining it to be love, took an occasion, when she was come home, to speak of him. 'Madam,' said she, 'did you not observe that fine young cordelier who brought the box?' At a question that named that object of her thoughts, Miranda blushed, and the finding she did so redoubled her confusion, and she had scarce courage enough to say, 'Yes, I did observe him.' And then, forcing herself to smile a little, continued, 'And I wondered to see so jolly a young friar of an order so severe, and mortified.' 'Madam,' replied Cornelia, 'when you know his story, you will not wonder.' Miranda, who was impatient to know all that concerned her new conqueror, obliged her to tell his story, and Cornelia obeyed, and proceeded.

The Story of Prince Henrick

'You must know, Madam, that this young holy man is a prince of Germany, of the house of ——, whose fate it was to fall most passionately in love with a fair young lady, who loved him with an ardour equal to what he vowed her. Sure of her heart, and wanting only the approbation of her parents and his own, which her quality did not suffer him to despair of, he boasted of his happiness to a young prince, his elder brother, a youth amorous and fierce, impatient of joys and sensible of beauty, taking fire with all fair eyes. He was his father's darling, and delight of his fond mother, and by an ascendant over both their hearts, ruled their wills.

'This young prince no sooner saw, but loved the fair mistress of his brother, and with an authority of a sovereign, rather than the advice of a friend, warned his brother Henrick (this now young friar) to approach no more this lady, whom he had seen and, seeing, loved.

'In vain the poor surprised prince pleads his right of love, his exchange of vows, and assurance of an heart that could never be but for himself. In vain he urges his nearness of blood, his friendship, his passion, or his life, which so entirely depended on the possession of the charming maid. All his pleading served but to blow his brother's flame, and the more he implores, the more the other burns, and while Henrick follows him on his knees with humble submissions, the other flies from him in rages of transported love. Nor could his tears that pursued his brother's steps move him to pity. Hot-headed, vain-conceited of his beauty, and greater quality as elder brother, he doubts not his success, and resolved to sacrifice all to the violence of his new-born passion.

'In short, he speaks of his design to his mother, who promised him her assistance, and accordingly proposing it first to the prince, her husband, urging the languishment of her son, she soon wrought so on him, that a match being concluded between the parents of this young beauty and Henrick's brother, the hour was appointed before she knew of the sacrifice she was to be made. And while this was in agitation, Henrick was sent on some great affairs up into Germany, far out of the way; not but his boding heart, with perpetual sighs and throbs, eternally foretold him his fate.

'All the letters he writ were intercepted, as well as those she writ to him. She finds herself every day perplexed with the addresses of the prince she hated; he was ever sighing at her feet. In vain were all her reproaches and all her coldness, he was on the surer side, for what he found love would not do, force of parents would.

'She complains in her heart on young Henrick, from whom she could never receive one letter, and at last could not forbear bursting into tears in spite of all her force and feigned courage, when on a day the prince told her that Henrick was withdrawn, to give him time to court her, to whom, he said, he confessed he had made some vows, but did repent of 'em, knowing himself too young to make 'em good; that it was for that reason he brought him first to see her, and for that reason that after that he never saw her more, nor so much as took leave of her (when, indeed, his death lay upon the next visit, his brother having sworn to murder him, and to that end, put a guard upon him till he was sent into Germany).

'All this he uttered with so many passionate asseverations, vows and seeming pity for her being so inhumanly abandoned, that she almost gave credit to all he had said, and had much ado to keep herself within the bounds of moderation and silent grief. Her heart was breaking, her eyes languished and her cheeks grew pale, and she had like to have fallen dead into the treacherous arms of him that had reduced her to this discovery; but she did what she could to assume her courage, and to show as little resentment as possible for a heart, like hers, oppressed with love, and now abandoned by the dear subject of its joys and pains.

'But, Madam, not to tire you with this adventure, the day arrived wherein our still weeping fair unfortunate was to be sacrificed to the capriciousness of love, and she was carried to Court by her parents, without knowing to what end, where she was almost compelled to marry the prince.

'Henrick, who, all this while, knew no more of his unhappiness than what his fears suggested, returns and passes even to the presence of his father, before he knew anything of his fortune, where he beheld his mistress and his brother with his father in such a familiarity as he no longer doubted his destiny. 'Tis hard to judge whether the lady or himself was most surprised; she was all pale and unmovable in her chair, and Henrick fixed like a statue. At last, grief and rage took place of amazement, and he could not forbear crying out, "Ah, traitor! Is it thus you have treated a friend and brother? And you, O perjured charmer! Is it thus you have rewarded all my vows?" He could say no more, but reeling against the door, had fallen in a swoon upon the floor, had not his page caught him in his arms, who was entering with him. The good old prince, the father, who knew not what all this meant, was soon informed by the young, weeping princess, who, in relating the story of her amour with Henrick, told her tale in so moving a manner, as brought tears to the old man's eyes, and rage to those of her husband. He immediately grew jealous to the last degree. He finds himself in possession ('tis true) of the beauty he adored, but the beauty adoring another: a prince young and charming as the light, soft, witty, and raging with an equal passion. He finds this dreaded rival in the same house with him, with an authority equal to his own, and fancies, where two hearts are so entirely agreed, and have so good an understanding, it would not be impossible to find opportunities to satisfy and ease that mutual flame that burnt so equally in both. He therefore resolved to send him out of the world, and to establish his own repose by a deed, wicked, cruel, and unnatural: to have him assassinated the first opportunity he could find. This resolution set him a little at ease, and he strove to dissemble kindness to Henrick with all the art he was capable of, suffering him to come often to the apartment of the princess, and to entertain her oftentimes with discourse, when he was not near enough to hear what he spoke; but still watching their eyes, he found those of Henrick full of tears ready to flow, but restrained, looking all dying, and yet reproaching, while those of the princess were ever bent to the earth, and she, as much as possible, shunning his conversation. Yet this did not satisfy the jealous husband; 'twas not her complaisance that could appease him. He found her heart was panting within whenever Henrick approached her, and every visit more and more confirmed his death.

'The father often found the disorders of the sons; the softness and address of the one gave him as much fear as the angry blushings, the fierce looks, and broken replies of the other whenever he beheld Henrick approach his wife. So that the father, fearing some ill consequence of this, besought Henrick to withdraw to some other country, or travel into Italy, he being now of an age that required a view of the world. He told his father that he would obey his commands, though he was certain that moment he was to be separated from the sight of the fair princess, his sister, would be the last of his life, and, in fine, made so pitiful a story of his suffering love as almost moved the old prince to compassionate him so far as to permit him to stay. But he saw inevitable danger in that, and therefore bid him prepare for his journey.

'That which passed between the father and Henrick being a secret, none talked of his departing from court, so that the design the brother had went on, and making an hunting match one day, where most young people of quality were, he ordered some whom he had hired to follow his brother, so as if he chanced to go out of the way, to dispatch him, and accordingly, fortune gave 'em an opportunity, for he lagged behind the company and turned aside into a pleasant thicket of hazels, where alighting, he walked on foot in the most pleasant part of

it, full of thought how to divide his soul between love and
obedience. He was sensible that he ought not to stay, that he
was but an affliction to the young princess, whose honour
could never permit her to ease any part of his flame; nor was
he so vicious to entertain a thought that should stain her
virtue. He beheld her now as his brother's wife, and that
secured his flame from all loose desires, if her native modesty
had not been sufficient of itself to have done it, and that
profound respect he paid her; and he considered, in obeying
his father, he left her at ease and his brother freed of a
thousand fears. He went to seek a cure, which if he could not
find, at last he could but die, and so he must, even at her feet;
however, that 'twas more noble to seek a remedy for his
disease than expect a certain death by staying. After a thousand
reflections on his hard fate, and bemoaning himself, and blaming his cruel stars, that had doomed him to die so young, after
an infinity of sighs and tears, resolvings and unresolvings, he
on the sudden was interrupted by the trampling of some
horses he heard, and their rushing through the boughs, and
saw four men make towards him. He had not time to mount,
being walked some paces from his horse. One of the men
advanced and cried, "Prince you must die—" "I do believe
thee," replied Henrick, "but not by a hand so base as thine."
And at the same time, drawing his sword, run him into the
groin. When the fellow found himself so wounded he wheeled
off and cried, "Thou art a prophet, and hast rewarded my
treachery with death." The rest came up, and one shot at the
prince and shot him into the shoulder; the other two hastily
laying hold (but too late) on the hand of the murderer, cried,
"Hold, traitor, we relent and he shall not die." He replied,
"'Tis too late, he is shot; and see, he lies dead. Let us provide
for ourselves, and tell the prince we have done the work, for
you are as guilty as I am." At that they all fled and left the
prince lying under a tree weltering in his blood.

'About the evening, the forester going his walks saw the
horse richly caparisoned, without a rider, at the entrance of
the wood, and going farther to see if he could find its owner,
found there the prince almost dead. He immediately mounts
him on the horse and, himself behind, bore him up and carried

him to the lodge, where he had only one old man, his father, well skilled in surgery, and a boy. They put him to bed, and the old forester, with what art he had, dressed his wound and, in the morning, sent for an abler surgeon, to whom the prince enjoined secrecy, because he knew him. The man was faithful and the prince, in time, was recovered of his wound and, as soon as he was well, he came for Flanders in the habit of a pilgrim and, after some time, took the order of St Francis, none knowing what became of him till he was professed, and then he writ his own story to the prince his father, to his mistress, and his ungrateful brother. The young princess did not long survive his loss; she languished from the moment of his departure and he had this to confirm his devout life: to know she died for him.

'My brother, Madam, was an officer under the prince his father, and knew his story perfectly well, from whose mouth I had it.'

'What!' replied Miranda then, 'is Father Henrick a man of quality?' 'Yes Madam,' said Cornelia, 'and has changed his name to Francisco.' But Miranda, fearing to betray the sentiments of her heart by asking any more questions about him, turned the discourse, and some persons of quality came in to visit her (for her apartment was, about six a clock, like the presence chamber of a queen, always filled with the greatest people). There meet all the *beaux esprits*,* and all the beauties. But it was visible Miranda was not so gay as she used to be, but pensive and answering malapropos* to all that was said to her. She was a thousand times going to speak against her will something of the charming friar, who was never from her thoughts, and she imagined if he could inspire love in a coarse, grey, ill-made habit, a shorn crown, a hair cord about his waist, bare legged in sandals instead of shoes, what must he do when, looking back on time, she beholds him in a prospect of glory, with all that youth and illustrious beauty set off by the advantage of dress and equipage. She frames an idea of him all gay and splendid, and looks on his present habit as some disguise proper for the stealths of love; some feigned put-on shape with the more security to approach a mistress and make himself happy; and that, the robe laid by, she has the lover in his proper beauty, the same he would have been if any other habit (though never so rich) were put off. In the bed, the silent, gloomy night, and the soft embraces of her arms, he loses all the friar and assumes all the prince; and that aweful reverence due alone to his holy habit he exchanges for a thousand dalliances for which his youth was made: for love, for tender embraces, and all the happiness of life. Some moments she fancies him a lover, and that the fair object that takes up all his heart has left no room for her there; but that was a thought that did not long perplex her, and which, almost as soon as born, she turned to her advantage. She beholds him a lover, and therefore finds he has a heart sensible and tender; he had youth to be fired, as well as to inspire; he was far from the loved object, and totally without hope, and she reasonably considered that flame would of itself soon die that had only despair to feed on. She beheld her own charms, and experience, as well as her glass, told her they never failed of conquest, especially where they designed it. And she believed Henrick would be glad at least to quench that flame in himself by an amour with her, which was kindled by the young princess of ——, his sister.

These, and a thousand other self-flatteries, all vain and indiscreet, took up her waking nights, and now more retired days, while love, to make her truly wretched, suffered her to soothe herself with fond imaginations, not so much as permitting her reason to plead one moment to save her from undoing. She would not suffer it to tell her he had taken holy orders, made sacred and solemn vows of everlasting chastity, that 'twas impossible he could marry her, or lay before her any argument that might prevent her ruin; but love, mad, malicious love, was always called to counsel, and, like easy monarchs, she had no ears but for flatterers.

Well then, she is resolved to love, without considering to what end and what must be the consequence of such an amour. She now missed no day of being at that little church where she had the happiness, or rather, the misfortune (so love ordained) to see this ravisher of her heart and soul, and every day she took new fire from his lovely eyes. Unawares, unknown, and unwillingly, he gave her wounds, and the difficulty of her cure made her rage the more. She burnt, she languished, and died for the young innocent, who knew not he was the author of so much mischief.

Now she revolves a thousand ways in her tortured mind to let him know her anguish, and at last pitched upon that of writing to him soft billets, which she had learnt the art of doing; or if she had not, she had now fire enough to inspire her with all that could charm and move. These she delivered to a young wench who waited on her and whom she had entirely subdued to her interest, to give to a certain lay brother of the order, who was a very simple, harmless wretch, and who served in the kitchen in the nature of a cook in the monastery of Cordeliers. She gave him gold to secure his faith and service, and not knowing from whence they came (with so good credentials), he undertook to deliver the letters to Father Francisco, which letters were all afterwards, as you shall hear, produced in open court. These letters failed not to come every day, and the sense of the first was to tell him that a very beautiful young lady, of a great fortune, was in love with him—without naming her, but it came as from a third person, to let him know the secret that she desired he would let her know whether she might hope any return from him, assuring him he needed but only see the fair languisher to confess himself her slave.

This letter being delivered him, he read by himself, and was surprised to receive words of this nature, being so great a stranger in that place, and could not imagine, or would not give himself the trouble of guessing, who this should be, because he never designed to make returns.

The next day Miranda, finding no advantage from her messenger of love, in the evening sends another (impatient of delay), confessing that she who suffered the shame of writing and imploring was the person herself who adored him. 'Twas there her raging love made her say all things that discovered the nature of its flame, and propose to flee with him to any part of the world, if he would quit the convent; that she had a fortune considerable enough to make him happy, and that his youth and quality were not given him to so unprofitable an end as to lose themselves in a convent, where poverty and ease* was all their business. In fine, she leaves nothing unurged that might debauch and invite him, not forgetting to send him her own character of beauty, and left him to judge of her wit and spirit by her writing, and her love by the extremity of passion she professed. To all which the lovely friar made no return, as believing a gentle capitulation or exhortation to her would but inflame her the more and give new occasions for her continuing to write. All her reasonings, false and vicious, he despised, pities the error of her love, and was proof against all she could plead. Yet notwithstanding his silence, which left her in doubt and more tormented her, she ceased not to pursue him with her letters, varying her style; sometimes all wanton, loose and raving; sometimes feigning a virgin modesty all over, accusing herself, blaming her conduct, and sighing her destiny, as one compelled to the shameful discovery by the austerity of his vow and habit, asking his pity and forgiveness, urging him in charity to use his fatherly care to persuade and reason with her wild desires, and by his counsel, drive the god from her heart, whose tyranny was worse than that of a fiend; and he did not know what his pious advice might do. But still she writes in vain, in vain she varies her style by a cunning peculiar to a maid possessed with such a sort of passion.

This cold neglect was still oil to the burning lamp, and she tries yet more arts which, for want of right thinking, were as fruitless. She has recourse to presents: her letters came loaded with rings of great price, and jewels which fops of quality had given her. Many of this sort he received before he knew where to return 'em or how, and on this occasion alone he sent her a letter and restored her trifles, as he called 'em. But his habit having not made him forget his quality and education, he writ to her with all the profound respect imaginable, believing by her presents and the liberality with which she parted with 'em, that she was of quality. But the whole letter, as he told me afterwards, was to persuade her from the honour she did him by loving him, urging a thousand reasons, solid and pious, and assuring her he had wholly devoted the rest of his days to heaven and had no need of those gay trifles she had sent him, which were only fit to adorn ladies so fair as herself, and who had business with this glittering world which he disdained and had forever abandoned. He sent her a thousand blessings, and told her she should be ever in his prayers, though not in his heart as she desired. And abundance of goodness more he expressed and counsel he gave her, which had the same effect with his silence: it made her love but the more, and the more impatient she grew. She now had a new occasion to write, she now is charmed with his wit; this was the new subject. She rallies his resolution and endeavours to recall him to the world by all the arguments that human invention is capable of.

But when she had above four months languished thus in vain, not missing one day wherein she went not to see him, without discovering herself to him, she resolved as her last effort to show her person and see what that, assisted by her tears, and soft words from her mouth, could do to prevail upon him.

It happened to be on the eve of that day when she was to receive the sacrament, that she, covering herself with her veil, came to vespers, purposing to make choice of the conquering friar for her confessor. She approached him and as she did so, she trembled with love. At last she cried, 'Father, my confessor is gone for some time from the town, and I am obliged tomorrow to receive,* and beg you will be pleased to take my confession.'

He could not refuse her, and led her into the sacristy, where there is a confession chair in which he seated himself, and on one side of him she kneeled down, over against a little altar where the priests' robes lie, on which was placed some lighted wax candles, that made the little place very light and splendid, which shone full upon Miranda.

After the little preparation usual in confession, she turned up her veil, and discovered to his view the most wondrous object of beauty he had ever seen, dressed in all the glory of a young bride, her hair and stomacher full of diamonds that gave a lustre all dazzling to her brighter face and eyes. He was surprised at her amazing beauty, and questioned whether he saw a woman or an angel at his feet. Her hands, which were elevated as if in prayer, seemed to be formed of polished alabaster, and he confessed he had never seen anything in nature so perfect and so admirable. He had some pain to compose himself to hear her confession, and was obliged to turn away his eyes, that his mind might not be perplexed with an object so diverting; when Miranda, opening the finest mouth in the world, and discovering new charms, began her confession.

'Holy Father,' said she, 'amongst the number of my vile offences, that which afflicts me to the greatest degree is that I am in love. Not', continued she, 'that I believe simple and virtuous love a sin, when 'tis placed on an object proper and suitable; but, my dear Father,' said she, and wept, 'I love with a violence which cannot be contained within the bounds of reason, moderation, or virtue. I love a man whom I cannot possess without a crime, and a man who cannot make me happy without becoming perjured.' 'Is he married?' replied the Father. 'No,' answered Miranda. 'Are you so?' continued he. 'Neither,' said she. 'Is he too near allied to you?' said Francisco. 'A brother, or relation?' 'Neither of these,' said she. 'He is unenjoyed, unpromised, and so am I. Nothing opposes our happiness or makes my love a vice, but you—'tis you deny me life. 'Tis you that forbids my flame. 'Tis you will have me die and seek my remedy in my grave, when I complain of tortures, wounds and flames. O cruel charmer, 'tis for you I languish, and here, at your feet, implore that pity which all my addresses have failed of procuring me—'

With that, perceiving that he was about to rise from his seat, she held him by his habit and vowed she would in that posture follow him wherever he flew from her. She elevated her voice so loud, he was afraid she might be heard, and therefore suffered her to force him into his chair again where, being seated, he began in the most passionate terms imaginable to dissuade her; but finding she but the more persisted in eagerness of passion, he used all the tender assurance that he could force from himself that he would have for her all the respect, esteem, and friendship that he was capable of paying; that he had a real compassion for her; and at last she prevailed so far with him by her sighs and tears, as to own he had a tenderness for her, and that he could not behold so many charms, without being sensibly touched by 'em, and finding all those effects that a maid so young and fair causes in the souls of men of youth and sense. But that as he was assured he could never be so happy to marry her, and as certain he could not grant anything but honourable passion, he humbly besought her not to expect more from him than such, and then began to tell her how short life was, and transitory its joys; how soon she would grow weary of vice, and how often change to find real repose in it, but never arrive to it. He made an end by new assurance of his eternal friendship, but utterly forbade her to hope.

Behold her now denied, refused, and defeated, with all her pleading, youth, beauty, tears, and knees; imploring, as she lay, holding fast his scapula,* and embracing his feet. What shall she do? She swells with pride, love, indignation, and desire; her burning heart is bursting with despair, her eyes grow fierce, and from grief she rises to a storm, and in her agony of passion, which looks all disdainful, haughty, and full of rage, she began to revile him as the poorest of animals. Tells him his soul was dwindled to the meanness of his habit, and his vows of poverty were suited to his degenerate mind. 'And,' said she, 'since all my nobler ways have failed me, and that, for a little hypocritical devotion, you resolve to lose the greatest blessings of life and to sacrifice me to your religious pride and vanity, I will either force you to abandon that dull dissimulation, or you shall die to prove your sanctity real. Therefore answer me immediately; answer my flame, my raging fire, which your eyes have kindled, or here, in this very moment, I will ruin thee, and make no scruple of revenging the pains I suffer, by that which shall take away your life and honour.'

The trembling young man who, all this while, with extreme anguish of mind and fear of the dire result, had listened to her ravings full of dread, demanded what she would have him do. When she replied, 'Do that which thy youth and beauty were ordained to do; this place is private, a sacred silence reigns here and no one dares to pry into the secrets of this holy place. We are as secure from fears of interruption as in deserts uninhabited, or caves forsaken by wild beasts. The tapers too shall veil their lights, and only that glimmering lamp shall be witness of our dear stealths of love.—Come to my arms, my trembling, longing arms, and curse the folly of thy bigotry that has made thee so long lose a blessing for which so many princes sigh in vain.'

At these words she rose from his feet and, snatching him in her arms, he could not defend himself from receiving a thousand kisses from the lovely mouth of the charming wanton, after which she ran herself and in an instant put out the candles. But he cried to her, 'In vain, O too indiscreet fair one, in vain you put out the light, for heaven still has eyes, and will look down upon my broken vows. I own your power, I own I have all the sense in the world of your charming touches; I am frail flesh and blood, but yet—yet——yet I can resist, and I prefer my vows to all your powerful temptations—I will be deaf and blind and guard my heart with walls of ice and make you know that when the flames of true devotion are kindled in a heart, it puts out all other fires, which are as ineffectual as candles lighted in the face of the sun.—Go, vain wanton, and repent, and mortify that blood which has so shamefully betrayed thee, and which will one day ruin both thy soul and body—'

At these words Miranda, more enraged the nearer she imagined herself to happiness, made no reply, but throwing herself in that instant into the confessing chair, and violently pulling the young friar into her lap, she elevated her voice to such a degree in crying out, 'Help, help; a rape; help, help!' that she was heard all over the church, which was full of people at the evening's devotion, who flocked about the door of the sacristy, which was shut with a spring lock on the inside, but they durst not open the door.

'Tis easily to be imagined in what condition our young friar was at this last devilish stratagem of his wicked mistress. He strove to break from those arms that held him so fast, and his bustling to get away, and hers to retain him, disordered her hair and her habit to such a degree as gave the more credit to her false accusation. The fathers had a door on the other side, by which they usually entered to dress in this little room, and at the report that was in an instant made 'em they hasted thither and found Miranda and the good father very indecently struggling, which they misinterpreted as Miranda desired, who, all in tears, immediately threw herself at the feet of the provincial, who was one of those that entered, and cried, 'O holy Father, revenge an innocent maid undone and lost to fame and honour by that vile monster, born of goats, nursed by tigers and bred up on savage mountains where humanity and religion are strangers. For, O holy Father, could it have entered into the heart of man to have done so barbarous and horrid a deed as to attempt the virgin honour of an unspotted maid, and one of my degree, even in the moment of my confession, in that holy time when I was prostrate before him and Heaven, confessing those sins that pressed my tender conscience, even then to load my soul with the blackest of infamies, to add to my number a weight that must sink me to Hell? Alas, under the security of his innocent looks, his holy habit, and his aweful function, I was led into this room to make my confession where, he locking the door, I had no sooner began but he, gazing on me, took fire at my fatal beauty and, starting up, put out the candles, and caught me in his arms, and raising me from the pavement set me in the confession chair and then——Oh, spare me the rest.'

With that, a shower of tears burst from her fair dissembling eyes, and sobs so naturally acted and so well managed as left no doubt upon the good men but all she had spoken was truth.

'——At first', proceeded she, 'I was unwilling to bring so great a scandal on his order as to cry out, but struggled as long as I had breath, pleaded the heinousness of the crime, urging my quality and the danger of the attempt. But he, deaf as the winds and ruffling as a storm, pursued his wild design with so much force and insolence as I at last, unable to resist, was wholly vanquished, robbed of my native purity. With what life and breath I had I called for assistance, both from men and Heaven; but Oh, alas, your succours come too late——You find me here a wretched, undone, and ravished maid. Revenge me, Fathers, revenge me on the perfidious hypocrite, or else give me a death that may secure your cruelty and injustice from ever being proclaimed o'er the world, or my tongue will be eternally reproaching you and cursing the wicked author of my infamy.' She ended as she began, with a thousand sighs and tears, and received from the provincial all assurances of revenge.

The innocent betrayed victim, all this while she was speaking, heard her with an astonishment that may easily be imagined, yet showed no extravagant signs of it, as those would do who feign it to be thought innocent; but being really so, he bore with an humble, modest, and blushing countenance all her accusations, which silent shame they mistook for evident signs of his guilt.

When the provincial demanded, with an unwonted severity in his eyes and voice, what he could answer for himself, calling him profaner of his sacred vows, and infamy to the holy order, the injured, but the innocently accused only replied, 'May Heaven forgive that bad woman and bring her to repentance'; for his part, he was not so much in love with life as to use many arguments to justify his innocence, unless it were to free that order from a scandal of which he had the honour to be professed. But, as for himself, life or death were things indifferent to him who heartily despised the world.

He said no more, and suffered himself to be led before the magistrate, who committed him to prison upon the accusation of this implacable beauty who, with so much feigned sorrow prosecuted the matter, even to his trial and condemnation, where he refused to make any great defence for himself. But being daily visited by all the religious, both of his own and other orders, they obliged him (some of 'em knowing the austerity of his life, others his cause of griefs that first brought him into orders, and others pretending a nearer knowledge even of his soul itself) to stand upon his justification, and discover what he knew of that wicked woman, whose life had not been so exemplary for virtue not to have given the world a thousand suspicions of her lewdness and prostitution.

The daily importunities of these fathers made him produce her letters, but as he had all the gownmen on his side, she had all the hats and feathers on hers, all the men of quality taking her part, and all the churchmen his. They heard his daily protestations and vows, but not a word of what passed at confession was yet discovered. He held that as a secret sacred on his part, and what was said in nature of a confession was not to be revealed, though his life depended on the discovery. But as to the letters, they were forced from him and exposed;

however, matters were carried with so high a hand against him, that they served for no proof at all of his innocence, and he was at last condemned to be burned at the market place.

After his sentence was passed, the whole body of priests made their addresses to Marquis Casteil Roderigo,* the then governor of Flanders, for a reprieve, which, after much ado, was granted him for some weeks, but with an absolute denial of pardon, so prevailing were the young cavaliers of his court, who were all adorers of this fair jilt.

About this time, while the poor innocent young Henrick was thus languishing in prison in a dark and dismal dungeon and Miranda, cured of her love, was triumphing in her revenge, expecting and daily gaining new conquests, and who, by this time, had reassumed all her wonted gaiety, there was a great noise about the town that a prince of mighty name and famed for all the excellencies of his sex, was arrived; a prince, young and gloriously attended, called Prince Tarquin.*

We had often heard of this great man, and that he was making his travels in France and Germany, and we had also heard that some years before, he being about eighteen years of age, in the time when our King Charles* of blessed memory was in Brussels, in the last year of his banishment, that all on a sudden this young man rose up upon 'em like the sun, all glorious and dazzling, demanding place of all the princes in that court. And when his pretence was demanded, he owned himself Prince Tarquin of the race of the last kings of Rome, made good his title, and took his place accordingly. After that he travelled for about six years up and down the world and then arrived at Antwerp about the time of my being sent thither by his late Majesty.*

Perhaps there could be nothing seen so magnificent as this prince. He was, as I said, extremely handsome, from head to foot exactly formed, and he wanted nothing that might adorn that native beauty to the best advantage. His parts were suitable to the rest: he had an accomplishment fit for a prince, an air haughty, but a carriage affable; easy in conversation and very entertaining, liberal and good natured, brave and inoffensive. I have seen him pass the streets with twelve footmen and four pages, the pages all in green velvet coats laced with gold, and white velvet trunks, the men in cloth richly laced with gold, his coaches and all other officers suitable to a great man.

He was all the discourse of the town; some laughing at his title, others reverencing it; some cried that he was an impostor, others that he had made his title as plain as if Tarquin had reigned but a year ago. Some made friendships with him, others would have nothing to say to him, but all wondered where this revenue was that supported this grandeur, and believed, though he could make his descent from the Roman kings very well out, that he could not lay so good a claim to the Roman land. Thus everybody meddled with what they had nothing to do, and, as in other places, thought themselves on the surer side if, in these doubtful cases, they imagined the worst.

But the men might be of what opinion they pleased concerning him, the ladies were all agreed that he was a prince, and a young, handsome prince, and a prince not to be resisted. He had all their wishes, all their eyes, and all their hearts. They now dressed only for him, and what church he graced was sure that day to have the beauties and all that thought themselves so.

You may believe our amorous Miranda was not the last conquest he made. She no sooner heard of him, which was as soon as he arrived, but she fell in love with his very name. Jesu!—A young king of Rome! Oh, 'twas so novel that she doted on the title, and had not cared whether the rest had been man or monkey almost, she was resolved to be the Lucretia* that this young Tarquin should ravish. To this end, she was no sooner up the next day, but she sent him a billet-doux, assuring him how much she admired his fame, and that being a stranger in the town, she begged the honour of introducing him to all the belle-conversations, etc.—which he took for the invitation of some coquette who had interest in fair ladies, and civilly returned her an answer that he would wait on her. She had him that day watched to church, and impatient to see what she heard so many people flock to see, she went also to the same church, those sanctified abodes being too often profaned by such devotees, whose business is to ogle and ensnare.

But what a noise and humming was heard all over the church when Tarquin entered; his grace, his mien, his fashion, his beauty, his dress, and his equipage surprised all that were present, and by the good management and care of Miranda, she got to kneel at the side of the altar just over against the prince, so that, if he would, he could not avoid looking full upon her. She had turned up her veil and all her face and shape appeared such, and so enchanting, as I have described, and her beauty heightened with blushes, and her eyes full of spirit and fire with joy to find the young Roman monarch so charming, she appeared like something more than mortal, and compelled his eyes to a fixed gazing on her face. She never glanced that way, but she met 'em, and then would feign so modest a shame, and cast her eyes downward with such inviting art, that he was wholly ravished and charmed, and she overjoyed to find he was so.

The ceremony being ended, he sent a page to follow that lady home, himself pursuing her to the door of the church, where he took some holy water and threw upon her and made her a profound reverence. She forced an innocent look, and a modest gratitude in her face, and bowed and passed forward, half assured of her conquest, leaving him to go home to his lodging and impatiently wait the return of his page. And all the ladies who saw this first beginning between the prince and Miranda began to curse and envy her charms, who had deprived 'em of half their hopes. After this, I need not tell you he made Miranda a visit and from that day never left her apartment but when he went home at nights or unless he had business, so entirely was he conquered by this fair one. But the bishop and several men of quality in orders, that professed friendship to him, advised him from her company, and spoke several things to him that might (if love had not made him blind) have reclaimed him from the pursuit of his ruin. But whatever they trusted him with, she had the art to wind herself about his heart, and make him unravel all his secrets, and then knew as well by feigned sighs and tears to make him disbelieve all. So that he had no faith but for her, and was wholly enchanted and bewitched by her. At last, in spite of all that would have opposed it, he married this famous woman, possessed by so many great men and strangers before, while all the world was pitying his shame and misfortunes.

Being married, they took a great house, and as she was indeed a great fortune, and now a great princess, there was nothing wanting that was agreeable to their quality; all was splendid and magnificent. But all this would not acquire 'em the world's esteem; they had an abhorrence for her former life, despised her, and for his espousing a woman so infamous, they despised him. So that though they admired, and gazed upon their equipage and glorious dress, they foresaw the ruin that attended it and paid her quality very little respect.

She was no sooner married but her uncle died, and dividing his fortune between Miranda and her sister,* leaves the young heiress and all her fortune entirely in the hands of the princess.

We will call this sister Alcidiana; she was about fourteen years of age, and now had chosen her brother the prince for her guardian. If Alcidiana were not altogether so great a beauty as her sister, she had charm sufficient to procure her a great many lovers, though her fortune had not been so considerable as it was; but with that addition you may believe she wanted no courtships from those of the best quality, though everybody deplored her being under the tutorage of a lady so expert in all the vices of her sex, and so cunning a manager of sin as was the princess, who, on her part, failed not by all the caresses and obliging endearments to engage the mind of this young maid, and to subdue her wholly to her government. All her senses were eternally regaled with the most bewitching pleasures they were capable of. She saw nothing but glory and magnificence, heard nothing but music of the sweetest sounds; the richest perfumes employed her smelling, and all she eat and touched was delicate and inviting, and being too young to consider how this state and grandeur was to be continued, little imagined her vast fortune was every day diminishing towards its needless support.

When the princess went to church she had her gentleman bare before her carrying a great velvet cushion with great golden tassels for her to kneel on, and her train borne up a most prodigious length, led by a gentleman-usher bare, followed by innumerable footmen, pages and women. And in this state she would walk in the streets, as in those countries 'tis the fashion for the great ladies to do who are well, and in her train two or three coaches, and perhaps a rich velvet chair embroidered, would follow in state.

'Twas thus for some time they lived, and the princess was daily pressed by young sighing lovers for her consent to marry Alcidiana; but she had still one art or other to put 'em off, and so continually broke all the great matches that were proposed to her, notwithstanding their kindred and other friends had industriously endeavoured to make several great matches for her, but the princess was still positive in her denial, and one way or other broke all. At last it happened there was one proposed yet more advantageous: a young count, with whom the young maid grew passionately in love, and besought her sister to consent that she might have him, and got the prince to speak in her behalf. But he had no sooner heard the secret reasons Miranda gave him but (entirely her slave) he changed his mind and suited it to hers and she, as before, broke off that amour, which so extremely incensed Alcidiana, that she, taking an opportunity, got from her guard, and ran away, putting herself into the hands of a wealthy merchant, her kinsman and one who bore the greatest authority in the city. Him she chooses for her guardian, resolving to be no longer a slave to the tyranny of her sister. And so well she ordered matters that she writ to this young cavalier, her last lover, and retrieved him, who came back to Antwerp again to renew his courtship.

Both parties being agreed, it was no hard matter to persuade all but the princess. But though she opposed it, it was resolved on, and the day appointed for marriage and the portion demanded—demanded only, but never to be paid, the best part of it being spent. However, she put 'em off from day to day by a thousand frivolous delays, and when she saw they would have recourse to force, and that all her magnificence would be at an end if the law should prevail against her, and that without this sister's fortune she could not long support her grandeur, she bethought herself of a means to make it all her own by getting her sister made away. But she being out of her tuition, she was not able to accomplish so great a deed of darkness. But since 'twas resolved it must be done, she revolves on a thousand stratagems, and at last pitches upon an effectual one.

She had a page called Van Brune, a youth of great address and wit, and one she had long managed for her purpose. This youth was about seventeen years of age, and extremely beautiful, and in the time when Alcidiana lived with the princess, she was a little in love with this handsome boy, but 'twas checked in its infancy and never grew up to a flame. Nevertheless, Alcidiana retained still a sort of tenderness for him, while he burned in good earnest with love for the princess.

The princess one day ordering this page to wait on her in her closet, she shut the door and, after a thousand questions of what he would undertake to serve her, the amorous boy, finding himself alone and caressed by the fair person he adored, with joyful blushes that beautified his face, told her there was nothing upon earth he would not do to obey her least commands. She grew more familiar with him to oblige him, and seeing love dance in his eyes, of which she was so good a judge, she treated him more like a lover than a servant; till at last the ravished youth, wholly transported out of himself, fell at her feet and impatiently implored to receive her commands quickly that he might fly to execute 'em, for he was not able to bear her charming words, looks, and touches, and retain his duty. At this she smiled and told him the work was of such a nature as would mortify all flames about him, and he would have more need of rage, envy, and malice than the aids of a passion so soft as what she now found him capable of. He assured her he would stick at nothing, though even against his nature, to recompense for the boldness he now, through indiscretion, had discovered. She, smiling, told him he had committed no fault, and that possibly the pay he should receive for the services she required at his hands should be—what he most wished for in the world. To this he bowed to the earth and, kissing her feet, bade her command. And then she boldly told him 'twas to kill her sister Alcidiana. The youth, without so much as starting, or pausing upon the matter, told her it should be done, and bowing low, immediately went out of the closet. She called him back and would have given him some instruction, but he refused it and said the

action and the contrivance should be all his own, and offering
to go again, she again recalled him, putting into his hands a
purse of a hundred pistols, which he took, and with a low bow,
departed.

He no sooner left her presence but he goes directly and
buys a dose of poison and went immediately to the house
where Alcidiana lived, where, desiring to be brought to her
presence, he fell a-weeping and told her his lady had fallen out
with him and dismissed him her service, and since from a child
he had been brought up in the family, he humbly besought
Alcidiana to receive him into hers, she being in a few days to
be married. There needed not much entreaty to a thing that
pleased her so well, and she immediately received him to
pension.* And he waited some days on her before he could get
an opportunity to administer his devilish potion. But one
night, when she drunk wine with roasted apples, which was
usual with her, instead of sugar, or with the sugar, the baneful
drug was mixed and she drank it down.

About this time, there was a great talk of this page's coming
from one sister to go to the other. And Prince Tarquin, who
was ignorant of the design from the beginning to the end,
hearing some men of quality at his table speaking of Van
Brune's change of place (the princess then keeping her chamber
upon some trifling indisposition), he answered that surely they
were mistaken, that he was not dismissed from the princess's
service. And calling some of his servants, he asked for Van
Brune, and whether anything had happened between her high-
ness and him that had occasioned his being turned off. They
all seemed ignorant of this matter, and those who had spoke of
it began to fancy there was some juggle in the case, which time
would bring to light.

The ensuing day 'twas all about the town that Alcidiana was
poisoned and, though not dead, yet very near it, and that the
doctors said she had taken mercury. So that there was never so
formidable a sight as this fair young creature; her head and
body swollen, her eyes starting out, her face black and all
deformed. So that diligent search was made who it should be
that did this, who gave her drink and meat. The cook and
butler were examined, the footmen called to an account, but

all concluded she received nothing but from the hand of her
new page since he came into her service. He was examined
and showed a thousand guilty looks, and the apothecary then
attending among the doctors proved he had bought mercury of
him three of four days before, which he could not deny, and
making excuses for his buying it betrayed him the more, so ill
he chanced to dissemble. He was immediately sent to be
examined by the margrave, or justice, who made his mittimus,*
and sent him to prison.

'Tis easy to imagine in what fears and confusion the princess
was at this news. She took her chamber upon it, more to hide
her guilty face than for any indisposition, and the doctors
applied such remedies to Alcidiana, such antidotes against the
poison, that in a short time she recovered, but lost the finest
hair in the world and the complexion of her face ever after.

It was not long before the trials for criminals came on, and
the day being arrived, Van Brune was tried the first of all,
everybody having already read his destiny according as they
wished it, and none would believe but just indeed as it was. So
that for the revenge they hoped to see fall upon the princess,
everyone wished he might find no mercy, that she might share
of his shame and misery.

The sessions-house was filled that day with all the ladies
and chief of the town to hear the result of his trial, and the sad
youth was brought, loaded with chains, and pale as death,
where every circumstance being sufficiently proved against
him, and he making but a weak defence for himself, he was
convicted and sent back to prison to receive his sentence of
death on the morrow, where he owned all and who set him on
to do it. He owned 'twas not reward of gain he did it for, but
hope he should command at his pleasure the possession of his
mistress, the princess, who should deny him nothing after
having entrusted him with so great a secret; and that besides
she had elevated him with the promise of that glorious reward
and had dazzled his young heart with so charming a prospect
that, blind and mad with joy, he rushed forward to gain the
desired prize, and thought on nothing but his coming happiness; that he saw too late the follies of his presumptuous flame
and cursed the deluding flatteries of the fair hypocrite, who

had soothed him to his undoing; that he was a miserable victim to her wickedness, and hoped he should warn all young men by his fall to avoid the dissimulation of the deceiving fair; that he hoped they would have pity on his youth and attribute his crime to the subtle persuasions alone of his mistress, the princess; and that since Alcidiana was not dead, they would grant him mercy and permit him to live to repent of his grievous crime in some part of the world whither they might banish him.

He ended with tears, that fell in abundance from his eyes, and immediately the princess was apprehended and brought to prison, to the same prison where yet the poor young Father Francisco was languishing, he having been from week to week reprieved by the intercession of the fathers, and possibly she there had time to make some reflections.

You may imagine Tarquin left no means unassayed to prevent the imprisonment of the princess, and the public shame and infamy she was likely to undergo in this affair, but the whole city being overjoyed that she should be punished, as an author of all this mischief, were so generally bent against her, both priests, magistrates and people, the whole force of the stream running that way, she found no more favour than the meanest criminal. The prince therefore, when he saw 'twas impossible to rescue her from the hands of justice, suffered with grief unspeakable what he could not prevent, and led her himself to the prison, followed by all his people, in as much state as if he had been going to his marriage, where, when she came, she was as well attended and served as before, he never stirring one moment from her.

The next day she was tried in open and common court, where she appeared in glory, led by Tarquin, and attended according to her quality, and she could not deny all the page had alleged against her, who was brought thither also in chains, and after a great many circumstances, she was found guilty and both received sentence: the page to be hanged till he was dead on a gibbet in the market place, and the princess to stand under the gibbet with a rope about her neck, the other end of which was to be fastened to the gibbet where the page was hanging and to have an inscription in large characters upon her back and breast of the cause why, where she was to stand from ten in the morning to twelve.

This sentence the people, with one accord, believed too favourable for so ill a woman, whose crimes deserved death equal to that of Van Brune, nevertheless, there were some who said it was infinitely more severe than the death itself.

The following Friday was the day of execution, and one need not tell of the abundance of people who were flocked together in the market place. All the windows were taken down and filled with spectators, and the tops of houses, when, at the hour appointed, the fatal beauty appeared. She was dressed in a black velvet gown, with a rich row of diamonds all down the fore part of the breast, and a great knot of diamonds at the peak behind, and a petticoat of flowered gold, very rich and laced, with all things else suitable. A gentleman carried her great velvet cushion before her, on which her prayer book, embroidered, was laid; her train was borne up by a page, and the prince led her, bare, followed by his footmen, pages and other officers of his house.

When they arrived to the place of execution, the cushion was laid on the ground upon a portugal-mat* spread there for that purpose, and the princess stood on the cushion, with her prayer book in her hand, and a priest by her side, and was accordingly tied up to the gibbet. She had not stood there ten minutes but she had the mortification (at least, one would think it so to her) to see her sad page Van Brune approach, fair as an angel but languishing and pale. That sight moved all the beholders with as much pity as that of the princess did disdain and pleasure.

He was dressed all in mourning and very fine linen, bare-headed, with his own hair, the fairest that could be seen, hanging all in curls on his back and shoulders very long. He had a prayer book of black velvet in his hand, and behaved himself with much penitence and devotion. When he was brought under the gibbet, he, seeing his mistress in that condition, showed an infinite concern, and his fair face was covered over with blushes, and, falling at her feet, he humbly asked her pardon for having been the occasion of so great an infamy to her, by a weak confession which the fears of youth and hopes of life had obliged him to make, so greatly to her dishonour, for, indeed, he had wanted that manly strength to bear the efforts of dying as he ought, in silence, rather than of committing so great a crime against his duty and honour itself, and that he could not die in peace unless she would forgive him. The princess only nodded her head, and cried, 'I do.'

And after having spoken a little to his father confessor who was with him, he cheerfully mounted the ladder, and in the sight of the princess he was turned off, while a loud cry was heard through all the market place, especially from the fair sex; he hanging there till the time the princess was to depart, and when she was put into a rich embroidered chair and carried away, Tarquin going into his, for he had all that time stood supporting the princess under the gallows, and was very weary, she was sent back till her releasement came, which was that night about seven of the clock, and then she was conducted to her own house in great state, with a dozen white wax flambeaux about her chair.

If the affairs of Alcidiana and her friends before were impatient of having the portion out of the hands of these extravagants, 'tis not to be imagined but they were now much more so, and the next day they sent an officer according to law to demand it, or to summon the prince to give reasons why he would not. And the officer received for answer that the money should be called in and paid in such a time, setting a certain time which I have not been so curious as to retain, or put in my journal observations, but I am sure it was not long, as may be easily imagined, for they every moment suspected the prince would pack up and be gone some time or other on the sudden, and for that reason they would not trust him without bail, or two officers to remain in his house to watch that nothing should be removed or touched. As for bail or security, he could give none; everyone slunk their heads out of the collar when it came to that, so that he was obliged at his own expense to maintain officers in his house.

The princess finding herself reduced to the last extremity, and that she must either produce the value of a hundred thousand crowns, or see the prince, her husband, lodged for ever in a prison and all their glory vanish, and that it was impossible to fly, since guarded, she had recourse to an extremity worse than the affair of Van Brune. And in order to this, she first puts on a world of sorrow and concern for what she feared might arrive to the prince. And indeed, if ever she shed tears which she did not dissemble, it was upon this occasion. But here she almost overacted. She stirred not from her bed, and refused to eat or sleep or see the light, so that the day being shut out of her chamber, she lived by wax lights, and refused all comfort and consolation.

The prince, all raving with love, tender compassion and grief, never stirred from her bedside, nor ceased to implore that she would suffer herself to live. But she, who was not now so passionately in love with Tarquin as she was with the prince, not so fond of the man as his titles and of glory, foresaw the total ruin of the last if not prevented by avoiding the payment of this great sum, which could no otherwise be than by the death of Alcidiana. And therefore, without ceasing, she wept and cried out she could not live unless Alcidiana died. 'This Alcidiana,' continued she, 'who has been the author of my shame, who has exposed me under a gibbet in the public market place——Oh!——I am deaf to all reason, blind to natural affection. I renounce her. I hate her as my mortal foe, my stop to glory, and the finisher of my days ere half my race of life be run.'

Then throwing her false but snowy, charming arms about the neck of her heartbreaking* lord and lover, who lay sighing and listening by her side, he was charmed and bewitched into saying all things that appeased her, and lastly, told her Alcidiana should be no longer an obstacle to her repose, but that, if she would look up, and cast her eyes of sweetness and love upon him as heretofore, forget her sorrows and redeem her lost health, he would take what measures she should propose to dispatch this fatal stop to her happiness out of the way. These words failed not to make her caress him in the most endearing manner that love and flattery could invent, and she kissed him to an oath, a solemn oath, to perform what he had promised, and he vowed liberally, and she assumed in an instant her good humour, and suffered a supper to be prepared and did eat, which in many days before she had not done, so obstinate and powerful was she in dissembling well.

The next thing to be considered was which way this deed
was to be done, for they doubted not but when 'twas done, all
the world would lay it upon the princess as done by her
command. But she urged suspicion was no proof, and that they
never put to death anyone but when they had great and
certain evidences who were the offenders. She was sure of her
own constancy, that racks and tortures should never get the
secret from her breast, and if he were as confident on his part,
there was no danger. Yet this preparation she made towards
the laying the fact on others: that she caused several letters to
be written from Germany, as from the relations of Van Brune,
who threatened Alcidiana with death for depriving their kinsman (who was a gentleman) of his life, though he had not
taken away hers. And it was the report of the town how this
young maid was threatened. And indeed, the death of the page
had so afflicted a great many, that Alcidiana had procured
herself abundance of enemies upon that account, because she
might have saved him if she had pleased, but on the contrary,
she was a spectator, and in full health and vigour at his
execution, and people were not so much concerned for her at
this report as they would have been.

The prince, who now had, by reasoning the matter soberly
with Miranda, found it absolutely necessary to dispatch Alcidiana, he resolved himself, and with his own hand, to execute it,
not daring to trust to any of his most favourite servants,
though he had many who, possibly, would have obeyed him,
for they loved him as he deserved, and so would all the world,
had he not been so poorly deluded by this fair enchantress.
He, therefore, as I said, resolved to keep this great secret to
himself, and taking a pistol charged well with two bullets, he
watched an opportunity to shoot her as she should go out, or
into her house or coach some evening. To this end he waited
several nights near her lodgings, but still either she went not
out, or when she returned, she was so guarded with friends or
her lover and flambeaux,* that he could not aim at her without
endangering the life of some other. But one night above the
rest, upon a Sunday, when he knew she would be at the
theatre, for she never missed that day seeing the play, he
waited at the corner of the Statt-house near the theatre with

his cloak cast over his face, and a black perrywig, all alone, with his pistol ready cocked, and remained not very long but he saw her kinsman's coach come along. 'Twas almost dark; day was just shutting up her beauties, and left such a light to govern the world as served only just to distinguish one object from another, and a convenient help to mischief. He saw alight out of the coach only one young lady, the lover, and then the destined victim, which he (drawing near) knew rather by her tongue than shape. The lady ran into the playhouse and left Alcidiana to be conducted by her lover into it, who led her to the door, and went to give some order to the coachman, so that the lover was about twenty yards from Alcidiana when she stood—the fairest mark in the world—on the threshold of the theatre, there being many coaches about the door, so that hers could not come so near. Tarquin was resolved not to lose so fair an opportunity, and advanced, but went behind the coaches, and when he came over against the door, through a great booted, velvet coach that stood between him and her, he shot, and she, having her train of her gown and petticoat on her arm in great quantity, he missed her body, and shot through her clothes between her arm and her body. She, frightened to find something hit her and to see the smoke and hear the report of the pistol, running in, cried, 'I am shot! I am dead!'

This noise quickly alarmed her lover, and all the coachmen and footmen immediately ran, some one way and some another. One of 'em, seeing a man haste away in a cloak, he being a lusty, bold German, stopped him, and drawing upon him, bade him stand and deliver his pistol, or he would run him through.

Tarquin, being surprised at the boldness of this fellow to demand his pistol, as if he positively knew him to be the murderer (for so he thought himself, since he believed Alcidiana dead), had so much presence of mind as to consider, if he suffered himself to be taken, he should poorly die a public death, and therefore resolved upon one mischief more to secure himself from the first, and in the moment that the German bade him deliver his pistol, he cried, 'Though I have no pistol to deliver, I have a sword to chastise thy insolence.' And throwing off his cloak and flinging his pistol from him, he drew, and wounded and disarmed the fellow.

This noise of swords brought everybody to the place, and immediately the bruit ran: 'The murderer was taken; the murderer was taken', though none knew which was he, nor the cause of the quarrel between the two fighting men, which none yet knew, for it now was darker than before. But at the noise of the murderer being taken, the lover of Alcidiana, who by this time found his lady unhurt, all but the trains of her gown and petticoat, came running to the place just as Tarquin had disarmed the German and was ready to have killed him, when laying hold of his arm, they arrested the stroke, and redeemed the footman.

They then demanded who this stranger was at whose mercy the fellow lay, but the prince, who now found himself venturing for his last stake, made no reply, but with two swords in his hands, went to fight his way through the rabble. And though there were above a hundred persons, some with swords, others with long whips (as coachmen), so invincible was the courage of this poor, unfortunate gentleman at that time, that all these were not able to seize him, but he made his way through the ring that encompassed him and ran away—but was, however, so closely pursued, the company still gathering as they ran, that, toiled with fighting, oppressed with guilt and fear of being taken, he grew fainter and fainter, and suffered himself, at last, to yield to his pursuers, who soon found him to be Prince Tarquin in disguise. And they carried him directly to prison, being Sunday, to wait the coming day to go before a magistrate.

In an hour's time, the whole fatal adventure was carried all over the city, and everyone knew that Prince Tarquin was the intended murderer of Alcidiana, and not one but had a real sorrow and compassion for him. They heard how bravely he had defended himself, how many he had wounded before he could be taken and what numbers he had fought through, and even those that saw his valour and bravery, and who had assisted at his being seized, now repented from the bottom of their hearts their having any hand in the ruin of so gallant a man, especially since they knew the lady was not hurt. A thousand addresses were made to her not to prosecute him, but her lover, a hot-headed fellow, more fierce than brave, would by no means be pacified, but vowed to pursue him to the scaffold.

The Monday came and the Prince, being examined, confessed the matter of fact, since there was no harm done, believing a generous confession the best of his game; but he was sent back to closer imprisonment, loaded with irons, to expect the next sessions. All his household goods were seized and all they could find for the use of Alcidiana. And the princess, all in rage, tearing her hair, was carried to the same prison to behold the cruel effects of her hellish designs. One need not tell here how sad and horrid this meeting appeared between her lord and she; let it suffice it was the most melancholy and mortifying object that ever eyes beheld. On Miranda's part, 'twas sometimes all rage and fire, and sometimes all tears and groans; but still 'twas sad love and mournful tenderness on his. Nor could all his sufferings and the prospect of death itself drive from his soul one spark of that fire the obstinate god had fatally kindled there. And in the midst of all his sighs, he would recall himself and cry, '—I have Miranda still.'

He was eternally visited by his friends and acquaintance, and this last action of bravery had got him more than all his former conduct had lost. The fathers were perpetually with him, and all joined with one common voice in this, that he ought to abandon a woman so wicked as the princess, and that however fate dealt with him, he could not show himself a true penitent while he laid the author of so much evil in his bosom; that Heaven would never bless him till he had renounced her, and on such conditions he would find those that would employ their utmost interest to save his life, who else would not stir in his affair. But he was so deaf to all, that he could not so much as dissemble a repentance for having married her.

He lay a long time in prison, and all that time the poor Father Francisco remained there also. And the good fathers, who daily visited these two amorous prisoners, the prince and princess, and who found by the management of matters it would go very hard with Tarquin, entertained 'em often with holy matters relating to the life to come, from which, before his trial, he gathered what his stars had appointed and that he was destined to die.

This gave an unspeakable torment to the now-repenting beauty, who had reduced him to it, and she began to appear with a more solid grief. Which being perceived by the good fathers, they resolved to attack her on the yielding side, and after some discourse upon the judgement for sin, they came to reflect on the business of Father Francisco, and told her she had never thrived since her accusing of that father, and laid it very home to her conscience, assuring her that they would do their utmost in her service if she would confess that secret sin to all the world, so that she might atone for the crime by the saving that good man. At first she seemed inclined to yield, but shame of being her own detector in so vile a matter recalled her goodness and she faintly persisted in it.

At the end of six months Prince Tarquin was called to his trial, where I will pass over the circumstances, which are only what is usual in such criminal cases, and tell you that he, being found guilty of the intent of killing Alcidiana, was condemned to lose his head in the market place and the princess to be banished her country.

After sentence pronounced, to the real grief of all the spectators, he was carried back to prison. And now the fathers attack her anew, and she, whose griefs daily increased, with a languishment that brought her very near her grave, at last confessed all her life, all the lewdness of her practices with several princes and great men, besides her lusts with people that served her and others in mean capacity, and lastly, the whole truth of the young friar, and how she had drawn the page and the prince her husband to this designed murder of her sister. This she signed with her hand in the presence of the prince her husband, and several holy men who were present. Which being signified to the magistrates, the friar was immediately delivered from his irons (where he had languished more than two whole years) in great triumph and with much honour, and lives a most exemplary, pious life, and as he did before; for he is yet living in Antwerp.

After the condemnation of these two unfortunate persons, who begot such different sentiments in the minds of the people (the prince all the compassion and pity imaginable, and the princess, all the contempt and despite), they languished almost

six months longer in prison, so great an interest there was
made in order to the saving his life by all the men of the robe.
On the other side, the princes and great men of all nations
who were at the court of Brussels, who bore a secret revenge
in their hearts against a man who had, as they pretended, set
up a false title only to take place of them, who, indeed, was
but a merchant's son of Holland, as they said, so incensed
them against him that they were too hard at court for the
churchmen. However, this dispute gave the prince his life
some months longer than was expected, which gave him also
some hope that a reprieve for ninety years would have been
granted, as was desired. Nay, Father Francisco so interested
himself in this concern that he writ to his father and several
princes of Germany with whom Marquis Casteil Roderigo was
well acquainted, to intercede with him for the saving of
Tarquin, since 'twas more by his persuasions than those of all
who attacked her that made Miranda confess the truth of her
affair with him. But at the end of six months, when all
applications were found fruitless and vain, the prince received
news that in two days he was to die, as his sentence had been
before pronounced, and for which he prepared himself with all
cheerfulness.

On the following Friday, as soon as it was light, all people
of any condition came to take their leaves of him, and none
departed with dry eyes or hearts unconcerned to the last
degree, for Tarquin, when he found his fate inevitable, bore it
with a fortitude that showed no signs of regret, but addressed
himself to all about him with the same cheerful, modest and
great air he was wont to do in his most flourishing fortune. His
valet was dressing him all the morning, so many interruptions
they had by visitors, and he was all in mourning and so were
all his followers, for even to the last he kept up his grandeur,
to the amazement of all people, and indeed, he was so passionately beloved by them that those he had dismissed served him
voluntarily and would not be persuaded to abandon him while
he lived.

The princess was also dressed in mourning, and her two
women, and notwithstanding the unheard of lewdness and
villainies she had confessed of herself, the prince still adored

her, for she had still those charms that made him first do so; nor, to his last moment, could be brought to wish that he had never seen her. But on the contrary, as a man yet vainly proud of his fetters, he said all the satisfaction this short moment of life could afford him was that he died in endeavouring to serve Miranda, his adorable princess.

After he had taken leave of all who thought it necessary to leave him to himself for some time, he retired with his confessor, where they were about an hour in prayer, all the ceremonies of devotions that were fit to be done being already passed. At last the bell tolled, and he was to take leave of the princess as his last work of life and the most hard he had to accomplish. He threw himself at her feet, and gazing on her as she sat, more dead than alive, o'erwhelmed with silent grief, they both remained some moments speechless, and then, as if one rising tide of tears had supplied both their eyes, it burst out in streams at the same instant, and when his sighs gave way, he uttered a thousand farewells, so soft, so passionate and moving, that all who were by were extremely touched with it, and said that nothing could be seen more deplorable and melancholy. A thousand times they bade farewell and still some tender look or word would prevent his going; then embrace and bid farewell again. A thousand times she asked his pardon for being the occasion of that fatal separation; a thousand times assuring him she would follow him, for she could not live without him. And heaven knows when their soft and sad caresses would have ended had not the officers assured him 'twas time to mount the scaffold. At which words the princess fell fainting in the arms of her women and they led Tarquin out of the prison.

When he came to the market place, whither he walked on foot followed by his own domestics, and some bearing a black, velvet coffin with silver hinges, the headsman before him with his fatal scimitar drawn, his confessor by his side, and many gentlemen and churchmen with Father Francisco attending him, the people showering millions of blessings on him and beholding with weeping eyes, he mounted the scaffold, which was strewed with some sawdust about the place where he was to kneel, to receive the blood, for they behead people kneeling,

and with the back stroke of a scimitar, and not lying on a block
and with an axe as we in England. The scaffold had a low rail
about it, that everybody might more conveniently see. This
was hung with black, and all that state that such a death could
have was here in most decent order.

He did not say much upon the scaffold; the sum of what he
said to his friends was to be kind and take care of the poor
penitent, his wife; to others, recommending his honest and
generous servants, whose fidelity was so well known and
commended that they were soon promised all preferment. He
was some time in prayer, and a very short time speaking to his
confessor; then he turned to the headsman and desired him to
do his office well, and gave him twenty louis d'ors, and
undressing himself with the help of his valet and page, he
pulled off his coat, and had underneath a white satin waistcoat.
He took off his perrywig and put on a white, satin cap with a
holland one done with point under it, which he pulled a little
over his eyes, then took a cheerful leave of all, and kneeled
down and said, when he lifted up his hands the third time, the
headsman should do his office; which accordingly was done,
and the headsman gave him his last stroke, and the prince fell
on the scaffold. The people, with one common voice, as if it
had been but one entire one, prayed for his soul, and murmurs
of sighs were heard from the whole multitude, who scrambled
for some of the bloody sawdust to keep for his memory.

The headsman, going to take up the head, as the manner is,
to show to the people, he found he had not struck it off, and
that the body stirred. With that he stepped to an engine which
they always carry with 'em to force those who may be refrac-
tory, thinking, as he said, to have twisted the head from the
shoulders, conceiving it to hang but by a small matter of flesh.
Though 'twas an odd shift of the fellow's, yet 'twas done, and
the best shift he could suddenly propose. The margrave and
another officer, old men, were on the scaffold with some of the
prince's friends and servants who, seeing the headsman put
the engine about the neck of the prince, began to call out, and
the people made a great noise. The prince, who found himself
yet alive, or rather, who was past thinking, but had some sense
of feeling left, when the headsman took him up and set his back

against the rail, and clapped the engine about his neck, got his two thumbs between the rope and his neck, feeling himself pressed there, and struggling between life and death, and bending himself over the rail backward, while the headsman pulled forward, he threw himself quite over the rail by chance, and not design, and fell upon the heads and shoulders of the people, who were crying out with amazing shouts of joy. The headsman leaped after him, but the rabble had liked to have pulled him to pieces. All the city was in an uproar, but none knew what the matter was, but those who bore the body of the prince, whom they found yet living; but how, or by what strange miracle preserved they knew not, nor did examine, but with one accord, as if the whole crowd had been one body and had had but one motion, they bore the prince on their heads about a hundred yards from the scaffold, where there is a monastery of Jesuits and there they secured him. All this was done—his beheading, his falling, and his being secured—almost in a moment's time, the people rejoicing as at some extraordinary victory won. One of the officers being, as I said, an old, timorous man, was so frightened at the accident, the bustle, the noise, and the confusion, of which he was wholly ignorant, that he died with amazement and fear, and the other was fain to be let blood.

The officers of justice went to demand the prisoner, but they demanded in vain; they had now a right to protect him and would do so. All his overjoyed friends went to see in what condition he was, and all of quality found admittance. They saw him in bed going to be dressed by the most skilful surgeons, who yet could not assure him of life. They desired nobody should speak to him, or ask him any questions. They found that the headsman had struck him too low and had cut him into the shoulder-bone—a very great wound you may be sure, for the sword in such executions carries an extreme force. However, so good care was taken on all sides, and so greatly the fathers were concerned for him, that they found an amendment and hopes of a good effect of their incomparable charity and goodness.

At last, when he was permitted to speak, the first news he asked was after the princess. And his friends were very much afflicted to find that all his loss of blood had not quenched that flame, nor let out that which made him still love that bad woman. He was solicited daily to think no more of her, and all her crimes were laid so open to him and so shamefully represented, and on the other side his virtues so admired, and which, they said, would have been eternally celebrated, but for his folly with this infamous creature, that at last, by assuring him of all their assistance if he abandoned her, and to renounce him and deliver him up if he did not, they wrought so far upon him as to promise he would suffer her to go alone into banishment, and would not follow her or live with her any more. But, alas, this was but his gratitude that compelled this complaisance, for in his heart he resolved never to abandon her, nor was he able to live and think of doing it. However, his reason assured him he could not do a deed more justifiable, and one that would regain his fame sooner.

His friends asked him some questions concerning his escape and that since he was not beheaded but only wounded, why he did not immediately rise up. But he replied, he was so absolutely prepossessed that at the third lifting up his hands he should receive the stroke of death, that at the same instant the sword touched him, he had no sense, nay, not even of pain, so absolutely dead he was with imagination, and knew not that he stirred as the headsman found he did, nor did he remember anything from the lifting up of his hands to his fall, and then awakened as out of a dream, or rather, a moment's sleep without dream, he found he lived, and wondered what was arrived to him, or how he came to live, having not, as yet, any sense of his wound, though so terrible an one.

After this, Alcidiana, who was extremely afflicted for having been the prosecutor of this great man, who, bating his last design against her, which she knew was the instigation of her sister, had obliged her with all the civility imaginable, now sought all means possible of getting his pardon and that of her sister; though of a hundred thousand crowns which she should have paid her, she could get but ten thousand, which was from the sale of her rich beds and some other furniture. So that the young count, who before should have married her, now went off for want of fortune, and a young merchant (perhaps the best of the two) was the man to whom she was destined.

At last, by great intercession, both their pardons were obtained and the prince, who would be no more seen in a place that had proved every way so fatal to him, left Flanders, promising never to live with the fair hypocrite more; but ere he departed, he writ her a letter, wherein he ordered her, in a little time, to follow him into Holland, and left a bill of exchange with one of his trusty servants, whom he had left to wait upon her, for money for her accommodations, so that she was now reduced to one woman, one page, and this gentleman. The prince, in this time of his imprisonment, had several bills of great sums from his father, who was exceeding rich, and this all the children he had in the world and whom he tenderly loved.

As soon as Miranda was come into Holland, she was welcomed with all imaginable respect and endearment by the old father, who was imposed upon so as that he knew not she was the fatal occasion of all these disasters to his son, but rather looked on her as a woman who had brought him a hundred and fifty thousand crowns, which his misfortunes had consumed. But, above all, she was received by Tarquin with a joy unspeakable, who, after some time, to redeem his credit and gain himself a new fame, put himself into the French army, where he did wonders, and after three campaigns, his father dying, he returned home and retired to a country house, where, with his princess, he lives as a private gentleman in all the tranquillity of a man of a good fortune. They say Miranda has been very penitent for her life past, and gives Heaven the glory for having given her these afflictions that have reclaimed her and brought her to as perfect a state of happiness as this troublesome world can afford.

Since I began this relation, I heard that Prince Tarquin died about three-quarters of a year ago.

MEMOIRS OF THE COURT OF
THE KING OF BANTAM

This money, certainly, is a most dev'lish thing! I'm sure, the
want of it had like to have ruined my dear Philibella in her
love to Valentine Goodland, who was, really, a pretty deserving
gentleman, heir to about fifteen hundred pound a year, which,
however, did not so much recommend him as the sweetness of
his temper, the comeliness of his person, and the excellency of
his parts, in all which circumstances my obliging acquaintance
equalled him, unless in the advantage of their fortune. Old Sir
George Goodland knew of his son's passion for Philibella, and
though he was generous, and of an humour sufficiently comply-
ing, yet he could by no means think it convenient that his only
son should marry with a young lady of so slender a fortune as
my friend, who had not above five hundred pound, and that
the gift of her uncle, Sir Philip Friendly, though her virtue and
beauty might have deserved and have adorned the throne of
an Alexander or Caesar.

Sir Philip himself, indeed, was but a younger brother, though
of a good family, and of a generous education, which with his
person, bravery, and wit recommended him to his lady Philadelphia, widow of Sir Bartholomew Banquier, who left her possessed of two thousand pound per annum, besides twenty
thousand pound in money and jewels, which obliged him to
get himself dubbed that she might not descend to an inferior
quality. When he was in town, he lived—let me see—in the
Strand; or, as near as I can remember, somewhere about
Charing Cross, where, first of all, Mr Wou'dbe King, a gentleman of a large estate in houses, land and money, of a haughty,
extravagant, and profuse humour, very fond of every new face,
had the misfortune to fall passionately in love with Philibella,
who then lived with her uncle.

This Mr Wou'dbe (it seems) had often been told, when he
was yet a stripling, either by one of his nurses, by his own
grandmother, or by some other gipsy, that he should infallibly

be what his surname implied, a king, by providence or chance, ere he died, or never. This glorious prophecy had so great an influence on all his thoughts and actions that he distributed and disbursed his wealth, sometimes so largely, that one would ha' thought he had undoubtedly been king of some part of the Indies, to see a present made today of a diamond ring worth two or three hundred pound to Madam Flippant, tomorrow a large chest of the finest china to my Lady Fleecewell, and next day (perhaps) a rich necklace of large oriental pearl with a locket to it of sapphires, emeralds, rubies, etc. to pretty Miss Ogleme, for an amorous glance, for a smile, and (it may be, though but rarely) for the mighty blessing of one single kiss. But such were his largesses, not to reckon his treats, his balls, and serenades besides, that at the same time he had married a virtuous lady, and of good quality. But her relation to him (it may be feared) made her very disagreeable, for a man of his humour and estate can no more be satisfied with one woman than with one dish of meat, and to say truth, 'tis something unmodish. However, he might ha' died a pure celibate, and altogether unexpert of woman, had his good or bad hopes only terminated in Sir Philip's niece. But the brave and haughty Mr Wou'dbe was not to be baulked by appearances of virtue, which he thought all womankind did only affect; besides, he promised himself the victory over any lady whom he attempted, by the force of his damned money, though her virtue were never so real and strict.

With Philibella he found another pretty young creature, very like her who had been a quondam* mistress to Sir Philip. He, with young Goodland, was then diverting his mistress and niece at a game of cards. When Wou'dbe came to visit him he found 'em very merry, with a flask of claret or two before 'em, and oranges roasting by a large fire (for it was Christmas time). The Lady Friendly, understanding that this extraordinary man was with Sir Philip in the parlour, came in to 'em to make the number of both sexes equal, as well as in hopes to make up a purse of guineas toward the purchase of some new, fine business that she had in her head, from his accustomed design of losing at play to her. Indeed, she had part of her wish, for she got twenty guineas of him; Philibella, ten; and Lucy, Sir

Philip's quondam, five. Not but that Wou'dbe intended better
fortune to the young ones than he did to Sir Philip's lady, but
her Ladyship was utterly unwilling to give him over to their
management, though at the last. When they were all tired with
the cards, after Wou'dbe had said as many obliging things as
his present genius would give him leave to Philibella and
Lucy, especially to the first, not forgetting his baisemains* to
the Lady Friendly, he bid the knight and Goodland adieu, but
with a promise of repeating his visit at six o'clock in the
evening o' twelfth-day, to renew the famous and ancient
solemnity of choosing king and queen,* to which Sir Philip
before invited him, with a design yet unknown to you, I hope.

As soon as he was gone, everyone made their remarks on
him, but with very little or no difference in all their figures of
him; in short, all mankind, had they ever known him, would
have universally agreed in this his character: that he was an
original, since nothing in humanity was ever so vain, so
haughty, so profuse, so fond, and so ridiculously ambitious as
Mr Wou'dbe King. They laughed and talked about an hour
longer, and then young Goodland was obliged to see Lucy
home in his coach, though he had rather have sat up all night
in the same house with Philibella, I fancy, of whom he took
but an unwilling leave, which was visible enough to everyone
there, since they were all acquainted with his passion for my
fair friend.

About twelve o'clock on the day prefixed, young Goodland
came to dine with Sir Philip, whom he found just returned
from court in a very good humour. On the sight of Valentine,
the knight ran to him and, embracing him, told him that he
had prevented his wishes in coming thither before he sent for
him, as he had just then designed. T'other returned that he
therefore hoped he might be of some service to him by so
happy a prevention of his intended kindness. 'No doubt,'
replied Sir Philip, 'the kindness, I hope, will be to us both; I
am assured it will, if you will act according to my measures.' 'I
desire no better prescriptions for my happiness', returned
Valentine, 'than what you shall please to set down to me. But
is it necessary or convenient that I should know 'em first?' 'It
is,' answered Sir Philip, 'let us sit and you shall understand

'em. I am very sensible', continued he, 'of your sincere and honourable affection and pretension to my niece, who, perhaps, is as dear to me as my own child could be, had I one; nor am I ignorant how averse Sir George your father is to your marriage with her, in so much that I am confident he would disinherit you immediately upon it, merely for want of a fortune somewhat proportionable to your estate; but I have now contrived the means to add two or three thousand pounds to the five hundred I designed to give with her: I mean, if you marry her, Val, not otherwise. For I will not labour so for any other man.' 'What inviolable obligations you put upon me!', cried Goodland. 'No returns by way of compliments, good Val,' said the knight. 'Had I not engaged to my wife before marriage that I would not dispose of any part of what she brought me without her consent, I would certainly make Philibella's fortune answerable to your estate. And besides, my wife is not yet full eight and twenty, and we may therefore expect children of our own, which hinders me from proposing anything more for the advantage of my niece—but now to my instructions. King will be here this evening without fail, and, at some time or other tonight, will show the haughtiness of his temper to you, I doubt not, since you are in a manner a stranger to him. Be sure therefore you seem to quarrel with him before you part, but suffer as much as you can first from his tongue, for I know he will give you occasions enough to exercise your passive valour. I must appear his friend, and you must retire home, if you please, for this night, but let me see you early as your convenience will permit tomorrow. My late friend Lucy must be my niece too—observe this and leave the rest to me.' 'I shall most punctually, and will in all things be directed by you,' returned Valentine. 'I had forgot to tell you', said Friendly, 'that I have so ordered matters that he must be king tonight and Lucy queen, by the lots in the cake.' 'By all means,' returned Goodland, 'it must be Majesty.'

Exactly at six o'clock came Wou'dbe in his coach and six, and found Sir Philip and his Lady Goodland, Philibella and Lucy ready to receive him; Lucy as fine as a duchess and almost as beautiful as she was before her fall. All things were in ample order for his entertainment. They played till supper

was served in, which was between eight and nine. The treat
was very seasonable and splendid. Just as the second course
was set on the table, they were all on a sudden surprised,
except Wou'dbe, with a flourish of violins and other instruments, which proceeded to entertain 'em with the best and
newest airs in the last new plays, being then in the year 1683.
The ladies were curious to know to whom they owed this
cheerful part of their entertainment, on which he called out,
'Hey! Tom Farmer! Aleworth! Eccles! Hall! And the rest of
you! Here's a health to these ladies, and all this honourable
company.' They bowed, he drank, and commanded another
glass to be filled, into which he put something yet better than
the wine—I mean, ten guineas. 'Here, Farmer,' said he then,
'this for you and your friends.' 'We humbly thank the honourable Mr Wou'dbe King,' they all returned, and struck up with
more sprightliness than before. For gold and wine, doubtless,
are the best rosin for musicians.

After supper, they took a hearty glass or two to the King,
Queen, Duke, etc. And then the mighty cake,* teeming with
the fate of this extraordinary personage, was brought in, the
musicians playing an overture at the entrance of the alimental
oracle, which was then cut and consulted, and the royal bean
and pea fell to those to whom Sir Philip had designed 'em.
'Twas then the knight began a merry bumper, with three
huzzahs, and, 'Long live King Wou'dbe' to Goodland, who
echoed and pledged him, putting the glass about to the harmoni-
ous attendants, while the ladies drank their own quantities
among themselves to His aforesaid Majesty. Then of course,
you may believe, Queen Lucy's health went merrily around
with the same ceremony. After which he saluted his royal
consort and condescended to do the same honour to the two
other ladies.

Then they fell a-dancing like lightning, I mean they moved
as swift and made almost as little noise. But His Majesty was
soon weary of that, for he longed to be making love both to
Philibella and Lucy, who (believe me) that night might well
enough have passed for a queen.

They fell then to questions and commands; to cross-pur-
poses; I think a thought, what is it like? etc.* In all which His

Wou'dbe Majesty took the opportunity of showing the excellency of his parts, as, how fit he was to govern, how dexterous at mining and counter-mining, and how he could reconcile the most contrary and distant thoughts. The music at last, good as it was, grew troublesome and too loud, which made him dismiss 'em, and then he began to this effect, addressing himself to Philibella: 'Madam, had fortune been just, and were it possible that the world should be governed and influenced by two suns, undoubtedly we had all been subjects to you from this night's chance, as well as to that lady, who, indeed, alone can equal you in the empire of beauty, which yet you share with Her Majesty here present, who only could dispute it with you and is only superior to you in title.' 'My wife is infinitely obliged to Your Majesty,' interrupted Sir Philip, 'who, in my opinion, has greater charms, and more than both of 'em together.' 'You ought to think so, Sir Philip,' returned the new-dubbed king. 'However, you should not so liberally have expressed yourself in opposition and derogation to Majesty. Let me tell you, 'tis a saucy boldness that thus has loosed your tongue. What think you, young kinsman and counsellor?', said he to Goodland. 'With all respect due to your sacred title,' returned Valentine, rising and bowing, 'Sir Philip spoke as became a truly affectionate husband, and it had been presumption in him unpardonable to have seemed to prefer Her Majesty or that other sweet lady in his thoughts, since Your Majesty has been pleased to say so much and so particularly of their merits, 'twould appear as if he durst lift up his eyes with thoughts too near the heaven you only would enjoy.' 'And only can deserve, you should have added,' said King, no longer Wou'dbe. 'How, may it please Your Majesty,' cried Friendly, 'both my nieces! Though you deserve ten thousand more, and better, would Your Majesty enjoy 'em both?' 'Are they then both your nieces?', asked chance's king. 'Yes, both, Sir,' returned the knight, 'Her Majesty's the eldest, and in that fortune has shown some justice.' 'So she has,' replied the titular monarch, 'my lot is fair,' pursued he, 'though I can be blessed but with one:

> "Let majesty with majesty be joined,
> To 'get* and leave a race of kings behind."

'Come, Madam,' continued he, kissing Lucy, 'this, as an earnest of our future endeavours.' 'I fear', returned the pretty queen, 'Your Majesty will forget the unhappy Statira, when you return to the embraces of your dear and beautiful Roxana.'* 'There is none beautiful but you,' replied the titular king, 'unless this lady, to whom I yet could pay my vows most zealously, were't not that fortune thus has pre-engaged me. But, Madam,' continued he, 'to show that still you hold our royal favour and that, next to our royal consort we esteem you, we greet you thus,' kissing Philibella, 'and, as a signal of our continued love, wear this rich diamond.' (Here he put a diamond ring on her finger worth three hundred pounds.) 'Your Majesty', pursued he to Lucy, 'may please to wear this necklace, with this locket of emeralds.' 'Your Majesty is bounteous as a god,' said Valentine. 'Art thou in want, young spark?' asked the King of Bantam, 'I'll give thee an estate shall make thee merit the mistress of thy vows, be she who she will.' 'That is my other niece, Sir,' cried Friendly. 'How! How! Presumptuous youth! How are thy eyes and thoughts exalted?' 'Ha! To bliss Your Majesty must never hope for,' replied Goodland. 'How now, thou creature of the basest mould! Not hope for what thou dost aspire to!' 'Mock King, thou canst not, darest not, shall not hope it,' returned Valentine in a heat. 'Hold, Val!' cried Sir Philip, 'you grow warm, forget your duty to Their Majesties and abuse your friends by making us suspected.' 'Goodnight, dear Philibella, and my queen!' 'Madam, I am your ladyship's servant,' said Goodland. 'Farewell, Sir Philip. Adieu thou pageant! Thou Property King! I shall see thy brother on the stage ere long; but first I'll visit thee, and in the meantime, by way of return to thy proffered estate, I will add a real territory to the rest of thy empty titles; for, from thy education, barbarous manner of conversation and complexion, I think I may justly proclaim thee King of Bantam. So, hail King that would be. Hail, thou King of Christmas. All hail, Wou'dbe, King of Bantam.' And so he left 'em. They all seemed amazed, and gazed on one another without speaking a syllable, till Sir Philip broke the charm and sighed out, 'O, the monstrous effects of passion!' 'Say rather, O, the foolish effects of a mean education!,' interrupted His Majesty of Bantam, 'for passions were given us for use, reason to govern and direct us in the use, and education to cultivate and refine that reason. But', pursued he, 'for all his impudence to me, which I shall take a time to correct, I am obliged to him that at last he has found me out a kingdom to my title, and if I were monarch of that place, believe me, ladies, I would make you all princesses and duchesses, and thou, my old companion Friendly, shouldst rule the roost with me. But these ladies should be with us there, where we would erect temples and altars to 'em, build golden palaces of love and castles—' 'In the air,' interrupted Her Majesty Lucy the First, smiling. ''Gad, take me,' cried King Wou'dbe, 'thou dear partner of my greatness, and shalt be of all my pleasures! Thy pretty satirical observation has obliged me beyond imitation.' 'I think Your Majesty is got into a vein of rhyming tonight,' said Philadelphia. 'Aye, pox o' that young, insipid fop, we could else have been as great as an emperor of China, and as witty as Horace in his wine; but let him go, like a pragmatical, captious, giddy fool, as he is. I shall take a time to see him.' 'Nay, Sir,' said Philibella, 'he has promised Your Majesty a visit in our hearing. Come, Sir, I beg Your Majesty to pledge me this glass to your long and happy reign, laying aside all thoughts of ungoverned youth. Besides, this discourse must needs be ungrateful to Her Majesty, to whom, I fear, he will be married within this month.' 'How!' cried King and No King, 'married to my queen! I must not, cannot, suffer it!' 'Pray restrain yourself a little, Sir,' said Sir Philip, 'and when once these ladies have left us, I will discourse Your Majesty further about this business.' 'Well, pray Sir Philip,' said his lady, 'let not Your Worship be pleased to sit up too long for His Majesty; about five o'clock I shall expect you. 'Tis your old hour.' 'And yours, Madam, to wake to receive me coming to bed. Your Ladyship understands me,' returned Friendly. 'You're merry, my love, you're merry,' cried Philadelphia. 'Come, niece, to bed, to bed!' 'Aye,' said the knight, 'go both of you and sleep together, if you can, without the thoughts of a lover or a husband.'

His Majesty was pleased to wish 'em a good repose, and so, with a kiss, they parted for that time.

'Now, we're alone,' said Sir Philip, 'let me assure you, Sir, I resent this affront done to you by Mister Goodland almost as highly as you can, and though I can't wish that you should take such satisfaction as, perhaps, some other hotter sparks would, yet let me say his miscarriage ought not to go unpunished in him.' 'Fear not,' replied t'other, 'I shall give him a sharp lesson.' 'No, Sir,' returned Friendly, 'I would not have you think of a bloody revenge, for 'tis that which, possibly, he designs on you. I know him brave as any man. However, were it convenient that the sword should determine betwixt you, you should not want mine: the affront is partly to me, since done in my house, but I've already laid down safer measures for us, though of more fatal consequence to him. That is, I formed 'em in my thoughts. Dismiss your coach and equipage, all but one servant, and I will discourse it to you at large. 'Tis now past twelve and, if you please, I would invite you to take up as easy a lodging here as my house will afford.' (Accordingly, they were dismissed, and he proceeded.) 'As I hinted to you before, he is in love with my youngest niece Philibella, but her fortune not exceeding five hundred pound, his father will assuredly disinherit him if he marries her, though he has given his consent that he should marry her eldest sister, whose father dying ere he knew his wife was with child of the youngest, left Lucy three thousand pounds, being as much as he thought convenient to match her handsomely, and accordingly the nuptials of young Goodland and Lucy are to be celebrated next Easter.' 'They shall not if I can hinder 'em,' interrupted His offended Majesty. 'Never endeavour the obstruction,' said the knight, 'for I'll show you the way to a dearer vengeance. Women are women, Your Majesty knows. She may be won to your embraces before that time, and then you antedate him your creature.' 'A cuckold, you mean,' cried King in Fancy, 'O exquisite revenge. But can you consent that I should attempt it?' 'What is it to me? We live not in Spain, where all the male relations of the family are obliged to vindicate a whore; no, I would wound him in his most tender part.' 'But how shall we compass it?' asked t'other. 'Why thus, throw away three thousand pounds on the youngest sister as a portion to make her as happy as she can be in her new lover,

Sir Frederick Flygold, an extravagant young fop, and wholly given over to gaming. So, ten to one but you may retrieve your money of him and have the two sisters at your devotion.' 'O, thou my better genius than that which was given to me by Heaven at my birth! What thanks, what praises shall I return and sing to thee for this!' cried King Conundrum. 'No thanks, no praises, I beseech Your Majesty, since in this I gratify myself. You think I am your friend, and you'll agree to this?' said Friendly, by way of question. 'Most readily,' returned the Fop-King, 'would it were broad day, that I might send for the money to my bankers, for in all my life, in all my frolics, encounters and extravagancies, I never had one so grateful and pleasant as this will be, if you are in earnest to gratify both my love and revenge.' 'That I am in earnest, you will not doubt when you see with what application I shall pursue my design. In the meantime, my duty to Your Majesty, to our good success in this affair.'

While he drank, t'other returned, 'With all my heart', and pledged him. Then Friendly began afresh: 'Leave the whole management of this to me. Only one thing more I think necessary: that you make a present of five hundred guineas to Her Majesty, the bride that must be.' 'By all means,' returned the wealthy King of Bantam, 'I had so designed before.' 'Well, Sir,' said Sir Philip, 'what think you of a set party of two at piquet* to pass away some few hours till we can sleep.' 'A seasonable and welcome proposition,' returned that King, 'but I won't play above twenty guineas the game and forty the lurch.' 'Agreed,' said Friendly, 'first call in your servant, mine is here already.' The slave came in, and they began with unequal fortune at first, for the knight had lost an hundred guineas to Majesty, which he paid in specie,* and then proposed fifty guineas the game and an hundred the lurch, to which t'other consented and without winning more than three games, and those not together, made shift to get three thousand two hundred guineas in debt to Sir Philip, for which Majesty was pleased to give him bond, whether Friendly would or no, sealed and delivered 'In the presence of The Mark of (W.) Will Watchful, and (S.) Sim. Slyboots', a couple of delicate beagles, their mighty attendants.

It was then about the hour that Sir Philip's and, it may be, other ladies, began to yawn and stretch, when the spirits, refreshed, troul'd* about and tickled the blood with desires of action, which made Majesty and Worship think of a retreat to bed, where, in less than half an hour, or before ever he could say his prayers, I'm sure the first fell fast asleep, but the last, perhaps, paid his accustomed devotion ere he began his progress to the shadow of death. However, he waked earlier than his cully* Majesty, and got up to receive young Goodland, who came to his word with the first opportunity. Sir Philip received him with more than usual joy, though not with greater kindness, and let him know every syllable and accident that had passed between 'em till they went to bed, which you may believe was not a little pleasantly surprising to Valentine, who began then to have some assurance of his happiness with Philibella. His friend told him that he must now be reconciled to his Mock Majesty, though with some difficulty. And so, taking one hearty glass a piece, he left Valentine in the parlour to carry the ungrateful news of his visit to him that morning. King — was in an odd sort of taking when he heard that Valentine was below, and had been, as Sir Philip informed Majesty, at Majesty's palace to enquire for him there, but when he told him that he had already schooled him on his own behalf for the affront done in his house, and that he believed he could bring His Majesty off without any loss of present honour, his countenance visibly discovered his past fear and present satisfaction, which was much increased too when Friendly, showing him his bond for the money he won of him at play, let him know that if he paid three thousand guineas to Philibella, he would immediately deliver him up his bond and not expect the two hundred guineas overplus. His Majesty of Bantam was then in so good an humour that he could have made love to Sir Philip, nay, I believe he could a kissed Valentine instead of seeming angry.

Down they came and saluted like gentlemen, but after the greeting was over, Goodland began to talk something of affront, satisfaction, honour, etc., when immediately Friendly interposed and, after a little seeming uneasiness, and reluctancy, reconciled the hot and choleric youth to the cold, phlegmatic King.

Peace was no sooner proclaimed than the King of Bantam took his rival and late antagonist with him in his own coach, not excluding Sir Philip by any means, to Locket's,* where they dined. Thence he would have 'em to court with him, where he met the Lady Flippant, the Lady Harpy, the Lady Crocodile, Madam Tattlemore, Miss Meddler, Mrs Gingerly, a rich grocer's wife, and some others, besides knights and gentlemen of as good humours as the ladies, all whom he invited to a ball at his own house the night following, his own lady being then in the country. Madam Tattlemore, I think, was the first he spoke to in court, and whom first he surprised with the happy news of his advancement to the title of King of Bantam. How wondrous hasty was she to be gone as soon as she heard it! 'Twas not in her power, because not in her nature, to stay long enough to take a civil leave of the company, but away she flew, big with the empty title of a fantastic king, proclaiming it to every one of her acquaintance as she passed through every room, till she came to the presence chamber, where she only whispered it, but her whispers made above half the honourable company quit the presence of the King of Great Britain to go make their court to His Majesty of Bantam; some cried, 'God bless Your Majesty!', some 'Long live the King of Bantam!', others 'All hail to Your Sacred Majesty!' In short, he was congratulated on all sides. Indeed, I don't hear that His Majesty King Charles II ever sent any ambassador to compliment him, though possibly he saluted him by his title the first time he saw him afterwards; for, you know, he is a wonderful good-natured and a well-bred gentleman.

After he thought the court of England was universally acquainted with his mighty honour, he was pleased to think fit to retire to his own, more private palace, with Sir Philip and Goodland, whom he entertained that night very handsomely till about seven a clock, when they went together to the play, which was that night *A King and No King.** His attendant friends could not forbear smiling to think how aptly the title of the play suited his circumstances. Nor could he choose but take notice of it behind the scenes between jest and earnest, telling the players how kind fortune had been the night past in disposing the bean to him, and justifying what one of her prophetesses had foretold some years since. 'I shall now no more regard', said he, 'that old, doting fellow Pythagoras' saying "abstineto à fabis", that is,' added he by way of construction, ' "abstain from beans". For I find the excellency of 'em in cakes and dishes; from the first they inspire the soul with mighty thoughts, and from the last our bodies receive a strong and wholesome nourishment.' 'That is,' said a wag among those sharp youths, I think 'twas my friend the count, 'these puff you up in mind, Sir, those in body.' They had some further discourse among the nymphs of the stage ere they went in to the pit, where Sir Philip spread the news of his friend's accession to the title, though not yet to the throne, of Bantam, upon which he was there again complimented on that occasion. Several of the ladies and gentlemen who saluted him he invited to the next night's ball at his palace.

The play done, they took each of 'em a bottle at the Rose,* and parted till seven the night following, which came not sooner than desired, for he had taken such care that all things were in readiness before eight, only he was to expect the music till the end of the play. About nine, Sir Philip, his lady, Goodland, Philibella and Lucy came. Sir Philip returned him Rabelais, which he had borrowed of him, wherein the knight had written in an old, odd sort of character, this prophecy of his own making, with which he surprised the Majesty of Bantam, who vowed he had never taken notice of 'em before, but he said he perceived they had been long written, by the character. And here it follows, as near as I can remember:

> When MDC come L before
> Three XXXs, two Is and one I more,*
> Then, king, though now but name to thee,
> Shall both thy name and title be.

They had hardly made an end of reading 'em, ere the whole company, and more than he had invited, came in and were received with a great deal of formality and magnificence. Lucy was there, attended as his queen, and Philibella, as the princess her sister. They danced then till they were weary, and afterwards retired to another large room, where they found the tables spread and furnished with all the most seasonable cold meats, which was succeeded by the choicest fruits and the richest dessert of sweetmeats that luxury could think on, or, at least, that this town could afford. The wines were all most excellent in their kind, and their spirits flew about through every corner of the house. There was scarce a spark sober in the whole company, with drinking repeated glasses to the health of the King of Bantam and his royal consort, with the princess Philibella's, who sate together under a royal canopy of state, His Majesty between the two beautiful sisters. Only Friendly and Goodland wisely managed that part of the engagement where they were concerned, and preserved themselves from the heat of the debauch.

Between three and four most of 'em began to draw off, laden with fruit and sweetmeats, and rich favours composed of yellow, green, red, and white, the colours of His new Majesty of Bantam. Before five, they were left to themselves, when the Lady Friendly was discomposed for want of sleep, and her usual cordial, which obliged Sir Philip to wait on her home with his two nieces. But His Majesty would by no means part with Goodland, whom, before nine that morning, he made as drunk as a lord, and by consequence one of his peers, for Majesty was then indeed as great as an emperor. He fancied himself Alexander, and young Valentine his Hephaestion, and did so bebuss* him, that the young gentleman feared he was fallen into the hands of an Italian. However, by the kind persuasions of His condescending and dissembling Majesty, he ventured to go into bed with him, where King Wou'dbe fell asleep, hand-over-head, and not long after Goodland, his new-made peer, followed him to the cool retreats of Morpheus.

About three the next afternoon they both waked as by consent, and called to dress. And after that business was over, I think they swallowed each of 'em a pint of old hock, with a little sugar, by the way of healing. Their coaches were got ready in the meantime, but the peer was forced to accept of the honour of being carried in His Majesty's to Sir Philip's, whom they found just risen from dinner with Philadelphia and his two nieces. They sat down, and asked for something to relish a glass of wine, and Sir Philip ordered a cold chine* to be set before 'em, of which they eat about an ounce a piece, but they drank more by the half, I dare say.

After their little repast, Friendly called the would-be monarch aside and told him that he would have him go [to]* the play that night, which was *The London Cuckolds,** promising to meet him there in less than half an hour after his departure, telling him withal that he would surprise him with a much better entertainment than the stage afforded. Majesty took the hint, imagining, and that rightly, that the knight had some intrigue in his head for the promotion of the commonwealth of cuckoldom. In order therefore to his advice, he took his leave about a quarter of an hour after.

When he was gone, Sir Philip thus bespoke his pretended niece. 'Madam, I hope Your Majesty will not refuse me the honour of waiting on you to a place where you will meet with better entertainment than Your Majesty can expect from the best comedy in Christendom. Val,' continued he, 'you must go with us to secure me against the jealousy of my wife.' 'That, indeed,' returned his lady, 'is very material, and you are mightily concerned not to give me occasion, I must own.' 'You see I am now,' replied he, 'but—come, on with hoods and scarf,' pursued he to Lucy. Then addressing himself again to his lady, 'Madam,' said he, 'we'll wait on you in less time than I could have drank a bottle to my share.' The coach was got ready, and on they drove to the playhouse. 'By the way,' said Friendly to Val, 'Your Honour, noble peer, must be set down at Long's,* for only Lucy and I must be seen to His Majesty of Bantam, and now, I doubt not, you understand what you must trust to.' 'To be robbed of Her Majesty's company, I warrant,' returned t'other, 'for these long three hours.' 'Why,' cried Lucy, 'you don't mean, I hope, to leave me with His Majesty of Bantam?' ''Tis for thy good, child, 'tis for thy good,' returned Friendly.

To the Rose they got then, where Goodland lighted and expected Sir Philip, who led Lucy into the King's box to His New Majesty, where, after the first scene, he left 'em together. The overjoyed fantastic monarch would feign have said some fine, obliging things to the knight as he was going out, but Friendly's haste prevented 'em, who went directly to Valentine, took one glass, called a reckoning, mounted chariot, and away home they came, where, I believe, he was welcome to his lady, for I never heard anything to the contrary.

In the meantime, His Majesty had not the patience to stay out half the play, at which he was saluted by above twenty gentlemen and ladies by his new and mighty title, but out he led Miss Majesty ere the third act was half done, pretending that it was so damned bawdy a play that he knew her modesty had been already but too much offended at it, so into his coach he got her. When they were seated, she told him she would go to no place with him, but to the lodgings her mother had taken for her when she first came to town, and which still she kept. 'Your mother, Madam!' cried he. 'Why, is Sir Philip's sister living then?' 'His brother's widow is, Sir,' she replied. 'Is she there?' he asked. 'No, Sir,' she returned, 'she's in the country.' 'O, then we'll go thither to choose.' The coachman was then ordered to drive to Germin's Street,* where, when he came into the lodgings, he found 'em very rich and modishly furnished. He presently called one of his slaves, and whispered him to get three or four pretty dishes for supper, and then getting a pen, ink and paper, writ a note to C——d,* the goldsmith, within Temple Bar, for five hundred guineas, which Watchwell brought him in little more than an hour's time when they were just in the height of supper, Lucy having invited her landlady for the better colour of the matter. His Bantamite Majesty took the gold from his slave, and threw it by him in the window, that Lucy might take notice of it, which you may assure yourself she did, and after supper, winked on the goodly matron of the house to retire, which she immediately obeyed. Then His Majesty began his court very earnestly and hotly, throwing the naked guineas into her lap, which she seemed to refuse with much disdain; but, upon his repeated promises, confirmed by unheard of oaths and imprecations, that he would give her sister three thousand guineas to her portion, she began by degrees to mollify, and let the gold lie quietly in her lap. And the next night after he had drawn notes on two or three of his bankers for the payment of three thousand guineas to Sir Philip, or order, and received his own bond made for what he had lost at play from Friendly, she made no great difficulty to admit His Majesty to her bed, where I think fit to leave 'em for the present, for (perhaps) they had some private business.

The next morning, before the titular king was (I won't say up or stirring, but) out o' bed, young Goodland and Philibella were privately married, the bills being all accepted and paid in two days' time. As soon as ever the fantastic monarch could find in his heart to divorce himself from the dear and charming embraces of his beautiful bedfellow, he came flying to Sir Philip with all the haste that imagination, big with pleasure, could inspire him with, to discharge itself to a supposed friend. The knight told him that he was really much troubled to find that his niece had yielded so soon and easily to him; however, he wished him joy. To which t'other returned, that he could never want it whilst he had the command of so much beauty, and that without the ungrateful obligations of matrimony, which certainly are the most nauseous, hateful, pernicious, and destructive of love imaginable. 'Think you so, Sir?' asked the knight. 'We shall hear what a friend of mine will say on such an occasion tomorrow about this time. But I beseech Your Majesty to conceal your sentiments of it to him, lest you make him as uneasy as you seem to be in that circumstance.' 'Be assured I will,' returned t'other. 'But when shall I see the sweet, the dear, the blooming, the charming Philibella?' 'She will be with us at dinner. Where's Her Majesty?' asked Sir Philip. 'Had you enquired before, she had been here, for, look, she comes.' Friendly seemed to regard her with a kind of displeasure, and whispered Majesty that he should express no particular symptoms of familiarity with Lucy in his house at any time, especially when Goodland was there, as then he was above with his lady and Philibella, who came down presently after to dinner.

About four o' clock, as His Majesty had intrigued with her, Lucy took a hackney coach and went to her lodgings, whither about an hour after he followed her. Next morning, at nine, he came to Friendly's, who carried him up to see his new-married friends—but (O damnation to thought!) what torments did he feel when he saw young Goodland and Philibella in bed together, the last of which returned him humble and hearty thanks for her portion and husband, as the first did for his wife. He shook his head at Sir Philip, and without speaking one word, left 'em and hurried to Lucy, to lament the ill treatment he had met with from Friendly. They cooed and billed as long as he was able; she (sweet hypocrite) seeming to 'moan his misfortunes, which he took so kindly that when he left her, which was about three in the afternoon, he caused a scrivener to draw up an instrument wherein he settled a hundred pounds a year on Lucy for her life, and gave her an hundred guineas more against her lying in, for she told him (and indeed 'twas true) that she was with child, and knew herself to be so from a very good reason. And indeed she was so—by the friendly knight.

When he returned to her, he threw the obliging instrument into her lap (it seems he had a particular kindness for that place), then called for wine, and something to eat, for he had not drank a pint to his share all the day (though he had plied it at the chocolate house). The landlady, who was invited to sup with 'em, bid 'em goodnight about eleven, when they went to bed and, partly, slept till about six, when they were entertained by some gentlemen of their acquaintance, who played and sung very finely by way of epithalamium these words and more:

> Joy to great Bantam!
> Live long love and wanton.
> And thy royal consort.
> For, both are of one sort, etc.

The rest I have forgot. He took some offence at the words, but more at the visit that Sir Philip and Goodland made him about an hour after, who found him in bed with his royal consort, and after having wished 'em joy, and thrown their Majesties' own shoes and stockings at their heads, retreated. This gave monarch in fancy so great a caution that he took his royal consort into the country (but above forty miles off the place where his own lady was), where, in less than eight months, she was delivered of a princely babe, who was christened by the heathenish name of Hayoumorecake Bantam, while Her Majesty lay in like a petty queen.

THE HISTORY OF THE NUN;

OR,

THE FAIR VOW-BREAKER

To the most illustrious princess, the Duchess of Mazarine.*

Madam, there are none of an illustrious quality who have not been made by some poet or other the patronesses of his distressed hero or unfortunate damsel, and such addresses are tributes due only to the most elevated, where they have always been very well received, since they are the greatest testimonies we can give of our esteem and veneration.

Madam, when I survey the whole toor* of ladies at court, which was adorned by you, who appeared there with a grace and majesty peculiar to your great self only, mixed with an irresistible air of sweetness, generosity, and wit, I was impatient for an opportunity to tell Your Grace how infinitely one of your own sex adored you, and that, among all the numerous conquest* Your Grace has made over the hearts of men, Your Grace had not subdued a more entire slave; I assure you, Madam, there is neither compliment, nor poetry in this humble declaration, but a truth which has cost me a great deal of inquietude, for that fortune has not set me in such a station as might justify my pretence to the honour and satisfaction of being ever near Your Grace, to view eternally that lovely person and hear that surprising wit; what can be more grateful to a heart than so great and so agreeable an entertainment? And how few objects are there that can render it so entire a pleasure as at once to hear you speak and to look upon your beauty? A beauty that is heightened, if possible, with an air of negligence in dress wholly charming, as if your beauty disdained those little arts of your sex which nicety alone is their greatest charm, while yours, Madam, even without the assistance of your exalted birth, begets an awe and reverence in all that do approach you, and everyone is proud and pleased in paying you homage their several ways according to their capacities and talents; mine, Madam, can only be expressed by my pen, which would be infinitely honoured in being permitted to celebrate your great name forever, and perpetually to serve where it has so great an inclination.

In the meantime, Madam, I presume to lay this little trifle at your feet; the story is true, as it is on the records of the town where it was transacted; and if my fair, unfortunate vow-breaker do not deserve the honour of Your Grace's protection, at least she will be found worthy of your pity, which will be a sufficient glory both for her and,

Madam,

Your Grace's most humble and most obedient servant,

A. Behn.

Of all the sins incident to human nature, there is none of which Heaven has took so particular, visible, and frequent notice and revenge as on that of violated vows, which never go unpunished, and the cupids may boast what they will for the encouragement of their trade of love, that Heaven never takes cognisance of lovers' broken vows and oaths, and that 'tis the only perjury that escapes the anger of the gods. But I verily believe, if it were searched into, we should find these frequent perjuries that pass in the world for so many gallantries only to be the occasion of so many unhappy marriages, and the cause of all those misfortunes which are so frequent to the nuptialled pair. For not one of a thousand but, either on his side, or on hers, has been perjured and broke vows made to some fond believing wretch, whom they have abandoned and undone. What man that does not boast of the numbers he has thus ruined, and who does not glory in the shameful triumph? Nay, what woman, almost, has not a pleasure in deceiving, taught, perhaps, at first by some dear false one, who had fatally instructed her youth in an art she ever after practised in revenge on all those she could be too hard for and conquer at their own weapons? For, without all dispute, women are by nature more constant and just than men, and did not their first lovers teach them the trick of change, they would be doves that would never quit their mate and, like Indian wives, would leap alive into the graves of their deceased lovers and be

buried quick with 'em. But customs of countries change, even
nature herself, and long habit takes her place. The women are
taught by the lives of the men to live up to all their vices, and
are become almost as inconstant, and 'tis but modesty that
makes the difference and, hardly, inclination; so depraved the
nicest appetites grow in time by bad examples.

But, as there are degrees of vows, so there are degrees of
punishments for vows. There are solemn matrimonial vows,
such as contract and are the most effectual marriage, and have
the most reason to be so; there are a thousand vows and
friendships that pass between man and man on a thousand
occasions, but there is another vow, called a sacred vow, made
to God only, and by which we oblige ourselves eternally to
serve Him with all chastity and devotion. This vow is only
taken and made by those that enter into holy orders, and, of all
broken vows, these are those that receive the most severe and
notorious revenges of God, and I am almost certain there is
not one example to be produced in the world where perjuries
of this nature have passed unpunished, nay, that have not been
pursued with the greatest and most rigorous of punishments. I
could myself of my own knowledge give an hundred examples
of the fatal consequences of the violation of sacred vows, and
whoever make it their business and are curious in the search of
such misfortunes shall find as I say that they never go unregarded.

The young beauty therefore who dedicates herself to
Heaven and weds herself forever to the service of God ought
first very well to consider the self-denial she is going to put
upon her youth, her fickle faithless deceiving youth, of one
opinion today, and of another tomorrow; like flowers which
never remain in one state or fashion but bud today and blow
by insensible degrees and decay as imperceptibly. The resolution we promise and believe we shall maintain, is not in our
power, and nothing is so deceitful as human hearts.

I once was designed an humble votary in the house of
devotion,* but fancying myself not endued with an obstinacy
of mind great enough to secure me from the efforts and
vanities of the world, I rather chose to deny myself that
content I could not certainly promise myself, than to languish

(as I have seen some do) in a certain affliction, though possibly since I have sufficiently bewailed that mistaken and inconsiderate approbation and preference of the false, ungrateful world (full of nothing but nonsense, noise, false notions, and contradiction) before the innocence and quiet of a cloister. Nevertheless, I could wish, for the prevention of abundance of mischiefs and miseries, that nunneries and marriages were not to be entered into till the maid so destined were of a mature age to make her own choice, and that parents would not make use of their justly assumed authority to compel their children neither to the one or the other, but since I cannot alter custom, nor shall ever be allowed to make new laws or rectify the old ones, I must leave the young nuns enclosed to their best endeavours of making a virtue of necessity, and the young wives, to make the best of a bad market.

In Iper,* a town not long since in the dominions of the King of Spain, and now in possession of the King of France, there lived a man of quality of a considerable fortune called Count Henrick de Vallary, who had a very beautiful lady, by whom he had one daughter called Isabella, whose mother dying when she was about two years old, to the unspeakable grief of the count, her husband, he resolved never to partake of any pleasure more that this transitory world could court him with, but determined with himself to dedicate his youth and future days to Heaven, and to take upon him holy orders, and, without considering that possibly the young Isabella when she grew to woman might have sentiments contrary to those that now possessed him, he designed she should also become a nun. However, he was not so positive in that resolution as to put the matter wholly out of her choice, but divided his estate; one half he carried with him to the monastery of Jesuits, of which number he became one, and the other half he gave with Isabella to the monastery, of which his only sister was lady abbess of the order of St Augustine. But so he ordered the matter that if at the age of thirteen Isabella had not a mind to take orders, or that the lady abbess found her inclination averse to a monastic life, she should have such a proportion of the revenue as should be fit to marry her to a nobleman, and left it to the discretion of the lady abbess, who was a lady of known piety, and admirable strictness of life, and so nearly related to Isabella, that there was no doubt made of her integrity and justice.

The little Isabella was carried immediately (in her mourning for her dead mother) into the nunnery and was received as a very diverting companion by all the young ladies and, above all, by her reverend aunt, for she was come just to the age of delighting her parents; she was the prettiest forward prattler in the world, and had a thousand little charms to please, besides the young beauties that were just budding in her little angel face, so that she soon became the dear loved favourite of the whole house; and as she was an entertainment to them all, so they made it their study to find all the diversions they could for the pretty Isabella, and as she grew in wit and beauty every day, so they failed not to cultivate her mind and delicate apprehension in all that was advantageous to her sex; and whatever excellency anyone abounded in, she was sure to communicate it to the young Isabella. If one could dance, another sing, another play on this instrument, and another on that, if this spoke one language, and that another, if she had wit, and she discretion, and a third the finest fashion and manners, all joined to complete the mind and body of this beautiful young girl, who, being undiverted with the less noble and less solid vanities of the world, took to these virtues and excelled in all, and her youth and wit being apt for all impressions, she soon became a greater mistress of their arts than those who taught her, so that at the age of eight or nine years, she was thought fit to receive and entertain all the great men and ladies and the strangers of any nation at the grate, and that with so admirable a grace, so quick and piercing a wit, and so delightful and sweet a conversation, that she became the whole discourse of the town, and strangers spread her fame as prodigious throughout the Christian world, for strangers came daily to hear her talk and sing and play, and to admire her beauty, and ladies brought their children to shame 'em into good fashion and manners with looking on the lovely young Isabella.

The lady abbess, her aunt, you may believe, was not a little proud of the excellencies and virtues of her fair niece, and omitted nothing that might adorn her mind, because not only of the vastness of her parts and fame, and the credit she would do her house by residing there forever, but also being very loathe to part with her considerable fortune, which she must resign if she returned into the world, she used all her arts and stratagems to make her become a nun, to which all the fair sisterhood contributed their cunning; but it was altogether needless: her inclination, the strictness of her devotion, her early prayers, and those* continual and innate steadfastness and calm she was mistress of, her ignorance of the world's vanities, and those that unenclosed young ladies count pleasures and diversions being all unknown to her, she thought there was no joy out of a nunnery, and no satisfactions on the other side of a grate.

The lady abbess, seeing that of herself she yielded faster than she could expect, to discharge her conscience to her brother, who came frequently to visit his darling Isabella, would very often discourse to her of the pleasures of the world, telling her how much happier she would think herself to be the wife of some gallant young cavalier, and to have coaches and equipage, to see the world, to behold a thousand rarities she had never seen, to live in splendour, to eat high and wear magnificent clothes, to be bowed to as she passed, and have a thousand adorers, to see in time a pretty offspring, the products of love that should talk and look and delight, as she did, the heart of their parents; but to all her father and the lady abbess could say of the world and its pleasures, Isabella brought a thousand reasons and arguments so pious, so devout, that the abbess was very well pleased to find her (purposely weak) propositions so well overthrown, and gives an account of her daily discourses to her brother which were no less pleasing to him, and though Isabella went already dressed as richly as her quality deserved, yet her father, to try the utmost that the world's vanity could do upon her young heart, orders the most glorious clothes should be bought her, and that the lady abbess should suffer her to go abroad with those ladies of quality that were her relations, and her mother's acquaintance; that she should visit and go on the Toor (that is, the Hyde Park there); that she should see all that was diverting, to try whether it were not for want of temptation to vanity that made her leave the world and love an enclosed life.

As the count had commanded, all things were performed, and Isabella, arriving at her thirteenth year of age, and being pretty tall of stature, with the finest shape that fancy can create, with all the adornment of a perfect brown-haired beauty, eyes black and lovely, complexion fair to a miracle, all her features of the rarest proportion, the mouth red, the teeth white, and a thousand graces in her mien and air, she came no sooner abroad but she had a thousand persons fighting for love of her; the reputation her wit had acquired got her adorers without seeing her, but when they saw her they found themselves conquered and undone; all were glad she was come into the world, of whom they had heard so much, and all the youth of the town dressed only for Isabella de Vallary. She rose like a new star that eclipsed all the rest, and which set the world a-gazing. Some hoped and some despaired, but all loved, while Isabella regarded not their eyes, their distant darling looks of love and their signs of adoration. She was civil and affable to all, but so reserved that none durst tell her his passion, or name that strange and abhorred thing, love, to her; the relations with whom she went abroad every day were fain to force her out, and when she went, 'twas the motive of civility, and not satisfaction, that made her go; whatever she saw, she beheld with no admiration, and nothing created wonder in her, though never so strange and novel. She surveyed all things with an indifference that, though it was not sullen, was far from transport, so that her evenness of mind was infinitely admired and praised. And now it was that, young as she was, her conduct and discretion appeared equal to her wit and beauty, and she increased daily in reputation, in so much that the parents of abundance of young noblemen made it their business to endeavour to marry their sons to so admirable and noble a maid, and one whose virtues were the discourse of all the world. The father, the lady abbess and those who had her abroad, were solicited to make an alliance; for the father, he would give no answer, but left it to the discretion of Isabella, who could not be persuaded to hear anything of that nature, so that for a long time she refused her company to all those who proposed anything of marriage to her; she said she had seen nothing in the world that was worth her care, or the venturing the losing of Heaven for, and therefore was resolved to dedicate herself to that; that the more she saw of the world, the worse she liked it, and pitied the wretches that were condemned to it; that she had considered it and found no one inclination that forbade her immediate entrance into a religious life, to which her father, after using all the arguments he could to make her take good heed of what she went about, to consider it well, and had urged all the inconveniencies of severe life: watchings, midnight risings in all weathers and seasons to prayers, hard lodging, coarse diet, and homely habit, with a thousand other things of labour and work used among the nuns, and finding her still resolved and inflexible to all contrary persuasion, he consented, kissed her, and told her she had argued according to the wish of his soul, and that he never believed himself truly happy till this moment that he was assured she would become a religious.

This news, to the heartbreaking of a thousand lovers, was spread all over the town, and there was nothing but songs of complaint and of her retiring after she had shown herself to the world and vanquished so many hearts; all wits were at work on this cruel subject, and one begat another, as is usual in such affairs. Amongst the number of these lovers there was a young gentleman, nobly born, his name was Villenoys, who was admirably made and very handsome, had travelled and accomplished himself as much as was possible for one so young to do. He was about eighteen, and was going to the siege of Candia* in a very good equipage, but, overtaken by his fate, surprised in his way to glory, he stopped at Iper, so fell most passionately in love with this maid of immortal fame. But, being defeated in his hopes by this news, was the man that made the softest complaints to this fair beauty, and whose violence of passion oppressed him to that degree that he was the only lover who durst himself tell her he was in love with her. He writ billets so soft and tender that she had, of all her lovers, most compassion for Villenoys, and deigned several times in pity of him to send him answers to his letters, but they were such as absolutely forbade him to love her, such as incited him to follow glory, the mistress that could noblest reward him, and that, for her part, her prayers should always be that he might be victorious and the darling of that fortune he was going to court, and that she, for her part, had fixed her mind on Heaven, and no earthly thought should bring it down, but she should ever retain for him all sisterly respect, and begged, in her solitudes, to hear whether her prayers had proved effectual or not, and if fortune was so kind to him as she should perpetually wish.

When Villenoys found she was resolved, he designed to pursue his journey, but could not leave the town till he had seen the fatal ceremony of Isabella's being made a nun, which was every day expected, and while he stayed, he could not forbear writing daily to her, but received no more answers from her, she already accusing herself of having done too much for a maid in her circumstances. But she confessed, of all she had seen, she liked Villenoys the best and if she ever could have loved, she believed it would have been Villenoys, for he had all the good qualities and grace that could render him agreeable to the fair; besides, that he was only son to a very rich and noble parent, and one that might very well presume to lay claim to a maid of Isabella's beauty and fortune.

As the time approached when he must eternally lose all hope by Isabella's taking orders, he found himself less able to bear the efforts of that despair it possessed him with; he languished with the thought so that it was visible to all his friends the decays it wrought on his beauty and gaiety. So that he fell at last into a fever, and 'twas the whole discourse of the town that Villenoys was dying for the fair Isabella; his relations, being all of quality, were extremely afflicted at his misfortune, and joined their interests yet to dissuade this fair young victoress from an act so cruel as to enclose herself in a nunnery while the finest of all the youths of quality was dying for her, and asked her if it would not be more acceptable to Heaven to save a life, and perhaps a soul, than to go and expose her own to a thousand tortures. They assured her Villenoys was dying, and dying adoring her; that nothing could save his life but her kind eyes turned upon the fainting lover, a lover that could breathe nothing but her name in sighs and find satisfaction in nothing but weeping and crying out, 'I die for Isabella!'. This discourse fetched abundance of tears from the fair eyes of this tender maid, but, at the same time, she besought them to believe these tears ought not to give them hope she should ever yield to save his life by quitting her resolution of becoming a nun, but, on the contrary, they were tears that only bewailed her own misfortune in having been the occasion of the death of any man, especially a man who had so many excellencies as might have rendered him entirely happy and glorious for a long race of years, had it not been his ill fortune to have seen her unlucky face. She believed it was for her sins of curiosity and going beyond the walls of the monastery to wander after the vanities of the foolish world that had occasioned this misfortune to the young Count of Villenoys, and she would put a severe penance on her body for the mischiefs her eyes had done him. She fears she might, by something in her looks, have enticed his heart, for she owned she saw him with wonder at his beauty, and much more she admired him when she found the beauties of his mind. She confessed she had given him hope by answering his letters, and that when she found her heart grow a little more than usually tender when she thought on him, she believed it a crime that ought to be checked by a virtue such as she pretended to profess, and hoped she should ever carry to her grave, and she desired his relations to implore him in her name to rest contented in knowing he was the first and should be the last that should ever make an impression on her heart; that what she had conceived there for him should remain with her to her dying day, and that she besought him to live that she might see he both deserved this esteem she had for him, and to repay it her, otherwise he would die in her debt, and make her life ever after reposeless.

This being all they could get from her, they returned with looks that told their message; however, they rendered those soft things Isabella had said in so moving a manner as failed not to please, and while he remained in this condition the ceremonies were completed of making Isabella a nun, which was a secret to none but Villenoys, and from him it was carefully concealed, so that in a little time he recovered his lost health, at least so well as to support the fatal news, and upon the first hearing it, he made ready his equipage and departed immediately for Candia, where he behaved himself very gallantly under the command of the Duke de Beaufort, and with him returned to France after the loss of that noble city to the Turks.

In all the time of his absence, that he might the sooner establish his repose, he forbore sending to the fair, cruel nun, and she heard no more of Villenoys in above two years, so that giving herself wholly up to devotion, there was never seen anyone who led so austere and pious a life as this young votress; she was a saint in the chapel and an angel at the grate. She there laid by all her severe looks and mortified discourse and being at perfect peace and tranquillity within, she was outwardly all gay, spritely, and entertaining, being satisfied no sights, no freedoms, could give any temptations to worldly desires. She gave a loose to all that was modest, and that virtue and honour would permit, and was the most charming conversation that ever was admired, and the whole world that passed through Iper of strangers came directed and recommended to the lovely Isabella; I mean, those of quality. But however diverting she was at the grate, she was most exemplary devout in the cloister, doing more penance and imposing a more rigid severity and task on herself than was required, giving such rare examples to all the nuns that were less devout that her life was a proverb and a precedent, and when they would express a very holy woman indeed, they would say she was a very Isabella.

There was in this nunnery a young nun called Sister Katteriena, daughter to the Grave Van Henault, that is to say, an earl, who lived about six miles from the town, in a noble villa. This Sister Katteriena was not only a very beautiful maid, but very witty, and had all the good qualities to make her be beloved, and had most wonderfully gained upon the heart of the fair Isabella; she was her chamber-fellow and companion in all her devotions and diversions, so that where one was, there was the other, and they never went but together to the grate, to the garden, or to any place whither their affairs called either. This young Katteriena had a brother, who loved her entirely, and came every day to see her. He was about twenty years of age, rather tall than middle statured, his hair and eyes brown, but his face exceeding beautiful, adorned with a thousand graces and the most nobly and exactly made that 'twas possible for nature to form; to the fineness and charms of his person, he had an air in his mien and dressing so very agreeable, besides rich, that 'twas impossible to look on him without wishing him happy because he did so absolutely merit being so. His wit and his manner were so perfectly obliging, a goodness and generosity so sincere and gallant, that it would even have atoned for ugliness. As he was eldest son to so great a father, he was kept at home while the rest of his brothers were employed in wars abroad; this made him of a melancholy temper and fit for soft impressions. He was very bookish, and had the best tutors that could be got for learning and languages and all that could complete a man, but was unused to action and of a temper lazy and given to repose, so that his father could hardly ever get him to use any exercise, or so much as ride abroad, which he would call losing time from his studies. He cared not for the conversation of men because he loved not debauch, as they usually did, so that for exercise, more than any design, he came on horseback every day to Iper to the monastery, and would sit at the grate entertaining his sister the most part of the afternoon and, in the evening, retire. He had often seen and conversed with the lovely Isabella, and found from the first sight of her, he had more esteem for her than any other of her sex. But as love very rarely takes birth without hope, so he never believed that the pleasure he took in beholding her and in discoursing with her was love, because he regarded her as a thing consecrate to Heaven, and never so much as thought to wish she were a mortal fit for his addresses; yet he found himself more and more filled with reflections on her, which was not usual with him. He found she grew upon his memory, and oftener came there than he used to do, that he loved his studies less and going to Iper more, and that every time he went he found a new joy at his heart that pleased him. He found he could not get himself from the grate without pain, nor part from the sight of that all-charming object without sighs, and if, while he was there, any persons

came to visit her whose quality she could not refuse the
honour of her sight to, he would blush and burn and pant with
uneasiness, especially if they were handsome and fit to make
impressions, and he would check this uneasiness in himself and
ask his heart what it meant by rising and beating in those
moments, and strive to assume an indifferency in vain, and
depart dissatisfied and out of humour.

On the other side, Isabella was not so gay as she used to be,
but, on the sudden, retired herself more from the grate than
she used to do, refused to receive visits every day, and her
complexion grew a little pale and languid. She was observed
not to sleep or eat as she used to do, nor exercise in those little
plays they made and diverted themselves with now and then.
She was heard to sigh often, and it became the discourse of the
whole house that she was much altered. The lady abbess, who
loved her with a most tender passion, was infinitely concerned
at this change, and endeavoured to find out the cause and
'twas generally believed she was too devout, for now she
redoubled her austerity, and in cold winter nights of frost and
snow would be up at all hours and lying upon the cold stones
before the altar prostrate at prayers, so that she received
orders from the lady abbess not to harass herself so very much,
but to have a care of her health as well as her soul. But she
regarded not these admonitions, though even persuaded daily
by her Katteriena, whom she loved every day more and more.

But, one night, when they were retired to their chamber,
amongst a thousand things that they spoke of to pass away a
tedious evening, they talked of pictures and likenesses, and
Katteriena told Isabella that before she was a nun, in her more
happy days, she was so like her brother Bernardo Henault
(who was the same that visited them every day), that she
would in men's clothes undertake she should not have known
one from t'other, and fetching out his picture she had in a
dressing box, she showed it to Isabella, who at the first sight of
it, turns as pale as ashes, and, being ready to swound,* she bid
her take it away and could not, for her soul, hide the sudden
surprise the picture brought. Katteriena had too much wit not
to make a just interpretation of this change and (as a woman)
was naturally curious to pry farther, though discretion should

have made her been silent, for talking in such cases does but make the wound rage the more. 'Why, my dear sister,' said Katteriena, 'is the likeness of my brother so offensive to you?' Isabella found by this she had discovered too much, and that thought put her by all power of excusing it; she was confounded with shame and the more she strove to hide it the more it disordered her, so that she (blushing extremely) hung down her head, sighed, and confessed all by her looks. At last, after a considering pause, she cried, 'My dearest sister, I do confess I was surprised at the sight of Monsieur Henault, and much more than ever you have observed me to be at the sight of his person, because there is scarce a day wherein I do not see that, and know beforehand I shall see him. I am prepared for the encounter, and have lessened my concern, or rather confusion, by that time I come to the grate, so much mistress I am of my passions when they give me warning of their approach, and sure I can withstand the greatest assaults of fate, if I can but foresee it, but if it surprise me, I find I am as feeble a woman as the most unresolved. You did not tell me you had this picture, nor say you would show me such a picture; but when I least expect to see that face, you show it me even in my chamber.'

'Ah, my dear sister!' replied Katteriena. 'I believe that paleness and those blushes proceed from some other cause than the nicety of seeing the picture of a man in your chamber.' 'You have too much wit', replied Isabella, 'to be imposed on by such an excuse, if I were so silly to make it; but O, my dear sister, it was in my thoughts to deceive you; could I have concealed my pain and sufferings you should never have known them, but since I find it impossible and that I am too sincere to make use of fraud in anything, 'tis fit I tell you from what cause my change of colour proceeds, and to own to you, I fear 'tis love. If ever therefore, O gentle pitying maid, thou wert a lover, if ever thy tender heart were touched with that passion, inform me, O inform me of the nature of that cruel disease and how thou found'st a cure!'

While she was speaking these words she threw her arms about the neck of the fair Katteriena, and bathed her bosom (where she hid her face) with a shower of tears. Katteriena, embracing her with all the fondness of a dear lover, told her, with a sigh, that she could deny her nothing and therefore confessed to her she had been a lover, and that was the occasion of her being made a nun; her father finding out the intrigue which fatally happened to be with his own page, a youth of extraordinary beauty.

'I was but young,' said she, 'about thirteen, and knew not what to call the new-known pleasure that I felt when e'en I looked upon the young Arnaldo; my heart would heave whene'er he came in view, and my disordered breath came doubly from my bosom; a shivering seized me and my face grew wan; my thought was at a stand and sense itself, for that short moment, lost its faculties. But when he touched me, O, no hunted deer, tired with his flight and just secured in shades, pants with a nimbler motion than my heart! At first I thought the youth had had some magic art to make one faint and tremble at his touches, but he himself, when I accused his cruelty, told me he had no art but aweful passion, and vowed that when I touched him, he was so: so trembling, so surprised, so charmed, so pleased. When he was present, nothing could displease me, but when he parted from me, then 'twas rather a soft, silent grief that eased itself by sighing and by hoping that some kind moment would restore my joy. When he was absent, nothing could divert me, howe'er I strove, howe'er I toiled for mirth; no smile, no joy dwelt in my heart or eyes; I could not feign, so very well I loved, impatient in his absence, I would count the tedious parting hours and pass them off like useless visitants whom we wish were gone. These are the hours where life no business has—at least, a lover's life. But, O, what minutes seemed the happy hours when on his eyes I gazed and he on mine, and half our conversation lost in sighs—sighs, the soft, moving language of a lover.'

'No more, no more,' replied Isabella, throwing her arms again about the neck of the transported Katteriena, 'thou blow'st my flame by thy soft words, and mak'st me know my weakness and my shame. I love! I love! And feel those differing passions!' Then, pausing a moment, she proceeded, 'Yet so didst thou but hast surmounted it. Now thou hast found the nature of my pain, O tell me thy saving remedy.' 'Alas,' replied

Katteriena, 'though there's but one disease, there's many remedies. They say possession's one, but that to me seems a riddle; absence, they say, another, and that was mine, for Arnaldo having by chance lost one of my billets, discovered the amour, and was sent to travel and myself forced into this monastery, where at last time convinced me I had loved below my quality, and that shamed me into holy orders.' 'And is it a disease', replied Isabella, 'that people often recover?' 'Most frequently,' said Katteriena, 'and yet some die of the disease, but very rarely.' 'Nay then,' said Isabella, 'I fear you'll find me one of these martyrs, for I have already opposed it with the most severe devotion in the world, but all my prayers are vain, your lovely brother pursues me into the greatest solitude; he meets me at my very midnight devotions and interrupts my prayers; he gives me a thousand thoughts that ought not to enter into a soul dedicated to Heaven. He ruins all the glory I have achieved, even above my sex, for piety of life and the observation of all virtues. O Katteriena, he has a power in his eyes that transcends all the world besides, and, to show the weakness of human nature, and how vain all our boastings are, he has done that in one fatal hour that the persuasions of all my relations and friends, glory, honour, pleasure, and all that can tempt, could not perform in years! I resisted all but Henault's eyes, and they were ordained to make me truly wretched. But yet, with thy assistance, and a resolution to see him no more, and my perpetual trust in Heaven, I may perhaps overcome this tyrant of my soul, who, I thought, had never entered into holy houses, or mixed his devotions and worship with the true religion. But, O, no cells, no cloisters, no hermitages, are secured from his efforts.'

This discourse she ended with abundance of tears, and it was resolved, since she was devoted forever to a holy life, that it was best for her to make it as easy to her as was possible; in order to it, and the banishing this fond and useless passion from her heart, it was very necessary she should see Henault no more. At first, Isabella was afraid that, in refusing to see him, he might mistrust her passion, but Katteriena, who was both pious and discreet, and endeavoured truly to cure her of so violent a disease, which must, she knew, either end in her death or destruction, told her she would take care of that matter that it should not blemish her honour; and so leaving her a while, after they had resolved on this, she left her in a thousand confusions. She was now another woman than what she had hitherto been; she was quite altered in every sentiment, thought, and notion; she now repented she had promised not to see Henault; she trembled and even fainted for fear she should see him no more. She was not able to bear that thought; it made her rage within like one possessed, and all her virtue could not calm her; yet since her word was passed and, as she was, she could not without great scandal break it in that point, she resolved to die a thousand deaths rather than not perform her promise made to Katteriena. But 'tis not to be expressed what she endured, what fits, pains, and convulsions she sustained, and how much ado she had to dissemble to Dame Katteriena, who soon returned to the afflicted maid. The next day, about the time that Henault was to come, as he usually did, about two or three a clock afternoon,* 'tis impossible to express the uneasiness of Isabella. She asked a thousand times, 'What, is not your brother come?', when Dame Katteriena would reply, 'Why do you ask?'. She would say, 'Because I would be sure not to see him.' 'You need not fear, Madam,' replied Katteriena, 'for you shall keep your chamber.' She need not have urged that, for Isabella was very ill without knowing it, and in a fever.

At last, one of the nuns came up and told Dame Katteriena that her brother was at the grate, and she desired he should be bid come about to the private grate above stairs, which he did, and she went to him, leaving Isabella even dead on the bed at the very name of Henault. But the more she concealed her flame, the more violently it raged, which she strove in vain by prayers, and those recourses of solitude, to lessen. All this did but augment the pain, and was oil to the fire, so that she now could hope that nothing but death would put an end to her griefs and her infamy.

She was eternally thinking on him, how handsome his face, how delicate every feature, how charming his air, how graceful his mien, how soft and good his disposition and how witty and entertaining his conversation. She now fancied she was at the grate talking to him as she used to be, and blessed those happy hours she passed then, and bewailed her misfortune that she is not more destined to be so happy, then gives a loose to grief; griefs at which no mortals but despairing lovers can guess, or how tormenting they are, where the most easy moments are those wherein one resolves to kill oneself, and the happiest thought is damnation. But from these imaginations she endeavours to fly all frighted with horror, but, alas, whither would she fly but to a life more full of horror? She considers well she cannot bear despairing love, and finds it impossible to cure her despair; she cannot fly from the thoughts of the charming Henault, and 'tis impossible to quit 'em, and, at this rate, she found life could not long support itself, but would either reduce her to madness and so render her an hated object of scorn to the censuring world, or force her hand to commit a murder upon herself. This she had found, this she had well considered; nor could her fervent and continual prayers, her nightly watchings, her mortifications on the cold marble in long winter season, and all her acts of devotion, abate one spark of this shameful fever of love that was destroying her within.

When she had raged and struggled with this unruly passion till she was quite tired and breathless, finding all her force in vain, she filled her fancy with a thousand charming ideas of the lovely Henault and, in that soft fit, had a mind to satisfy her panting heart and give it one joy more by beholding the lord of its desires and the author of its pains. Pleased, yet trembling at this resolve, she rose from the bed where she was laid, and softly advanced to the staircase from whence there opened that room where Dame Katteriena was, and where there was a private grate at which she was entertaining her brother; they were earnest in discourse and so loud that Isabella could easily hear all they said, and the first words from Katteriena who, in a sort of anger, cried, 'Urge me no more, my virtue is too nice to become an advocate for a passion that can tend to nothing but your ruin, for, suppose I should tell the fair Isabella you die for her, what can it avail you? What hope can any man have to move the heart of a virgin so averse to love, a virgin whose modesty and virtue is

so very curious it would fly the very word love as some
monstrous witchcraft or the foulest of sins, who would loathe
me for bringing so lewd a message, and banish you her sight as
the object of her hate and scorn. Is it unknown to you how
many of the noblest youths of Flanders have addressed themselves to her in vain, when yet she was in the world? Have you
been ignorant how the young Count de Villenoys languished
in vain almost to death for her, and that no persuasions, no
attractions in him, no worldly advantages, or all his pleadings,
who had a wit and spirit capable of prevailing on any heart
less severe and harsh than hers? Do you not know that all was
lost on this insensible fair one, even when she was a proper
object for the adoration of the young and amorous? And can
you hope, now she has so entirely wedded her future days to
devotion, and given all to Heaven, nay, lives a life here more
like a saint than a woman, rather an angel than a mortal
creature? Do you imagine, with any rhetoric you can deliver,
now to turn the heart and whole nature of this divine maid to
consider your earthly passion? No, 'tis fondness and an injury
to her virtue to harbour such a thought; quit it, quit it, my dear
brother, before it ruin your repose.'

'Ah, sister!', replied the dejected Henault, 'your counsel
comes too late, and your reasons are of too feeble force to
rebate those arrows the charming Isabella's eyes have fixed in
my heart and soul, and I am undone, unless she know my pain,
which I shall die before I shall ever dare mention to her; but
you young maids have a thousand familiarities together, can
jest and play and say a thousand things between raillery and
earnest that may first hint what you would deliver and insinuate into each other's hearts a kind of curiosity to know more,
for naturally (my dear sister) maids are curious and vain and,
however divine the mind of the fair Isabella may be, it bears
the tincture still of mortal woman.'

'Suppose this true, how could this mortal part about her
advantage you?' said Katteriena. 'All that you can expect from
this discovery (if she should be content to hear it and to return
your pity) would be to make her wretched like yourself. What
farther can you hope?' 'O, talk not', replied Henault, 'of so
much happiness! I do not expect to be so blessed that she

should pity me, or love to a degree of inquietude; 'tis sufficient for the ease of my heart that she know its pains, and what it suffers for her; that she would give my eyes leave to gaze upon her, and my heart to vent a sigh now and then, and, when I dare, to give me leave to speak and tell her of my passion. This, this is all, my sister.'

And, at that word, the tears glided down his cheeks, and he declined his eyes and set a look so charming and so sad that Isabella, whose eyes were fixed upon him, was a thousand times ready to throw herself into the room and to have made a confession how sensible she was of all she had heard and seen. But, with much ado, she contained and satisfied herself with knowing that she was adored by him whom she adored and, with a prudence that is natural to her, she withdrew and waited with patience the event of their discourse. She impatiently longed to know how Katteriena would manage this secret her brother had given her, and was pleased that the friendship and prudence of that maid had concealed her passion from her brother; and now contented and joyful beyond imagination to find herself beloved, she knew she could dissemble her own passion and make him the first aggressor, the first that loved, or, at least, that should seem to do so. This thought restores her so great a part of her peace of mind, that she resolved to see him, and to dissemble with Katteriena so far as to make her believe she had subdued that passion she was really ashamed to own. She now, with her woman's skill, begins to practise an art she never before understood and has recourse to cunning and resolves to seem to reassume her former repose. But hearing Katteriena approach, she laid herself again on her bed where she had left her, but composed her face to more cheerfulness and put on a resolution that indeed deceived the sister, who was extremely pleased, she said, to see her look so well. When Isabella replied, 'Yes, I am another woman now; I hope Heaven has heard and granted my long and humble supplications and driven from my heart this tormenting god that has so long disturbed my pure thoughts.' 'And are you sure', said Dame Katteriena, 'that this wanton deity is repelled by the noble force of your resolution? Is he never to return?' 'No,' replied Isabella, 'never to my heart.'

'Yes,' said Katteriena, 'if you should see the lovely murderer of your repose, your wound would bleed anew.' At this, Isabella, smiling with a little disdain, replied, 'Because you once to love and Henault's charms defenceless found me, ah, do you think I have no fortitude, but so in fondness lost, remiss in virtue, that when I have resolved (and see it necessary for my after quiet) to want the power of keeping that resolution? No, scorn me, and despise me then as lost to all the glories of my sex, and all that nicety I have hitherto preserved.'

There needed no more from a maid of Isabella's integrity and reputation to convince anyone of the sincerity of what she said since, in the whole course of her life, she never could be charged with an untruth or an equivocation, and Katteriena assured her she believed her, and was infinitely glad she had vanquished a passion that would have proved destructive to her repose. Isabella replied she had not altogether vanquished her passion, she did not boast of so absolute a power over her soft nature, but had resolved things great and time would work the cure; that she hoped Katteriena would make such excuses to her brother for her not appearing at the grate so gay and entertaining as she used and, by a little absence, she should retrieve the liberty she had lost. But she desired such excuses might be made for her that young Henault might not perceive the reason. At the naming him she had much ado not to show some concern extraordinary, and Katteriena assured her she had now a very good excuse to keep from the grate when he was at it, 'For', said she, 'now you have resolved, I may tell you he is dying for you, raving in love, and has this day made me promise to him to give you some account of his passion and to make you sensible of his languishment. I had not told you this', replied Katteriena, 'but that I believe you fortified with brave resolution and virtue, and that this knowledge will rather put you more upon your guard than you were before.' While she spoke, she fixed her eyes on Isabella, to see what alteration it would make in her heart and looks, but the masterpiece of this young maid's art was shown in this minute, for she commanded herself so well that her very looks dissembled and showed no concern at a relation that made her soul dance with joy, but it was what she was prepared for, or else I question her fortitude. But, with a calmness which absolutely subdued Katteriena, she replied, 'I am almost glad he has confessed a passion for me, and you shall confess to him you told me of it, and that I absent myself from the grate on purpose to avoid the sight of a man who durst love me and confess it; and I assure you, my dear sister,' continued she, dissembling, 'you could not have advanced my cure by a more effectual way than telling me of his presumption.' At that word, Katteriena joyfully related to her all that had passed between young Henault and herself and how he implored her aid in this amour; at the end of which relation Isabella smiled and carelessly replied, 'I pity him.' And so going to their devotion, they had no more discourse of the lover.

In the meantime, young Henault was a little satisfied to know his sister would discover his passion to the lovely Isabella, and though he dreaded the return, he was pleased that she should know she had a lover that adored her, though even without hope, for though the thought of possessing Isabella was the most ravishing that could be, yet he had a dread upon him when he thought of it, for he could not hope to accomplish that without sacrilege, and he was a young man very devout and even bigoted in religion, and would often question and debate within himself that, if it were possible he should come to be beloved by this fair creature, and that it were possible for her to grant all that youth and love could require, whether he should receive the blessing offered, and though he adored the maid, whether he should not abhor the nun in his embraces. 'Twas an undetermined thought that chilled his fire as often as it approached, but he had too many that rekindled it again with the greater flame and ardour.

His impatience to know what success Katteriena had with the relation she was to make to Isabella in his behalf brought him early to Iper the next day. He came again to the private grate, where his sister receiving him and finding him with a sad and dejected look expect what she had to say, she told him that look well became the news she had for him, it being such as ought to make him both grieved and penitent, for, to obey him, she had so absolutely displeased Isabella that she was resolved never to believe her her friend more, 'Or, to see you,' said she, 'therefore, as you have made me commit a crime against my conscience, against my order, against my friendship, and against my honour, you ought to do some brave thing, take some noble resolution worthy of your courage to redeem all for your repose. I promised I would let Isabella know you loved and, for the mitigation of my crime, you ought to let me tell her you have surmounted your passion as the last remedy of life and fame.'

At these her last words, the tears gushed from his eyes and he was able only a good while to sigh; at last cried, 'What! See her no more! See the charming Isabella no more!' And then vented the grief of his soul in so passionate a manner as his sister had all the compassion imaginable for him, but thought it great sin and indiscretion to cherish his flame, so that, after a while, having heard her counsel, he replied, 'And is this all, my sister, you will do to save a brother?' 'All,' replied she, 'I would not be the occasion of making a nun violate her vow to save a brother's life, no, nor my own; assure yourself of this and take it as my last resolution. Therefore, if you will be content with the friendship of this young lady and so behave yourself that we may find no longer the lover in the friend, we shall reassume our former conversation and live with you as we ought; otherwise, your presence will continually banish her from the grate and, in time, make both her you love, and yourself, a town-discourse.'

Much more to this purpose she said to dissuade him, and bid him retire, and keep himself from thence till he could resolve to visit them without a crime, and she protested if he did not do this and master his foolish passion, she would let her father understand his conduct, who was a man of a temper so very precise that should he believe his son should have a thought of love to a virgin vowed to Heaven, he would abandon him to shame and eternal poverty by disinheriting him of all he could. Therefore, she said, he ought to lay all this to his heart and weigh it with his unheedy passion. While the sister talked thus wisely, Henault was not without his thoughts, but considered as she spoke, but did not consider in the right place; he was not considering how to please a father and save an estate, but how to manage the matter so to establish himself

as he was before with Isabella, for he imagined, since already
she knew his passion, and that if after that she would be
prevailed with to see him, he might, some lucky minute or
other, have the pleasure of speaking for himself—at least he
should again see and talk to her, which was a joyful thought in
the midst of so many dreadful ones, and, as if he had known
what passed in Isabella's heart, he, by a strange sympathy, took
the same measures to deceive Katteriena, a well-meaning
young lady, and easily imposed on from her own innocence;
he resolved to dissemble patience, since he must have that
virtue and owned his sister's reasons were just and ought to be
pursued, that she had argued him into half his peace and that
he would endeavour to recover the rest; that youth ought to be
pardoned a thousand failings, and years would reduce him to a
condition of laughing at his follies of youth, but that grave
direction was not yet arrived. And so, desiring she would pray
for his conversion, and that she would recommend him to the
devotions of the fair Isabella, he took his leave and came no
more to the nunnery in ten days; in all which time none but
impatient lovers can guess what pain and languishments Isabella suffered, not knowing the cause of his absence, nor
daring to enquire. But she bore it out so admirably that Dame
Katteriena never so much as suspected she had any thoughts
of that nature that perplexed her, and now believed indeed she
had conquered all her uneasiness. And, one day, when Isabella
and she were alone together, she asked that fair dissembler if
she did not admire at the conduct and resolution of her
brother. 'Why?' replied Isabella unconcernedly, while her heart
was fainting within for fear of ill news. With that, Katteriena
told her the last discourse she had with her brother, and how
at last she had persuaded him (for her sake) to quit his passion;
and that he had promised he would endeavour to surmount it,
and that that was the reason he was absent now and they were
to see him no more till he had made a conquest over himself.
You may assure yourself this news was not so welcome to
Isabella as Katteriena imagined. Yet still she dissembled with a
force beyond what the most cunning practitioner could have
shown, and carried herself before people as if no pressures had
lain upon her heart; but when alone retired in order to her

devotion, she would vent her griefs in the most deplorable manner that a distressed distracted maid could do and which, in spite of all her severe penances, she found no abatement of.

At last Henault came again to the monastery and, with a look as gay as he could possible assume, he saw his sister and told her he had gained an absolute victory over his heart, and desired he might see Isabella only to convince both her and Katteriena that he was no longer a lover of that fair creature that had so lately charmed him, that he had set five thousand pounds a year against a fruitless passion, and found the solid gold much the heavier in the scale. And he smiled and talked the whole day of indifferent things with his sister and asked no more for Isabella; nor did Isabella look or ask after him, but in her heart. Two months passed in this indifference, till it was taken notice of that Sister Isabella came not to the grate when Henault was there as she used to do; this being spoken to Dame Katteriena, she told it to Isabella and said the nuns would believe there was some cause for her absence if she did not appear again; that if she could trust her heart, she was sure she could trust her brother, for he thought no more of her, she was confident. This in lieu of pleasing was a dagger to the heart of Isabella, who thought it time to retrieve the flying lover, and therefore told Katteriena she would the next day entertain at the low grate as she was wont to do, and, accordingly, as soon as any people of quality came, she appeared there, where she had not been two minutes, but she saw the lovely Henault, and it was well for both that people were in the room, they had else both sufficiently discovered their inclinations, or rather, their not to be concealed passions. After the general conversation was over, by the going away of the gentlemen that were at the grate, Katteriena being employed elsewhere, Isabella was at last left alone with Henault. But who can guess the confusion of these two lovers, who wished, yet feared, to know each other's thoughts? She trembling with a dismal apprehension that he loved no more; and he almost dying with fear she should reproach or upbraid him with his presumption, so that both being possessed with equal sentiments of love, fear, and shame, they both stood fixed with dejected looks and hearts that heaved with stifled sighs. At last,

Isabella, the softer and tender-hearted of the two, though not the most a lover, perhaps, not being able to contain her love any longer within the bounds of dissimulation or discretion, being by nature innocent, burst out into tears and all fainting with pressing thoughts within, she fell languishly into a chair that stood there, while the distracted Henault, who could not come to her assistance, and finding marks of love rather than anger or disdain in that confusion of Isabella's, throwing himself on his knees at the grate, implored her to behold him, to hear him, and to pardon him, who died every moment for her and who adored her with a violent ardour, but yet, with such an one as should (though he perished with it) be conformable to her commands, and as he spoke, the tears streamed down his dying eyes that beheld her with all the tender regard that ever lover was capable of. She recovered a little and turned her too beautiful face to him and pierced him with a look that darted a thousand joys and flames into his heart, with eyes that told him her heart was burning and dying for him, for which assurances he made ten thousand asseverations of his never-dying passion and expressing as many raptures and excesses of joy to find her eyes and looks confess he was not odious to her, and that the knowledge he was her lover did not make her hate him. In fine, he spoke so many things all soft and moving, and so well convinced her of his passion, that she at last was compelled by a mighty force, absolutely irresistible, to speak.

'Sir,' said she, 'perhaps you will wonder where I, a maid, brought up in the simplicity of virtue, should learn the confidence not only to hear of love from you, but to confess I am sensible of the most violent of its pain myself, and I wonder, and am amazed at my own daring, that I should have the courage rather to speak than die and bury it in silence. But such is my fate. Hurried by an unknown force which I have endeavoured always, in vain, to resist, I am compelled to tell you I love you and have done so from the first moment I saw you, and you are the only man born to give me life or death, to make me happy or blessed. Perhaps, had I not been confined, and, as it were, utterly forbid by my vow, as well as my modesty, to tell you this, I should not have been so miserable to have fallen thus low as to have confessed my shame, but our opportunities of speaking are so few, and letters so impossible to be sent without discovery, that perhaps this is the only time I shall ever have to speak with you alone.'

And at that word the tears flowed abundantly from her eyes and gave Henault leave to speak. 'Ah, Madam,' said he, 'do not, as soon as you have raised me to the greatest happiness in the world, throw me with one word beneath your scorn; much easier 'tis to die and know I am loved than never, never hope to hear that blessed sound again from that beautiful mouth. Ah, Madam, rather let me make use of this one opportunity our happy luck has given us and contrive how we may forever see and speak to each other; let us assure one another there are a thousand ways to escape a place so rigid as denies us that happiness, and denies the fairest maid in the world the privilege of her creation and the end to which she was formed so angelical.' And seeing Isabella was going to speak, lest she should say something that might dissuade from an attempt so dangerous and wicked, he pursued to tell her it might be indeed the last moment Heaven would give 'em, and besought her to answer him what he implored, whether she would fly with him from the monastery. At this word, she grew pale and started as at some dreadful sound, and cried, 'Ha! What is it you say? Is it possible you should propose a thing so wicked? And can it enter into your imagination because I have so far forgot my virtue and my vow to become a lover, I should therefore fall to so wretched a degree of infamy and reprobation? No, name it to me no more, if you would see me, and if it be as you say, a pleasure to be beloved by me, for I will sooner die than yield to what—alas—I but too well approve!' These last words she spoke with a fainting tone, and the tears fell anew from her fair, soft eyes. 'If it be so,' said he (with a voice so languishing it could scarce be heard), 'if it be so, and that you are resolved to try if my love be eternal without hope, without expectation of any other joy than seeing and adoring you through the grate, I am, and must, and will be contented, and you shall see I can prefer the sighing to these cold irons that separate us before all the possessions of the rest of the world; that I choose rather to lead my life here at this cruel distance from you forever than before the embrace of all the fair, and you shall see how pleased I will be to languish here; but as you see me decay (for surely so I shall), do not triumph o'er my languid looks, and laugh at my pale and meagre face, but, pitying, say, "How easily I might have preserved that face, those eyes and all that youth and vigour, now no more from this total ruin I now behold it in", and love your slave that dies and will be daily and visibly dying as long as my eyes can gaze on that fair object and my soul be fed and kept alive with her charming wit and conversation; if love can live on such airy food (though rich in itself, yet unfit, alone, to sustain life) it shall be forever dedicated to the lovely Isabella. But, O, that time cannot be long, fate will not lend her slave many days, who loves too violently to be satisfied to enjoy the fair object of his desires no otherwise than at a grate.'

He ceased speaking, for sighs and tears stopped his voice, and he begged the liberty to sit down and his looks being quite altered, Isabella found herself touched to the very soul with a concern the most tender that ever yielding maid was oppressed with. She had no power to suffer him to languish while she, by one soft word, could restore him, and being about to say a thousand things which would have been agreeable to him, she saw herself approached by some of the nuns and only had time to say, 'If you love me, live and hope.' The rest of the nuns began to ask Henault of news, for he always brought them all that was novel in the town, and they were glad still of his visits above all other, for they heard how all amours and intrigues passed in the world by this young cavalier. These last words of Isabella's were a cordial to his soul, and he from that and to conceal the present affair, endeavoured to assume all the gaiety he could and told 'em all he could either remember or invent to please 'em, though he wished them a great way off at that time.

Thus they passed the day till it was a decent hour for him to quit the grate and for them to draw the curtain; all that night did Isabella dedicate to love. She went to bed with a resolution to think over all she had to do and to consider how she should manage this great affair of her life. I have already said she had tried all that was possible in human strength to perform in the design of quitting a passion so injurious to her honour and virtue, and found no means possible to accomplish it. She had tried fasting long, praying fervently, rigid penances and pains, severe disciplines, all the mortification almost to the destruction of life itself, to conquer the unruly flame, but still it burnt and raged but the more; so, at last, she was forced to permit that to conquer her she could not conquer, and submitted to her fate as a thing destined her by Heaven itself, and, after all this opposition, she fancied it was resisting even divine providence to struggle any longer with her heart, and this being her real belief, she the more patiently gave way to all the thoughts that pleased her.

As soon as she was laid, without discoursing as she used to do to Katteriena after they were in bed, she pretended to be sleepy and turning from her, settled herself to profound thinking and was resolved to conclude the matter between her heart and her vow of devotion that night; that she, having no more to determine, might end the affair accordingly the first opportunity she should have to speak to Henault, which was to fly and marry him, or, to remain forever fixed to her vow of chastity. This was the debate. She brings reason on both sides; against the first, she sets the shame of a violated vow and considers where she shall show her face after such an action; to the vow, she argues that she was born in sin and could not live without it; that she was human and no angel and that, possibly, that sin might be as soon forgiven as another; that since all her devout endeavours could not defend her from the cause, Heaven ought to excuse the effect; that as to showing her face, so she saw that of Henault always turned (charming as it was) towards her with love; what had she to do with the world or cared to behold any other?

Sometimes she thought it would be more brave and pious to die than to break her vow; but she soon answered that as false arguing, for self-murder was the worst of sins and in the deadly number. She could, after such an action, live to repent and, of two evils, she ought to choose the least; she dreads to think, since she had so great a reputation for virtue and piety, both in the monastery and in the world, what they both would say when she should commit an action so contrary to both these she professed. But, after a whole night's debate, love was strongest and gained the victory. She never went about to think how she should escape, because she knew it would be easy, the keeping of the key of the monastery often entrusted in her keeping and was by turns in the hands of many more whose virtue and discretion was infallible and out of doubt; besides, her aunt being the lady abbess, she had greater privilege than the rest, so that she had no more to do, she thought, than to acquaint Henault with her design as soon as she should get an opportunity, which was not quickly. But, in the meantime, Isabella's father died, which put some little stop to our lover's happiness, and gave her a short time of grief; but love, who, while he is new and young, can do us miracles, soon wiped her eyes and chased away all sorrow from her heart and grew every day more and more impatient to put her new design in execution, being every day more resolved. Her father's death had removed one obstacle and secured her from his reproaches, and now she only wants opportunity, first to acquaint Henault, and then to fly.

She waited not long, all things concurring to her desire, for Katteriena falling sick, she had the good luck, as she called it then, to entertain Henault at the grate oftentimes alone. The first moment she did so she entertained him with the good news and told him she had at last vanquished her heart in favour of him and loving him above all things—honour, her vow, or reputation—had resolved to abandon herself wholly to him, to give herself up to love and serve him, and that she had no other consideration in the world. But Henault, instead of returning her an answer all joy and satisfaction, held down his eyes and, sighing with a dejected look, he cried, 'Ah, Madam, pity a man so wretched and undone as not to be sensible of this blessing as I ought!' She grew pale at this reply, and trembling, expected he would proceed. ''Tis not', continued he, 'that I want love, tenderest passion, and all the desire youth and love can inspire. But, O Madam, when I consider (for raving, mad in love as I am for your sake, I do consider) that if I should take you from this repose, nobly born and educated as you are, and, for that act, should find a rigid father deprive me of all that ought to support you, and afford your birth, beauty, and merits their due, what would you say? How would you reproach me?' He, sighing, expected her answer, when blushes overspreading her face, she replied in a tone all haughty and angry, 'Ah Henault, am I then refused, after having abandoned all things for you? Is it thus you reward my sacrificed honour, vows and virtue? Cannot you hazard the loss of fortune to possess Isabella, who loses all for you?' Then bursting into tears at her misfortune of loving, she suffered him to say, 'O, charming fair one, how industrious is your cruelty to find out new torments for an heart already pressed down with the severities of love! Is it possible you can make so unhappy a construction of the tenderest part of my passion? And can you imagine it want of love in me to consider how I shall preserve and merit the vast blessing Heaven has given me? Is my care a crime? And would not the most deserving beauty of the world hate me if I should, to preserve my life and satisfy the passion of my fond heart, reduce her to the extremities of want and misery, and is there anything in what I have said but what you ought to take for the greatest respect and tenderness?' 'Alas,' replied Isabella, sighing, 'young as I am, all unskilful in love I find, but what I feel, that discretion is no part of it, and consideration inconsistent with the nobler passion, who will subsist of its own nature, and live unmixed with any other sentiment. And 'tis not pure if it be otherwise. I know, had I mixed discretion with mine, my love must have been less; I never thought of living but by love and, if I considered at all, it was that grandeur and magnificence were useless trifles to lovers, wholly needless and troublesome. I thought of living in some lonely cottage far from the noise of crowded busy cities, to walk with thee in groves and silent shades where I might hear no voice but thine, and when we had been tired, to sit us down by some cool, murmuring rivulet and be to each a world, my monarch thou, and I thy sovereign queen, while wreaths of flowers shall crown our happy heads, some fragrant bank our throne and Heaven our canopy. Thus we might laugh at fortune and the proud, despise the duller world who place their joys in mighty show and equipage. Alas, my nature could not bear it, I am unused to worldly vanities and would boast of nothing but my Henault; no riches but his love; no grandeur but his presence.'

She ended speaking with tears, and he replied, 'Now, now, I find my Isabella loves indeed, when she's content to abandon the world for my sake. O, thou hast named the only happy life that suits my quiet nature: to be retired has always been my joy! But to be so with thee! O, thou hast charmed me with a thought so dear as has forever banished all my care but how to receive thy goodness. I'll think no more what my angry parent may do when he shall hear how I have disposed of myself against his will and pleasure, but trust to love and providence. No more, begone all thoughts but those of Isabella.'

As soon as he had made an end of expressing his joy, he fell to consulting how and when she should escape; and since it was uncertain when she should be offered the key, for she would not ask for it, she resolved to give him notice either by word of mouth or a bit of paper she would write in and give him through the grate the first opportunity, and, parting for that time, they both resolved to get up what was possible for their support, till time should reconcile affairs and friends, and to wait the happy hour.

Isabella's dead mother had left jewels of the value of two thousand pounds to her daughter, at her decease, which jewels were in the possession now of the lady abbess, and were upon sale to be added to the revenue of the monastery, and as Isabella was the most prudent of her sex—at least had hitherto been so esteemed—she was entrusted with all that was in possession of the lady abbess, and 'twas not difficult to make herself mistress of all her own jewels, as also some three or four hundred pounds in gold, that was hoarded up in her ladyship's cabinet against any accidents that might arrive to the monastery. These Isabella also made her own and put up with the jewels, and having acquainted Henault with the day and hour of her escape, he got together what he could, and waiting for her with his coach one night when nobody was awake but herself, when rising softly as she used to do in the night to her devotion, she stole so dexterously out of the monastery as nobody knew anything of it. She carried away the keys with her, after having locked all the doors, for she was entrusted often with all. She found Henault waiting in his coach and trusted none but an honest coachman that loved him. He received her with all the transports of a truly ravished lover, and she was infinitely charmed with the new pleasure of his embraces and kisses.

They drove out of town immediately and, because she durst not be seen in that habit (for it had been immediate death for both), they drove into a thicket some three miles from the town, where Henault, having brought her some of his younger sister's clothes, he made her put off her habit and put on those, and, rending the other, they hid them in a sandpit covered over with broom and went that night forty miles from Iper to a little town upon the river Rhine where, changing their names, they were forthwith married and took a house in a country village, a farm, where they resolved to live retired by the name of Beroone, and drove a farming trade. However, not forgetting to set friends and engines at work to get their pardon as criminals first that had transgressed the law and, next, as disobedient persons who had done contrary to the will and desire of their parents. Isabella writ to her aunt the most moving letters in the world, so did Henault to his father, but she was a long time before she could gain so much as an answer from her aunt, and Henault was so unhappy as never to gain one from his father, who no sooner heard the news that was spread over all the town and country that young Henault was fled with the so-famed Isabella, a nun, and singular for devotion and piety of life, but he immediately settled his estate on his younger son, cutting Henault off all his birthright, which was five thousand pounds a year. This news, you may believe, was not very pleasing to the young man, who though in possession of the loveliest virgin and now wife that ever man was blessed with, yet when he reflected he should have children by her, and these and she should come to want (he having been magnificently educated, and impatient of scanty fortune), he laid it to heart and it gave him a thousand uneasinesses in the midst of unspeakable joys, and the more he strove to hide his sentiments from Isabella, the more tormenting it was within. He durst not name it to her, so insuperable a grief it would cause in her, to hear him complain, and though she could live hardly, as being bred to a devout and severe life, he could not, but must let the man of quality show itself even

in the disguise of an humbler farmer; besides all this, he found
nothing of his industry thrive, his cattle still died in the midst
of those that were in full vigour and health of other people's;
his crops of wheat and barley and other grain, though managed
by able and knowing husbandmen, were all either mildewed or
blasted or some misfortune still arrived to him; his coach
horses would fight and kill one another, his barns sometimes
be fired; so that it became a proverb all over the country if any
ill luck had arrived to anybody, they would say, they had
Monsieur Beroone's luck. All these reflections did but add to
his melancholy, and he grew at last to be in some want, in so
much that Isabella, who had by her frequent letters and
submissive supplications to her aunt (who loved her tenderly)
obtained her pardon and her blessing, she now pressed her for
some money, and besought her to consider how great a fortune
she had brought to the monastery, and implored she would
allow her some salary out of it, for she had been married two
years and most of what she had was exhausted. The aunt, who
found that what was done could not be undone, did from time
to time supply her so as one might have lived very decently
on that very revenue, but that would not satisfy the great heart
of Henault. He was now about three and twenty years old, and
Isabella about eighteen: too young and too lovely a pair to
begin their misfortunes so soon. They were both the most just
and pious in the world; they were examples of goodness and
eminent for holy living, and for perfect loving, and yet nothing
thrived they undertook. They had no children and all their joy
was in each other. At last, one good fortune arrived to them by
the solicitations of the lady abbess, and the bishop, who was
her near kinsman. They got a pardon for Isabella's quitting the
monastery and marrying, so that she might now return to her
own country again. Henault having also his pardon, they
immediately quit the place where they had remained for two
years, and came again into Flanders, hoping the change of
place might afford 'em better luck.

Henault then began again to solicit his cruel father, but
nothing would do, he refused to see him or to receive any
letters from him. But, at last he prevailed so far with him as
that he sent a kinsman to him to assure him if he would leave

his wife and go into the French campaign he would equip him as well as his quality required, and that, according as he behaved himself, he should gain his favour, but if he lived idly at home, giving up his youth and glory to lazy love, he would have no more to say to him but raze him out of his heart and out of his memory.

He had settled himself in a very pretty house furnished with what was fitting for the reception of anybody of quality that would live a private life, and they found all the respect that their merits deserved from all the world, everybody entirely loving and endeavouring to serve them, and Isabella so perfectly had the ascendant over her aunt's heart that she procured from her all that she could desire and much more than she could expect. She was perpetually progging* and saving all that she could to enrich and advance her and at last, pardoning and forgiving Henault, loved him as her own child, so that all things looked with a better face than before and never was so dear and fond a couple seen as Henault and Isabella. But at last, she proved with child, and the aunt, who might reasonably believe so young a couple would have a great many children, and foreseeing there was no provision likely to be made them unless he pleased his father, for if the aunt should chance to die all their hope was gone, she therefore daily solicited him to obey his father and go to the camp, and that having achieved fame and renown, he would return a favourite to his father and comfort to his wife. After she had solicited in vain, for he was not able to endure the thought of leaving Isabella, melancholy as he was with his ill fortune, the bishop, kinsman to Isabella, took him to task and urged his youth and birth and that he ought not to waste both without action when all the world was employed, and that since his father had so great a desire he should go into a campaign, either to serve the Venetian against the Turks, or into the French service, which he liked best, he besought him to think of it and since he had satisfied his love, he should and ought to satisfy his duty, it being absolutely necessary for the wiping off the stain of his sacrilege and to gain him the favour of Heaven which, he found, had hitherto been averse to all he had undertaken. In fine, all his friends and all who loved him joined in this design, and all thought it convenient; nor was he insensible of the advantage it might bring him, but love, which every day grew fonder and fonder in his heart, opposed all their reasonings, though he saw all the brave youth of the age preparing to go either to one army or the other.

At last, he lets Isabella know what propositions he had made him, both by his father and his relations; at the very first motion, she almost fainted in his arms while he was speaking, and it possessed her with so entire a grief that she miscarried, to the insupportable torment of her tender husband and lover, so that to re-establish her repose, he was forced to promise not to go. However, she considered all their circumstances and weighed the advantages that might redound both to his honour and fortune by it, and, in a matter of a month's time, with the persuasions and reasons of her friends, she suffered him to resolve upon going, herself determining to retire to the monastery till the time of his return. But when she named the monastery, he grew pale and disordered and obliged her to promise him not to enter into it any more, for fear they should never suffer her to come forth again, so that he resolved not to depart till she had made a vow to him never to go again within the walls of a religious house which had already been so fatal to them. She promised and he believed.

Henault at last overcame his heart, which pleaded so for his stay, and sent his father word he was ready to obey him and to carry the first efforts of his arms against the common foes of Christendom, the Turks. His father was very well pleased at this and sent him two thousand crowns, his horses and furniture suitable to his quality, and a man to wait on him, so that it was not long ere he got himself in order to be gone, after a dismal parting.

He made what haste he could to the French army, then under the command of the Monsignior the Duke of Beaufort, then at Candia, and put himself a volunteer under his conduct, in which station was Villenoys, who, you have already heard, was so passionate a lover of Isabella, who no sooner heard of Henault's being arrived and that he was husband to Isabella, but he was impatient to learn by what strange adventure he came to gain her, even from her vowed retreat, when he, with all his courtship, could not be so happy, though she was then free in the world and unvowed to Heaven.

As soon as he sent his name to Henault he was sent for up, for Henault had heard of Villenoys and that he had been a lover of Isabella. They received one another with all the endearing civility imaginable, for the aforesaid reason and for that he was his countryman, though unknown to him, Villenoys being gone to the army just as Henault came from the Jesuits' College. A great deal of endearment passed between them and they became, from that moment, like two sworn brothers, and he received the whole relation from Henault of his amour.

It was not long before the siege began anew, for he arrived at the beginning of the spring, and, as soon as he came almost, they fell to action, and it happened upon a day that a party of some four hundred men resolved to sally out upon the enemy, as, whenever they could, they did; but as it is not my business to relate the history of the war, being wholly unacquainted with the terms of battles, I shall only say that these men were led by Villenoys and that Henault would accompany him in this sally, and that they acted very noble and great things worthy of a memory in the history of that siege. But this day particularly they had an occasion to show their valour, which they did very much to their glory; but, venturing too far, they were ambushed in the pursuit of the party of the enemy's and being surrounded, Villenoys had the unhappiness to see his gallant friend fall fighting and dealing of wounds around him, even as he descended to the earth, for he fell from his horse at the same moment that he killed a Turk, and Villenoys could neither assist him nor had the satisfaction to be able to rescue his dead body from under the horses, but with much ado escaping with his own life, got away in spite of all that followed him, and recovered the town before they could overtake him. He passionately bewailed the loss of this brave young man, and offered any recompense to those that would have ventured to have searched for his dead body among the slain, but it was not fit to hazard the living for unnecessary services to the dead, and though he had a great mind to have interred him, he rested content with what he wished to pay his friend's memory, though he could not. So that all the service

now he could do him was to write to Isabella to whom he had
not writ, though commanded by her so to do, in three years
before, which was never since she took orders. He gave her an
account of the death of her husband and how gloriously he fell
fighting for the holy cross, and how much honour he had won
if it had been his fate to have outlived that great but unfortunate day where, with four hundred men, they had killed
fifteen hundred of the enemy. The General Beaufort himself
had so great a respect and esteem for this young man, and
knowing him to be of quality, that he did him the honour to
bemoan him and to send a condoling letter to Isabella how
much worth her esteem he died, and that he had eternised his
memory with the last gasp of his life.

When this news arrived, it may be easily imagined what
impressions, or rather ruins, it made in the heart of this fair
mourner. The letters came by his man who saw him fall in
battle, and came off with those few that escaped with Villenoys.
He brought back what money he had, a few jewels, with
Isabella's picture that he carried with him, and had left in his
chamber in the fort at Candia for fear of breaking it in action.
And now Isabella's sorrow grew to the extremity she thought
she could not suffer more than she did by his absence, but she
now found a grief more killing. She hung her chamber with
black and lived without the light of day, only wax lights that
let her behold the picture of this charming man before which
she daily sacrificed floods of tears. He had now been absent
about ten months, and she had learnt just to live without him,
but hope preserved her then, but now she had nothing for
which to wish to live. She, for about two months after the news
arrived, lived without seeing any creature but a young maid
that was her woman; but extreme importunity obliged her to
give way to the visits of her friends, who endeavoured to
restore her melancholy soul to its wonted easiness, for however
it was oppressed within by Henault's absence, she bore it off
with a modest cheerfulness, but now she found that fortitude
and virtue failed her when she was assured he was no more.
She continued thus mourning and thus enclosed the space of a
whole year, never suffering the visit of any man but of a near
relation, so that she acquired a reputation such as never any

young beauty had, for she was now but nineteen and her face and shape more excellent than ever. She daily increased in beauty, which, joined to her exemplary piety, charity, and all other excellent qualities, gained her a wondrous fame and begat an awe and reverence in all that heard of her, and there was no man of any quality that did not adore her. After her year was up, she went to the churches, but would never be seen anywhere else abroad, but that was enough to procure her a thousand lovers, and some, who had the boldness to send her letters which, if she received, she gave no answer to, and many she sent back unread and unsealed, so that she would encourage none, though their quality was far beyond what she could hope; but she was resolved to marry no more, however her fortune might require it.

It happened that, about this time, Candia being unfortunately taken by the Turks, all the brave men that escaped the sword returned, among them Villenoys, who no sooner arrived, but he sent to let Isabella know of it and to beg the honour of waiting on her. Desirous to learn what fate befell her dear lord, she suffered him to visit her, where he found her in her mourning a thousand times more fair (at least, he fancied so) than ever she appeared to be; so that if he loved her before, he now adored her; if he burnt then, he rages now; but the aweful sadness and soft languishment of her eyes hindered him from the presumption of speaking of his passion to her, though it would have been no new thing, and his first visit was spent in the relation of every circumstance of Henault's death, and, at his going away, he begged leave to visit her sometimes, and she gave him permission. He lost no time, but made use of the liberty she had given him, and when his sister, who was a great companion of Isabella's, went to see her, he would still wait on her, so that, either with his own visits and those of his sister's, he saw Isabella every day and had the good luck to see he diverted her by giving her relations of transactions of the siege and the customs and manners of the Turks. All he said was with so good a grace that he rendered everything agreeable; he was, besides, very beautiful, well made, of quality and fortune, and fit to inspire love.

He made his visits so often and so long that, at last, he took

the courage to speak of his passion, which, at first, Isabella
would by no means hear of, but, by degrees, she yielded more
and more to listen to his tender discourse, and he lived thus
with her two years before he could gain any more upon her
heart than to suffer him to speak of love to her, but that which
subdued her quite was that her aunt, the lady abbess, died and,
with her, all the hopes and fortune of Isabella, so that she was
left with only a charming face and mien, a virtue, and a
discretion above her sex, to make her fortune within the world.
Into a religious house she was resolved not to go, because her
heart deceived her once and she durst not trust it again,
whatever it promised.

The death of this lady made her look more favourably on
Villenoys, but yet she was resolved to try his love to the
utmost and keep him off as long as 'twas possible she could
subsist, and 'twas for interest she married again, though she
liked the person very well, and since she was forced to submit
herself to be a second time a wife, she thought she could live
better with Villenoys than any other, since for him she ever
had a great esteem, and fancied the hand of Heaven had
pointed out her destiny, which she could not avoid without a
crime.

So that when she was again importuned by her impatient
lover, she told him she had made a vow to remain three years
at least before she would marry again after the death of the
best of men and husbands and him who had the fruits of her
early heart; and, notwithstanding all the solicitations of Villenoys, she would not consent to marry him till her vow of
widowhood was expired.

He took her promise, which he urged her to give him, and
to show the height of his passion in his obedience, he conde-
scends to stay her appointed time, though he saw her every
day and all his friends and relations made her visits upon this
new account, and there was nothing talked on but this designed
wedding, which, when the time was expired, was performed
accordingly with great pomp and magnificence, for Villenoys
had no parents to hinder his design, or, if he had, the reputation
and virtue of this lady would have subdued them.

The marriage was celebrated in this house where she lived

ever since her return from Germany from the time she got her pardon, and when Villenoys was preparing all things in a more magnificent order at his villa some ten miles from the city, she was very melancholy and would often say she had been used to such profound retreat and to live without the fatigue of noise and equipage that she feared she should never endure that grandeur which was proper for his quality and, though the house in the country was the most beautifully situated in all Flanders, she was afraid of a numerous train and kept him for the most part in this pretty, city mansion, which he adorned and enlarged as much as she would give him leave, so that there wanted nothing to make this house fit to receive the people of the greatest quality, little as it was. But all the servants and footmen, all but one valet and the maid, were lodged abroad, for Isabella, not much used to the sight of men about her, suffered them as seldom as possible to come in her presence, so that she lived more like a nun still than a lady of the world, and very rarely any maids came about her but Maria, who had always permission to come whenever she pleased, unless forbidden.

As Villenoys had the most tender and violent passion for his wife in the world, he suffered her to be pleased at any rate and to live in what method she best liked, and was infinitely satisfied with the austerity and manner of her conduct, since, in his arms and alone with him, she wanted nothing that could charm, so that she was esteemed the fairest and best of wives, and he the most happy of all mankind. When she would go abroad, she had her coaches rich and gay, and her livery ready to attend her in all the splendour imaginable, and he was always buying one rich jewel or necklace or some great rarity or other that might please her, so that there was nothing her soul could desire which it had not, except the assurance of eternal happiness, which she laboured incessantly to gain. She had no discontent, but because she was not blessed with a child; but she submits to the pleasure of Heaven and endeavoured by her good works and her charity to make the poor her children and was ever doing acts of virtue to make the proverb good, 'that more are the children of the barren than the fruitful woman'. She lived in this tranquillity beloved by all for the space of five years and time (and perpetual obligations from Villenoys, who was the most indulgent and endearing man in the world) had almost worn out of her heart the thoughts of Henault, or if she remembered him, it was in her prayers, or sometimes with a short sigh and no more, though it was a great while before she could subdue her heart to that calmness; but she was prudent and wisely bent all her endeavours to please, oblige, and caress the deserving living, and to strive all she could to forget the unhappy dead, since it could not but redound to the disturbance of her repose to think of him. So that she had now transferred all that tenderness she had for him to Villenoys.

Villenoys, of all diversions, loved hunting and kept at his country house a very famous pack of dogs, which he used to lend sometimes to a young lord, who was his dear friend and his neighbour in the country, who would often take them and be out two or three days together where he heard of game, and oftentimes Villenoys and he would be a whole week at a time exercising in this sport, for there was no game near at hand. This young lord had sent him a letter to invite him fifteen miles farther than his own villa to hunt and appointed to meet him at his country house in order to go in search of this promised game. So that Villenoys got about a week's provision of what necessaries he thought he should want in that time, and taking only his valet, who loved the sport, he left Isabella for a week to her devotion and her other innocent diversions of fine work, at which she was excellent, and left the town to go meet this young challenger.

When Villenoys was at any time out, it was the custom of Isabella to retire to her chamber and to receive no visits, not even the ladies', so absolutely she devoted herself to her husband. All the first day she passed over in this manner and, evening being come, she ordered her supper to be brought to her chamber and, because it was washing day the next day, she ordered all her maids to go very early to bed that they might be up betimes and to leave only Maria to attend her, which was accordingly done. This Maria was a young maid that was very discreet and, of all things in the world, loved her lady, whom she had lived with ever since she came from the monastery.

When all were in bed, and the little light supper just carried up to the lady, and only, as I said, Maria attending, somebody knocked at the gate, it being about nine of the clock at night, so Maria, snatching up a candle, went to the gate to see who it might be. When she opened the door, she found a man in a very odd habit and a worse countenance, and asking who he would speak with, he told her, her lady. 'My lady', replied Maria, 'does not use to receive visits at this hour; pray, what is your business?' He replied, 'That which I will deliver only to your lady, and that she may give me admittance, pray deliver her this ring.' And pulling off a small ring, with Isabella's name and hair in it, he gave it Maria, who, shutting the gate upon him, went in with the ring. As soon as Isabella saw it, she was ready to swound on the chair where she sat, and cried, 'Where had you this?'. Maria replied, 'An old, rusty fellow at the gate gave it me, and desired it might be his passport to you; I asked his name, but he said you knew him not, but he had great news to tell you.' Isabella replied, almost swounding again, 'O, Maria, I am ruined!' The maid all this while knew not what she meant, nor that that was a ring given to Henault by her mistress, but endeavouring to recover her, only asked her what she should say to the old messenger. Isabella bid her bring him up to her (she had scarce life to utter these last words) and before she was well recovered, Maria entered with the man, and Isabella making a sign to her to depart the room, she was left alone with him.

Henault (for it was he) stood trembling and speechless before her, giving her leisure to take a strict survey of him. At first finding no feature nor part of Henault about him, her fears began to lessen and she hoped it was not he as her first apprehensions had suggested, when he (with the tears of joy standing in his eyes, and not daring suddenly to approach her for fear of increasing that disorder he saw in her pale face) began to speak to her and cried, 'Fair creature, is there no remains of your Henault left in this face of mine all o'ergrown with hair? Nothing in these eyes sunk with eight years absence from you and sorrows? Nothing in this shape bowed with labour and griefs that can inform you I was once that happy man you loved?' At these words, tears stopped his speech and

Isabella's kept them company, for yet she wanted words. Shame and confusion filled her soul and she was not able to lift her eyes up to consider the face of him whose voice she knew so perfectly well. In one moment, she run over a thousand thoughts. She finds, by his return, she is not only exposed to all the shame imaginable, to all the upbraiding on his part when he shall know she is married to another, but all the fury and rage of Villenoys, and the scorn of the town, who will look on her as an adulteress. She sees Henault poor and knew she must fall from all the glory and tranquillity she had for five happy years triumphed in, in which time she had known no sorrow or care, though she had endured a thousand with Henault. She dies to think, however, that he should know she had been so lightly in love with him to marry again, and she dies to think that Villenoys must see her again in the arms of Henault. Besides, she could not recall her love, for love, like reputation, once fled, never returns more. 'Tis impossible to love and cease to love (and love another) and yet return again to the first passion, though the person have all the charms or a thousand times more than it had when it first conquered. This mystery in love, it may be, is not generally known, but nothing is more certain. One may a while suffer the flame to languish, but there may be a reviving spark in the ashes raked up that may burn anew, but when 'tis quite extinguished it never returns or rekindles.

'Twas so with the heart of Isabella: had she believed Henault had been living she had loved to the last moment of their lives, but, alas, the dead are soon forgotten, and she now loved only Villenoys.

After they had both thus silently wept, with very different sentiments, she thought 'twas time to speak, and dissembling as well as she could, she caressed him in her arms and told him she could not express her surprise and joy for his arrival. If she did not embrace him heartily or speak so passionately as she used to do, he fancied it her confusion and his being in a condition not so fit to receive embraces from her, and evaded them as much as 'twas possible for him to do in respect to her, till he had dressed his face and put himself in order. But the supper being just brought up when he knocked, she ordered

him to sit down and eat and he desired her not to let Maria
know who he was, to see how long it would be before she
knew him or would call him to mind. But Isabella commanded
Maria to make up a bed in such a chamber, without disturbing
her fellows, and dismissed her from waiting at table. The maid
admired what strange, good, and joyful news this man had
brought her mistress that he was so treated and alone with her,
which never any man had yet been, but she never imagined
the truth and knew her lady's prudence too well to question
her conduct. While they were at supper, Isabella obliged him
to tell her how he came to be reported dead, of which she
received letters both from Monsieur Villenoys and the Duke
of Beaufort, and by his man the news, who saw him dead. He
told her that, after the fight, of which first he gave her an
account, he being left among the dead, when the enemy came
to plunder and strip 'em, they found he had life in him. 'And
appearing as an eminent person, they thought it better booty
to save me', continued he, 'and get my ransom, than to strip
me and bury me among the dead, so they bore me off to a tent
and recovered me to life, and, after that, I was recovered of my
wounds and sold by the soldier that had taken me to a spahee,*
who kept me a slave, setting a great ransom on me such as I
was not able to pay. I writ several times to give you and my
father an account of my misery, but received no answer, and
endured seven years of dreadful slavery, when I found at last
an opportunity to make my escape, and from that time resolved
never to cut the hair of this beard till I should either see my
dearest Isabella again, or hear some news of her. All that I
feared was that she was dead,' and at that word he fetched a
deep sigh, and viewing all things so infinitely more magnificent
than he had left 'em, or believed she could afford, and that she
was far more beautiful in person and rich in dress than when
he left her, he had a thousand torments of jealousy that seized
him, of which he durst not make any mention, but rather chose
to wait a little and see whether she had lost her virtue. He
desired he might send for a barber to put his face in some
handsomer order and more fit for the happiness 'twas that
night to receive, but she told him no dress, no disguise, could
render him more dear and acceptable to her and that tomorrow

was time enough and that his travels had rendered him more fit for repose than dressing. So that after a little while, they had talked over all they had a mind to say, all that was very endearing on his side, and as much concern as she could force on hers; she conducted him to his chamber, which was very rich and which gave him a very great addition of jealousy. However he suffered her to help him to bed, which she seemed to do with all the tenderness in the world, and when she had seen him laid, she said she would go to her prayers and come to him as soon as she had done, which being before her usual custom, it was not a wonder to him she stayed long and he, being extremely tired with his journey, fell asleep.

'Tis true Isabella assayed to pray, but, alas, it was in vain. She was distracted with a thousand thoughts what to do, which the more she thought, the more it distracted her. She was a thousand times about to end her life and, at one stroke, rid herself of the infamy that she saw must inevitably fall upon her. But nature was frail and the tempter strong, and after a thousand convulsions, even worse than death itself, she resolved upon the murder of Henault, as the only means of removing all obstacles to her future happiness. She resolved on this, but after she had done so, she was seized with so great horror that she imagined if she performed it she should run mad, and yet, if she did not, she should be also frantic with the shames and miseries that would befall her, and believing the murder the least evil, since she could never live with him, she fixed her heart on that, and causing herself to be put immediately to bed in her own bed, she made Maria go to hers, and when all was still, she softly rose and taking a candle with her, only in her nightgown and slippers, she goes to the bed of the unfortunate Henault with a pen-knife in her hand. But considering she knew not how to conceal the blood should she cut his throat, she resolves to strangle him, or smother him with a pillow. That last thought was no sooner born but put in execution, and, as he soundly slept, she smothered him without any noise or so much as his struggling. But when she had done this dreadful deed, and saw the dead corpse of her once loved lord lie smiling (as it were) upon her, she fell into a swound with the horror of the deed, and it had been well for her she had there died; but she revived again, and, awakened to more and new horrors, she flies all frighted from the chamber and fancies the phantom of her dead lord pursues her. She runs from room to room and starts and stares as if she saw him continually before her. Now all that was ever soft and dear to her with him comes into her heart, and she finds he conquers anew, being dead, who could not gain her pity while living.

While she was thus flying from her guilt in vain, she hears one knock with authority at the door. She is now more affrighted if possible and knows not whither to fly for refuge. She fancies they are already the officers of justice and that ten thousand tortures and wracks are fastening on her to make her confess the horrid murder. The knocking increases and so loud that the laundry maids, believing it to be the woman that used to call them up, and help them to wash, rose and, opening the door, let in Villenoys who, having been at his country villa and finding there a footman instead of his friend, who waited to tell him his master was fallen sick of the smallpox and could not wait on him, he took horse and came back to his lovely Isabella. But running up as he used to do to her chamber, he found her not, and seeing a light in another room, he went in, but found Isabella flying from him out at another door with all the speed she could. He admires at this action and the more because his maid told him her lady had been abed a good while. He grows a little jealous and pursues her, but still she flies. At last, he caught her in his arms, where she fell into a swound, but quickly recovering, he set her down in a chair and, kneeling before her, implored to know what she ailed, and why she fled from him who adored her. She only fixed a ghastly look upon him and said she was not well. 'O,' said he, 'put not me off with such poor excuses. Isabella never fled from me when ill, but came to my arms and to my bosom to find a cure; therefore, tell me what's the matter?' At that she fell a-weeping in a most violent manner, and cried she was forever undone. He, being moved with love and compassion, conjured her to tell what she ailed. 'Ah,' said she, 'thou and I and all of us are undone!' At this, he lost all patience and raved and cried, 'Tell me, and tell me immediately, what's the matter?' When she saw his face pale and his eyes fierce, she fell on her knees and cried, 'O, you can never pardon me if I should tell you, and yet, alas, I am innocent of ill, by all that's good I am.' But her conscience accusing her at that word, she was silent. 'If thou art innocent,' said Villenoys, taking her up in his arms and kissing her wet face, 'by all that's good I pardon thee, whatever thou hast done.' 'Alas,' said she, 'O, but I dare not name it till you swear!' 'By all that's sacred,' replied he, 'and by whatever oath you can oblige me to, by my inviolable love to thee and by thy own dear self, I swear whate'er it be I do forgive thee. I know thou art too good to commit a sin I may not with honour pardon.'

With this, and heartened by his caresses, she told him that Henault was returned, and repeating to him his escape, she said she had put him to bed, and when he expected her to come, she fell on her knees at the bedside and confessed she was married to Villenoys. 'At that word', said she, 'he fetched a deep sigh or two and presently after with a very little struggling, died, and yonder he lies still in the bed.' After this, she wept so abundantly that all Villenoys could do could hardly calm her spirits. But after, consulting what they should do in this affair, Villenoys asked her who of the house saw him. She said, 'Only Maria, who knew not who he was.' So that, resolving to save Isabella's honour, which was the only misfortune to come, Villenoys himself proposed the carrying him out to the bridge and throwing him into the river, where the stream would carry him down to the sea and lose him; or, if he were found, none could know him. So Villenoys took a candle and went and looked on him, and found him altogether changed that nobody would know who he was. He therefore put on his clothes, which was not hard for him to do, for he was scarce yet cold, and comforting again Isabella as well as he could, he went himself into the stable and fetched a sack such as they used for oats, a new sack, whereon stuck a great needle with a packthread in it. This sack he brings into the house and shows to Isabella, telling her he would put the body in there for the better convenience of carrying it on his back. Isabella all this while said but little, but filled with thoughts all black and hellish, she pondered within while the fond and passionate Villenoys was endeavouring to hide her shame and to make this an absolute secret. She imagined that could she live after a deed so black, Villenoys would be eternal reproaching her, if not with his tongue, at least with his heart, and emboldened by one wickedness, she was the readier for another, and another of such a nature as has, in my opinion, far less excuse than the first. But when fate begins to afflict, she goes throughstitch with her black work.

When Villenoys, who would for the safety of Isabella's honour, be the sole actor in the disposing of this body, and since he was young, vigorous, and strong, and able to bear it, would trust no one with the secret, he having put up the body and tied it fast, set it on a chair, turning his back towards it with the more conveniency to take it upon his back, bidding Isabella give him the two corners of the sack in his hands, telling her they must do this last office for the dead, more in order to the securing their honour and tranquillity hereafter, than for any other reason, and bid her be of good courage till he came back, for it was not far to the bridge and it being the dead of the night, he should pass well enough. When he had the sack on his back and ready to go with it, she cried, 'Stay, my dear, some of his clothes hang out, which I will put in', and with that, taking the packneedle with the thread, sewed the sack with several strong stitches to the collar of Villenoys's coat without his perceiving it, and bid him go now. 'And when you come to the bridge', said she, 'and that you are throwing him over the rail, which is not above breast high, be sure you give him a good swing, lest the sack should hang on anything at the side of the bridge and not fall into the stream.' 'I'll warrant you', said Villenoys, 'I know how to secure his falling.' And going his way with it, love lent him strength, and he soon arrived at the bridge where, turning his back to the rail, and heaving the body over, he threw himself with all his force backward the better to swing the body into the river, whose weight (it being made fast to his collar) pulled Villenoys after it and both the live and the dead man falling into the river, which, being rapid at the bridge, soon drowned him, especially when so great a weight hung to his neck, so that he died without considering what was the occasion of his fate.

Isabella remained the most part of the night sitting in her

chamber without going to bed to see what would become of
her damnable design, but when it was towards morning and
she heard no news, she put herself into bed, but not to find
repose or rest there, for that she thought impossible after so
great a barbarity as she had committed. 'No,' said she, 'it is but
just I should forever wake, who have in one fatal night
destroyed two such innocents. O, what fate, what destiny is
mine? Under what cursed planet was I born, that Heaven itself
could not divert my ruin? It was not many hours since I
thought myself the most happy and blessed of women, and
now am fallen to the misery of one of the worst fiends of Hell.'

Such were her thoughts, and such her cries, till the light
brought on new matter for grief. For, about ten of the clock,
news was brought that two men were found dead in the river,
and that they were carried to the town hall to lie there till
they were owned. Within an hour after news was brought in
that one of these unhappy men was Villenoys; his valet, who
all this while imagined him in bed with his lady, ran to the hall
to undeceive the people, for he knew if his lord were gone out,
he should have been called to dress him, but finding it as 'twas
reported, he fell a-weeping and wringing his hands, in a most
miserable manner. He ran home with the news, where, knocking at his lady's chamber door and finding it fast locked, he
almost hoped again he was deceived. But Isabella rising, and
opening the door, Maria first entered weeping with the news
and then brought the valet to testify the fatal truth of it.
Isabella, though it were nothing but what she expected to hear,
almost swounded in her chair; nor did she feign it, but felt
really all the pangs of killing grief, and was so altered with her
night's watching and grieving that this new sorrow looked very
natural in her. When she was recovered, she asked a thousand
questions about him and questioned the possibility of it. 'For',
said she, 'he went out this morning early from me and had no
signs in his face of any grief or discontent.' 'Alas,' said the
valet, 'Madam, he is not his own murderer. Someone has done
it in revenge.' And then told her how he was found fastened to
a sack with a dead, strange man tied up within it, and everybody concludes that they were both first murdered and then
drawn to the river and thrown both in. At the relation of this

strange man, she seemed more amazed than before, and commanding the valet to go to the hall, and to take order about the Coroner's sitting on the body of Villenoys, and then to have it brought home. She called Maria to her and, after bidding her shut the door, she cried, 'Ah Maria, I will tell thee what my heart imagines, but first,' said she, 'run to the chamber of the stranger and see if he be still in bed, which I fear he is not.' She did so, and brought word he was gone. 'Then,' said she, 'my forebodings are true. When I was in bed last night with Villenoys' (and at that word she sighed as if her heart strings had broken) 'I told him I had lodged a stranger in my house who was by when my first lord and husband fell in battle, and that, after the fight, finding him yet alive, he spoke to him and gave him that ring you brought me last night, and conjured him if ever his fortune should bring him to Flanders, to see me and give me that ring and tell me—' (with that she wept, and could scarce speak) 'a thousand tender and endearing things, and then died in his arms. For my dear Henault's sake', said she, 'I used him nobly and dismissed you that night because I was ashamed to have any witness of the griefs I paid his memory. All this I told to Villenoys, whom I found disordered and, after a sleepless night, I fancy he got up and took this poor man and has occasioned his death.' At that she wept anew and Maria, to whom all that her mistress said was gospel, verily believed it so without examining reasons, and Isabella conjuring her since none of the house knew of the old man's being there (for old he appeared to be), that she would let it forever be a secret and to this she bound her by an oath, so that none knowing Henault, although his body was exposed there for three days to public view, when the Coroner had set* on the bodies, he found they had been first murdered some way or other and then afterwards tacked together and thrown into the river. They brought the body of Villenoys home to his house, where, it being laid on a table, all the house infinitely bewailed it and Isabella did nothing but swound away almost as fast as she recovered life. However, she would, to complete her misery, be led to see this dreadful victim of her cruelty and, coming near the table, the body, whose eyes were before close shut, now opened themselves wide and fixed them on Isabella, who, giving a great shriek, fell down in a swound, and the eyes closed again. They had much ado to bring her to life but, at last, they did so, and led her back to her bed where she remained a good while. Different opinions and discourses were made concerning the opening of the eyes of the dead man and viewing Isabella. But she was a woman of so admirable a life and conversation, of so undoubted a piety and sanctity of living, that not the least conjecture could be made of her having a hand in it, besides the improbability of it. Yet the whole thing was a mystery which they thought they ought to look into. But a few days after, the body of Villenoys being interred in a most magnificent manner, and, by will, all he had was long since settled on Isabella, the world, instead of suspecting her, adored her the more and everybody of quality was already hoping to be next, though the fair mourner still kept her bed and languished daily.

It happened not long after this, there came to the town a French gentleman who was taken at the siege of Candia and was fellow-slave with Henault for seven years in Turkey, and who had escaped with Henault and came as far as Liège with him, where, having some business and acquaintance with a merchant, he stayed some time, but when he parted with Henault, he asked him where he should find him in Flanders. Henault gave him a note with his name and place of abode, if his wife were alive; if not, to enquire at his sister's or his father's. This Frenchman came, at last, to the very house of Isabella, enquiring for this man, and received a strange answer and was laughed at. He found that was the house, and that the lady, and enquiring about the town, and speaking of Henault's return, describing the man, it was quickly discovered to be the same that was in the sack. He had his friend taken up (for he was buried) and found him the same and, causing a barber to trim him, when his bushy beard was off, a great many people remembered him, and the Frenchman affirming, he went to his own home. All Isabella's family and herself were cited before the magistrate of justice where, as soon as she was accused, she confessed the whole matter of fact and, without any disorder, delivered herself in the hands of justice as the murderess of two husbands (both beloved) in one night. The whole world stood amazed at this, who knew her life a holy and charitable life, and how dearly and well she had lived with her husbands, and everyone bewailed her misfortune, and she alone was the only person that was not afflicted for herself. She was tried and condemned to lose her head, which sentence she joyfully received and said Heaven and her judges were too merciful to her and that her sins had deserved much more.

While she was in prison, she was always at prayers and very cheerful and easy, distributing all she had amongst and for the use of the poor of the town, especially to the poor widows, exhorting daily the young and the fair that came perpetually to visit her never to break a vow, for that was first the ruin of her and she never since prospered, do whatever other good deeds she could. When the day of execution came, she appeared on the scaffold all in mourning, but with a mien so very majestic and charming and a face so surprising fair, where no languishment or fear appeared, but all cheerful as a bride, that she set all hearts a-flaming, even in that mortifying minute of preparation for death. She made a speech of half an hour long, so eloquent, so admirable a warning to the vow-breakers, that it was as amazing to hear her, as it was to behold her.

After she had done, with the help of Maria, she put off her mourning veil and, without anything over her face, she kneeled down and the executioner, at one blow, severed her beautiful head from her delicate body, being then in her seven and twentieth year. She was generally lamented and honourably buried.

THE ADVENTURE OF
THE BLACK LADY

About the beginning of last June (as near as I can remember)
Bellamora came to town from Hampshire and was obliged to
lodge the first night at the same inn where the stagecoach set
up. The next day she took coach for Covent Garden, where
she thought to find Madam Brightly, a relation of hers, with
whom she designed to continue for about half a year undiscov-
ered, if possible, by her friends in the country, and ordered
therefore her trunk, with her clothes, and most of her money
and jewels, to be brought after her to Madam Brightly's, by a
strange porter whom she spoke to in the street as she was
taking coach, being utterly unacquainted with the neat practices of this fine city. When she came to Bridges Street, where
indeed her cousin had lodged near three or four years since,
she was strangely surprised that she could not learn anything
of her; no, nor so much as meet with anyone that had ever
heard of her cousin's name. Till, at last, describing Madam
Brightly to one of the housekeepers* in that place, he told her
that there was such a kind of lady, whom he had sometimes
seen there about a year and a half ago, but that he believed she
was married and removed towards Soho. In this perplexity she
quite forgot her trunk and money etc. and wandered in her
hackney coach all over St Ann's parish, enquiring for Madam
Brightly, still describing her person, but in vain, for no soul
could give her any tale or tidings of such a lady. After she had
thus fruitlessly rambled, till she, the coachman, and the very
horses were e'en tired, by good fortune for her, she happened
on a private house, where lived a good, discreet, ancient
gentlewoman, who was fallen a little to decay, and was forced
to let lodgings for the best part of her livelihood, from whom
she understood that there was such a kind of a lady who had
lain there somewhat more than a twelvemonth, being near
three months after she was married. But that she was now gone
abroad with the gentleman her husband, either to the play, or

to take the fresh air, and she believed would not return till night. This discourse of the good gentlewoman's so elevated Bellamora's drooping spirits, that after she had begged the liberty of staying there till they came home, she discharged the coachman in all haste, still forgetting her trunk, and the more valuable furniture of it.

When they were alone, Bellamora desired she might be permitted the freedom to send for a pint of sack,* which, with some little difficulty, was at last allowed her. They began then to chat for a matter of half an hour of things indifferent, and, at length, the ancient gentlewoman asked the fair innocent (I must not say foolish) one, of what country, and what her name was. To both which she answered very directly and truly, though it might have proved not discreetly. She then enquired of Bellamora if her parents were living, and the occasion of her coming to town. The fair unthinking creature replied, that her father and mother were both dead, and that she had escaped from her uncle, under pretence of making a visit to a young lady, her cousin, who was lately married, and lived above twenty miles from her uncle's in the road to London, and that the cause of her quitting the country was to avoid the hated importunities of a gentleman, whose pretended love to her she feared had been her eternal ruin. At which she wept and sighed most extravagantly.

The discreet gentlewoman endeavoured to comfort her by all the softest and most powerful argument* in her capacity, promising her all the friendly assistance that she could expect from her during Bellamora's stay in town, which she did with so much earnestness and visible integrity, that the pretty innocent creature was going to make her a full and real discovery of her imaginary, insupportable misfortunes. And (doubtless) had done it, had she not been prevented by the return of the lady, whom she hoped to have found her cousin Brightly. The gentleman her husband just saw her within doors, and ordered the coach to drive to some of his bottle-companions, which gave the women the better opportunity of entertaining one another, which happened to be with some surprise on all sides. As the lady was going up to her apartment, the gentlewoman of the house told her there was a young lady in the parlour, who came out o' the country that very day on purpose to visit her. The lady stepped immediately to see who it was, and Bellamora approaching to receive her hoped for cousin, stopped on the sudden just as she came to her, and sighed out aloud, 'Ah Madam! I am lost—It is not your Ladyship I seek.' 'No, Madam,' returned t'other, 'I am apt to think you did not intend me this honour. But you are as welcome to me as you could be to the dearest of your acquaintance. Have you forgot me, Madam Bellamora?' continued she. That name startled both the other. However, it was with a kind of joy. 'Alas, Madam,' replied the young one, 'I now remember that I have been so happy to have seen you, but where, and when, my memory can't show me.' ''Tis indeed some years since,' returned the lady, 'but of that another time. Meanwhile, if you are unprovided of a lodging, I dare undertake you shall be welcome to this gentlewoman.' The fair unfortunate returned her thanks, and whilst a chamber was preparing for her, the lady entertained her in her own. About ten a clock they parted, Bellamora being conducted to her new lodging by the mistress of the house, who then left her to take what rest she could amidst her so many seeming misfortunes, returning to the other lady, who desired her to search into the cause of Bellamora's retreat to town.

The next morning the good gentlewoman of the house, coming up to her, found Bellamora almost drowned in tears, which by many kind and sweet words she at last stopped, and asking whence so great signs of sorrow should proceed, vowed a most profound secrecy if she would discover to her their occasion, which, after some little reluctancy, she did, in this manner.

'I was courted', said she, 'above three years ago, when my mother was yet living, by one Mr Fondlove, a gentleman of a good estate and true worth, and one who, I dare believe, did then really love me. He continued his passion for me with all the earnest and honest solicitations imaginable, till some months before my mother's death, who at that time was most desirous to see me disposed of in marriage to another gentleman, of a much better estate than Mr Fondlove, but one whose person and humour did by no means hit with my inclinations, and this gave Fondlove the unhappy advantage over me. For, finding me one day all alone in my chamber, and lying on my bed, in as mournful and wretched a condition, to my then foolish apprehension, as now I am, he urged his passion with such violence and accursed success for me, with reiterated promises of marriage, whenever I pleased to challenge 'em, which he bound with the most sacred oaths and most dreadful execrations, that partly with my aversion to the other, and partly with my inclinations to pity him, I ruined myself'— Here she relapsed into a greater extravagance of grief than before, which was so extreme, that it did not continue long. When therefore she was pretty well come to herself, the ancient gentlewoman asked her why she imagined herself ruined. To which she answered, 'I am great with child by him (Madam) and wonder you did not perceive it last night. Alas, I have not a month to go; I am shamed, ruined, and damned, I fear forever lost.' 'O fie, Madam, think not so,' said t'other, 'for the gentleman may yet prove true and marry you.' 'Aye, Madam,' replied Bellamora, 'I doubt not that he would marry me, for, soon after my mother's death, when I came to be at my own disposal, which happened about two months after, he offered, nay, most earnestly solicited me to it, which still he perseveres to do.' 'This is strange,' returned t'other, 'and it appears to me to be your own fault that you are yet miserable. Why did you not, or why will you not consent to your own happiness?' 'Alas, alas,' cried Bellamora, ''tis the only thing I dread in this world, for I am certain he can never love me after. Besides, ever since, I have abhorred the sight of him, and this is the only cause that obliges me to forsake my uncle and all my friends and relations in the country, hoping this populous and public place to be most private, especially, Madam, in your house and in your fidelity and discretion.' 'Of the last you may assure yourself, Madam,' said t'other, 'but what provision have you made for the reception of the young stranger that you carry about you?' 'Ah, Madam,' cried Bellamora, 'you have brought to mind another misfortune.'

Then she acquainted her with the supposed loss of her money and jewels, telling her withal that she had but three guineas and some silver left, and the rings she wore, in her present possession. The good gentlewoman of the house told her she would send to enquire at the inn where she lay the first night she came to town, for happily they might give some account of the porter to whom she had entrusted her trunk, and withal repeated her promise of all the help in her power, and for that time left her much more composed than she found her. The good gentlewoman went directly to the other lady, her lodger, to whom she recounted Bellamora's mournful confession, at which the lady appeared mighty concerned, and at last she told her landlady that she would take care that Bellamora should lie in according to her quality. 'For', added she, 'the child (it seems) is my own brother's.'

As soon as she had dined, she went to the Exchange* and bought child-bed linen, but desired that Bellamora might not have the least notice of it, and at her return dispatched a letter to her brother Fondlove in Hampshire, with an account of every particular, which soon brought him up to town, without satisfying any of his or her friends with the reason of his sudden departure; meanwhile, the good gentlewoman of the house had sent to the Star-inn on Fish Street-hill, to demand the trunk, which she rightly supposed to have been carried back thither. For, by good luck, it was a fellow that plied thereabouts, who brought it to Bellamora's lodgings that very night, but unknown to her. Fondlove no sooner got to London, but he posts to his sister's lodgings, where he was advised not to be seen of Bellamora till they had worked farther upon her, which the landlady began in this manner. She told her that her things were miscarried, and she feared lost; that she had but little money herself, and if the overseers of the poor* (justly so called from their over-looking 'em) should have the least suspicion of a strange and unmarried person, who was entertained in her house big with child and so near her time as Bellamora was, she should be troubled, if they could not give security to the parish of twenty or thirty pound that they should not suffer by her, which she could not; or otherwise, she must be sent to the house of correction,* and her child to a parish-nurse.

This discourse, one may imagine, was very dreadful to a person of her youth, beauty, education, family, and estate.

However, she resolutely protested that she had rather undergo all this than be exposed to the scorn of her friends and relations in the country. The other told her then that she must write down to her uncle a farewell letter as if she were just going aboard the packet-boat for Holland, that he might not send to enquire for her in town, when he should understand she was not at her new-married cousin's in the country, which accordingly she did, keeping herself a close prisoner to her chamber, where she was daily visited by Fondlove's sister and the landlady, but by no soul else, the first dissembling the knowledge she had of her misfortunes. Thus she continued for above three weeks, not a servant being suffered to enter her chamber, so much as to make her bed, lest they should take notice of her great belly. But for all this caution, the secret had taken wing, by the means of an attendant of the other lady below, who had overheard her speaking of it to her husband. This soon got out o' doors and spread abroad, till it reached the long ears of the wolves of the parish, who next day designed to give her an ungrateful visit. But Fondlove, by good providence, prevented it, who, the night before, was ushered into Bellamora's chamber by his sister, his brother-in-law, and the landlady. At the sight of him she had like to have swooned away, but he taking her in his arms, began again, as he was wont to do, with tears in his eyes, to beg that she would marry him ere she was delivered, if not for his, nor her own, yet for the child's sake, which she hourly expected, that it might not be born out of wedlock, and so be made uncapable of inheriting either of their estates, with a great many more pressing arguments on all sides. To which at last she consented, and an honest officious gentleman, whom they had before provided, was called up, who made an end of the dispute. So to bed they went together that night, and next day to the Exchange, for several pretty businesses that ladies in her condition want. Whilst they were abroad, came the vermin of the parish, (I mean, the overseers of the poor, who eat the bread from 'em) to search for a young black-haired lady (for so was Bellamora) who was either brought to bed, or just ready to lie down. The landlady showed 'em all the rooms in her house, but no such lady could be found. At last she bethought herself, and led 'em into her parlour, where she opened a little closet-door, and showed 'em her black cat that had just kittened; assuring 'em, that she should never trouble the parish as long as she had rats or mice in the house, and so dismissed 'em like logger-heads as they came.

THE UNFORTUNATE BRIDE;

OR,

THE BLIND LADY A BEAUTY

Frankwit and Wildvill were two young gentlemen of very
considerable fortunes, both born in Staffordshire, and during
their minority both educated together, by which opportunity
they contracted a very inviolable friendship, a friendship which
grew up with them, and though it was remarkably known to
everybody else, they knew it not themselves; they never made
profession of it in words, but actions; so true a warmth their
fires could boast, as needed not the effusion of their breath to
make it live. Wildvill was of the richest family, but Frankwit of
the noblest; Wildvill was admired for outward qualifications,
as strength and manly proportions, Frankwit for a much softer
beauty, for his inward endowments, pleasing in his conversation, of a free, and moving air, humble in his behaviour, and if
he had any pride, it was but just enough to show that he did
not affect humility, his mind bowed with a motion as uncon-
strained as his body, nor did he force this virtue in the least,
but he allowed it only; so amiable he was, that every virgin
that had eyes, knew too she had a heart, and knew as surely
she should lose it. His Cupid could not be reputed blind: he
never shot for him, but he was sure to wound. As every other
nymph admired him, so he was dear to all the tuneful sisters:
the Muses were fired with him as much as their own radiant
God Apollo, not their loved springs and fountains were so
grateful to their eyes as he, him they esteemed their Helicon
and Parnassus too; in short, whenever he pleased, he could
enjoy them all. Thus he enamoured the whole female sex, but
amongst all the sighing captives of his eyes, Belvira only
boasted charms to move him; her parents lived near his, and
even from their childhood they felt mutual love, as if their
eyes at their first meeting had struck out such glances as had
kindled into amorous flame. And now Belvira in her fourteenth
year (when the fresh spring of young virginity began to cast

more lively bloomings in her cheeks, and softer longings in her eyes) by her indulgent father's care was sent to London to a friend, her mother being lately dead, when, as if fortune ordered it so, Frankwit's father took a journey to the other world, to let his son the better enjoy the pleasures and delights of this. The young lover now with all imaginable haste interred his father, nor did he shed so many tears for his loss as might in the least quench the fires which he received from his Belvira's eyes, but (master of seventeen hundred pounds a year, which his father left him) with all the wings of love he flies to London, and solicits Belvira with such fervency, that it might be thought he meant death's torch should kindle Hymen's, and now as soon as he arrives at his journey's end, he goes to pay a visit to the fair mistress of his soul, and assures her, that though he was absent from her, yet she was still with him, and that all the road he travelled her beauteous image danced before him, and like the ravished prophet, he saw his deity in every bush; in short, he paid her constant visits, the sun ne'er rose or set, but still he saw it in her company, and every minute of the day he counted by his sighs. So incessantly he importuned her that she could no longer hold out, and was pleased in the surrender of her heart, since it was he was conqueror, and therefore felt a triumph in her yielding; their flames, now joined, grew more and more, glowed in their cheeks, and lightened in their glances; eager they looked, as there were pulses beating in their eyes, and all endearing, at last she vowed that, Frankwit living, she would ne'er be any other man's. Thus they passed on some time, while every day rolled over fair, Heaven showed an aspect all serene, and the sun seemed to smile at what was done; he still caressed his charmer with an innocence becoming his sincerity, he lived upon her tender breath, and basked in the bright lustre of her eyes, with pride and secret joy.

He saw his rivals languish for that bliss, those charms, those rapturous and ecstatic transports which he engrossed alone. But now some eighteen months (some ages in a lover's calendar) winged with delights, and fair Belvira, now grown fit for riper joys, knows hardly how she can deny her pressing lover and herself to crown their vows and join their hands as well as hearts. All this while the young gallant washed himself clean of that shining dirt, his gold; he fancied little of Heaven dwelt in his yellow angels, but let them fly away as it were on their own golden wings, he only valued the smiling babies in Belvira's eyes. His generosity was boundless as his love, for no man ever truly loved that was not generous. He thought his estate, like his passion, was a sort of a Pontic ocean, it could never know an ebb. But now he found it could be fathomed, and that the tide was turning, therefore he solicits with more impatience the consummation of their joys, that both might go like martyrs from their flames immediately to Heaven, and now at last it was agreed between them that they should both be one, but not without some reluctancy on the female side, for 'tis the humour of our sex, to deny most eagerly those grants to lovers for which most tenderly we sigh: so contradictory are we to ourselves, as if the deity had made us with a seeming reluctancy to his own designs, placing as much discords in our minds, as there is harmony in our faces. We are a sort of airy clouds, whose lightning flash out one way, and the thunder another. Our words and thoughts can ne'er agree.

So, this young charming lady thought her desires could live in their own longings, like misers' wealth-devouring eyes, and ere she consented to her lover, prepared him first with speaking looks, and then with a fore-running sigh, applied to the dear charmer thus: 'Frankwit, I am afraid to venture the matrimonial bondage, it may make you think yourself too much confined, in being only free to one.' 'Ah! My dear Belvira,' he replied, 'that one, like manna, has the taste of all; why should I be displeased to be confined to Paradise, when it was the curse of our forefathers to be set at large, though they had the whole world to roam in. You have, my love, ubiquitary charms, and you are all in all, in every part.' 'Aye but', replied Belvira, 'we are all like perfumes, and too continual smelling makes us seem to have lost our sweets. I'll be judged by my cousin Celesia here, if it be not better to live still in mutual love, without the last enjoyment.' (I had forgot to tell my reader that Celesia was an heiress, the only child of a rich Turkey merchant, who when he died, left her fifty thousand pound in money, and some estate in land; but, poor creature, she was blind to all these riches, having been born without the use of sight, though in all other respects charming to a wonder.) 'Indeed,' says Celesia (for she saw clearly in her mind), 'I admire you should ask my judgement in such a case, where I have never had the least experience; but I believe it is but a sickly soul which cannot nourish its offspring of desires without preying upon the body.' 'Believe me,' replied Frankwit, 'I bewail your want of sight, and I could almost wish you my own eyes for a moment, to view your charming cousin, where you would see such beauties as are too dazzling to be long beheld, and if too daringly you gazed, you would feel the misfortune of the loss of sight, much greater than the want on't, and you would acknowledge that in too presumptuously seeing, you would be blinder then, than now unhappily you are.'

'Ah! I must confess', replied Belvira, 'my poor dear cousin is blind, for I fancy she bears too great an esteem for Frankwit, and only longs for sight to look on him.' 'Indeed,' replied Celesia, 'I would be glad to see Frankwit, for I fancy he's as dazzling as he but now described his mistress, and if I fancy I see him, sure I do see him, for sight is fancy, is it not? Or do you feel my cousin with your eyes?' 'This is indeed a charming blindness,' replied Frankwit, 'and the fancy of your sight excels the certainty of ours; strange that there should be such glances even in blindness! You, fair maid, require not eyes to conquer, if your knight has such stars, what sunshine would your day of sight have, if ever you should see?' 'I fear those stars you talk of', said Belvira, 'have some influence on you, and by the compass you sail by now, I guess you are steering to my cousin. She is indeed charming enough to have been another offspring of bright Venus, blind like her brother Cupid.' 'That Cupid', replied Celesia, 'I am afraid has shot me, for methinks I would not have you marry Frankwit, but rather live as you do without the least enjoyment, for methinks if he were married, he would be more out of my sight than he already is.' 'Ah, Madam,' returned Frankwit, 'love is no camelion, it cannot feed on air alone.' 'No but', rejoined Celesia, 'you lovers that are not blind like love itself, have amorous looks to feed on.' 'Ah! Believe it,' said Belvira, ''tis better, Frankwit, not to lose Paradise by too much knowledge; marriage-enjoyment does but wake you from your sweet golden dreams. Pleasure is but a dream, dear Frankwit, but a dream, and to be wakened.' 'Ah, dearest but unkind Belvira,' answered Frankwit, 'sure there's no waking from delight, in being lulled on those soft breasts of thine.' 'Alas,' replied the bride to be, 'it is that very lulling wakes you; women enjoyed, are like romances read, or raree-shows,* once seen, mere tricks of the sleight of hand, which, when found out, you only wonder at yourselves for wondering so before at them. 'Tis expectation endears the blessing; Heaven would not be Heaven, could we tell what 'tis. When the plot's out you have done with the play, and when the last act's done, you see the curtain drawn with great indifferency.' 'Oh my Belvira,' answered Frankwit, 'that expectation were indeed a monster which enjoyment could not satisfy; I should take no pleasure', he rejoined, 'running from hill to hill, like children chasing that sun which I could never catch.' 'Oh thou shalt have it then, that sun of love,' replied Belvira, fired by this complaint, and gently rushed into his arms, rejoining, 'so Phoebus rushes radiant, and unsullied into a gilded cloud.' 'Well then, my dear Belvira,' answered Frankwit, 'be assured I shall be ever yours, as you are mine; fear not, you shall never draw bills of love upon me so fast as I shall wait in readiness to pay them; but now I talk of bills, I must retire into Cambridgeshire, where I have a small concern as yet unmortgaged; I will return thence with a brace of thousand pounds within a week at farthest, with which our nuptials by their celebration shall be worthy of our love. And then, my life, my soul, we shall be joined, never to part again.'

This tender expression moved Belvira to shed some few tears, and poor Celesia thought herself most unhappy that she had not eyes to weep with too; but if she had, such was the greatness of her grief, that sure she would have soon grown blind with weeping. In short, after a great many soft vows, and promises of an inviolable faith, they parted with a pompous sort of pleasing woe; their concern was of such a mixture of joy and sadness as the weather seems when it both rains and shines. And now the last, the very last of last adieus was over, for the farewells of lovers hardly ever end, and Frankwit (the

time being summer) reached Cambridge that night, about nine
a clock (strange, that he should have made such haste to fly
from what so much he loved), and now, tired with the fatigue
of his journey, he thought fit to refresh himself by writing
some few lines to his beloved Belvira, for a little verse after
the dull prose company of his servant, was as great an ease to
him (from whom it flowed as naturally and unartificially, as his
love or his breath) as a pace or hand gallop after a hard,
uncouth, and rugged trot. He therefore, finding his Pegasus
was no way tired with his land travel, takes a short journey
through the air, and writes as follows:

> 'My dearest dear Belvira,
>
> you knew my soul, you knew it yours before,
> I told it all, and now can tell no more;
> Your presence never wants fresh charms to move,
> But now more strange, and unknown pow'r you prove,
> For now your very absence 'tis I love.
> Something there is which strikes my wand'ring view,
> And still before my eyes I fancy you.
> Charming you seem, all charming, heavenly fair,
> Bright as a goddess does my love appear,
> You seem, Belvira, what indeed you are:
> Like the angelic offspring of the skies
> With beatific glories in your eyes,
> Sparkling with radiant lustre all divine.
> Angels and gods! Oh heavens, how bright they shine!
> Are you Belvira? Can I think you mine!
> Beyond ev'n thought, I do thy beauties see,
> Can such a heaven of heavens be kept from me?
> O be assured, I shall be ever true,
> I must——
> For if I would, I can't be false to you.
> Oh! How I wish I might no longer stay,
> Though I resolve I will no time delay,
> One tedious week, and then I'll fleet away.
> Though love be blind, he shall conduct my road,
> Winged with almighty love to your abode,
> I'll fly, and grow immortal as a god.
> Short is my stay, yet my impatience strong,
> Short though it is, alas, I think it long!

> I'll come, my life, new blessings to pursue,
> Love then shall fly a flight, he never flew,
> I'll stretch his balmy wings; I'm yours—adieu.

Frankwit.'

This letter Belvira received with unspeakable joy, and laid it up safely in her bosom, laid it where the dear author of it lay before, and wonderfully pleased with his humour of writing in verse, resolved not to be at all behind hand with him, and so writ as follows:

> 'My dear charmer,
>
> You knew before what power your love could boast,
> But now your constant faith confirms me most.
> Absent sincerity the best assures,
> Love may do much, but faith much more allures,
> For now your constancy has bound me yours.
> I find, methinks, in verse some pleasure too,
> I cannot want a Muse, who write to you.
> Ah! Soon return, return my charming dear,
> Heav'n knows how much we mourn your absence here;
> My poor Celesia now would charm your soul,
> Her eyes, once blind, do now divinely roll.
> An aged matron has by charms unknown
> Given her clear sight as perfect as thy own.
> And yet, beyond her eyes, she values thee,
> 'Tis for thy sake alone she's glad to see.
> She begged me, pray remember her to you,
> That is a task which now I gladly do.
> Gladly, since so I only recommend,
> A dear relation, and a dearer friend,
> Ne'er shall my love——but here my note must end.

Your ever true Belvira.'

When this letter was written, it was straight shown to Celesia, who looked upon anything that belonged to Frankwit with rejoicing glances; so eagerly she perused it, that her tender eyes beginning to water, she cried out (fancying she saw the words dance before her view) 'Ah! Cousin, cousin, your letter is running away, sure it can't go itself to Frankwit.' A great deal of other pleasing innocent things she said, but still her eyes flowed more bright with lustrous beams, as if they were to shine out now all that glancing radiancy which had been so long kept secret, and as if, as soon as the cloud of blindness once was broke, nothing but lightnings were to flash forever after. Thus in mutual discourse they spent their hours, while Frankwit was now ravished with the receipt of this charming answer of Belvira's, and blessed his own eyes, which discovered to him the much welcome news of fair Celesia's. Often he reads the letter o'er and o'er, but there his fate lay hid, for 'twas that very fondness proved his ruin. He lodged at a cousin's house of his, and there (it being a private family) lodged likewise a blackamoor lady,* then a widow; a whimsical knight had taken a fancy to enjoy her; enjoy her, did I say? Enjoy the devil in the flesh at once? I know not how it was, but he would fain have been a-bed with her, but she not consenting on unlawful terms (but sure all terms are with her unlawful), the knight soon married her, as if there were not Hell enough in matrimony, but he must wed the devil too. The knight a little after died, and left this lady of his (whom I shall call Moorea) an estate of six thousand pounds per annum. Now this Moorea observed the joyous Frankwit with an eager look, her eyes seemed like stars of the first magnitude glaring in the night; she greatly importuned him to discover the occasion of his transport, but he denying it (as 'tis the humour of our sex) made her the more inquisitive, and being jealous that it was from a mistress, employed her maid to steal it, and if she found it such to bring it her; accordingly it succeeded, for Frankwit having drank hard with some of the gentlemen of that shire, found himself indisposed, and soon went to bed, having put the letter in his pocket. The maid therefore to Moorea contrived that all the other servants should be out of the way, that she might plausibly officiate in the warming the bed of the indisposed lover, but likely, had it not been so, she had warmed it by his entreaties in a more natural manner; he being in bed in an inner room, she slips out the letter from his pocket, carries it to her mistress to read, and so restores it whence she had it. In the morning the poor lover wakened in a violent fever, burning with a fire more hot than that of love. In short, he continued sick a considerable while, all which time the lady Moorea constantly visited him, and he as unwillingly saw her (poor gentleman) as he would have seen a parson; for as the latter would have persuaded, so the former scared him to repentance. In the meanwhile, during his sickness, several letters were sent to him by his dear Belvira, and Celesia too (then learning to write) had made a shift to give him a line or two in postscript with her cousin, but all was intercepted by the jealousy of the black Moorea, black in her mind, and dark, as well as in her body. Frankwit too writ several letters as he was able, complaining of her unkindness, those likewise were all stopped by the same blackmoor devil. At last, it happened that Wildvill (who I told my reader was Frankwit's friend) came to London, his father likewise dead, and now master of a very plentiful fortune, he resolves to marry, and paying a visit to Belvira, enquires of her, concerning Frankwit; she all in mourning for the loss, told him his friend was dead. 'Ah! Wildvill, he is dead,' said she, 'and died not mine, a blackmoor lady had bewitched him from me; I received a letter lately which informed me all; there was no name subscribed to it, but it intimated that it was written at the request of dying Frankwit.' 'Oh! I am sorry at my soul,' said Wildvill, 'for I loved him with the best, the dearest friendship; no doubt then', rejoined he, ''tis witchcraft indeed that could make him false to you; what delight could he take in a blackmoor lady, though she had received him at once with a soul as open as her longing arms, and with her petticoat put off her modesty. Gods! How could he change a whole field argent into downright sables!' ''Twas done', returned Celesia, 'with no small blot, I fancy, to the female scutcheon.' In short, after some more discourse, but very sorrowful, Wildvill takes his leave, extremely taken with the fair Belvira, more beauteous in her cloud of woe; he paid her afterwards frequent visits, and found her wonder for the odd inconstancy of Frankwit greater than her sorrow, since he died so unworthy of her.

Wildvill attacked her with all the force of vigorous love, and she (as she thought) fully convinced of Frankwit's death, urged by the fury and impatience of her new ardent lover, soon surrendered, and the day of their nuptials now arrived, their hands were joined. In the meantime Frankwit (for he still lived) knew nothing of the injury the base Moorea practised, knew not that 'twas through her private order, that the forementioned account of his falsehood and his death was sent; but impatient to see his dear Belvira, though yet extremely weak, rid post to London, and that very day arrived there, immediately after the nuptials of his mistress and his friend were celebrated. I was at this time in Cambridge, and having some small acquaintance with this blackamoor lady, and sitting in her room that evening, after Frankwit's departure thence, in Moorea's absence, saw inadvertently a bundle of papers, which she had gathered up, as I suppose, to burn, since now they grew but useless, she having no further hopes of him. I fancied I knew the hand, and thence my curiosity only led me to see the name, and finding Belvira subscribed, I began to guess there was some foul play in hand, Belvira being my particularly intimate acquaintance; I read one of them, and finding the contents, conveyed them all secretly out with me, as I thought, in point of justice, I was bound, and sent them to Belvira by that night's post, so that they came to her hands soon after the minute of her marriage, with an account how, and by what means, I came to light on them.

No doubt but they exceedingly surprised her; but oh, much more she grew amazed immediately after, to see the poor, and now unhappy, Frankwit, who privately had enquired for her below, being received as a stranger, who said he had some urgent business with her in a back chamber below stairs. What tongue, what pen can express the mournful sorrow of this scene; at first they both stood dumb, and almost senseless; she took him for the ghost of Frankwit, he looked so pale, new risen from his sickness, he (for he had heard at his entrance in the house, that his Belvira married Wildvill) stood in a maze, and like a ghost indeed, wanted the power to speak, till spoken to the* first. At last, he draws his sword, designing there to fall upon it in her presence; she then imagining it his ghost too sure, and come to kill her, shrieks out and swoons; he ran immediately to her, and catched her in his arms, and while he strove to revive and bring her to herself, though that he thought could never now be done, since she was married, Wildvill missing his bride, and hearing the loud shriek, came running down, and entering the room, sees his bride lie clasped in Frankwit's arms, 'Ha! Traitor!' he cries out, drawing his sword with an impatient fury, 'have you kept that strumpet all this while, cursed Frankwit, and now think fit to put your damned cast-mistress upon me; could not you forbear her neither even on my wedding day? Abominable wretch!' Thus saying, he made a full pass at Frankwit, and run him through the left arm, and quite through the body of the poor Belvira; that thrust immediately made her start, though Frankwit's endeavours all before were useless. Strange, that her death revived her! For ah, she felt that now she only lived to die. Striving through wild amazement to run from such a scene of horror as her apprehensions showed her, down she dropped, and Frankwit seeing her fall (all friendship disanulled by such a chain of injuries) draws, fights with, and stabs his own loved Wildvill. Ah! Who can express the horror and distraction of this fatal misunderstanding! The house was alarmed, and in came poor Celesia, running in confusion just as Frankwit was offering to kill himself, to die with a false friend, and perjured mistress, for he supposed them such. Poor Celesia now bemoaned her unhappiness of sight and wished she again were blind. Wildvill died immediately, and Belvira only survived him long enough to unfold all their most unhappy fate, desiring Frankwit with her dying breath, if ever he loved her (and now she said that she deserved his love, since she had convinced him that she was not false) to marry her poor dear Celesia, and love her tenderly for her Belvira's sake, leaving her, being her nearest relation, all her fortune, and he, much dearer than it all, to be added to her own; so joining his and Celesia's hands, she poured her last breath upon his lips, and said, 'Dear Frankwit, Frankwit, I die yours.' With tears and wondrous sorrow he promised to obey her will, and in some months after her interment, he performed his promise.

PART TWO

Poetry

Song. Love Armed

Love in fantastic triumph sat,
Whilst bleeding hearts around him flowed,
For whom fresh pains he did create,
And strange tyrannic power he showed;
From thy bright eyes he took his fire,
Which round about, in sport he hurled;
But 'twas from mine, he took desire,
Enough to undo the amorous world.

From me he took his sighs and tears,
From thee his pride and cruelty;
From me his languishments and fears,
And every killing dart from thee;
Thus thou and I the God have armed,
And set him up a deity;
But my poor heart alone is harmed,
Whilst thine the victor is, and free.

On A Juniper Tree, Cut Down to Make Busks*

Whilst happy I triumphant stood,
The pride and glory of the wood;
My aromatic boughs and fruit,
Did with all other trees dispute.
Had right by nature to excel,
In pleasing both the taste and smell:
But to the touch I must confess,
Bore an ungrateful sullenness.
My wealth, like bashful virgins, I
Yielded with some reluctancy;
For which my value should be more,
Not giving easily my store.

My verdant branches all the year
Did an eternal beauty wear;
Did ever young and gay appear.
Nor needed any tribute pay,
For bounties from the god of day:
Nor do I hold supremacy,
(In all the wood) o'er every tree.
But even those too of my own race,
That grow not in this happy place.
But that in which I glory most,
And do myself with reason boast,
Beneath my shade the other day,
Young Philocles and Cloris* lay
Upon my root she leaned her head,
And where I grew, he made their bed:
Whilst I the canopy more largely spread.
Their trembling limbs did gently press,
The kind supporting yielding grass:
Ne'er half so blessed as now, to bear
A swain so young, a nymph so fair:
My grateful shade I kindly lent,
And every aiding bough I bent.
So low, as sometimes had the bliss,
To rob the shepherd of a kiss,
Whilst he in pleasures far above
The sense of that degree of love:
Permitted every stealth I made,
Unjealous of his rival shade.
I saw 'em kindle to desire,
Whilst with soft sighs they blew the fire:
Saw the approaches of their joy,
He growing more fierce, and she less coy,
Saw how they mingled melting rays,
Exchanging love a thousand ways.
Kind was the force on every side,
Her new desire she could not hide:
Nor would the shepherd be denied.
Impatient he waits no consent
But what she gave by languishment,

The blessed minute he pursued;
While love and shame her soul subdued.
And now transported in his arms,
Yields to the conqueror all her charms,
His panting breast, to hers now joined,
They feast on raptures unconfined;
Vast and luxuriant such as prove
The immortality of love.
For who but a divinity,
Could mingle souls to that degree?
Now like the phoenix, both expire,
While from the ashes of their fire,
Sprung up a new, and soft desire.
Like charmers, thrice they did invoke
The god and thrice new vigour took.
Nor had the mystery ended there,
But Cloris reassumed her fear,
And chid the swain, for having pressed,
What she alas could not resist:
Whilst he in whom love's sacred flame,
Before and after was the same,
Fondly implored she would forget
A fault which he would yet repeat.
From active joys with some they hast*
To a reflection on the past;
A thousand times my covert bless,
That did secure their happiness:
Their gratitude to every tree
They pay, but most to happy me;
The shepherdess my bark caressed,
Whilst he my root, love's pillow, kissed;
And did with sighs their fate deplore,
Since I must shelter them no more;
And if before my joys were such,
In having heard, and seen too much,
My grief must be as great and high,
When all abandoned I shall be,
Doomed to a silent destiny.
No more the charming strife to hear,

The shepherd's vows, the virgin's fear:
No more a joyful looker on,
Whilst love's soft battle's lost and won.
With grief I bowed my murmuring head,
And all my crystal dew I shed.
Which did in Cloris pity move,
(Cloris whose soul is made of love;)
She cut me down, and did translate,
My being to a happier state.
No martyr for religion died
With half that unconsidering pride;
My top was on that altar laid,
Where love his softest offerings paid:
And was as fragrant incense burned,
My body into busks was turned,
Where I still guard the sacred store,
And of love's temple keep the door.

A Ballad on Mr J. H. to Amoret, Asking Why I Was So Sad

My Amoret, since you must know,
The grief you say my eyes do show:
Survey my heart, where you shall find,
More love than for yourself confined.
And though you chide, you'll pity too,
A passion which even rivals you.

Amyntas on a holy-day
As fine as any lord of May,
Amongst the nymphs and jolly swains,
That feed their flocks upon the plains:
Met in a grove beneath whose shade,
A match of dancing they had made.

His cassock was of green, as trim
As grass upon a river brim;
Untouched or sullied with a spot,
Unpressed by either lamb or goat:
And with the air it loosely played,
With every motion that he made.

His sleeves a-many ribbons ties,
Where one might read love-mysteries:
As if that way he would impart,
To all, the sentiments of his heart,
Whose passions by those colours known,
He with a charming pride would own.

His bonnet with the same was tied,
A silver scrip* hung by his side:
His buskins* garnished a-la-mode,
Were graced by every step he trod;
Like Pan a majesty he took,
And like Apollo when he spoke.

His hook a wreath of flowers did braid,
The present of some love-sick maid.
Who all the morning had bestowed,
And to her fancy now composed:
Which fresher seemed when near that place,
To whom the giver captive was.

His eyes their best attracts put on,
Designing some should be undone;
For he could at his pleasure move,
The nymphs he liked to fall in love:
Yet so he ordered every glance,
That still they seemed but wounds of chance.

He well could feign an innocence,
And taught his silence eloquence;
Each smile he used, had got the force,
To conquer more than soft discourse:

Which when it served his ends he'd use,
And subtly through a heart infuse.

His wit was such it could control
The resolutions of a soul;
That a religious vow had made,
By love it ne'er would be betrayed:
For when he spoke he well could prove
Their errors who dispute with love.

With all these charms he did address
Himself to every shepherdess:
Until the bagpipes which did play,
Began the business of the day;
And in the taking forth to dance,
The lovely swain became my chance.

To whom much passion he did vow,
And much his eyes and sighs did show;
And both employed with so much art,
I strove in vain to guard my heart;
And ere the night our revels crossed,
I was entirely won and lost.

Let me advise thee, Amoret,
Fly from the baits that he has set
In every grace; which will betray
All beauties that but look that way:
But thou hast charms that will secure
A captive in this conqueror.

Song. The Invitation

Damon, I cannot blame your will,
'Twas chance and not design did kill;
For whilst you did prepare your charms,
On purpose Sylvia to subdue:

I met the arrows as they flew,
And saved her from their harms.

Alas she cannot make returns,
Who for a swain already burns,
A shepherd whom she does caress:
With all the softest marks of love,
And 'tis in vain thou seek'st to move,
The cruel shepherdess.

Content thee with this victory,
Think me as fair and young as she:
I'll make thee garlands all the day,
And in the groves we'll sit and sing;
I'll crown thee with the pride o'th' spring,
When thou art lord of May.

Song

When Jemmy* first began to love,
He was the gayest swain
That ever yet a flock had drove,
Or danced upon the plain.
'Twas then that I, weighs me poor heart
My freedom threw away,
And finding sweets in every smart,
I could not say him nay.

And ever when he talked of love,
He would his eyes decline;
And every sigh, a heart would move,
Gued faith and why not mine?
He'd press my hand, and kiss it oft,
In silence spoke his flame.
And whilst he treated me thus soft,
I wished him more to blame.

Sometimes to feed my flocks with him,
My Jemmy would invite me:

Where he the gayest songs would sing,
On purpose to delight me.
And Jemmy every grace displayed,
Which were enough I trow,*
To conquer any princely maid,
So did he me I vow.

But now for Jemmy must I mourn,
Who to the wars must go;
His sheephook to a sword must turn:
Alack what shall I do?
His bagpipe into warlike sounds,
Must now exchanged be:
Instead of bracelets,* fearful wounds;
Then what becomes of me?

On the Death of the Late Earl of Rochester

Mourn, mourn, ye Muses, all your loss deplore
The young, the noble Strephon* is no more.
Yes, yes, he fled quick as departing light,
And ne'er shall rise from death's eternal night,
So rich a prize the Stygian* gods ne'er bore,
Such wit, such beauty, never graced their shore.
He was but lent this duller world t'improve
In all the charms of poetry, and love;
Both were his gift, which freely he bestowed,
And like a god, dealt to the wondering crowd.
Scorning the little vanity of fame,
Spite of himself attained a glorious name.
But oh, in vain was all his peevish pride,
The sun as soon might his vast lustre hide,
As piercing, pointed, and more lasting bright,
As suffering no vicissitudes of night.
Mourn, mourn, ye muses, all your loss deplore,
The young, the noble Strephon is no more.

Now uninspired upon your banks we lie,
Unless when we would mourn his elegy;
His name's a genius that would wit dispense,
And give the theme a soul, the words a sense.
But all fine thought that ravished when it spoke,
With the soft youth eternal leave has took;
Uncommon wit that did the soul o'ercome,
Is buried all in Strephon's worshipped tomb;
Satire has lost its art, its sting is gone,
The fop and cully* now may be undone;
That dear instructing rage is now allayed,
And no sharp pen dares tell 'em how they've strayed;
Bold as a god was every lash he took,
But kind and gentle the chastising stroke.
Mourn, mourn, ye youths whom fortune has betrayed,
The last reproacher of your vice is dead.

Mourn all ye beauties, put your cypress on,
The truest swain that e'er adored you's gone;
Think how he loved, and writ, and sighed, and spoke,
Recall his mien, his fashion, and his look.
By what dear arts the soul he did surprise,
Soft as his voice, and charming as his eyes.
Bring garlands all of never-dying flowers,
Bedewed with everlasting falling showers;
Fix your fair eyes upon your victim'd slave,
Sent gay and young to his untimely grave.
See where the noble swain extended lies,
Too sad a triumph of your victories;
Adorned with all the graces Heaven e'er lent,
All that was great, soft, lovely, excellent
You've laid into his early monument.
Mourn, mourn, ye beauties, your sad loss deplore,
The young, the charming Strephon is no more.

Mourn, all ye little gods of love, whose darts
Have lost their wonted power of piercing hearts;
Lay by the gilded quiver and the bow,
The useless toys can do no mischief now,

Those eyes that all your arrows' points inspired,
Those lights that gave ye fire are now retired,
Cold as his tomb, pale as your mother's doves;
Bewail him then, oh all ye little loves,
For you the humblest votary have lost
That ever your divinities could boast;
Upon your hands your weeping heads decline,
And let your wings encompass round his shrine;
Instead of flowers your broken arrows strow,
And at his feet lay the neglected bow.
Mourn, all ye little gods, your loss deplore,
The soft, the charming Strephon is no more.

Large was his fame, but short his glorious race,
Like young Lucretius* lived and died apace.
So early roses fade, so over all
They cast their fragrant scents, then softly fall,
While all the scattered perfumed leaves declare,
How lovely 'twas when whole, how sweet, how fair.
Had he been to the Roman Empire known,
When great Augustus filled the peaceful throne,
Had he the noble wondrous poet seen,
And known his genius, and surveyed his mien,
(When wits, and heroes graced divine abodes)
He had increased the number of their gods;
The royal judge had temples reared to's name,
And made him as immortal as his fame;
In love and verse his Ovid* he 'ad out-done
And all his laurels, and his Julia* won.
Mourn, mourn, unhappy world his loss deplore,
The great, the charming Strephon is no more.

To Mrs W. On Her Excellent Verses
(Writ in Praise of Some I Had Made
On the Earl of Rochester)
Written in a Fit of Sickness

Enough kind Heaven! To purpose I have lived,
And all my sighs and languishments survived.
My stars in vain their sullen influence have shed,
    Round my till now unlucky head:
  I pardon all the silent hours I've grieved,
  My weary nights and melancholy days;
    When no kind power my pain relieved,
  I lose you all, you sad remembrances,
    I lose you all in new-born joys,
  Joys that will dissipate my falling tears.
  The mighty soul of Rochester's revived,
  Enough kind Heaven to purpose I have lived.
  I saw the lovely phantom, no disguise
  Veiled the blessed vision from my eyes,
'Twas all o'er Rochester that pleased and did surprise.
Sad as the grave I sat by glimmering light,
Such as attends departing souls by night.
Pensive as absent lovers left alone,
Or my poor dove, when his fond mate was gone.
Silent as groves when only whispering gales
    Sigh through the rushing leaves,
As softly as a bashful shepherd breathes
    To his loved nymph his amorous tales.
So dull I was, scarce thought a subject found,
Dull as the light that gloomed around;
    When lo the mighty spirit appeared,
    All gay, all charming to my sight;
    My drooping soul it raised and cheered,
    And cast about a dazzling light.
    In every part there did appear,
    The great, the god-like Rochester,
His softness all, his sweetness everywhere.

It did advance, and with a generous look,
To me addressed, to worthless me it spoke:
With the same wonted grace my Muse it praised,
With the same goodness did my faults correct:
And careful of the fame himself first raised,
Obligingly it schooled my loose neglect.
The soft, the moving accents soon I knew
The gentle voice made up of harmony;
Through the known paths of my glad soul it flew;
I knew it straight, it could no other's be,
'Twas not allied but very very he.
  So the all-ravished swain that hears
  The wondrous music of the spheres,
For ever does the grateful sound retain,
  Whilst all his oaten pipes and reeds
The rural music of the groves and meads
Strive to divert him from the heavenly song in vain.
  He hates their harsh and untuned lays,
Which now no more his soul and fancy raise.
  But if one note of the remembered air
  He chance again to hear,
He starts, and in a transport cries,—'tis there!
He knows it all by that one little taste,
And by that grateful hint remembers all the rest.
Great, good, and excellent, by what new way
  Shall I my humble tribute pay,
For this vast glory you my Muse have done,
For this great condescension shown!
  So gods of old sometimes laid by
  Their aweful trains of majesty,
And changed even Heaven awhile for groves and
         [plains,
And to their fellow gods preferred the lowly swains.
  And beds of flowers would oft compare,
  To those of downy clouds or yielding air;
  At purling streams would drink in homely shells,
  Put off the god, to revel it in woods and shepherds'
         [cells;
  Would listen to their rustic songs, and show

Such divine goodness in commending too,
Whilst the transported swain the honour pays
With humble adoration, humble praise.

The Disappointment

I

One day the amorous Lysander,
By an impatient passion swayed,
Surprised fair Cloris, that loved maid,
Who could defend herself no longer.
All things did with his love conspire;
The gilded planet of the day,
In his gay chariot drawn by fire,
Was now descending to the sea,
And left no light to guide the world,
But what from Cloris' brighter eyes was hurled.

II

In a lone thicket made for love,
Silent as yielding maids' consent,
She with a charming languishment,
Permits his force, yet gently strove;
Her hands his bosom softly meet,
But not to put him back designed,
Rather to draw 'em on inclined:
Whilst he lay trembling at her feet,
Resistance 'tis in vain to show;
She wants the power to say—'Ah! what d'ye do?'

III

Her bright eyes sweet, and yet severe,
Where love and shame confusedly strive,
Fresh vigour to Lysander give;
And breathing faintly in his ear,
She cried 'Cease, cease your vain desire,
Or I'll call out——what would you do?
My dearer honour even to you
I cannot, must not give—retire,
Or take this life, whose chiefest part
I gave you with the conquest of my heart.'

IV

But he as much unused to fear,
As he was capable of love,
The blessed minutes to improve,
Kisses her mouth, her neck, her hair;
Each touch her new desire alarms,
His burning trembling hand he pressed
Upon her swelling snowy breast,
While she lay panting in his arms.
All her unguarded beauties lie
The spoils and trophies of the enemy.

V

And now without respect or fear,
He seeks the object of his vows,
(His love no modesty allows)
By swift degrees advancing—where
His daring hand that altar seized,
Where gods of love do sacrifice:
That aweful throne, that paradise
Where rage is calmed, and anger pleased;
That fountain where delight still flows,
And gives the universal world repose.

VI

Her balmy lips encountering his,
Their bodies, as their souls, are joined;
Where both in transports unconfined
Extend themselves upon the moss.
Cloris half dead and breathless lay;
Her soft eyes cast a humid light,
Such as divides the day and night;
Or falling stars, whose fires decay:
And now no signs of life she shows,
But what in short-breathed sighs returns and goes.

VII

He saw how at her length she lay;
He saw her rising bosom bare;
Her loose, thin robes, through which appear
A shape designed for love and play;
Abandoned by her pride and shame.
She does her softest joys dispense,
Offering her virgin-innocence
A victim to love's sacred flame;
While the o'er-ravished shepherd lies
Unable to perform the sacrifice.

VIII

Ready to taste a thousand joys,
The too transported hapless swain
Found the vast pleasure turned to pain;
Pleasure which too much love destroys:
The willing garments by he laid,
And Heaven all opened to his view,
Mad to possess, himself he threw
On the defenceless lovely maid.
But oh what envying god conspires
To snatch his power, yet leave him the desire!

IX

Nature's support, (without whose aid
She can no human being give)
Itself now wants the art to live;
Faintness its slackened nerves invade:
In vain th'enraged youth essayed
To call its fleeting vigour back,
No motion 'twill from motion take;
Excess of love his love betrayed:
In vain he toils, in vain commands;
The insensible fell weeping in his hand.

X

In this so amorous cruel strife,
Where love and fate were too severe,
The poor Lysander in despair
Renounced his reason with his life:
Now all the brisk and active fire
That should the nobler part inflame,
Served to increase his rage and shame,
And left no spark for new desire:
Not all her naked charms could move
Or calm that rage that had debauched his love.

XI

Cloris returning from the trance
Which love and soft desire had bred,
Her timorous hand she gently laid
(Or guided by design or chance)
Upon that fabulous Priapus,*
That potent god, as poets feign;
But never did young shepherdess,
Gathering of fern upon the plain,
More nimbly draw her fingers back,
Finding beneath the verdant leaves a snake:

XII

Than Cloris her fair hand withdrew,
Finding that god of her desires
Disarmed of all his aweful fires,
And cold as flowers bathed in the morning dew.
Who can the nymph's confusion guess?
The blood forsook the hinder place,
And strewed with blushes all her face,
Which both disdain and shame expressed:
And from Lysander's arms she fled,
Leaving him fainting on the gloomy bed.

XIII

Like lightning through the grove she hies
Or Daphne* from the Delphic god,
No print upon the grassy road
She leaves, t'instruct pursuing eyes.
The wind that wantoned in her hair,
And with her ruffled garments played,
Discovered in the flying maid
All that the gods e'er made, if fair.
So Venus, when her love was slain,
With fear and haste flew o'er the fatal plain.

XIV

The nymph's resentments none but I
Can well imagine or condole:
But none can guess Lysander's soul,
But those who swayed his destiny.
His silent griefs swell up to storms,
And not one god his fury spares;
He cursed his birth, his fate, his stars;
But more the shepherdess's charms,
Whose soft bewitching influence
Had damned him to the Hell of impotence.

The Dream. A Song

I

The grove was gloomy all around
Murm'ring the streams did pass,
Where fond Astrea* laid her down
Upon a bed of grass.

I slept and saw a piteous sight,
Cupid a-weeping lay,
Till both his little stars of light
Had wept themselves away.

II

Methought I asked him why he cried,
My pity led me on:
All sighing the sad boy replied,
'Alas, I am undone!

As I beneath yon myrtles lay,
Down by Diana's springs,
Amyntas stole my bow away,
And pinioned both my wings.'

III

'Alas!' cried I, ''twas then thy darts
Wherewith he wounded me:
Thou mighty deity of hearts,
He stole his power from thee.

Revenge thee, if a god thou be
Upon the amorous swain;
I'll set thy wings at liberty,
And thou shalt fly again.

IV

And for this service on my part,
All I implore of thee,
Is, that thou't wound Amyntas' heart,
And make him die for me.'

His silken fetters I untied,
And the gay wings displayed;
Which gently fanned, he mounts and cried,
'Farewell fond easy maid.'

V

At this I blushed, and angry grew
I should a god believe;
And waking found my dream too true,
Alas, I was a slave.

A Letter to a Brother of the Pen in Tribulation

Poor Damon! Art thou caught? Is't ev'n so?
Art thou become a¹ tabernacler* too?
Where sure thou dost not mean to preach or pray,
Unless it be the clean contrary way:
This holy² time I little thought thy sin
Deserved a tub* to do its penance in.
Oh how you'll for th'Aegyptian flesh-pots wish,
When you're half-famished with your Lenten-dish,
Your almonds, currants, biscuits hard and dry,
Food that will soul and body mortify:
Damned penitential drink, that will infuse
Dull principles into thy grateful Muse.
—Pox on't that you must needs be fooling now,

¹ So he called a sweating-tub.
² Lent.

Just when the wits had greatest[3] need of you.
Was Summer then so long a-coming on,
That you must make an artificial one?
Much good may't do thee; but 'tis thought thy brain
Ere long will wish for cooler days again.
For honesty no more will I engage:
I durst have sworn thou'dst had thy pusillage.
Thy looks the whole cabal* have cheated too;
But thou wilt say, most of the wits do so.
Is this thy writing[4] plays? Who thought thy wit
An interlude of whoring would admit.
To poetry no more thou'lt be inclined,
Unless in verse to damn all womankind:
And 'tis but just thou shouldst in rancour grow
Against that sex that has confined thee so.
All things in nature now are brisk and gay
At the approaches of the blooming May:
The new-fletched* birds do in our arbours sing
A thousand airs to welcome in the Spring;
Whilst ev'ry swain is like a bridegroom dressed,
And ev'ry nymph as going to a feast:
The meadows now their flowery garments wear,
And ev'ry grove does in its pride appear:
Whilst thou poor Damon in close rooms art pent
Where hardly thy own breath can find a vent.
Yet that too is a Heaven, compared to th'task
Of coddling every morning in a cask.
Now I could curse this female, but I know,
She needs it not, that thus could handle you.
Besides, that vengeance does to thee belong,
And 'twere injustice to disarm thy tongue.
Curse then, dear swain, that all the youth may hear,
And from thy dire mishap be taught to fear.
Curse till thou hast undone the race, and all
That did contribute to thy spring and fall.

---

[3] I wanted a prologue to a play.
[4] He pretended to retire to write.

Song. On Her Loving Two Equally
Set by Captain Pack*

I

How strongly does my passion flow,
Divided equally 'twixt two?
Damon had ne'er subdued my heart,
Had not Alexis took his part;
Nor could Alexis powerful prove,
Without my Damon's aid to gain my love.

II

When my Alexis present is,
Then I for Damon sigh and mourn;
But when Alexis I do miss,
Damon gains nothing but my scorn.
But if it chance they both are by,
For both alike I languish, sigh, and die.

III

Cure then, thou mighty winged god,
This restless fever in my blood;
One golden-pointed dart take back:
But which, oh Cupid, wilt thou take?
If Damon's, all my hopes are crossed;
Or that of my Alexis, I am lost.

The Counsel. A Song
Set by Captain Pack

I

A pox upon this needless scorn:
Sylvia for shame the cheat give o'er:
The end to which the fair are born,
Is not to keep their charms in store:
But lavishly dispose in haste
Of joys which none but youth improve;
Joys which decay when beauty's past;
And who, when beauty's past, will love?

II

When age those glories shall deface,
Revenging all your cold disdain;
And Sylvia shall neglected pass,
By every once-admiring swain;
And we no more shall homage pay:
When you in vain too late shall burn,
If love increase, and youth decay,
Ah Sylvia! Who will make return?

III

Then haste, my Sylvia, to the grove,
Where all the sweets of May conspire
To teach us every art of love,
And raise our joys of pleasure higher:
Where while embracing we shall lie
Loosely in shades on beds of flowers,
The duller world while we defy,
Years will be minutes, ages hours.

Song. The Surprise.
Set by Mr Farmer*

I

Phyllis, whose heart was unconfined,
And free as flowers on meads and plains,
None boasted of her being kind,
'Mongst all the languishing and amorous swains.
No sighs or tears the nymph could move,
To pity or return their love.

II

Till on a time the hapless maid
Retired to shun the heat o'th' day
Into a grove, beneath whose shade
Strephon the careless shepherd sleeping lay:
But oh such charms the youth adorn,
Love is revenged for all her scorn.

III

Her cheeks with blushes covered were,
And tender sighs her bosom warm,
A softness in her eyes appear;
Unusual pain she feels from every charm:
To woods and echoes now she cries,
For modesty to speak denies.

On Mr J. H. in a Fit of Sickness

If when the god of day retires,
The pride of all the Spring decays and dies:

Wanting those life-begetting fires
From whence they draw their excellencies;
Each little flower hangs down its gaudy head,
Losing the lustre which it did retain;
No longer will its fragrant face be spread,
But languishes into a bud again:
    So with the sighing crowd it fares
Since you Amyntas, have your eyes withdrawn,
    Ours lose themselves in silent tears,
    Our days are melancholy dawn;
    The groves are unfrequented now,
    The shady walks are all forlorn;
    Who still were throng to gaze on you:
With nymphs, whom your retirement has undone.

II

Our bagpipes now away are flung,
    Our flocks a-wandering go;
Garlands neglected, on the boughs are hung,
    That used to adorn each cheerful brow,
    Forsaken looks the enamelled May:
    And all its wealth uncourted dies;
Each little bird forgets its wonted lay,
That sung good morrow to the welcome day,
    Or rather to thy lovely eyes.
    The cooling streams do backward glide:
    Since on their banks they saw not thee,
    Losing the order of their tide,
    And murmuring, chide thy cruelty:
Then haste to lose themselves i'th' angry sea.

III

Thus everything in its degree,
    Thy said* retreat deplore;
Haste then, Amyntas and restore
    The whole world's loss in thee.
For like an Eastern monarch, when you go,

(If such a fate the world must know)
   A beauteous and a numerous host
Of love-sick maids, will wait upon thy ghost;
And death that secret will reveal,
   Which pride and shame did here conceal;
   Live then thou loveliest of the plains,
   Thou beauty of the envying swains;
   Whose charms even death itself would court,
And of his solemn business make a sport.

IV

In pity to each sighing maid,
Revive, come forth, be gay and glad;
Let the young god of love implore,
   In pity lend him darts,
For when thy charming eyes shall shoot no more;
He'll lose his title of the god of hearts.
   In pity to Astrea live,
Astrea, whom from all the sighing throng,
   You did your oft won garlands give:
For which she paid you back in grateful song:
Astrea, who did still the glory boast,
To be adored by thee, and to adore thee most.

V

With pride she saw her rivals sigh and pine,
And vainly cried, the lovely youth is mine!
By all thy charms I do conjure thee, live;
By all the joys thou canst receive, and give:
By each recess and shade where thou and I,
   Love's secrets did unfold;
And did the dull unloving world defy:
   Whilst each the heart's fond story told.
If all these conjurations naught prevail,
Not prayers or sighs, or tears avail,
But Heaven has destined we deprived must be,
Of so much youth, wit, beauty, and of thee;

I will the deaf and angry powers defy,
Curse thy decease, bless thee, and with thee die.

The Cabal at Nickey Nackeys

I

A pox of the statesman that's witty,
Who watches and plots all the sleepless night:
For seditious harangues, to the Whigs* of the city;
And maliciously turns a traitor in spite.
Let him wear and torment his lean carrion:
    To bring his sham-plots about,
    Till at last king, bishop, and baron,
For the public good he have quite rooted out.

II

But we that are no politicians,
But rogues that are impudent, bare faced and great,
Boldly head the rude rabble in times of sedition;
And bear all down before us, in church and in state.
Your impudence is the best state-trick;
    And he that by law means to rule,
    Let his history with ours be related;
And though we are the knaves, we know who's the fool.

Song

Cease, cease, Amynta to complain
    Thy languishment give o'er,
Why should'st thou sigh because the swain
    Another does adore.
Those charms fond maid that vanquished thee,

Have many a conquest won,
And sure he could not cruel be,
    And leave 'em all undone.

The youth a noble temper bears,
    Soft and compassionate,
And thou canst only blame thy stars,
    That made thee love too late;
Yet had their influence all been kind,
    They had not crossed my fate,
The tenderest hours must have an end,
    And passion has its date.

The softest love grows cold and shy,
    The face so late adored,
Now unregarded passes by,
    Or grows at last abhorred;
All things in nature fickle prove,
    See how they glide away;
Think so in time thy hopeless love
    Will die, as flowers decay.

On The Death of E. Waller, Esquire

How to thy sacred memory shall I bring
(Worthy thy fame) a grateful offering?
I, who by toils of sickness, am become
Almost as near as thou art to a tomb.
While every soft and every tender strain
Is ruffled, and ill-natured grown with pain.
But, at thy name, my languished Muse revives,
And a new spark in the dull ashes strives.
I hear thy tuneful verse, thy song divine;
And am inspired by every charming line.
But, oh————
What inspiration at the second hand,
Can an immortal elegy command?

Unless, like pious offerings, mine should be
Made sacred, being consecrate to thee.
Eternal, as thy own almighty verse,
Should be those trophies that adorn thy hearse.
The thought illustrious, and the fancy young;
The wit sublime, the judgement fine and strong;
Soft, as thy notes to Sacharissa* sung.
Whilst mine, like transitory flowers, decay,
That come to deck thy tomb a short-lived day.
Such tributes are, like tenures, only fit
To show from whom we hold our right to wit.

    Hail, wondrous Bard, whose Heaven-born genius first
My infant Muse, and blooming fancy nursed!
With thy soft food of love I first began,
Then fed on nobler panegyric strain,
Numbers seraphic and at every view,
My soul extended, and much larger grew:
Where e'er I read, new raptures seized my blood;
Methought I heard the language of a god.

    Long did the untuned world in ignorance stray,
Producing nothing that was great and gay,
Till taught, by thee, the true poetic way.
Rough were the tracts before, dull and obscure;
Nor pleasure, nor instruction could procure.
Their thoughtless labour could no passion move;
Sure, in that age, the poets knew not love:
That charming god, like apparitions, then
Was only talked on, but ne'er seen by men:
Darkness was o'er the Muses' land displayed,
And even the chosen tribe unguided strayed.
Till, by thee rescued from th'Egyptian night,
They now look up, and view the god of light,
That taught them how to love, and how to write;
And to enhance the blessing which Heaven lent,
When for our great instructor thou wert sent.

Large was thy life, but yet thy glory's more;
And, like the sun, did still dispense thy power,
Producing something wondrous every hour:
And, in thy circulary course, didst see
The very life and death of poetry.
Thou saw'st the generous nine neglected lie,
None listening to their heavenly harmony;
The world being grown to that low ebb of sense,
To disesteem the noblest excellence;
And no encouragement to prophets shown,
Who in past ages got so great renown
Though fortune elevated thee above
Its scanty gratitude, or fickle love;
Yet, sullen with the world, untired by age,
Scorning th'unthinking crowd, thou quit'st the stage.

To Mr Creech (*Under The Name of Daphnis*) *On His*
Excellent Translation of Lucretius

Thou great young man, permit amongst the crowd
Of those that sing thy mighty praises loud,
My humble Muse to bring its tribute too.
    Inspired by thy vast flight of verse,
Methinks I should some wondrous thing rehearse,
Worthy divine Lucretius, and diviner thou.
    But I of feebler seeds designed
    Whilst the slow moving atoms strove,
    With careless heed to form my mind:
    Composed it all of softer love.
In gentle numbers all my songs are dressed,
    And when I would thy glory sing,
    What in strong manly verse I would express,
Turns all to womanish tenderness within.
Whilst that which admiration does inspire,
In other souls, kindles in mine a fire.
Let them admire thee on—whilst I this newer way
Pay thee yet more than they;

For more I owe, since thou hast taught me more
Than all the mighty bards that went before.
Others long since have paled the vast delight;
In duller Greek and Latin satisfied the appetite:
But I unlearned in schools, disdain that mine
Should treated be at any feast but thine.
Till now, I cursed my birth, my education,
And more the scanted customs of the nation:
Permitting not the female sex to tread,
The mighty paths of learned heroes dead.
The god-like Virgil and great Homer's verse,
Like divine mysteries are concealed from us.
 We are forbid all grateful themes,
  No ravishing thoughts approach our ear
  The fulsome jingle of the times,
Is all we are allowed to understand or hear.
 But as of old, when men unthinking lay,
Ere gods were worshipped, or ere laws were framed,
The wiser bard that taught 'em first t'obey,
Was next to what he taught, adored and famed;
Gentler they grew, their words and manners changed,
And salvage* now no more the woods they ranged.
So thou by this translation dost advance
Our knowledge from the state of ignorance,
And equals us to man, ah, how can we
Enough adore, or sacrifice enough to thee!

The mystic terms of rough philosophy,
Thou dost so plain and easily express:
Yet deckst them in so soft and gay a dress:
So intelligent to each capacity
That they at once instruct and charm the sense,
With heights of fancy, heights of eloquence;
And reason over all unfettered plays,
Wanton and undisturbed as Summer's breeze;
 That gliding murmurs o'er the trees:
And no hard notion meets or stops its way.
 It pierces, conquers, and compels,
Beyond poor feeble faith's dull oracles.

Faith, the despairing soul's content,
Faith, the last shift of routed argument.

Hail sacred Wadham,* whom the Muses grace
And from the rest of all the reverend pile
Of noble palaces, designed thy space:
    Where they in soft retreat might dwell.
They blessed thy fabric, and said—'Do thou
    Our darling sons contain;
We thee our sacred nursery ordain.'
    They said and blessed and it was so.
And if of old the fanes* of sylvian gods,
    Were worshipped as divine abodes
    If courts are held as sacred things,
    For being the aweful seats of kings
    What veneration should be paid
To thee that hast such wondrous poets made!
    To gods for fear, devotion was designed,
    And safety made us bow to majesty;
    Poets by nature awe and charm the mind,
Are born not made by dull religion or necessity.

The learned Thyrsis* did to thee belong,
Who Athens' plague has so divinely sung.
Thyrsis to wit, as sacred friendship true,
Paid mighty Cowley's* memory its due.
Thyrsis who whilst a greater plague did reign,
Than that which Athens did depopulate,
Scattering rebellious fury o'er the plain,
That threatened ruin to the church and state,
Unmoved he stood, and feared no threats of fate.
That loyal champion for the church and crown,
That noble ornament of the sacred gown,
Still did his sovereign's cause* espouse,
And was above the thanks of the mad Senate house.
Strephon* the great, whom last you sent abroad,
Who writ, and loved, and looked like any god;
For whom the Muses mourn, the love-sick maids
Are languishing in melancholy shades.

The Cupids flag their wings, their bows untie,
And useless quivers hang neglected by,
And scattered arrows all around 'em lie.
By murmuring brooks the careless deities are laid
Weeping their rifled power now noble Strephon's dead.
    Ah, sacred Wadham! Shouldst thou never own
    But this delight of all mankind and thine
    For ages past of dullness, this alone,
        This charming hero would atone.
    And make thee glorious to succeed in time;
    But thou like nature's self disdainst to be,
        Stinted to singularity.
Even as fast as she thou dost produce,
And over all the sacred mystery infuse.
    No sooner was famed Strephon's glory set,
    Strephon, the soft, the lovely, and the great;
    But Daphnis rises like the morning-star
    That guides the wandering traveller from afar.
    Daphnis whom every grace and Muse inspires,
Scarce Strephon's ravishing poetic fires
    So kindly warm, or so divinely cheer.

Advance young Daphnis, as thou hast begun
    So let thy mighty race be run.
    Thou in thy large poetic chase,
    Beginst where others end the race.
If now thy grateful numbers are so strong,
If they so early can such graces show,
Like beauty so surprising, when so young,
What Daphnis will thy riper judgement do,
When thy unbounded verse in their own streams shall
                                                    [flow!
What wonder will they not produce,
    When thy immortal fancy's loose
Unfettered, unconfined by any other Muse!
    Advance young Daphnis then, and mayest thou prove
    Still sacred in thy poetry and love.
    May all the groves with Daphnis's songs be blessed,
    Whilst every bark is with thy distichs* dressed.

May timorous maids learn how to love from thence
And the glad shepherd, arts of eloquence.
And when to solitude thou wouldst retreat,
May their tuned pipes thy welcome celebrate.
And all the nymphs strew garlands at thy feet.
May all the purling streams that murmuring pass,
    The shady groves and banks of flowers,
    The kind reposing beds of grass,
    Contribute to their softer hours.
Mayest thou thy Muse and mistress there caress,
And may one heighten t'other's happiness.
And whilst thou so divinely dost converse,
We are content to know and to admire thee in thy
                  [sacred verse.

A Letter to Mr Creech at Oxford
Written in the Last Great Frost

Daphnis, because I am your debtor
(And other causes which are better)
I send you here my debt of letter.
You should have had a scrap of nonsense,
You may remember left at Tonson's.*
(Though by the way that's scurvy rhyme, Sir,
But yet 'twill serve to tag a line, Sir.)
A billet-doux I had designed then,
But you may think I was in wine then;
Because it being cold, you know,
We warmed it with a glass—or so,
I grant you that shie* wine's the devil,
To make one's memory uncivil;
But when 'twixt every sparkling cup,
I so much brisker wit took up;
Wit, able to inspire a thinking;
And make one solemn even in drinking;
Wit that would charm and stock a poet,

Even instruct ———— who has no wit;
Wit that was hearty, true, and loyal,
Of wit, like Bays',* Sir, that's my trial;
I say 'twas most impossible,
That after that one should be dull.
Therefore because you may not blame me,
Take the whole truth as ———— shall sa' me,
    From White-Hall, Sir, as I was coming
His sacred Majesty from dunning;*
Who oft in debt is, truth to tell,
For Tory farce, or doggerell,*
When every street as dangerous was,
As ever the Alpian hills to pass,
When melted snow and ice confound one,
Whether to break one's neck, or drown one,
And billet-doux in pocket lay,
To drop as coach should jolt that way,
Near to that place of fame called Temple,*
(Which I shall note by sad example)
Where college dunce is cured of simple,
Against that sign of whore called scarlet,
My coachman fairly laid pilgarlick.*
    Though scribbling fist was out of joint,
And every limb made great complaint;
Yet missing the dear assignation,
Gave me most cause of tribulation.
To honest H—le* I should have shown ye,
A wit that would be proud t'have known ye;
A wit uncommon, and facetious,
A great admirer of Lucretius,
But transitory hopes do vary,
And high designments oft miscarry,
Ambition never climbed so lofty,
But may descend too fair and softly,
But would you'd seen how sneakingly
I looked with this catastrophe
So saucy Whig, when plot broke out,*
Dejected hung his snivelling snout,
So Oxford member looked, when Rowley*

Kicked out the rebel crew so foully;
So Perkin* once that god of Wapping,
Whom slippery turn of state took napping,
From hope of James the Second fell
Into the native scounderel.
So lover looked of joy defeated,
When too much fire his vigour cheated,
Even so looked I, when bliss depriving,
Was caused by over-hasty driving,
Who saw me could not choose but think,
I looked like brawn in sousing drink.*
Or Lazarello* who was showed
For a strange fish, to th' gaping crowd.
    Thus you by fate (to me sinister),
At shop of book my billet missed, Sir.
And home I went as discontent,
As a new routed parliament,
Not seeing Daphnis ere he went.
And sure his grief beyond expressing,
Of joy proposed to want the blessing;
Therefore to pardon pray incline,
Since disappointment all was mine;
Of Hell we have no other notion,
Than all the joys of Heaven's privation;
So, Sir, with recommendments fervent,
I rest your very humble servant.

Postscript

On twelfth-night, Sir, by that good token,
When lamentable cake was broken,
You had a friend, a man of wit,
A man whom I shall ne'er forget;
For every word he did impart,
'Twas worth the keeping in a heart:
True Tory all, and when he spoke,
A god in wit, though man in look.
—To this your friend—Daphnis address

The humblest of my services;
Tell him how much—yet do not too,
My vast esteem no words can show;
Tell him—that he is worthy—you.

To Lysander, Who Made Some Verses on a Discourse of Love's Fire

I

In vain, dear youth, you say you love,
And yet my marks of passion blame;
Since jealousy alone can prove,
The surest witness of my flame:
And she who without that, a love can vow,
Believe me, shepherd, does not merit you.

II

Then give me leave to doubt that fire
I kindle, may another warm,
A face that cannot move desire,
May serve at least to end the charm:
Love else were witchcraft, that on malice bent,
Denies ye joys, or makes ye impotent.

III

'Tis true, when cities are on fire,
Men never wait for crystal springs;
But to the neighbouring pools retire;
Which nearest, best assistance bring;
And serves as well to quench the raging flame,
As if from god-delighting streams it came.

IV

A fancy strong may do the feat
Yet this to love a riddle is,

And shows that passion but a cheat;
    Which men but with their tongues confess.
For 'tis a maxim in love's learned school,
Who blows the fire, the flame can only rule.

V

Though honour does your wish deny,
    Honour! The foe to your repose;
    Yet 'tis more noble far to die,
    Than break love's known and sacred laws:
What lover would pursue a single game,
That could amongst the fair deal out his flame?

VI

Since then Lysander you desire,
    Aminta only to adore;
    Take in no partners to your fire,
    For who well loves, that loves one more?
And if such rivals in your heart I find,
'Tis in my power to die, but not be kind.

On the First Discovery of Falsehood in Amintas

Make haste! Make haste my miserable soul,
    To some unknown and solitary grove,
Where nothing may thy languishment control
    Where thou mayest never hear the name of love.
Where unconfined, and free as whispering air,
Thou mayest caress and welcome thy despair:

Where no dissembled complaisance may veil
    The griefs with which, my soul, thou art oppressed.

But dying, breathe thyself out in a tale
   That may declare the cause of thy unrest:
The toils of death 'twill render far more light
And soon convey thee to the shades of night.

Search then, my soul, some unfrequented place,
   Some place that nature meant her own repose:
When she herself withdrew from human race,
   Displeased with wanton lovers' vows and oaths.
Where sol could never dart a busy ray,
And where the softer winds ne'er met to play.

By the sad purling of some rivulet
   O'er which the bending yew and willow grow,
That scarce the glimmerings of the day permit,
   To view the melancholy banks below,
Where dwells no noise but what the murmurs make,
When the unwilling stream the shade forsakes.

There on a bed of moss and new-fallen leaves,
   Which the triumphant trees once proudly bore,
Though now thrown off by every wind that breathes
   Despised by what they did adorn before,
And who, like useless me, regardless lie
While springing beauties do the boughs supply.

There lay thee down, my soul, and breathe thy last,
   And calmly to the unknown regions fly;
But ere thou dost thy stock of life exhaust,
   Let the ungrateful know, why 'tis you die.
Perhaps the gentle winds may chance to bear
Thy dying accents to Amintas' ear.

Breathe out thy passion; tell him of his power
   And how thy flame was once by him approved.
How soon as wished he was thy conqueror
   No sooner spoke of love, but was beloved.
His wondrous eyes, what weak resistance found,
While every charming word begat a wound.

Here thou wilt grow impatient to be gone,
    And through my willing eyes will silent pass,
Into the stream that gently glides along,
    But stay thy hasty flight (my soul), alas,
A thought more cruel will thy flight secure,
Thought, that can no admittance give to cure.

Think, how the prostrate infidel now lies,
    An humble suppliant at another's feet,
Think, while he begs for pity from her eyes.
    He sacrifices thee without regret.
Think, how the faithless treated thee last night,
And then, my tortured soul, assume thy flight.

From Of Plants, *Book VI*

O thou*——
Of all the woody nations happiest made
Thou greatest princess of the fragrant shade.
But should the goddess Dryas not allow
That royal title to thy virtue due,
At least her justice must this truth confess
If not a princess, thou'rt a prophetess,
And all the glories of immortal fame
Which conquering monarchs so much strive to gain,
Is but at best from thy triumphing boughs
To reach a garland to adorn their brows,
And after monarchs, poets claim a share
As the next worthy thy prized wreaths to wear.
Among that number, do not me disdain,
Me, the most humble of that glorious train.
I by a double right thy bounties claim,   The
Both from my sex, and in Apollo's name: translatress
Let me with Sappho* and Orinda* be   in her
O ever sacred nymph adorned by thee;   own person
And give my verses immortality.   speaks

From Aesop's Fables

LXXI

THE YOUNG MAN AND HIS CAT

A youth in love with puss, to
　　Venus prayed
To change the useless beauty to
　　A maid.

Venus consents, but in the
　　Height of charms
'A mouse!' she cried, and leaves
　　His ravished arms.

Moral

Ill principles no mercy can reclaim,
And once a rebel still will be the same.

LXXXVII

THE BEAR AND TWO TRAVELLERS

A bear approached two travellers
　　One fled
To a safe tree, th'other lay still
　　As dead,

The bear but smelling to his
　　face retired
The friend descends and
　　laughing thus enquired

Moral

What was't he whispered in his ear. Quoth he:
'He bade me shun a treacherous friend like thee.'

A Pindaric on the Death of Our Late Sovereign: With an Ancient Prophecy on His Present Majesty

I

Sad was the morn, the sadder week began,
And heavily the god of day came on:
From ominous dreams my wondering soul looked out,
And saw a dire confusion round about.
My bed like some sad monument appeared,
Round which the mournful statues wring their hands
         [and weep;
Distracted objects all, with mighty grief prepared
 To rouse me from my painful sleep.
Not the sad bards that wailed Jerusalem's woes,
(With wild neglect throughout the peopled street,
With a prophetic rage affrighting all they meet)
Had mightier pangs of sorrow, mightier throes;
'Ah! Wretch, undone,' they cry, 'awake forlorn,
The King! The King is dead! Rise! Rise and mourn.'

II

Again I bid 'em tell their sorrow's theme,
Again they cry, 'The King! The King is dead!
Extended, cold and pale, upon the royal bed.'
 Again I heard, and yet I thought it dream.
  'Impossible!' I raving cry,
'That such a monarch! Such a God should die!
And no dire warning to the world be given:
No hurricanes on earth! No blazing fires in Heaven!
 The sun and tide their constant courses keep:
 That cheers the world with its life-giving reign,
 This hastes with equal motion to the deep;
And in its usual turns revives the banks again,

And in its soft and easy way,
Brings up no storms or monsters from the sea,
No showers of blood, no temple's veil is rent,
But all is calm, and all is innocent.
When nature in convulsions should be hurled,
And fate should shake the fabric of the world;
Impossible! Impossible!' I cry.
'So great a King! So much a God! So silently should die!

III

True, I divined, when lo a voice arrived,
Welcome as that which did the crowd surprise
When the dead Lazarus from the tomb revived,
And saw a pitying God attend his rise.
'Our sovereign lives!' it cried. 'Rise and adore!
Our sovereign lives! Heaven adds one wonder more
To the miraculous history of his numerous store.'
Sudden as thought or winged lightning flies,
This chased the gloomy terrors from our eyes,
And all from sorrows, fall to sacrifice.
Whole hecatombs* of vows the altars crown,
To clear our sins that brought this vengeance down;
So the great saviour of the world did fall,
A bleeding victim to atone for all!
Nor were the blessed apostles more revived
When in the resurrection they beheld
Their faith established, and their Lord survived,
And all the holy prophecies fulfilled.
Their mighty love, by mighty joy they showed!
    And if from feebler faith before,
They did the deity and man adore:
What must they pay, when he confirmed the God?
Who having finished all his wonders here,
    And full instructions given,
To make his bright divinity more clear;
Transfigured all to glory, mounts to Heaven!

IV

So fell our earthly God! So loved, so mourned,
    So like a God again returned.
For of his message, yet a part was unperformed,
    But oh, our prayers and vows were made too late,
    The sacred dictates were already passed:
    And open laid the mighty book of fate,
    Where the great monarch read his life's short date;
    And for eternity prepared in haste.
      He saw in th'ever lasting chains
Of long passed time and numerous things,
    The fates, vicissitudes, and pains,
Of mighty monarchies, and mighty kings;
And blessed his stars that in an age so vain,
Where zealous mischiefs, frauds, rebellions, reign,
Like Moses, he had lead the murm'ring crowd,
Beneath the peaceful rule of his almighty wand;
    Pulled down the golden calf to which they bowed,
    And left 'em safe, entering the promised land;
    And to good Joshua,* now resigns his sway,
Joshua, by Heaven and nature pointed out to lead the way.

V

Full of wisdom and the power of God,
The royal prophet now before him stood:
On whom his hands the dying monarch laid,
And wept with tender joy, and blessed and said:
'To thee, kind aid in all my fates and powers,
Dear partner of my sad and softest hours,
Thy parting King and brother recommends
His frighted nations, and his mourning friends,
Take to thy pious care my faithful flock.
    And though the sheltering cedar fade,
Regard,' said he, 'regard my tender stock;
    The noble stems may shoot and grow
    To grace the spacious plains, and bow
Their spreading branches round thee a defensive shade.'

The royal successor to all he hears
With sighs assented, and confirming tears.
Much more he spoke, much more he had expressed,
But that the charming accents of his tongue
Flew upwards, to compose a Heavenly song,
And left his speaking eyes to bless and tell the rest,
His eyes so much adored! Whose less'ning light
Like setting suns that hasten on the night;
(Lending their glories to another sphere)
Those sacred lights are fading here,
Whilst every beam above informs a star,

VI

Which shall a nobler business know,
And influence his best loved friends below.
But, oh!
No human thought can paint the grief and love,
With which the parting heroes strove.
Sad was the scene, soft looks the voice supplies,
Anguish their hearts, and languishment their eyes;
Not God-like Jonathan* with greater pain,
Sigh'd his last farewell to the royal swain;
While aweful silence filled the gloomy place,
And death and midnight hung on ev'ry face.
And now the fatal hour came on,
And all the blessed pow'rs above
In haste to make him all their own,
Around the royal bed in shining order move.
Once more he longs to see the breaking day,
The last his mortal eyes shall e'er behold,
And oft he asked if no kind ray,
Its near approach foretold.
And when he found 'twas dawning in,
(With the cold tide of death that flowed all o'er)
'Draw, draw,' said he, 'this cloud that hangs between,
And let me take my last adieu;
Oh let me take my last last view,
For I shall never, never see it more.'
And now——

Officious angels catch his dying sighs,
And bear 'em up in triumph to the skies,
Each forms a soul! Of the divinest dress!
For new-born kings and heroes to possess.
The last, that from the sacred fabric flew,
Made Charles a God! And James a monarch too!

To His Sacred Majesty, King James the Second

All hail great Prince, whom ev'ry miracle
    Preserved for universal rule;
        When time your wondrous story shall unfold,
Your glorious deeds in arms, when yet but young;
Your strange escapes, and danger shall be told,
Your battles fought, your gilded laurels won,
When yet the elder generals (not in fame)
        Your perils dar'st not share,
Alone the raging torrent you would stem,
And bear before you the fierce tide of war.

    How Spain* records your glorious name;
And how when danger called, for Britain's good,
You paid the lavish ransom of your blood.
    When the ingrates shall blushing read,
How far great souls the vulgar can exceed
In patience, suffering, and humility,
Your condescension, and your banishment,*
Then let the obstinate (convinced) agree;
You only were preserved, and fit for sacred government.

Come listen all whom needless fears* possess,
And hear how Heav'n confirms your happiness:
    Behold the sacred promised prince,
    Whom wondrous prophets* ages since
Told, when the mystic figures of the year,
    To such a number should amount,
    (As fill this lucky year's account)
O'er England there should reign a star
Of that divine and gracious influence,
Should make proud neighbouring nations fear,
And mightier Britain's happy genius prove,

And bless the land with plenty, peace, and love.
'Tis you, oh sacred Sir, for empire born,
   Shall make the great prediction true,
   And this last miracle perform,
To make us blessed and make us own it too.
Oh may your lustre with your life renew;
Long may you shine, and spread your beams as far,
As from the morning to the ev'ning star;
Till your convincing rays, your foes o'ercome,
And for your glorious magnitude the scanted globe want
                               [room.

On Desire. A Pindaric

What art thou, oh thou new-found pain?
   From what infection dost thou spring?
Tell me——oh! Tell me thou enchanting thing,
     Thy nature, and thy name;
   Inform me by what subtle art,
     What powerful influence,
You got such vast dominion in a part
Of my unheeded, and unguarded, heart,
That fame and honour cannot drive ye thence.

Oh! Mischievous usurper of my peace;
Oh! Soft intruder on my solitude,
   Charming disturber of my ease,
   That hast my nobler fate pursued,
And all the glories of my life subdued.

Thou haunt'st my inconvenient hours;
The business of the day, nor silence of the night,
   That should to cares and sleep invite,
   Can bid defiance to thy conquering powers.
Where hast thou been this live-long age
   That from my birth till now,
Thou never couldst one thought engage,

Or charm my soul with the uneasy rage
That made it all its humble feebles* know?

    Where wert thou, oh malicious sprite,
    When shining honour did invite?
    When interest called, then thou wert shy,
Nor to my aid one kind propension brought,
    Nor wouldst inspire one tender thought,
    When princes at my feet did lie.
When thou couldst mix ambition with my joy,
Then peevish phantom thou wert nice and coy,
    Not beauty could invite thee then
    Nor all the arts of lavish men!
Not all the powerful rhetoric of the tongue
    Not sacred wit could charm thee on;
    Not the soft play that lovers make,
Nor sigh could fan thee to a fire,
Not pleading tears, nor vows could thee awake,
Or warm the unformed something——to desire.

    Oft I've conjured thee to appear
    By youth, by love, by all their powers,
    Have searched and sought thee everywhere,
In silent groves, in lonely bowers:
On flowery beds where lovers wishing lie,
    In sheltering woods where sighing maids
    To their assigning shepherds hie,
And hide their blushes in the gloom of shades:
    Yet there, even there, though youth assailed,
Where beauty prostrate lay and fortune wooed,
My heart insensible to neither bowed
Thy lucky aid was wanting to prevail.

In courts I sought thee then, thy proper sphere
    But thou in crowds wert stifled there,
Int'rest did all the loving business do,
Invites the youths and wins the virgins too.
Or if by chance some heart thy empire own
(Ah power ingrate!) the slave must be undone.

Tell me, thou nimble fire that dost dilate
　　Thy mighty force through every part,
What god, or human power did thee create
　　In my, till now, unfacile heart?
Art thou some welcome plague sent from above
　　In this dear form, this kind disguise?
　　Or the false offspring of mistaken love,
　　Begot by some soft thought that faintly strove,
With the bright piercing beauties of Lysander's eyes?
　　Yes, yes, tormentor, I have found thee now;
　　And found to whom thou dost thy being owe:
　　'Tis thou the blushes dost impart,
　　For thee this languishment I wear,
　　'Tis thou that tremblest in my heart
　　When the dear shepherd does appear,
　　I faint, I die with pleasing pain,
　　My words intruding sighing break
　　When e'er I touch the charming swain
　　When e'er I gaze, when e'er I speak.
Thy conscious fire is mingled with my love,
　　As in the sanctified abodes
　　Misguided worshippers approve
　　The mixing idol with their gods.
　　In vain, alas, in vain I strive
With errors, which my soul do please and vex,
　　For superstition will survive,
　　Purer religion to perplex.

Oh! Tell me you, philosophers, in love,
That can its burning feverish fits control,
　　By what strange arts you cure the soul,
　　And the fierce calenture* remove?

Tell me, ye fair ones, that exchange desire,
　　How 'tis you hid the kindling fire.
　　Oh! Would you but confess the truth,
It is not real virtue makes you nice:
But when you do resist the pressing youth,
'Tis want of dear desire, to thaw the virgin ice.

And while your young adorers lie
All languishing and hopeless at your feet,
 Raising new trophies to your chastity,
 Oh tell me, how you do remain discreet?
 How you suppress the rising sighs,
And the soft yielding soul that wishes in your eyes?
 While to th'admiring crowd you nice are found;
 Some dear, some secret youth that gives the wound
 Informs you, all your virtue's but a cheat
  And honour but a false disguise,
 Your modesty a necessary bait
 To gain the dull repute of being wise.

Deceive the foolish world—deceive it on,
 And veil your passions in your pride;
But now I've found your feebles by my own,
From me the needful fraud you cannot hide.
 Though 'tis a mighty power must move
 The soul to this degree of love
And though with virtue I the world perplex,
Lysander finds the weakness of my sex,
So Helen while from Theseus' arms she fled,
To charming Paris yields her heart and bed.

A Pindaric to Mr P. Who Sings Finely

Damon, although you waste in vain,
 That precious breath of thine,
Where lies a power in every strain,
 To take in any other heart, but mine;
Yet do not cease to sing, that I may know,
 By what soft charms and arts,
What more than human 'tis you do,
 To take, and keep your hearts,
Or have you vowed never to waste your breath,
 But when some maid must fall a sacrifice,
As Indian priest[s]* prepare a death,

For slaves t'adorn their victories,
Your charm's as powerful, if I live,
    For I as sensible shall be,
What wound you can, to all that hear you, give,
    As if you wounded me;
And shall as much adore your wondrous skill
As if my heart each dying note could kill.

And yet I should not tempt my fate,
    Nor trust my feeble strength,
Which does with every softening note abate,
    And may at length
Reduce me to the wretched slave I hate;
'Tis strange extremity in me,
To venture on a doubtful victory,
Where if you fail, I gain no more,
Than what I had before;
But 'twill certain comfort bring,
    If I unconquered do escape from you;
If I can live, and hear you sing,
No other forces can my soul subdue;
Sing Damon then, and let each shade,
Which with thy heavenly voice is happy made,
Bear witness if my courage be not great,
To hear thee sing, and make a safe retreat.

To Alexis in Answer to His Poem Against Fruition. Ode

Ah hapless sex! Who bear no charms,
But what like lightning flash and are no more
    False fires sent down for baneful harms,
Fires which the fleeting lover feebly warms
    And given like past Beboches* o'er,
        Like songs that please (though bad) when new,
        But learned by heart neglected grew.

In vain did Heav'n adore the shape and face
With beauties which by angels' forms it drew:
In vain the mind with brighter glories grace,
While all our joys are stinted to the space
    Of one betraying interview,
With one surrender to the eager will
We're short lived nothing or a real ill.

Since man with that inconstancy was born,
To love the absent, and the present scorn.
    Why do we deck, why do we dress
    For such a short-lived happiness?
    Why do we put attraction on,
Since either way 'tis we must be undone?

    They fly if honour take our part,
    Our virtue drives 'em o'er the field.
    We lose 'em by too much desert,
    And oh! They fly us if we yield.
Ye gods! Is there no charm in all the fair
To fix this wild, this faithless, wanderer.

Man! Our great business and our aim,
    For whom we spread out fruitless snares,
No sooner kindles the designing flame,
    But to the next bright object bears
The trophies of his conquest and our shame:
    In constancy's the good supreme
The rest is airy notion, empty dream!

    Then, heedless nymph, be ruled by me
    If e'er your swain the bliss desire;
    Think like Alexis he may be
    Whose wished possession damps his fire;
    The roving youth in every shade
Has left some sighing and abandoned maid,
For 'tis a fatal lesson he has learned,
After fruition ne'er to be concerned.

To The Fair Clarinda, Who Made Love To Me,
Imagined More Than Woman

Fair lovely maid, or if that title be
Too weak, too feminine for nobler thee,
Permit a name that more approaches truth:
And let me call thee, lovely charming youth.
This last will justify my soft complaint,
While that may serve to lessen my constraint;
And without blushes I the youth pursue,
When so much beauteous woman is in view,
Against thy charms we struggle but in vain
With thy deluding form thou giv'st us pain,
While the bright nymph betrays us to the swain.
In pity to our sex sure thou wert sent,
That we might love, and yet be innocent:
For sure no crime with thee we can commit;
Or if we should——thy form excuses it.
For who, that gathers fairest flowers believes
A snake lies hid beneath the fragrant leaves.

    Thou beauteous wonder of a different kind,
Soft Cloris with the dear Alexis joined;
When ere the manly part of thee, would plead
Thou tempts us with the image of the maid,
While we the noblest passions do extend
The love to Hermes, Aphrodite* the friend.

To Lysander, On Some Verses He Writ,
and Asking More for His Heart Than 'Twas Worth

I

Take back that heart, you with such caution give,
    Take the fond valued trifle back;

I hate love-merchants that a trade would drive;
    And meanly cunning bargains make.

II

I care not how the busy market goes,
    And scorn to chaffer* for a price:
Love does one staple rate on all impose,
    Nor leaves it to the trader's choice.

III

A heart requires a heart unfeigned and true,
    Though subtly you advance the price,
And ask a rate that simple love ne'er knew:
    And the free trade monopolise.

IV

An humble slave the buyer must become,
    She must not bate a look or glance,
You will have all, or you'll have none;
    See how love's market you enhance.

V

Is't not enough, I gave you heart for heart,
    But I must add my lips and eyes;
I must no friendly smile or kiss impart;
    But you must dun* me with advice.

VI

And every hour still more unjust you grow,
    Those freedoms you my life deny,
You to Adraste are obliged to show,
    And give her all my rifled joy.

VII

Without control she gazes on that face,
    And all the happy envied night,
In the pleased circle of your fond embrace:
    She takes away the lover's right.

VIII

From me she ravishes those silent hours,
    That are by sacred love my due:
Whilst I in vain accuse the angry powers,
    That make me hopeless love pursue.

IX

Adraste's ears with that dear voice are blessed,
    That charms my soul at every sound,
And with those love-enchanting touches pressed:
    Which I ne'er felt without a wound.

X

She has thee all, whilst I with silent grief,
    The fragments of thy softness feel,
Yet dare not blame the happy licensed thief:
    That does my dear-bought pleasures steal.

XI

Whilst like a glimmering taper still I burn,
    And waste myself in my own flame,
Adraste takes the welcome rich return:
    And leaves me all the hopeless pain.

XII

Be just, my lovely swain, and do not take
    Freedoms you'll not to me allow;

Or give Aminta so much freedom back:
That she may rove as well as you.

XIII

Let us then love upon the honest square,
   Since interest neither have designed,
For the sly gamester, who ne'er plays me fair,
   Must trick for trick expect to find.

A Pindaric Poem to the Reverend Doctor Burnet,
   On The Honour He Did Me of
   Enquiring After Me and My Muse

I

When old Rome's candidates aspired to fame,
And did the people's suffrages obtain
For some great consul, or a Caesar's name;
The victor was not half so pleased and vain,
As I, when given the honour of your choice.
And preference had in that one single voice;
That voice, from whence immortal wit still flows
Wit that at once is solemn all and sweet,
Where noblest eloquence and judgement shows
The inspiring mind illustrious, rich and great;
A mind that can inform your wond'rous pen
In all that's perfect and sublime:
And with an art beyond the wit of men,
On what e'er theme on what e'er great design,
It carries a commanding force, like that of writ divine.

II

With pow'rful reasoning dressed in finest sense,
A thousand ways my soul you can invade,

And spite of my opinion's weak defence,
   Against my will, you conquer and persuade.
Your language soft as love, betrays the heart,
And at each period fixes a resistless dart,
    While the fond listener, like a maid undone,
    Inspired with tenderness she fears to own;
In vain essays her freedom to regain:
The fine ideas in her soul remain:
And please, and charm, even while they grieve and pain.

III

But yet how well this praise can recompense
For all the welcome wounds (before) you'd given!
   Scarce anything but you and Heaven
   Such grateful bounties can dispense,
As that eternity of life can give;
So famed by you my verse eternally shall live:
Till now, my careless Muse no higher strove
T'inlarge her glory and extend her wings;
    Than underneath Parnassus grove,
To sing of shepherds and their humble loves;
But never durst, like Cowley,* tune her strings,
    To sing of heroes and of kings.
But since by an authority divine,
She is allowed a more exalted thought;
She will be valued now as current coin,
Whose stamp alone gives it the estimate,
Though out of an inferior metal wrought.

IV

   But oh, if from your praise I feel
   A joy that has no parallel
What must I suffer when I cannot pay
   Your goodness, your own generous way?
And make my stubborn Muse your just commands obey.
   My Muse that would endeavour fain to glide
With the fair prosperous gale, and the full driving tide

But loyalty commands with pious force,
   That stops me in the thriving course.
The breeze that wafts the crowding nations o'er,
   Leaves me unpitied far behind
   On the forsaken barren shore,
To sigh with echo, and the murmuring wind;
While all the inviting prospect I survey,
With melancholy eyes I view the plains,
Where all I see is ravishing and gay,
And all I hear is mirth in loudest strains,
Thus while the chosen seed possess the promised land,
   I, like the excluded prophet, stand,
    The fruitful happy soul can only see,
    But am forbid by fate's decree
To share the triumph of the joyful victory.

V

'Tis to your pen, great Sir, the nation owes
For all the good this mighty change has wrought;
'Twas that the wondrous method did dispose,
Ere the vast work was to perfection brought.
O strange effect of a seraphic quill!
   That can by unperceptible degrees
Change every notion, every principle
   To any form, its great dictator please:
The sword a feeble pow'r compar'd to that,
   And to the nobler pen subordinate;
And of less use in bravest turns of state:
While that to blood and slaughter has recourse,
This conquers hearts with soft prevailing force:
So when the wiser Greeks o'ercame their foes,
It was not by the barbarous force of blows.
When a long ten years' fatal war had failed,
With luckier wisdom they at last assailed,
Wisdom and counsel which alone prevailed.
Not all their numbers the famed town could win
'Twas nobler stratagem that let the conqueror in.

VI

Though I the wond'rous change deplore,
That makes me useless and forlorn
Yet I the great design adore,
Though ruined in the universal turn.
Nor can my indigence and lost repose,
Those meagre furies that surround me close,
        Convert my sense and reason more
    To this unprecedented enterprise
    Than that a man so great, so learned, so wise,
The brave achievement owns and nobly justifies.
        'Tis you, great Sir, alone by Heaven preserved,
        Whose conduct has so well the nation served,
        'Tis you that to posterity shall give
            This age's wonders, and its history.
And great Nassau* shall in your annals live
            To all futurity.
            Your pen shall more immortalise his name,
Than even his own renowned and celebrated fame.

EXPLANATORY NOTES

The following abbreviations have been used:

O'Donnell   Mary Ann O'Donnell, *Aphra Behn: An Annotated Bibliography of Primary and Secondary Sources* (New York, 1986), entries listed by item number.

Greer   *The Uncollected Verse of Aphra Behn*, ed. Germaine Greer (Stump Cross, 1989).

Todd   *The Works of Aphra Behn*, ed. Janet Todd, Vol. 1: *Poetry* (London, 1992).

Todd, Penguin   Aphra Behn, *Oroonoko, The Rover and Other Works*, ed. Janet Todd (Penguin Classics, Harmondsworth, 1992).

Goreau   Angeline Goreau, *Reconstructing Aphra* (New York, 1980).

Duffy   Maureen Duffy, *The Passionate Shepherdess* (London, 1977).

PSO   Aphra Behn, *Poems Upon Several Occasions* (1684).

3   OROONOKO: the text is taken from the first edition of 1688 (O'Donnell, A31.1a), checked against a copy of *Three Histories* (1688), O'Donnell, 32, in which *Oroonoko* was reissued.

    Maitland: Richard Maitland, 4th Earl of Lauderdale (1653–95). Jacobite, who went into exile after the revolution of 1688.

4   *gust*: taste.

    nation sighs for: at this point, in the copy of *Oroonoko* in the Bodleian Library bound with *The Fair Jilt* and *Agnes de Castro* as *Three Histories*, O'Donnell notes the existence of a unique stop-press variant, emphasizing Behn's admiration for Maitland's Catholic sympathies: 'Where is it amongst all our nobility we shall find so great a champion for the Catholic church? With what divine knowledge have you writ in defence of the faith! How unanswerably have you cleared all these intricacies in religion which even the gown-men have left dark and difficult. With what unbeaten arguments you convince the faithless and instruct the ignorant.'

    incommode: i.e. inconvenient.

5 *true story*: despite early debate on the subject, it is now clear that Behn did indeed travel to Surinam (see the accounts in W. J. Cameron, *New Light on Aphra Behn* (Auckland, 1961); Duffy; and Goreau), though no independent evidence of the story of Oroonoko has, as yet, been discovered.

6 *Surinam*: in South America. An English colony was established in Surinam in 1652, but it was ceded to the Dutch in 1667. For a brief account, see Cornelis Goslinga, *A Short History of the Netherlands Antilles and Surinam* (The Hague, 1979).

cousheries: possibly couchari, the Galibi word for a deer (Todd, Penguin).

7 *Indian Queen*: John Dryden and Robert Howard, *The Indian Queen*, first performed 1663/4, set, not in Surinam, but in Peru and Mexico.

quarter of an ell: an ell = 45 inches.

Fall: here and elsewhere Behn evokes an image of Surinam as a Paradise which is later tainted by the violence of the colonists.

8 *liar*: an interesting anticipation of Swift's houyhnhnms, in *Gulliver's Travels*, who have no word for liar. Oroonoko is easily duped because his notion of honour is no match for those who lie.

9 *negroes*: i.e. from Africa, rather than the native Indians of Surinam.

Coromantien: Coromantyn, in modern Ghana. For a general account of African slavery, see Patrick Manning, *Slavery and African Life* (Cambridge, 1990).

12 *bating*: excepting.

29 *maugre*: in spite of.

31 *him on*: possibly a mistake for put on him; thus in all editions.

32 *and*: emended for sense, cf. Todd, Penguin.

efforts: emended by Todd to 'effects', but 'efforts' does make a certain amount of sense in relation to Oroonoko's actions after hearing of Imoinda's supposed death.

37 *chanced to be*: there has been a great deal of controversy over the details of Behn's stay in Surinam, though the general consensus now is that she was indeed there: see note above.

38 *Trefry*: a John Treffry is recorded as being Willoughby's agent in Surinam; see Cameron, *New Light on Aphra Behn*.

mien: bearing/expression.

39 *Backearary*: master; slave owner.

40 *female pen*: Behn's sense of herself as a woman writer is complex; cf. her reference in the prologue to *The Lucky Chance* to 'my masculine part, the poet in me'.

42 *shock dog*: shaggy-haired dog, usually a poodle.

43 *novel*: i.e. new thing, though perhaps with a reference to the *nouvelle*/novel as a literary form in the Restoration concerned with such narrative turns.

45 *stories of nuns*: cf. Behn's stories of Nuns in this volume: *The Fair Jilt* and *The History of the Nun*. Another example is *The Nun, or The Perjured Beauty*.

47 *my father*: there is no corroboration of this account by Behn of her father, though it is accepted by all recent biographical accounts (e.g. Goreau, Duffy, Sara Heller Mendelson, *The Mental World of Stuart Women* (Brighton, 1987)), including the most recent hypothesis about her birth: Jane Jones, 'New Light on the Background and Early Life of Aphra Behn', *Notes and Queries*, 235 (1990), 288–93.

late Majesty: Charles II, who died in 1685.

Dutch: Surinam was ceded to the Dutch in 1667 through the Treaty of Breda, by which the English, in turn, acquired New York.

48 *armadilly*: armadillo.

St John's Hill: this was a plantation owned by Robert Harley and, later, by Willoughby.

raving: perhaps an error or abbreviation for 'ravishing' (emended thus in 3rd edition, see Todd, Penguin).

Marl: the Mall in St James'.

49 *he*: i.e. she (Behn refers to tigers as both he and she simultaneously).

Harry Martin, the great Oliverian: Henry Marten, who was an important parliamentarian and a regicide. Behn may mean only that by the term Oliverian (i.e. supporter of Oliver Cromwell), as Marten actually fell out with Cromwell and lost power during the protectorate. After the Restoration, he was imprisoned until his death in 1680. His brother George is recorded as writing to him from Barbados in 1657/8, see Ivor Waters, *Henry Marten and the Long Parliament* (Chepstow, 1973).

51 *numb-eel*: electric eel.

52 *Indians*: such disputes were not, in fact, the reason behind the English abandonment of Surinam.

55 *Comitias*: linked by Todd to the Spanish word *camisa*, citing Biel's French account of the Galibi language (spoken by the Surinam Caribee Indians).

58 *salvages*: savages.

    humane: probably = human, though humane may well be implied.

60 *hamaca*: hammock, described in Sir Walter Raleigh's *Discovery of Guiana* (1596) as 'Indian beds'.

61 *Byam*: William Byam was associated with the English colony in Surinam from a very early stage, ending as general governor in 1663.

64 *Colonel Martin*: the character of 'George Marteen' appears in *The Younger Brother, Or, The Amorous Jilt* (not performed until 1696), a comedy of intrigue.

65 *chirurgeon*: surgeon.

66 *nemine contradicente*: without dissension.

67 *mobile*: the mob.

70 [*who*]: emended differently by Todd, who inserts a period after 'on'.

71 *gashly*: ghastly.

72 *Banister*: a Major James Bannister is reported as entering into negotiations with the Dutch over the fate of remaining English settlers in 1688.

74 THE FAIR JILT: the text is taken from a copy of the first edition of 1688 (O'Donnell A28.1a), checked against a copy of *Three Histories* (1688), in which *The Fair Jilt* was reissued (O'Donnell A32).

    Henry Pain Esq.: Henry Neville Payne was a Catholic playwright who became an active Jacobite after 1688, and was imprisoned and tortured in 1690 for his part in the Montgomery Plot. He wrote three known plays between 1672 and 1674.

    matter of fact: Maureen Duffy has located support for the origins of *The Fair Jilt* in an item in *The London Gazette* in 1666, describing the abortive execution of a Prince Tarquino at Antwerp.

Tarquin: the pretender to the line of the last kings of Rome was certainly recorded as being in Antwerp at the time (see note above), and was generally regarded as an impostor.

75 *imprisonment and sufferings*: Payne was described by Gilbert Burnet (see note below) as 'the most active and determined of all King James's agents' after the 1688 revolution.

76 *opinionatreism*: erroneous; conformed to opinion.

perrywig: a wig.

scrutore: escritoire = writing desk.

billet-doux: billets doux = love letters.

cravat-string: part by which a cravat (scarf worn around the throat) was tied.

77 *pit and boxes*: i.e. the whole audience of the theatre, who either sat in the pit (modern stalls) or boxes.

78 *galloping nuns*: term for nuns without binding or perpetual vows.

Chanonesses, Beguines, Quests, Swart-Sisters, and Jesuitesses: respectively a community of women not under perpetual vows; a similar order centred in Flanders; a mendicant order; black (habited) sisters: Dominicans; an order of Jesuit nuns suppressed by Pope Urban VIII in 1638. All are orders without perpetual vows.

fille-devotes: filles dévotes = devout girls: those who have taken a vow.

bando: bandeau = narrow band around a headdress.

80 *attack*: i.e. affect her; perhaps also 'attach' her.

81 *cordeliers*: Franciscan friars.

pistole: Spanish gold coin.

87 *beaux esprits*: suitors of spirit; eligible men.

malapropos: inappropriately.

90 *ease*: i.e. lack of any burden or responsibility.

91 *receive*: i.e. the sacrament.

93 *scapula*: scapular: short cloak worn by Benedictine monks.

97 *Marquis Casteil Roderigo*: mentioned in the *London Gazette* account as the man who issued Tarquino's pardon, see Duffy.

97   *Prince Tarquin*: see previous note for Tarquin's identity. Tar-
      quin was (in legend) the last king of the Romans.

      King Charles: Charles II left Brussels at the end of March in 1660
      to negotiate the Treaty of Breda.

      my being sent thither by his late Majesty: Behn, apparently at the
      recommendation of Thomas Killigrew, was sent by Lord Arling-
      ton to act as a spy in the low countries in July 1666. Her main
      mission involved converting the republican William Scot, with
      whom she apparently had had a romantic conne~ion in Surinam,
      into an agent for the Crown in the war with the Dutch. Behn's
      activities were concentrated in Bruges and Antwerp. Her reports
      survive in the Public Records Office. She was always underpaid,
      and ended up in debt when ordered home in 1667. For a detailed
      account, which reprints all relevant documents and letters, see
      W. J. Cameron, *New Light on Aphra Behn* (Auckland, 1961).

98   *Lucretia*: Prince Tarquin's rape of Lucretia was, according to
      legend, instrumental in causing the uprising which drove the
      Tarquins out of Rome.

100   *sister*: 'and' deleted.

03   *to pension*: gave him a salary; employed him.

104   *mittimus*: warrant.

106   *portugal-mat*: woven rush matting.

108   *heartbreaking*: i.e. his heart is breaking.

109   *flambeaux*: torch-bearers.

120   MEMOIRS OF THE COURT OF THE KING OF BANTAM: the text is
      taken from the first printing, in *All The Histories and Novels
      Written by the Late Ingenious Mrs Behn* (1698), O'Donnell A40.3.
      Mendelson suggests without any explanation that this work is a
      'prose satire on Mulgrave (p. 213 n. 119). John Sheffield, third
      Earl of Mulgrave, courted James's daughter Anne and was
      exiled from court in disgrace in 1682. He is satirized in Behn's
      poem 'Ovid to Julia' and was certainly made fun of for preten-
      sions (via the courtship of Anne) to great things, one of his
      nicknames being King John (Greer). The events in Bantam and
      its probable date make it possible that Mulgrave was a target,
      but no proof for such an assertion seems evident.

121   *quondam*: one time; former.

122   *baisemains*: a kiss of the hands: compliment.

      choosing king and queen: the king and queen chosen to preside
      over Twelfth Night festivities derive from earlier ritual inver-

sions of authority involving a Lord of Misrule and a mock court. Gambling was also traditional at this time. Such Christmas festivities had a renewed gusto at the Restoration after their partial suppression during the Interregnum.

124 *mighty cake*: this custom of choosing the king and queen of Twelfth Night via favours in the cake was evidently dying out in the Restoration, and being replaced by the drawing of lots or characters. See J. Pimlott, *The Englishman's Christmas* (Brighton, 1978).

questions and commands; to cross purposes; I think a thought; what is it like? etc.: word games and party games all clearly concerned with riddles and guessing identities. In cross questions, players in a circle pass questions and answers on to each other in whispers.

125 *'get*: beget.

126 *Statira ... Roxana*: in Nathaniel Lee's popular play *The Rival Queens* (1677), Statira and Roxana are, respectively, the present and former wives of Alexander. The parts were made famous by Anne Bracegirdle and Mrs Barry (see note on Rochester below).

129 *piquet*: a popular card game played with a 32-card pack.

in specie: in kind; specifically.

130 *troul'd*: trawled.

cully: dupe.

131 *Locket's*: Locket's Eating House, in St James's Park, was a famous 'ordinary' (dining room or restaurant).

A King and No King: by Beaumont and Fletcher, revived frequently during the Restoration; e.g. in 1676 at the Theatre Royal.

132 *the Rose*: a tavern in Covent Garden.

one I more: i.e. 1683.

133 *bebuss*: kiss.

chine: roast beef.

134 *to*: added for sense.

The London Cuckolds: popular comedy by Edward Ravenscroft, first performed in 1682 and frequently thereafter.

134 *Long's*: another famous ordinary, Long's was located in the Hay-market.

135 *Germin's Street*: present Jermyn Street, a fashionable part of London.

C——d: possibly Francis Child, recorded in the Goldsmith's Register as at Marygold within Temple Bar in the 1680s.

138 THE HISTORY OF THE NUN, OR THE FAIR VOW-BREAKER: the text is taken from the first edition of 1689, O'Donnell A37.1.

Duchess of Mazarine: Hortense Mancini (1645–99) almost married Charles II in 1659. Renowned for her independent spirit, she left her husband and, after travelling throughout Europe, arrived in England in 1675, riding to London in male costume. She became Charles's mistress, but had many other lovers.

toor: promenade, parade.

conquest: (*sic*) conquests.

140 *votary in the house of devotion*: there is still some argument amongst Behn's biographers over the exact nature of her Catholic sympathies (evident in a good deal of her writing) and her background (which is still uncertain). No evidence exists to support or deny this contention by Behn (or perhaps her narrator).

141 *Iper*: modern Ypres (Flemish Ieper), near the present French border of Belgium.

143 *those*: sic, implies the plural.

145 *Candia*: in 1645, the Turks laid siege to Candia (Crete), held by Venice since 1200, and finally captured it in 1669.

150 *swound*: swoon or faint.

154 *afternoon*: in the afternoon.

172 *progging*: foraging or economizing.

182 *spahee*: spahi = Turkish cavalryman.

188 *set*: sat, i.e. sat in judgement.

191 THE ADVENTURE OF THE BLACK LADY: the text is taken from the first printing in *All The Histories and Novels Written by the Late Ingenious Mrs Behn* (1698), O'Donnell A40.3.

housekeepers: householder; the sense here is like the modern sense of owner as opposed to tenant.

192   *sack*: a kind of white wine, usually from Spain or the Canaries; sometimes short for sherry-sack.

   argument: *sic*; plural implied.

195   *the Exchange*: Royal Exchange, re-erected in 1670 after the fire and, in this context, the surrounding shops.

   the overseers of the poor: the officials who administered the Poor Law within the parish. Social historians have noted more benevolent aspects of the Poor Law during this period, which in London made special provision for foundlings, rather than echoing Behn's criticism of the exploitation by the overseers of their potential clients. See Valerie Pearl, 'Social Policy in Early Modern London', in *History and Imagination* (London, 1981). The potential for such exploitation is evident, however, and undoubtedly did occur. Recently, Jane Jones has put forward an identification of Behn's father as a Bartholomew Johnson, who was appointed an Overseer of the Poor for the parish of St Margaret's in Canterbury, though her case seems, to me, still unproven. See 'New Light on the Background and Early Life of Aphra Behn', *Notes and Queries* 235 (1990), 291.

   house of correction: such as Bridewell, a much harsher institution than a workhouse, both intended for those who fell under the jurisdiction of the Poor Law.

198   THE UNFORTUNATE BRIDE: OR, THE BLIND LADY A BEAUTY: the text is taken from the first printing in *Histories, Novels and Translations* (1700), O'Donnell A43.1. The dedication of this posthumously published work, by Samuel Briscoe to Richard Norton, has been omitted.

202   *raree-shows*: peep-shows.

205   *blackamoor lady*: from Elizabethan times, there are records of some hundreds of 'blackamoors', often brought to England as slaves. Apart from Shakespeare's Othello and dark mistress, the literary portrayals tended to be negative, and continued to be during the seventeenth century, as Behn's treatment here indicates—her attitude here is much more shaped by convention than her treatment of Oroonoko. (See Eldred Jones, *Othello's Countrymen*, Sierra Leone, 1965.) James Walvin notes that 'In the years after the Restoration, Negroes became everyday sights on the streets of London', in *Black and White* (London, 1973), 10. See also Folarin Olowale Shyllon, *Black People in Britain 1555–1833* (London, 1977).

207   *the*: *sic*, probably should be omitted.

211   SONG. LOVE ARMED: first printed in *Abdelazar* (1677), where it
       opens the play. The text here is from PSO.

       ON A JUNIPER TREE, CUT DOWN TO MAKE BUSKS: text from PSO.
       First printed in Rochester's *Poems on Several Occasions* (1680), and
       attributed to him until corrected by David M. Vieth, *Attributions
       in Restoration Poetry* (New Haven, Conn. 1963). For the quite
       substantial and interesting variants, see Todd.

       busks: corsets, or the wood/bone used to stiffen them.

212   *Philocles and Cloris*: the use of such classical and pseudo-classical
       names was part of the tradition of pastoral poetry. These names
       often stood for real people.

213   *hast*: i.e. haste.

214   A BALLAD ON MR J. H. TO AMORET, ASKING WHY I WAS SO SAD: text
       from PSO. J. H.: John Hoyle, Behn's lover (probably during the
       1670s, but perhaps also the early 1680s as well), the subject of a
       number of poems which catalogue the rise and fall of the affair
       and its consequences, and generally taken to be the subject of
       the posthumously published *Love Letters to a Gentleman* (reprinted
       in Todd, Penguin). Hoyle was a member of Gray's Inn and a
       controversial figure, tried for sodomy in 1687, seen generally as
       a republican, but also admired for his wit and learning (he
       apparently read seven languages). He was killed in a fight in
       1692. Amoret: usually identified as the first great English actress,
       Elizabeth Barry (1658–1713), who acted in a number of Behn's
       plays, and in those of Behn's friend Thomas Otway.

215   *scrip*: small bag or satchel carried by a shepherd.

       buskins: half-boots.

216   SONG. THE INVITATION: text from PSO. First printed in *The
       Young King* (1683), Act I Scene I.

217   SONG: text from PSO. First printed in *Covent Garden Drollery*
       (1672), a miscellany generally thought to have been edited by
       Behn (O'Donnell BA1).

       Jemmy: James in Scottish dialect. The poem is seen by Todd as
       possibly referring to James Scott, Duke of Monmouth, illegiti-
       mate son of Charles II and the focus of Protestant resistance to
       the accession of the Catholic James II. He was executed for his
       part in the rebellion against James in 1685.

218   *trow*: trust, believe.

bracelets: 'garlands' in 1672 version.

ON THE DEATH OF THE LATE EARL OF ROCHESTER: text from *Miscellany* (1685), a collection edited by Behn containing poems by a number of writers (O'Donnell BA2). This poem belongs to the elegy tradition exemplified in the seventeenth century by Milton's *Lycidas*.

John Wilmot, Earl of Rochester (1647–80), was the most renowned, and most infamous of the Restoration court wits. Elizabeth Barry (see note above) was one of his mistresses, and he apparently first taught her to act. Behn clearly knew Rochester reasonably well, though the details of their friendship remain obscure. He was thought at one time to have been the model for Willmore in Behn's *The Rover* (1677).

Strephon: the name of a pastoral lover.

Stygian: of the Styx, i.e. the Underworld.

219 *cully*: dupe.

220 *Lucretius*: Roman poet whose *De Rerum Natura* (On the Nature of Things), early first century BC, an Epicurean poem, was translated by Thomas Creech (see below). Said to have committed suicide.

Ovid: Roman poet (43 BC–AD 18), famous for his love poetry, much imitated in seventeenth-century lyrics.

Julia: daughter of the emperor Augustus, in legend model for Ovid's Corinna.

221 TO MRS W.: text from PSO. Mrs W: Anne Wharton (1659–85), Rochester's cousin, unhappily married to Thomas Wharton. She was an accomplished poet, who wrote her own elegy on Rochester's death, as well as an unperformed play about Ovid, 'Love's Martyr'. Wharton's poem, 'To Mrs Behn on What She Writ of the Earl of Rochester', praises her, but alludes to Behn's shaky reputation (implicitly as opposed to Wharton's own): 'May yours excell the matchless Sappho's name | May you have all her wit, without the shame', as well as advising Behn to 'Scorn meaner themes, declining low desire, | And bid your muse maintain a vestal fire'. Behn's reply, not to mention her *œuvre*, makes it clear that she refuted this advice.

223 THE DISAPPOINTMENT: text from PSO. First published in Rochester's *Poems on Several Occasions* (1680), and misattributed to him. Todd notes that the poem is an adaptation of a French original.

See also Richard E. Quaintance, 'French Sources of the Restoration "Imperfect Enjoyment" Poem', *PQ* 42 (1963), and Carole Fabricant, 'Rochester's World of Imperfect Enjoyment', *JEGP* 73 (1974). A number of Restoration poems on impotence exist, but all emphasize the male perspective, in contrast to some of Behn's poem. For an interesting anonymous example, see 'One Writing Against His Prick', in Harold Love (ed.), *The Penguin Book of Restoration Verse* (Harmondsworth, 1968).

226 *Priapus*: term for penis, derived from classical god of procreation.

227 *Daphne*: a nymph pursued by Apollo until she turned into a laurel.

228 THE DREAM. A SONG: text from PSO.

Astrea: Behn's most commonly recorded literary name. Referring to the classical goddess of justice, it is a seventeenth-century romance name, taken from d'Urfé's popular French romance *l'Astrée*. Behn used the name when acting as a spy. Duffy notes that her burial is entered in the Westminster Abbey registers as 'Astrea Behn'.

229 A LETTER TO A BROTHER OF THE PEN IN TRIBULATION: text from PSO. Summers speculates (though without any evidence) that the brother is the dramatist Edward Ravenscroft, who wrote the epilogue for Behn's play *The Town Fop* (1677).

tabernacler: puns on the wooden sweating tub as a house of prayer, a tabernacler being someone who used the temporary churches erected after the fire of London (1666). The pun continues throughout the poem, e.g. in the images of penance and Lent which follow.

tub: the treatment for venereal disease involved being placed in a sweating tub, usually together with a dose of mercury.

230 *cabal*: a group of associates; the name derived from the alliance of Clifford, Arlington, Buckingham, Ashley (Shaftesbury), and Lauderdale in 1672, and has the sense of a secret grouping of powerful people.

new-fletched: new-feathered.

231 SONG. ON HER LOVING TWO EQUALLY: text from PSO. First printed in *The False Count* (1682), II. ii.

Captain Pack: Simon Pack composed many songs for plays (as well as being a soldier).

232 THE COUNSEL. A SONG: text from PSO. First printed in *The Rover Part Two* (1681) and separately as *Beauties Triumph*. Sung by Abevile, Beaumond's page, in Act IV, sc. i. Uncollated in Todd, variants as follows: l. 13 And we no more shall homage pay [And we can only pity pay]; l. 20 joys [charms]; l. 21 shall [should].

233 SONG. THE SURPRISE: text from PSO. First printed in *The Rover Part Two* (1681), sung by Lucia, Act II, sc. ii, and in *Female Poems Upon Several Occasions* (1682), as 'Love's Revenge'.

Mr Farmer: Thomas Farmer, song-writer and musician at court.

ON MR J. H. IN A FIT OF SICKNESS: text from PSO. J. H.: John Hoyle, see note above.

234 *said*: presumably misprint for 'sad', though 'said' is just possible in the sense of aforesaid.

236 THE CABAL AT NICKEY NACKEYS: text from PSO. First printed in *The Roundheads* (1682), a satirical play set in the late days of the Commonwealth, sung by Lambert, Act IV, sc. iii. No collation in Todd, variants as follows: l. 5 wear [rack]; l. 7 at last [religion]; l. 8 he have [be]; l. 10 impudent [resolute]; l. 11 times of [open]; l. 12 And bear all down [Bearing all down]; l. 16 we know who's ['tis he is]. For cabal, see note above.

Nickey Nackeys: in Behn's friend Thomas Otway's popular play, *Venice Preserved* (1682), Nicky Nacky is a pet name used by Antonio, a figure said to represent Shaftesbury. As a whole, the play presents a Tory response to the Popish Plot. In the context of its place in *The Roundheads*, this song associates Behn with the general Tory 'line' at the time.

Whigs: in this context, Whigs are those, like Shaftesbury, opposed to the accession of James II.

SONG: text from *Miscellany* (1685).

237 ON THE DEATH OF E. WALLER ESQ.: text from *Poems to the Memory of That Incomparable Poet Edmund Waller, Esquire* (1688), O'Donnell BB17. The poem also exists in Behn's autograph manuscript (in the Pierpont Morgan Library). Edmund Waller (1606–87) was much acclaimed as a poet in the seventeenth century, especially for his lyric facility. Dryden praised him highly, calling him 'the father of English numbers', an idea echoed in Behn's poem.

238 *Saccharissa*: a figure in many of Waller's lyrics, representing Lady Dorothy Sidney, pursued (unsuccessfully) by Waller in the 1630s.

239 TO MR CREECH (UNDER THE NAME OF DAPHNIS): text from PSO.

First printed together with other commendatory poems (by
Otway and Waller, among others) in the second edition of
Creech's translation of Lucretius (1683) as 'To The Unknown
Daphnis on his Excellent Translation of Lucretius' (O'Donnell
BB11). The PSO version lays greater emphasis on Lucretius'
atheism; e.g. l. 56 in the earlier version read 'As strong as faith's
resistless oracles'. Todd lists all variants and prints 1683 as her
copytext. Thomas Creech (1659–1700) was most famous for his
translation of Lucretius' *De Rerum Natura*, 'Done into English
verse, with notes' (for Lucretius, see note above).

240   *salvage*: savage.

241   *Wadham*: Creech was a scholar of Wadham College, Oxford,
and became a fellow of All Souls in 1683.

fanes: temples.

Thyrsis: another common name in Renaissance pastoral, identified here as Thomas Sprat (1635–1713), fellow of Wadham and
historian of the Royal Society. He wrote a life of Cowley (see
below), and imitated his Pindaric poetry, earning the title
'Pindaric Sprat'.

Cowley's: Abraham Cowley (1618–67), originator of the English
irregular Pindaric ode, a form often used by Behn (as well as
Dryden and others). Cowley wrote a Royalist epic during the Interregnum.

sovereign's cause: Sprat preached before the House of Commons
in 1680, strongly defending the King and accusing the House of
'undutifulness'.

Strephon: Rochester (see note above), who was a student at
Wadham.

242   *distichs*: couplets/lines of verse.

243   A LETTER TO MR CREECH AT OXFORD, WRITTEN IN THE LAST
GREAT FROST: text from *Miscellany* (1685). The famous frost of
1683/4 caused the Thames to freeze to the extent that a veritable
fun-fair could be held on it.

Tonson's: Jacob Tonson (*c*.1656–1736), stationer and bookseller,
famous as Dryden's early publisher, and publisher of many
Restoration writers, including Otway, and a number of Behn's
works, including PSO. A surviving letter from Behn to Tonson
indicates her financial plight (and that of many authors of the
time): 'good dear Mr Tonson, let it be £5 more' (quoted in
Duffy and Goreau).

shie: Greer suggests an abbreviation for sherry.

244 *Bays'*: Dryden's nickname as poet laureate (i.e. crowned with a laurel [bay] wreath).

dunning: demanding money.

Tory farce, or doggerell: Tory propaganda against the Whigs, perhaps works like *The Roundheads*. Behn's Tory doggerell has generally remained lost or unidentified; see Janet Todd and Virginia Crompton, ' "Rebellions Antidote": A New Attribution to Aphra Behn', *Notes and Queries*, 238 (1991), 175–7.

Temple: quarters of members of the Inns of Court (i.e. lawyers, but also fashionable men about town) such as John Hoyle.

pilgarlick: peelgarlic (bald): foolish creature.

H—le: Hoyle, see note above on John Hoyle.

plot broke out: the 1678 Popish Plot involved a fabricated Catholic conspiracy. The Tory counterplot, referred to here, was the 1683 Rye House Plot, a supposed Whig conspiracy, involving Monmouth and Lord Grey, to assassinate Charles and James. Behn depicted scandalous events surrounding the Rye House Plot in her *Love Letters Between a Nobleman and His Sister* (part one, 1684). See the detailed study by John Kenyon, *The Popish Plot* (London, 1972), which offers a helpful sense of an important background to much of Behn's work which has political implications.

Rowley: nickname for Charles II, either from his horse (Greer) or a lecherous goat (Todd). The Oxford Parliament of 1681 marked a shift away from the Whig power produced by the Popish Plot; the Parliament was quickly dismissed by Charles. See Ronald Hutton, *Charles II* (Oxford, 1989).

245 *Perkin*: Monmouth (nicknamed after Perkin Warbeck, a fifteenth-century pretender to the throne, subject of a popular play by John Ford in 1634). Wapping was a centre of popular revolt during the Popish Plot. Monmouth, as Charles's illegitimate son, was at the centre of attempts to exclude the Catholic James from the throne. After a stormy relationship with his father, Monmouth finally went into exile in 1684.

brawn in sousing drink: pickled (soused) boar's meat.

Lazarello: Lazarillo de Tormes, eponymous hero of a Spanish sixteenth-century picaresque work popular in England in the seventeenth century. In the continuation, by Juan de Luna, he is exhibited as a fish.

246 TO LYSANDER: text from PSO.

247 ON THE FIRST DISCOVERY OF FALSEHOOD IN AMINTAS: text from *Lycidus* (1688), O'Donnell BA4. Amintas is used as a name for John Hoyle in a number of poems. For an important analysis of this poem's links with a number of other poems, all versions of 'The Willing Mistress', see Bernard Duyfhuizen, '"That Which I Dare Not Name": Aphra Behn's "The Willing Mistress"', *ELH* 58 (1991), 63–82.

249 FROM *OF PLANTS*: text from *The Second and Third Parts of the Works of Mr Abraham Cowley* (1689), O'Donnell BB18. Behn contributed to an English translation of Cowley's Latin poem of 1668 (modelled on Virgil's *Georgics*). Behn's version of Book VI was written without a knowledge of Latin, presumably using someone's literal translation. As with her translations elsewhere, the version is imbued with much of her own writing. Behn's work consists of nearly 2,000 lines; this extract is ll. 575–95.

O thou: the laurel tree is addressed at this point in the poem.

Sappho: mid-seventh century BC; first known female poet.

Orinda: Katherine Philips (1632–64), known as 'the matchless Orinda', much praised as a female poet of unsullied reputation (in contrast to Behn). Her poems were published without her consent in 1664, then posthumously in 1667. She also translated two plays by Corneille.

250 FROM *AESOP'S FABLES*: text from *Aesop's Fables* (1687), O'Donnell BB16. Behn wrote new poems to accompany a reissue of Francis Barlow's 1666 engravings, originally with English verses by Thomas Philipott. There are 110 altogether.

251 A PINDARIC ON THE DEATH OF OUR LATE SOVEREIGN: text from the 1685 publication (O'Donnell A19.1), checked against the reissue in the same year. For Pindaric poetry, see notes on Cowley and Sprat, above.

Charles II collapsed on the morning of 2 February 1685 and died four days later, having been received into the Catholic church on the last night of his life. As Behn's poem notes, the public were given false hope by an optimistic medical bulletin on the morning of his death, quickly emended as his worsening state became apparent. Greer notes 78 elegies on Charles's death. For a detailed account, see Antonia Fraser, *Charles II* (London, 1979).

252   *hecatombs*: large public sacrifice (originally a hundred oxen).

253   *Joshua*: i.e. Charles's brother, James, who will succeed Charles as Joshua succeeded Moses.

254   *Jonathan*: friend in youth of David, King of Israel.

255   *Spain*: James was indeed a highly successful soldier and leader. He had notable successes fighting with the Spanish in the Interregnum, and was offered the command of the Spanish army in 1660. See Jock Haswell, *James II: Soldier and Sailor* (London, 1972).

   banishment: under pressure during the exclusion crisis, Charles 'banished' James in 1679; he went first to Brussels, then to Scotland, and did not return until 1682.

   needless fears: i.e. fears about James as a Catholic monarch, which had been fuelled by the Popish Plot and its aftermath.

   prophets: prophecy was popular in the seventeenth century, for royal and all other events. An example connected with James is *Prince-Protecting Providences* (1682). See Keith Thomas, *Religion and the Decline of Magic* (London, 1971), who notes a great increase in prophecies during the Civil War.

256   ON DESIRE. A PINDARIC: text from *Lycidus* (1688), O'Donnell BA4.

257   *feebles*: feebless = feebleness, infirmity.

258   *calenture*: tropical disease affecting sailors with delirium; fever (literal and metaphorical).

259   A PINDARIC TO MR P. WHO SINGS FINELY: text from *Miscellany* (1685). Without any real evidence available, Mr P. has been identified as Henry Purcell (Summers) or his brother Daniel (Duffy).

   priest[s]: emended from 'Priest' in the original.

260   TO ALEXIS IN ANSWER TO HIS POEM AGAINST FRUITION: text from *Lycidus* (1688). Behn's answer is to 'A Poem Against Fruition on the Reading in Mountain's Essay' [i.e. Montaigne, bk 2 essay 15, 'Our Desire is Increased By Difficulty']:

   > Ah wretched man! whom neither fate can please
   > Nor Heavens indulgent to his wish can bless,
   > Desire torments him, or fruition cloys,
   > Fruition which shou'd make his bliss, destroys;
   > Far from our eyes th'enchanting object's set

Advantage by the friendly distance get.
Fruition shows the cheat, and views 'em near,
Then all their borrow'd splendours plain appears
And we what with much care we gain and skill
An empty nothing find, or real ill.
Thus disappointed, our mistaken thought,
Not finding satisfaction which it sought
Renews its search, and with much toil and pain
Most wisely strives to be deceived again
Hurried by our fantastic wild desire
We loathe the present, absent things admire.
Those we adore, and fair ideas frame
And those enjoyed we think wou'd quench the flame,
In vain, the ambitious fever still returns
And with redoubled fire more fiercely burns
Our boundless vast desires can know no rest
But travel forward still and labour to be blest
Philosophers and poets strive in vain
The restless anxious progress to restrain
And to their loss soon found their good supreme
An airy notion and a pleasing dream
For happiness is nowhere to be found
But flies the searcher like enchanted ground.
Are we then masters or the slaves of things?
Poor wretched vassals or terrestrial kings?
Left to our reason, and by that betrayed,
We lose a present bliss to catch a shade.
Unsatisfied with beauteous nature's store,
The universal monarch man is only poor.

260 *Beboches*: deboches = debauches.

262 TO THE FAIR CLARINDA, WHO MADE LOVE TO ME IMAGINED MORE
THAN WOMAN: text from *Lycidus* (1688).

Hermes, Aphrodite: a reference to Hermaphroditus, son of Hermes
(Mercury) and Aphrodite (Venus), who grew together with the
nymph Salmacis while bathing in her fountain, and thus com-
bined male and female sexual characteristics. (Goreau notes
that 'Aphrodite' also puns on Behn's first name.) Behn's treatment of lesbian desire in this poem may also be related to her
use of 'hermaphroditic' self-conceptions elsewhere; e.g. her
sense of 'my masculine part' (see note above).

TO LYSANDER . . . WORTH: text from PSO.

263 *chaffer*: haggle.

dun: make demands (usually for money).

265 A PINDARIC POEM TO THE REVEREND DOCTOR BURNET ... MUSE: text from the 1689 publication, O'Donnell A35. Gilbert Burnet (1643–1715) was an influential bishop and important historian. He began as a political moderate, though implicated in the after effects of the Rye House Plot. He was out of favour and lived in France during James's reign, then moved to The Hague and became close to William and Mary, offering them advice leading to the revolution of 1688. He entered England with William and Mary and offered important support during the early part of their reign. Burnet did not succeed in persuading Behn, as a strong supporter of James, to write a commendatory poem for William, but Behn did write 'A Congratulatory Poem to her Sacred Majesty Queen Mary, Upon Her Arrival in England' (1689). Greer reads the poem as containing, underneath the praise, a barbed attack on Burnet as an 'arch traitor'.

266 *Cowley*: see note above on Cowley. Behn did indeed sing of 'kings', and her recent translation of Cowley included a celebration of Charles and James, now superseded by William and Mary.

268 *Nassau*: William, who was Count of Nassau.

INDEX TO POETRY:
FIRST LINES AND TITLES